S0-AXW-584

BRAVE, BOLD, AND BRASH

Her eyes slid to his chest, noting with alarm the incredible width of his torso, the way his shoulders filled out the fine material of his jacket, then continued downward to his narrow waist and slim hips. With naughty delight, Tia's gaze skimmed past thickly muscled thighs to that part of him that was blatantly sexual. Her eyes jerked upward when she saw his unconscious reaction to her bold journey over his six-foot-three-inch frame.

"Do you like what you see?" Ben drawled. His voice was fraught with lazy humor, making Tia aware of her rude perusal. "I suppose turnabout is fair play, since I saw much more of you than you saw of me."

A deep red crawled up Tia's cheek and neck. "Now who's being crude?"

"If you're thinking of seducing me, you're wasting your time. I've already encountered more trouble with women than I need."

BRAVE LAND, BRAVE LOVE

CONNIE MASON

LOVE SPELL BOOKS   ◆   NEW YORK CITY

LOVE SPELL®

October 1998

Published by

Dorchester Publishing Co., Inc.
276 Fifth Avenue
New York, NY 10001

ISBN 0-505-52282-9

The name "Love Spell" and its logo are trademarks of Dorchester Publishing Co., Inc.

Printed in the United States of America.

*To my beautiful granddaughters,
Beth and Paula, and grandsons,
Joe, Matt, Alex, James, and Aaron.*

Prologue

London, 1815

Her fingertips were losing their grip on the bruising roughness of the brick ledge. Clinging tenuously to the slim thread of life, she turned her head to glance downward. There were no bushes beneath her to break her fall, only the hard-packed earth of the circular driveway below. Blood stained one cheek where she had scraped it against the unforgiving brick wall. She must not fail. She was so young; her life was too precious to waste.

Better death than the life fate had dealt her.

Frantically she twisted her head, seeking the sturdy branches of the stately old oak that had stood long before the house had been built.

Mere moments ago she had desperately studied the tree from her window and perceived it as her only link to salvation. Its spreading branches, thickly leafed with spring foliage, beckoned to her, and she had recklessly answered its call.

But it looked so far away.

Dare she release one hand to seize the safety it offered? What if she fell? A smile far too cynical for one so young curved her soft red lips. She had already considered that possibility but had discarded the threat to life and limb as she sucked in a ragged breath and lowered herself out of the window.

What good was life when it offered so little?

Swallowing her fear, she released one hand—time was running out—and twisted her body as she sought frantically to embrace the branch closest to her. The effort cost her her precious hold as the weight became too great for her other hand and arm to bear. Realizing she was in danger of plunging to her death, she braced her feet against the wall and made a desperate lunge toward the tree. Her fingers clutched convulsively at the elusive branch.

She had it within her grasp!

Her arms felt as if they might separate from their sockets, but she clung with fervent tenacity to the slim hope fate had offered her. She swung her legs over the branch; then, with the agility of youth, she climbed down the tree. The last branch was still quite high. Even when she lowered herself as far as possible, the ground was six feet from her dangling legs.

One by one the lights in the huge brick house flickered out. With courage born of desperation, she closed her eyes and released the branch. She hit the ground and rolled, coming to a bone-jarring halt against the stone wall that surrounded the estate. Being young, healthy, and resilient, she earned from her wild, impulsive escape through the window little more than a few bloody scrapes, bruises, and an ankle that was already beginning to swell.

Picking herself up off the ground, she limped through the gate that had been left unlatched to accommodate the guests who had just recently attended the celebration. Within minutes she was swallowed up by the restless fog that swirled in misty tendrils along the narrow alleyways and broader streets of London.

She didn't look back.

Nor did she regret leaving behind the stately ivy-covered mansion.

No matter what the future dealt her, it couldn't be worse than what she had left behind.

Chapter One

London, 1818

The door banged open, nearly flying off its hinges as a man burst into the room and stopped mere inches from the bed where Ben Penrod was engaged in vigorous love-making with Caroline Battersby. It wasn't the first time that he and Caroline had shared passion, and Ben had hoped it wouldn't be the last. What rotten luck had brought her outraged father barging into the room when he wasn't expected home until tomorrow?

"I hope you enjoyed yourself, young man, for it will be the last time you make love to anyone, unless you do the right thing by Caroline and make her your wife."

Ben groped frantically for the sheet, flinging it over himself and Caroline before attempting to placate the irate man. In his haste he failed to note the conspiratorial look that passed between father and daughter, for if he had he would have had an inkling of what was in store for him.

"If you're speaking of marriage," Ben replied when he was sufficiently protected by the sheet, "I'm afraid that's out of the question."

Aggressively handsome, Ben Penrod had spent the better part of his twenty-seven years keeping one step ahead of marriage. Since there was no reason to marry and provide an heir—his brother Dare had already done that—he felt no need to saddle himself with a wife. Both Dare and his friend Robin Fletcher had encountered so much difficulty winning their wives that Ben had solemnly sworn to remain a bachelor the rest of his life.

"You—you have ruined my daughter," Lord Battersby sputtered angrily. Ben's blatant refusal to marry Caroline served only to increase his outrage. "It's obvious now that these past two years you have been in London you have engaged in a clandestine affair with my daughter, and I demand you do the honorable thing."

"That's not entirely true," Ben said with a calmness that belied his agitation. "Caroline is but one of the many women I have escorted about London since my arrival."

"I don't know how things are done in

Australia, but in England a man is expected to marry the woman he has ruined."

Ben swallowed an angry retort, too much of a gentleman to reveal that he wasn't Caroline's first lover nor likely to be the last. Having taken London by storm two years ago upon his arrival from Australia, Ben was having the time of his life sampling the women from one end of England to the other. During a visit to France he had perfected his sexual skills and honed his charm until he was nearly irresistible to the opposite sex. Countless women aspired to the position of wife to the handsome, wealthy Australian, even if it meant living in the convict colony, though most doubted that fun-seeking Ben Penrod would abandon London gaiety for the remote outback of Australia. But then few knew Ben Penrod well enough to predict what the future held for him or where he intended to spend the rest of his life.

"I doubt if Caroline and I would suit," Ben offered lamely.

Suddenly Caroline, who until now had allowed her father to control the conversation, came alive. "That's not true, Ben, we would suit very well!"

Ben ground his teeth in frustration. He had no intention of marrying Caroline, or anyone else. Within the first year of marriage to the little baggage she would put horns on him. No thanks, he silently vowed. He refused to be coerced into wedding Caroline, no matter how great the inducement.

"You don't understand, Caroline, marriage—"

"No, Penrod," Battersby interrupted rudely, "*you* don't understand. I will not have my daughter's name bandied about London. You *will* marry her. I have sufficient clout to see that you are brought to the altar. If force must be employed, then so be it."

Ben groaned. Bloody hell, how did this happen? It wasn't the first time he had bedded Caroline, and she had assured him her parents wouldn't be home until late tomorrow. It wasn't as if she were some young innocent he had seduced. Hell, no! Seducing innocents was not his cup of tea. Caroline had come eagerly to his bed, nearly as experienced as he. He glanced at her now, realizing with a sudden jolt of intuition that he had been duped. Her face was far too complacent for all this to be an accident. The little bitch had planned this to bring him to heel! For months she had been trying to wheedle a proposal from him, and his reluctance to make a commitment angered her. When he threatened to break off their relationship, she begged him to come to her tonight for old time's sake.

"I told you before, marriage is out of the question," Ben insisted stubbornly.

"I would be interested to know why," Battersby prodded.

"I—I'm already married!" Ben blurted in a moment of madness. His lie certainly couldn't

17

make things worse and might even help.

"What!" This from Caroline who bolted upright, nearly forgetting to bring the sheet up to shield her naked breasts. Her full red lips formed a vivid expression of shock in her white face. She was beautiful in a dark, sensual way, her pale skin contrasting starkly with her ebony hair and bold black eyes. "This is the first I heard of a wife."

"Nevertheless, I do have a wife. She accompanied me to London from Australia."

"Where is this woman you claim to have married?" Battersby challenged. "Have you hidden her in your apartment these two years?"

"Certainly not!" Ben declared, becoming more deeply involved in his lie than he intended. "My wife has been in the country, visiting relatives."

"Then it should be little trouble for you to produce this elusive wife of yours."

"Bloody hell, don't you believe me?"

"No. If you can't produce a wife in one week from today, you'll marry Caroline. And if you know what's good for you, I'd advise you not to leave the country."

Ben bristled indignantly. He certainly didn't want a wife, but he wasn't the type to run away from his problems. Cowardice didn't run in the Penrod family, and he was no exception. "I have no intention of leaving England."

"Then you'll marry me?" Caroline gloated happily.

"I'm already married," Ben repeated, aggravated with himself for inventing a nonexistent wife. If he had been given more time he might have come up with a more plausible excuse.

"We'll see," Battersby replied tersely. "Meanwhile, I suggest you leave."

"Of course," Ben replied, overjoyed to escape an embarrassing situation even though he was certain he had been skillfully manipulated by Caroline and her father. "If you'd be so kind to allow me to dress—"

Abruptly Battersby turned and strode from the bedroom, leaving Caroline and Ben alone.

"Darling, I hope you don't think I'd—"

"That's exactly what I think, *darling*," Ben stressed. His voice was ripe with sarcasm and his gray eyes hardened with icy contempt. "Excuse me if I don't fall in with your plans."

"You do me an injustice, Ben," Caroline pouted, allowing the sheet to drop to her waist. "I'd never try to manipulate you like that." Suddenly her black eyes narrowed slyly. "Are you *really* married?"

Ben leaped from bed and shrugged into his clothes, disdaining an answer until he had his hand on the doorknob. "I'm afraid you'll have to wait a week to learn the answer to that question, Caroline."

Deeper into the bowels of London Ben strode, unaware of where he was or how late the hour. He'd been walking for hours, ever since he left

Caroline's fashionable townhouse on St. George Square. He went where his feet led him, through the park, over the bridge, and now into streets he was unfamiliar with. Streets boasting dark alleys, twisting lanes, and garbage-strewn walkways. Acrid smells assailed his nostrils. Smells of rotting food, human waste, and the salty, fetid odor of fish and the river. Squalid inns inhabited the area, and grubby, foul-mouthed streetwalkers attempted to distract Ben as he passed.

But Ben neither saw the seedy inns nor heard the invitations offered by the prostitutes. His mind was focused on one thought and one thought only. Where was he going to find a wife in one week? And if he didn't produce a wife, how could he escape the wedding Lord Battersby was determined to force him into? His mind whirled in endless speculation, but every road led to the inescapable fact that he had no wife.

Briefly Ben considered asking one of his many female acquaintances to impersonate his wife, but quickly discarded the idea when he realized most of his acquaintances were members of the ton and easily recognized. The notion of paying one of the higher-class prostitutes to portray his wife was swiftly rejected when Ben couldn't think of a single one who would be suitable. And if he did by chance find one, she would certainly be known to most of his London friends.

Ben trudged on, unmindful of the midnight

darkness or the drifting, impenetrable fog swirling around him in thick, damp fingers that chilled him to the bone. The infernal fog was a part of London he had never learned to appreciate. At times like this he longed for the sunny, temperate climes of New South Wales, where fog was a novelty except in the upper reaches of the Blue Mountains. So engrossed was he in his mental misery that he paid little heed to a small, ragged figure crouching in the black void of an alleyway that Ben was approaching.

The waif's eyes narrowed in avid speculation when Ben came into view, alone and apparently lost in concentration. Giving him a brief once-over, the waif, no bigger than a half-grown lad, noted the fine cut of Ben's clothes, his proud bearing, and came to the conclusion that Ben was a member of the ton out slumming. It mattered little. One-eyed Bertha was expecting blunt tonight, and there would be a beating if none was forthcoming.

Ben drew closer to the alley, blissfully unaware that he was a prime target for a robbery. It was a miracle that he hadn't been accosted already. Perhaps his size had scared off most would-be thieves. He was outlandishly tall, and the breadth of his shoulders was indeed intimidating.

In a moment of triumph, the moon slid out from beneath a thick bank of clouds to provide the waif unrestricted view of the man. Permanently tanned from the relentless Australian

21

sun, he was marked by lazy arrogance and exotic good looks.

Keeping in mind the hard-learned lessons taught by One-eyed Bertha, the waif located the bulge of Ben's wallet and flexed long, nimble fingers in anticipation. Then all thought ceased as instinct came into play. As Ben drew abreast of the darkened alley, the waif darted out, extending a well-placed foot and tripping Ben. Ben fell with a thud and a curse, and before he knew what was happening the little thief had delved into his pocket, lifted his wallet, and scampered off into the alley.

"Bloody hell! Come back here, you bloody little thief!"

Recovering quickly, Ben lurched to his feet and gave chase, nearly as nimble as the thief despite his size. To Ben's chagrin, the alley led to a dead end. But he could tell by the way the empty crates were piled one atop another that the boy had scaled the high wall and dropped to the other side. Angry determination lent wings to Ben's feet as he easily vaulted over the fence with the aid of the crates and was over the top in time to see the thief disappear around a corner.

"Damn bloody scamp," Ben muttered beneath his breath as he chased after the thief. He'd been in London two years and this was the first time he had been accosted on the streets and robbed. Though he had to admit this was the first time he'd been foolish enough to venture alone in this section of London.

22

Ben's long-muscled legs stretched to amazing lengths as he closed the distance between himself and the pickpocket. In superb condition despite his two years in London, Ben's body responded easily as it obeyed his command for greater speed. Living most of his life in the untamed wilds of Australia, he was accustomed to pushing himself to incredible lengths. And his great strength showed in his vigorous pursuit of the pickpocket who had lifted his blunt.

Ben caught up with the urchin just as the bundle of rags was about to duck into a building. The waif grunted in surprise when Ben hurtled out of the darkness and wrestled the slim youth to the filth-littered ground in an alley behind a large deserted warehouse.

"Got you, you bloody thief!" Ben crowed, grabbing the boy by the scruff of the neck and shaking him until he heard the rattle of teeth. "There are too many characters like you in New South Wales for me to fall victim to one in London. Hand over the blunt, vermin."

The waif was being shaken so thoroughly that words were impossible. If this big ox didn't stop his infernal jostling, the pickpocket expected to be minus a head. When Ben finally desisted, the waif opened a surprisingly soft mouth and spit out a string of vile curses that stung Ben's ears.

"Ye bloody bastard, take yer bleedin' 'ands off me!"

"You foul-mouthed little viper!" Ben hissed

between clenched teeth. "I have half a notion to throttle you here and now, boy. Why wait for the law to deal with you when I can do just as well?"

The thief blanched, revealing a white face beneath smeared dirt, then turned and viciously attacked the back of Ben's hand with sharp little teeth.

"Ow! Dammit to hell! You'll pay for that, you ragged little beggar!" Ben cried as he resumed his relentless shaking. He really did feel like throttling the little wretch but wisely resisted.

"Yer 'urtin' me, ye black-hearted devil!"

"Serves you right. Now hand over the wallet."

"Will ye let me go if I give ye yer wallet?"

"No. I'm carting you off to the constable as soon as you return my blunt."

"Blast and damn!"

"Aren't you rather young for this kind of work?" Ben demanded, as he pocketed the reluctantly returned wallet.

"I'm older than I look," the thief replied sourly.

"What's your name?" Ben asked.

"None of yer business!"

"Watch your tongue. You need a damn good beating."

"I've 'ad me share of 'em," the waif admitted defiantly. The moment Ben's grip slackened, the ragged urchin struggled anew.

The waif's startling words caused Ben's resolve to falter. The poor homeless boy probably had been living on the streets, fending off predators since he was a wee child, Ben reflected guiltily, and here he was acting like a bloody bully. He was twice the boy's size and could easily crush him in one powerful hand, so why was he acting with unnecessary cruelty? Because he is a bloody thief and pickpocket, he told himself. If he relented now, the boy would probably end up dangling from a rope or be transported to a convict colony like Australia. Still, Ben felt pity for one so young and helpless. . . .

Taking advantage of Ben's preoccupation, the waif twisted from Ben's grasp and bolted. But Ben was faster. Reaching out with one long arm, he made a desperate lunge for the fleeing thief. His hand came away with the woolen cap that had been jammed down over the waif's ears. Ben's breath caught painfully in his throat as long pale strands of blond hair floated out from under the cap and settled around the thief's shoulders like a silver mantle. Intrigued, Ben was hard on the urchin's heels, seizing a silken strand of hair and putting an abrupt halt to the thief's desperate flight.

"What are you? Who are you?" Ben asked. Ragged little puffs of air escaped from his chest as he fought to catch his breath.

It was obvious now to Ben that the thief wasn't a lad as he assumed, but a young girl. How young he wasn't certain, but he damn well intended to find out.

25

"None of yer business, ye bleedin' swell!" the girl shouted as Ben wound a silver strand of hair around his fist, dragging her up against the unyielding wall of his chest.

"You have a foul tongue for a child," Ben said tightly as he stared down into the urchin's grimy face. "I have a good notion to warm your britches good and proper."

"Ye wouldn't dare! Ye got yer bloody blunt, let me go."

An arrested look came over Ben's features. He certainly couldn't let the little termagant loose to continue her wicked ways. And turning her over to the constable didn't appeal to him. He'd seen too many just like her in New South Wales. Perhaps if he took her home and cleaned her up a bit he might find a home for the child. Or he could send her to an orphanage. Those two options seemed infinitely more palatable than letting her go or sending her to prison.

"If I let you go, you'll only continue your life of crime," Ben decided aloud. "What's your name?"

Silence.

"Tell me your name or I'll take you straight-away to the constable."

"Tia!" the girl spit out defiantly.

"Tia what? What's your last name?"

"I ain't got none."

"All right, Tia, I'll let that go for now. How old are you?"

"Old enough."

"That's no answer," Ben said, his patience waning.

"Eighteen."

"You're a liar as well as a thief. You can't be more than thirteen or fourteen at the most."

"Suit yerself. What are ya gonna do with me?"

"I haven't decided, but one thing is certain. I won't throw you back on the streets to rob unsuspecting victims like you did me. Where are your parents?"

"I ain't got none."

A spark of pity softened Ben's gray eyes. "You have no guardian? No one to care for you?"

Tia stiffened. Ben's question seemed to ignite a strange reaction in the girl. Her chin shot up and one corner of her lip curved into a snarl. "I told ya, I ain't got no one."

Suddenly Ben came to a decision. "Very well, Tia, have it your way. But don't expect sympathy from me. Come along, I suspect there's a constable nearby."

"No! I told ye the truth. There ain't a soul what cares about me except fer One-eyed Bertha. And she'd lose interest right fast if the blunt don't come in regular. Don't send me to jail, yer honor, please!"

It was the "please" that persuaded Ben. He hadn't the stomach to send this mere slip of a girl to jail. He might be a rogue but he wasn't heartless. "Don't call me your honor. My name is Ben Penrod. And I won't take you to jail if you do as I say and come along peacefully."

27

Connie Mason

Tia's eyes narrowed suspiciously. There was nothing she hadn't seen or heard in London's squalid underworld that would shock her. "Just what do ye 'ave in mind? I ain't no streetwalker."

"Bloody hell! Do I look like a man who abuses children?" Disgust colored his words. "There are enough willing women in London without forcing young girls."

"I'll bet there are, fer the likes of you," Tia hinted slyly. She wasn't unaware of Ben's masculine appeal no matter how much of a bully she thought him.

"That's enough, brat," Ben warned, grabbing her by the scruff of the neck.

"Where ye takin' me?"

"To my lodging. Once you're cleaned up I stand a better chance of finding someone willing to pound some manners into you. The first thing you need is to have your mouth washed out with soap. Once the dirt is scraped off your hide you might even be tolerable to look at. An education wouldn't hurt either. Of course, I can always send you to an orphanage."

"Orphanage! Like hell, ya bleedin' idiot! I'm too old to go to an orphanage. I ain't no bloody slave."

Ben's mouth tightened into a grim line. Why in the hell did these things have to happen to him? First Caroline and her scheming father conspire to trap him into marriage, and now this foul-mouthed little baggage turns up to disrupt his life. He had thought Dare's and Robin's

28

life was complicated, but suddenly his own life was surpassing anything Dare and Robin had experienced.

"You'll do as I say, brat."

Grasping Tia's arm, he dragged her with relentless determination down dark, deserted streets until he reached a less seedy section of town and hailed a passing hack. Lifting her by her collar and the seat of her baggy pants, he shoved her inside and quickly followed, shouting directions to the driver. Relaxing against the squabs, he studied Tia through narrowed lids. Actually, he could see little of her features. And what he could see was coated in a layer of grime. She was small-boned and appeared oddly fragile and vulnerable within the ragged folds of the oversized rags she wore.

Tia said little, her mind racing in all directions at once. Should she throw herself from the hack, she wondered bleakly, and risk serious injury? Or wait for a more propitious time to escape, possibly when the arrogant bully had his back turned? From the looks of him, he wouldn't be easy to fool. Why did this have to happen to her now? she wondered. Except for an occasional close call, she'd never been apprehended before. *Jail.* The thought sent tremors racing down her spine. Once before she had escaped a similar fate, and if she didn't do as this stranger said she'd find herself in a situation nearly as unacceptable as the one she left.

The hack drew to a halt and Ben stepped out,

dragging Tia behind him while he paused to pay the driver. His firm grip kept her from bolting. While Ben was occupied with counting out the correct fare, Tia glanced around. Though not nearly as impressive as St. George Park or Bedford Square, Ben's rented house sat on a quiet street in an upper-class neighborhood around the corner from the park. The street was deserted, the houses nearly all dark, and Tia's quick mind memorized the lay of the street and position of the houses, storing it away for future use. Then her thoughts ceased when the hack drove off. Tia felt the grip on her arm tighten as Ben started toward the front door of a small brick dwelling.

Fumbling for his key, Ben unlocked the door and flung Tia inside. A tall man with thinning hair and erect bearing stepped from one of the rear rooms carrying a lamp. Tia could tell by his dark, drab clothing and well-modulated voice that the man was a servant.

"I'm glad you waited up, Jeevers, I have need of your services tonight."

"Of course, Mr. Penrod, what is it you wish?" His gaze fell on Tia, but being a proper servant he exhibited only mild curiosity.

"A bath, Jeevers. Bring the tub to my room immediately, and hot water, plenty of it."

"Yes, sir," Jeevers answered, wondering what Ben was up to now. He'd been with Ben the entire two years of the Australian's visit to London and by now was surprised at nothing the impulsive young man did. Jeevers had seen many beautiful women come and go from the house during that time, but never had he seen anyone like the grubby urchin Ben now had in tow. Fortunately, his lot in life was not to understand the whims of the gentry but to serve their needs, no matter how strange they may seem.

"I don't need no bath!" Tia protested vigorously. Actually, it sounded heavenly.

"You're filthy," Ben observed, wrinkling his nose in obvious distaste. "Have you ever bathed in your life?"

"Only when I'm dirty," Tia returned saucily. The sight of Ben imploring the heavens sent a giggle tumbling past Tia's lips. She couldn't recall when she'd laughed last and it felt good.

A few minutes later a discreet knock on Ben's bedroom door announced Jeevers. Ben opened the door and the servant wrestled a big brass tub into the room. "It will be a few minutes before the water is hot, sir," Jeevers advised as he left the room. Ben spent the time coaxing answers out of Tia. Most of his questions were met with sullen silence.

"Surely you have a last name."

"None that I can recall," Tia said sourly.

"Are you a bastard?" Ben asked. "Was your mother a streetwalker?"

"Hell, no, my mother wasn't no streetwalker!" Tia refuted, enraged over Ben's unjust accusation.

"How do you expect me to learn the truth if you don't tell me?" Ben asked in a wheedling tone.

"It ain't none of yer business," Tia repeated for the fourth time that night.

"I'm making it my business. If I'm going to help you, I need to know more about you."

"I ain't askin' fer yer help."

"Contrary little brat, aren't you?" Ben muttered, growing more aggravated by the minute. "Who is One-eyed Bertha? You mentioned her earlier."

Tia thought a moment before deciding to answer. "She's the woman what took me in when I needed 'elp. She kept the—the others from 'urtin' me."

Ben flushed, realizing that Tia was talking about men who might abuse her. Which led to another question. "Are you a whore? Prostitutes ply their trade at an early age in the bowels of London Town."

"Ye bloody bastard! I ain't no whore!" The words had no sooner left her mouth than she flew at Ben, nails extended, teeth bared to sink into soft flesh. She managed to dig a deep groove down Ben's cheek before he caught her hands, keeping her from inflicting further damage.

"You filthy little vixen! You're going to pay for that."

Dragging her behind him, he sat down on the bed, threw her over his knee, and flipped her over on her stomach. "You've needed this beating since the moment I laid eyes on you."

"No, please!"

Ignoring her plea, Ben yanked down her britches, baring two perfect white mounds that gave him momentary pause. Her skin was the texture of soft, fine velvet—and clean. Stunned, he stared as if hers was the first female buttocks he'd ever seen. She looked strangely vulnerable and innocent upended like she was, and Ben suddenly lost all desire to inflict punishment.

"Well, what are ye waitin' fer, ya bleedin' bully? Get it over with if yer gonna beat me. I can take it." Gritting her teeth, Tia waited for the first blow.

It never came.

Chapter Two

An arrested look came over Ben's features as he gazed down at the soft white mounds of Tia's buttocks. Suddenly the last thing he wanted to do was hurt the girl. She might be a thief and whore despite her youth and denial, but he didn't have the heart to hurt her more than life had already done. Twisting her head around, Tia opened her eyes and flashed him a look of open defiance. When the first blow failed to connect, she drew in a ragged breath. Then abruptly Ben stood and she went tumbling off his lap. Without a backward glance, he strode briskly to the door.

"I'll help Jeevers carry up the hot water." His voice was low and strangely taut, revealing nothing of his reason for changing his mind.

Tia barely had time to pick herself up off the floor before Ben and Jeevers returned, each carrying a bucket of water. They made several trips, and when the tub was full, Jeevers discreetly left the room, closing the door softly behind him.

"Strip and get in the tub," Ben ordered curtly.

"Not bloody likely! Not with you watchin'."

"I've seen children before," Ben intoned dryly.

Tia's face turned a dull red beneath the grime. "I ain't gonna strip in front of no man."

Ben made a disparaging sound deep in his throat. " 'Tis more than likely you've done more than strip before men," he suggested crudely.

Clenching her fists, Tia swung at him. "Take that back, ye arrogant bastard!"

Neatly sidestepping the attack, Ben grasps her wrists. Her long silvery tresses caught the glint of lamplight, and for the space of a heartbeat Ben was seized by the uncanny feeling that his entire life was about to unravel. There's a limit on time, a limit on what one can accomplish in life, and a limit on luck, and Ben felt that luck had just deserted him.

Tia glared with mute belligerence at Ben. He stood so tall she was intimidated by his height, and from the moment of their first meeting she had detested his arrogance and his obnoxious demand for instant obedience. Blacker than raven wings, his long hair touched his broad shoulders with a keen disregard for convention. Thick brows arched over his

35

arresting silver-gray eyes, eyes that revealed contradictions of character with greater reliability than his handsome face, fine nose, or sensual curve of his mouth set against a firm, strong chin. Tia flinched beneath Ben's heavy-lidded gaze and felt a curl of something strange and unfamiliar unwind within her.

A tense silence prevailed as the unlikely pair mutely appraised one another. Ben was the first to look away.

"Very well, I'll leave. But if you're not in the tub by the time I return, I'll tear those filthy rags off you myself." Turning abruptly, he stormed from the room.

Once he left, Tia eyed the tub with longing. She couldn't remember when she'd had a real bath in a real tub. For the past few years she'd had to make do with furtive washes when no one was about or quick dunkings in the river when weather permitted. She glanced apprehensively toward the door, wondering how long she had before Ben returned and if he really would strip her if she didn't comply with his wishes. He certainly looked capable of doing everything he threatened. Deciding not to test his short temper again, Tia quickly undressed, tossing her filthy clothes aside, and climbed in the tub. It felt heavenly.

Picking up the fragrant soap and washcloth placed on the rim of the tub for her use, Tia worked up a rich lather and sighed blissfully as the cleansing suds soothed her skin. It felt wonderful. Bathing was a luxury when one was afforded little opportunity to do so. Once her skin was clean and pink, she attacked her long blond hair with a vengeance. Twice she worked the suds into her hair and rinsed until the water ran clean. And then she washed it again just for good measure. One-eyed Bertha had threatened many times to hack off her glorious tresses, but Tia had managed to talk her out of it each time. It was all Tia had left to remind her of the life she had once led, a life she had willingly abandoned for freedom.

The sad truth was that the quality of freedom she had acquired was little better than what she had abandoned. But at least she was free to come and go. And life on the streets wasn't nearly as abhorrent as what she had fled from. Until she met Ben Penrod, who threatened to take away her freedom. Resting her head on the rim of the tub, Tia sank deeper into the soothing water. She closed her eyes, dreaming of the time when she could once again stroll the better sections of London without worrying about being found and returned to . . . No, she wouldn't think about that, she vowed with stubborn determination. Somehow she would escape from Ben Penrod and make her way back to the life she had grown comfortable with. Hadn't One-eyed Bertha always said that bathing regularly was bad for your health?

Ben stood lazily in the doorway, one broad shoulder resting against the jamb, arms crossed over his massive chest. He wondered what devious plot Tia was hatching in her mind. Her eyes were closed and her head was resting against the rim, her blond hair trailing over the edge to the floor. One white arm, looking surprisingly soft and curvacious, rested on the side of the tub. Water pooled on the floor beneath her fingertips, and Ben couldn't tear his eyes away from the amazingly full upper curves of her breasts, all that was visible beneath the scum rising to the top of the water. He realized that Tia hadn't heard him open the door, else she would be spitting defiance at him, so he lingered, thoroughly enjoying the tantalizing vision.

"If you're through with your bath, Jeevers will bring up something for you to eat."

Tia's eyes flew open and she slid down even farther into the dirty water. "Wha—what are ye doin' here?" she sputtered indignantly.

"This is my house and my room." He walked farther into the room, spied the bath sheet draped over a chair, and picked it up. Approaching the tub, he held it out. "Unless you want Jeevers to see you in your bath, I suggest you get out now."

Tia made a grab for the towel, but Ben held it just out of reach. She settled back down. "I ain't gonna get out til ye leave."

How easy it was to taunt this child, Ben thought, suddenly disgusted with his actions. It wasn't like him to act so cruelly toward one so young. Not that Tia was an innocent young thing unaccustomed to such treatment. She was a pickpocket, thief, and Lord only knows what else. Still, he reflected, it wouldn't hurt to find a spark of kindness in his heart for her. Hopefully he'd find her a home with a family who would teach her manners befitting a young lady. With proper training she might even become a ladies' maid, or governess.

"Get out of the tub, Tia. I'll see to the fire while you wrap yourself in the bath sheet." Placing the sheet on a bench near the tub, Ben turned away to poke at the fire in the hearth. He was adding more wood to the flames when he heard a thud and shriek. Whirling on his heel, he was startled to find Tia sprawled on the floor beside the tub.

Unmindful of the puddle of water that had dripped from her fingertips, Tia had stepped out of the tub into the puddle, which had made the highly polished wood floor slick as ice. Her foot had flown out from under her and she hit the floor with a resounding whack. Her head had smacked the rim of the tub, knocking her nearly senseless.

The sight of Tia sprawled in all her naked glory on the floor rendered Ben speechless. Her skin was all pink and white and glowing from her bath. She lay in a cloud of blond hair that glittered like moonbeams in the firelight. Her legs were long and shapely for all her short stature. Her waist was impossibly slim and gave way to gently rounded hips. She was thin, as if she had missed many meals, but as Ben's eyes riveted on her full, coral-tipped breasts, he realized that Tia was not the child he had assumed. Shifting his gaze downward to the womanly triangle between her thighs, Ben felt his loins react violently as he noted that the curls crowning her mound were a deeper gold than the silvery hair on her head.

"Bloody hell, you're no child!"

Shaking her head to clear away the cobwebs, Tia tried to rise, found the effort too great, and fell back with a moan. The curiously vulnerable sound released Ben's frozen limbs. Shock was the only word he could think of to describe how he felt when he discovered that Tia was a young beauty with the full bloom of womanhood upon her. Her body was magnificently fashioned and her features lovely beyond all imagination! She had the face of an angel, all peaches-and-cream beneath the dirt she had washed away. And her eyes. They were the most incredible shade of blue-green he had ever seen. Almost jewel-like, rimmed with incredibly long dark gold lashes situated beneath delicately arched brows the same bright shade as her lashes. How had he failed to notice those full pouty lips? he asked himself wonderingly. Or skin so soft and velvety he ached to touch it?

"Are you hurt?"

Tia's temper flared when she saw Ben staring down at her with something akin to awe. She didn't like it one damn bit. Her anger exploded and she lit into him with all the fury of an enraged tigress.

"Ye damn bloody pervert, stop starin' at me! I ain't no different from any other woman."

Scowling fiercely, Ben picked up the bath sheet, draped it over Tia's naked body, and helped her to her feet. "You've got some explaining to do, young lady."

"What's to explain?" Tia replied furiously as she wrapped herself in the sheet. "I told ye I wasn't no kid, but ya didn't believe me."

"Bloody hell. You're no bigger than a minute, what was I to think? Besides, it's difficult to believe that a young lady could spout the obscenities that come out of your mouth. How old are you?"

"I told ye. I'm eighteen."

"No more than a child," Ben muttered disparagingly. For some unknown reason he was unwilling to think of the little termagant as a full-grown woman. In a matter of hours his luck had gone from bad to worse. He might have found a home for a child, but what in the hell was he going to do with a full-grown woman?

Jeevers arrived with the food Ben had ordered, putting an end to the conversation for the time being. But the moment the servant set the tray down on the table and left, Ben once again demanded answers.

"How long have you lived on the streets?"

"Long enough."

"What kind of answer is that?"

41

"Look, yer honor, kin I eat? The food is gettin' cold and my stomach is growlin'."

Ben grit his teeth in barely contained rage. "Don't call me your honor. My name is Ben. Go ahead and eat, Tia, I'll wait."

Tia needed no second invitation. Grasping the fork, she dug into the food with a gusto that startled Ben. The poor girl must be starving, he thought with a jolt of pity that thoroughly unnerved him. He watched in consternation as she shoveled food into her mouth with amazing speed. When nothing was left on the tray, she sat back and sighed in obvious contentment.

"Kin I go to bed now, yer—Ben?" She gazed longingly at the bed. It had been longer than she cared to remember since she'd slept in an honest-to-God bed with a feather mattress that looked soft enough to drown in. Too bad she'd not be able to use the bed, she thought as she looked away.

"In good time," Ben replied sternly. "Your crude speech and foul language leads me to believe you've been raised in the worst slums of London. Have you always lived in such dismal circumstances?"

A pained look spread over Tia's lovely features, mesmerizing Ben. Her beauty was so enchanting he found it difficult to believe he hadn't spotted it right off. Her features were delicately defined, not coarse or heavy as one would expect of a child of the streets. What was she thinking? he wondered. There were times when the depths of her emotions rose to the surface and revealed more than she would have liked. Like now. Ben swore that Tia was concealing something from him. Something that might change the course of her life.

"I can speak as well as you," Tia said with quiet dignity.

"What? What did you say?"

"You heard me correctly." She spoke in well-modulated tones devoid of all slang and crudeness. "I am sick and tired of listening to you make fun of me."

Ben's mouth flew open, aghast by what he had just heard. "Who in bloody hell are you?"

"Tia. Who are you?"

"You may have cleaned up your language but you're still a fresh-mouthed little tart," Ben said, his voice laced with disgust.

Tia bristled angrily. "I'm no tart! How dare you judge me when you know nothing about me?"

"Why don't you tell me?" Ben said, his tone gentling. "From whom did you learn your fancy language? And if by some remote chance you are educated, what are you doing living on the streets and picking pockets for a living?"

Obviously Ben was asking the wrong questions, for Tia's blue-green eyes hardened and her mouth grew taut. "None of your business."

"I'm only trying to help," Ben ventured when he realized that Tia had no intention of enlightening him.

"I don't need your help," Tia insisted stubbornly.

"Judging from your activity a few hours ago, I'd say you need all the help you can get. Are you running away from someone? Your parents, perhaps?"

Tia stiffened. For a brief moment she had the look of a trapped animal. "I told you before, I have no parents. They died long ago."

"Dammit, Tia, how can I decide what's best for you when you continually block my efforts?"

"Let me go. I promise you'll never see me again if you turn me loose."

"I can't do that," Ben said slowly. "Beneath all that dirt and grime covering your face and those baggy clothes disguising your body, you're a beautiful young lady. I can't toss you back on the streets to continue your life of crime. One day someone will discover you're not a young lad, and then what? Are you prepared to deal with that? Will you become a whore, if you're not already one, and use your body to earn a living?"

"It's not my intention to be a pickpocket the rest of my life. When the time is right I'll— I'll know," she finished lamely, refusing to say more. "There is nothing you or anyone can do to help me."

"Lord preserve me from stubborn, independent, and ornery women," Ben muttered darkly.

"And save me from arrogant, nosy men," Tia returned tartly. "Besides, how do I know you really want to help me? I know nothing about you. From what I know of men, they are over-bearing, insufferable bullies who expect total obedience from a woman. They care nothing for a woman's feelings as long as she serves them in whatever capacity they demand. Most men are crude, demanding animals."

Stung by Tia's biased tirade, Ben was tempted to throw the little termagant back on the streets where she obviously belonged. But he couldn't do that. Whether Tia liked it or not, he was determined to help her find a different way of life. "Have you always had such a low opinion of men? Or are you perhaps referring to me?"

"If the shoe fits . . ." Tia said with a hint of malice.

Ben sighed, so aggravated with the little witch he wanted to shake her until her good senses returned. "For your information, I am a respected sheep rancher from New South Wales, Australia. As I said before, my name is Ben Penrod. My father and I own and operate—quite profitably, I might add—Penrod station on the Hawkesbury River. I have one brother, Dare, a sister-in-law, Casey, two nephews, and one niece. I am in England on holiday."

Tia said nothing, studying Ben through heavi-ly lashed lids. Truthfully, she didn't know what to make of the man. She knew little of the gen-try, having lived among thieves and riffraff for so long. And before that, from the age of twelve, she was shunted off to the country where she had lived in quiet obscurity. She was brought to

London only once, and that was the day she left forever the life she was born to. To her knowledge, few if any of her parents' friends would recognize her today. Except for one . . .

Something about Ben disturbed her. He was too handsome, too male, so damned virile she felt intimidated by his very presence. She was certain of only one thing: she had to leave his house—soon. Just looking at him raised emotions in her she never knew existed. Unfamiliar feelings that made her body react in strange ways. For the first time in her life she was aware of a man in a manner that was totally foreign to her, and she wasn't certain she liked it.

Her eyes slid to his chest, noting with alarm the incredible width of his torso, the way his shoulders filled out the fine material of his jacket, then continued downward to his narrow waist and slim hips. With naughty delight, Tia's gaze skimmed past thickly muscled thighs to that part of him that was blatantly sexual. Her eyes jerked upward when she saw his unconscious reaction to her bold journey over his six-foot-three-inch frame.

"Do you like what you see?" Ben drawled. His voice was fraught with lazy humor, making Tia aware of her rude perusal. "I suppose turnabout is fair play, since I saw much more of you than you saw of me."

A deep red crawled up Tia's cheeks and neck. "Now who's being crude?"

"If you're thinking of seducing me, you're wasting your time. I've already encountered more trouble with women than I need."

"Blast and damn!" Tia shouted, reverting back to street language. "Ye bleedin' bastard! I don't have to sit here and listen to yer insults." She jumped to her feet, pulling the towel tightly about her as she searched frantically for her clothes.

"You're not going anywhere," Ben said tightly. "Not until I decide what's to be done with you."

"You can't keep me here against my will," Tia charged defiantly.

"I can and I will. I still hold the upper hand. I caught you lifting my blunt. The authorities will be most happy to take someone like you off the streets permanently. I'll leave you now, to think on your crimes and punishment. Meanwhile, get some sleep, we'll continue this conversation tomorrow." He rose to leave, carefully picking up her dirty garments and holding them at arm's length as if they offended him. "And don't think about leaving. The door will be bolted from the other side and the windows are tightly shuttered." Tia's foul curses turned the air blue as Ben let himself out the door.

Once Ben was gone, Tia ran first to one window and then the other. Sure enough, they were tightly shuttered and her meager strength refused to budge them. Next she tried the door, rattling the latch several times before conceding that it offered no avenue of escape. Sighing despondently, she walked slowly to the bed, eyeing it somewhat wistfully before pulling off the blanket and pillow and tossing them to the floor. Then, bolstering her resolve, she lowered herself to the hard, unyielding floor and pulled the blanket over her. She'd be damned if she'd yield to luxury when it was so fleeting. Tomorrow she'd either be back on the streets snatching sleep wherever she could find it or in jail sleeping on a hard pallet.

Ben slowly made his way to the small den he much preferred to the more formal parlor. Pouring himself a generous splash of brandy, he sank into an upholstered leather chair and sipped thoughtfully at the amber liquid. It was good. Damn good, lending him the courage to concentrate on his problems, which had multiplied within an amazingly short time.

With all the obliging women in London, why did he have to pick Caroline Battersby to dally with? he wondered bleakly. What was he going to do about the coil he had gotten himself into? Where in bloody hell was he going to find a wife in a week? Not a real wife, heaven forbid, but one who would willingly act the part for as long as he had need of her. Why had he invented a wife in the first place, when the lie was doomed from the beginning? Because nothing short of marriage would satisfy Battersby and his daughter, he told himself.

Bolting down the brandy, Ben poured himself another, and another, but his problems remained. Not only did the Battersbys plague him, but the little termagant sleeping upstairs in his room added a new dimension to his dilemma. He certainly didn't want the responsibility of rehabilitating Tia, and he knew of no one else willing to undertake so monumental a task. If only he could get her to reveal her past. Ben was certain she was keeping something from him, something that would solve the mystery of her past. She had deceived him into thinking she was a dirty street urchin, and perhaps she was, but obviously she hadn't always been a ragged pickpocket. Tia was an enigma, one Ben wasn't certain he wanted to become involved with.

Much to Ben's distress, Tia affected him in strange ways. One minute he wanted to shake her until her head rattled, and the next ... Bloody hell! What was he thinking? Tia was a child of the streets. Lord only knows what she had been forced to do or what vile germs she was infected with. Dear God, she was beautiful! She looked like an angel with all that silky blond hair swirling around her face and head like a halo. And there certainly was nothing childish about her body. It was soft and womanly and rounded in all the right places. She was all woman—and probably accustomed to using that incredible body to survive. Shaking his head to clear it from such disturbing thoughts, Ben rose unsteadily to his feet. Just then the hall clock struck two, and he was startled to find it so late—or early, however one wanted to look at it. Since his problems seemed no closer to being solved now than they were several hours ago, Ben decided to seek his bed. Things usually looked brighter after a good night's sleep.

Slowly he mounted the stairs, grateful for the lamp left burning on the landing to guide his steps. When he came to his room, he paused outside the door, listening for some indication that Tia was still awake. He heard nothing. He had every intention of seeking his rest in a spare bedroom, but some perverse devil made him slip the key into the lock and open the door. The lamp on the nightstand emitted a soft glow, and one quick glance at the bed told Ben it was empty. His gaze flew to the window. He noted that it was still shuttered and wondered if the minx could have disappeared into thin air. Or was she a figment of his imagination, conjured up in a moment of madness?

He entered the room, thinking Tia was such a tiny creature she might easily be lost somewhere amidst the bed covers. He was ten steps into the room when he stumbled over some kind of obstruction on the floor. Muttering a curse, Ben looked down, surprised to find Tia stretched out at his feet. What was she up to now? She was sound asleep, her bright hair spread about her like a shimmering mantle. It cascaded over her bare shoulders and covered one naked breast that had escaped from beneath the blanket. She slept with her hands beneath her cheek like a child, and her face was serene and angelic. Yet Ben knew that Tia was neither child nor angel. She was a full-grown woman whose generous curves were blatantly sexual beneath the thin blanket.

She was all innocence and vulnerable womanhood.

She was a filthy little guttersnipe who would have stolen his blunt and afterward laughed about it with her fellow pickpockets.

She was a sensual feast.

She was a contradiction to the rules of society.

She was . . . Bloody hell! Why hadn't he thought of it before? Ben's gray eyes shimmered with laughter and perverse humor. If he could pull it off, it would solve all his problems. All he had to do was convince Tia. And that wouldn't be too difficult once he presented the alternatives.

Unfortunately, Ben hadn't counted on Tia's stubborn nature or her sense of outrage.

"What! Your brains are in your arse! You want me to pose as your wife?"

Ben had awakened Tia and presented his proposition before she was fully awake. His words stunned her like a dash of cold water in the face.

"It wouldn't be for long," Ben cajoled. "Just long enough to get the Battersbys off my back. I never intend to marry, and certainly not Caroline Battersby."

"It serves you right, you horny devil," Tia said sourly. "It's no more than you deserve. How

51

many innocents have you seduced in London? Not to mention those in Australia, wherever that may be."

"Caroline was no innocent," Ben protested. "Nor do I make a habit of bedding virgins. There are too many obliging women in London and the world to resort to seducing innocents."

Tia stared at him in disbelief. He was too wickedly handsome not to attract all sorts of women, virgins and otherwise, and it made her even less inclined to fall in with his plans. She doubted that anyone would remember her after all this time, but there was always the possibility that—"Find someone else to do your dirty work. I wouldn't pose as your wife for all the blunt in England."

"Not even if it meant your freedom?" Ben asked slyly.

"Are you saying you'll free me once I convince this Caroline and her father that I'm your wife?"

"Exactly," Ben said blandly. "And I'll pay you well for your trouble. I have one week to produce a bogus wife. If I don't, I'll soon find myself saddled with a real one."

"Is that so bad?" Tia asked, her eyes narrowed suspiciously. "You're not the kind who prefers boys, are you?" Though she was still technically innocent, she had seen and heard everything. The streets were a cruel teacher.

"Damn your vulgar little tongue! No, I don't like boys, not in the way you suggest, anyway.

Women consider me a damn fine lover, but I have no need of a wife. I don't ever intend to marry."

"If women find you so irresistible, why not ask someone better suited for the job than me to act as your wife?" Tia suggested.

"If I knew someone like that I'd have already asked her," Ben bit out angrily. "Truth is, all my—acquaintances are members of the ton and well known about town. And the prostitutes who would oblige aren't suitable."

"And I am?"

Tia stirred uneasily beneath Ben's heavy-lidded gaze. His sharp gray eyes raked her from head to toe, assessing, measuring, calculating the odds of passing Tia off as his wife. "I believe you can be. You're clever enough." Tia bristled indignantly. "And beautiful enough. With a whole week to polish you up and teach you proper deportment befitting a lady, you should do nicely. All you have to remember is to speak only when spoken to, smile beguilingly, bat those long lashes, and pretend to be empty-headed. I'll teach you all you need to know about Australia and me."

"And if I refuse?" Tia challenged.

"Then I'll turn you over to the authorities immediately. As I see it, you have two choices. Either you agree to my proposition or rot in jail. Which will it be, Tia?

Chapter Three

Frustration gripped Tia as she stared at Ben.
Obviously he was quite capable of carrying out
his threats. A man like Ben wouldn't think twice
about putting a woman behind bars. Could she
trust him to keep his word if she complied with
his wishes?

"Well, I'm waiting for your answer," Ben said
with smug confidence. He held the upper hand
and knew it. Tia wouldn't dare defy him.

He was wrong.

"Go to hell! I'd rather go to jail than pretend
to be your wife."

"What? What kind of woman are you to
prefer prison to a few weeks of pretending
to be someone you're not? Do you know what
prison is like? Are you aware of the vile things

that could happen to a woman in a place like that?"

Tia flushed and her incredible eyes grew bleak as she thought of the horrible stories she'd heard about Newgate Prison. She'd grow old and die in those moldy depths without ever having known love or fulfillment. Is that what she wanted from life? Faced with the terrible prospect of never seeing daylight again, she found that Ben's proposal didn't seem quite as preposterous as when he first offered it. In fact, the alternative he offered sounded more attractive by the minute.

"Tell me more," Tia asked curiously. "If I agree to this harebrained scheme, how long would I be forced to pose as your wife? And exactly what would it involve?"

Ben grinned cheekily. "Don't worry, brat, this would be a 'marriage' in name only. I told you, I already had enough trouble with women, I don't need any more. A few weeks should suffice. I can always say you didn't like London and went back to the country to visit relatives."

"And you swear to free me once I've convinced everyone I'm your wife?"

"I always keep my word," Ben said solemnly. "Once Battersby and his daughter see that I am no longer available to coerce into marriage, I swear you can rejoin your seedy companions and continue your life of crime with no interference from me."

Tia's mind worked furiously as she digested Ben's words. A few weeks? Could she endure his imposing presence and arrogant manner that long? It wasn't the first time in her life that Tia viewed men as creatures who used women shamelessly. Though she didn't know Ben Penrod well enough to judge him, he seemed no different than others of his species. Wasn't he scheming to escape marriage and planning to hoodwink his prospective father-in-law? One thing puzzled her, though. Ben might be arrogant and overbearing, but he didn't seem to be deliberately cruel.

"Why are you so dead set against marriage?" Tia asked suddenly. "What is wrong with Caroline Battersby?"

"There is nothing wrong with Caroline Battersby. She's a damn fine lover. But I decided long ago not to marry," Ben said carelessly. "I'm not so vain that I feel compelled to reproduce sons and daughters in my image. Nor do I need an heir for the Penrod name. My brother Dare and his wife Casey are taking care of that nicely, thank you. Caroline was no innocent to begin with, and I won't be trapped into taking a wife I don't want."

"Is—is she beautiful?" Tia asked timidly, then nearly bit her tongue for asking such a personal question. What did it matter how beautiful the woman was? Still, she couldn't help but be curious about the type of women Ben Penrod bedded.

Ben grew thoughtful as the picture of Caroline's lovely features formed in his mind. Dark, exotic, with a body generously endowed in all the right places; any man would be pleased to claim her. And she was good in bed—damn good. But she was sly, conniving, and manipulative, all the characteristics he despised most in a woman. Ben had decided long ago that no woman could measure up to Casey O'Cain Penrod or Kate McKenzie Fletcher. Besides, remaining single suited him just fine. There were plenty of women in the world he hadn't sampled yet, and enough of them were willing to indulge his sensual nature.

"I suppose you could call Caroline beautiful," he said at length. "But that's beside the point. You still haven't answered my question."

"Do I have a choice?" Tia asked tightly.

"None that I can see." His smug answer made Tia bristle indignantly.

"Were ye always such an arrogant bastard?"

"Do you always use gutter language?"

Ben had won and he knew it.

"What do I have to do?"

"You can begin by becoming comfortable with my name. We are intimate, remember? And try to contain your outbursts of outrageous language. Most of it is unacceptable."

Tia's expression grew stormy. "Very well—Ben," she said with bitter emphasis. "I'll convince Caroline we're husband and wife, but afterward I'll expect you to honor your promise. And make it worth my while," she added bluntly.

"Mercenary little brat, aren't you?" Ben muttered beneath his breath. "You'll be well paid for your little deception. I just hope you're a good actress."

In the week that followed, Tia found herself wishing time and again that she had never agreed to Ben's preposterous scheme to pass her off as his wife. Some men would go to any lengths to escape marriage, and Ben was more determined than most. The dressmaker was hastily summoned to Ben's lodgings, and the next day Tia had two day dresses made to Ben's specifications, though it surprised Tia that Ben knew so much about women's fashions. An entire wardrobe was to follow before Saturday, the day of the Battersbys' party.

Every day brought something new. One day it was undergarments, the next, nightclothes. Then came a parade of day dresses and walking costumes. Finally, two lovely ball gowns arrived, one in a blue-green shade to match her eyes and another in pure white that made her look like an angel. Tia was astounded by Ben's thoroughness and his determination to transform her into the kind of wife people would expect of a wealthy sheep farmer. Obviously, Ben was dedicated to remain unencumbered by a wife. Though Tia enjoyed the clothes, having dressed as a boy for the past three years, she resented Ben's relentless hounding.

Each day Ben sat her down in the study and pounded facts into her head, until Tia thought her poor brain would burst.

"I'll never remember all that," Tia wailed when Ben was describing Australia. "Besides, I don't believe any country could be as you described."

" 'Tis true, Tia. There is no place in the world like Australia," Ben said wistfully. "All I'm asking is that you try to remember pertinent facts like climate, names of cities, and something of the flora and fauna."

"What you ask is impossible," Tia said sullenly. "Until three years ago I had never even seen London."

Ben looked at her strangely. Did Tia realize what she had just let slip? Ben thought not. She had as good as admitted that she wasn't born in London's slums, that she had lived most of her life in the country. From the beginning, he had sensed an aura of mystery about her, but she had adamantly refused to divulge one iota of information about her past.

"Nevertheless, you'll be expected to know something of the country. Pay attention now while I tell you about my family. I have one brother, Dare. He and his wife Casey have three children. Two boys and a girl. Their names are Brandon, Lucy, and Justin. My father's name is Roy. He is just recently married to Maude, an emancipist."

"What's an emancipist?" Tia asked.

"An emancipist is a convict who has served his or her time," Ben explained patiently.

Tia's eyes grew wide. "Your father married a convict?"

"As did my brother. But Robin married an Englishwoman newly arrived in New South Wales."

"Robin? Is he another brother?"

"No, but we are as close as brothers. Robin is also an emancipist."

"Damn and blast! Is everyone in Australia a convict?"

"Watch your language, Tia," Ben warned sternly. "No, everyone is not a convict. None of the Penrods are. And there are many immigrants and currency lads and lasses."

Tia opened her mouth to ask another question, but Ben forestalled her. "Currency lads and lasses are sons and daughters of ex-convicts. Have you got that all straight?"

Tia nodded slowly, her head whirling with snippets of information she was certain she'd never retain. Besides, Ben was far too intimidating for her to concentrate for long periods of time. His mesmerizing gray eyes were ever relentless, ever probing, ever elusive. She was aware of him as a man; an attractive man whose piercing look had the ability to turn her insides to mush. Tia had never thought of a man in a romantic sense, and if Ben wasn't such an arrogant rogue she might be persuaded to view him in a different light.

Ben's voice droned on, explaining to Tia the difference in landscape between England and Australia. But his mind wasn't on his words, they were focused on Tia's lips. They were luscious, red, and parted slightly as she listened intently to his words. He almost lost his train of thought when the tip of her tongue darted out between her teeth to moisten her lips. Ben could almost taste the sweet moistness glistening there. Reluctantly his gaze slid upward to her eyes, struck anew by their incredible jewel-like brilliance. How could he have ever thought her a child? Ben asked himself in silent wonder. What mystery was she hiding? Was she a whore as well as a pickpocket?

"Enough, Ben!" Tia cried suddenly, clapping her hands over her ears. "I can't remember so much at one time."

It took several seconds for Ben to realize that Tia was speaking. She intrigued him, goaded him, made him want to learn every facet of her complex personality. What was she? Vixen? Victim? Whore? Thief? Was her past too gruesome to recall?

"What? What did you say?"

"I said I've heard enough for today. I want to go back to my room now."

The day Tia had agreed to Ben's proposal, she was given the guest room in the small house and had occupied it gladly. She was still leery of Ben's intentions where she was concerned, having little faith regarding men.

Her experience had proven that men couldn't be trusted, and Ben Penrod was no exception. Wasn't he dishonest in his dealings with the Battersbys, using fraudulent means to escape marriage? Though Ben had made no advances toward her, she was still skittish in his presence.

"You've little time left to learn all the knowledge you'll need to fool the Battersbys," Ben insisted, strangely loath to let her go. Something about Tia intrigued him—perhaps the mystery surrounding her. He didn't trust her.

There, it was out. He didn't trust Tia. She seemed skittish as a young mare around him, and as likely to run out on him after their agreement as she was to remain. The way she was staring at him made him uncomfortable. Something in her eyes—was she trying to seduce him? The thought carried a familiar surge of hot blood to his loins. Her whore's tricks wouldn't work on him, yet he couldn't help but wonder what it would feel like to shove himself deep—deeper into her body. She was such a tiny thing he doubted she could stretch enough to take all of him.

Bloody hell! Just thinking about her soft white flesh filled with him nearly unmanned him. All women were alike in that respect, he reasoned. Some of them were better at it than others, but they all came with the same equipment.

"I'm sorry, Ben, I've had enough," Tia said, rising shakily to her feet.

"Sit down, Tia, we're not finished."

"I'm finished," Tia said defiantly. "I'm tired. There's still tomorrow."

"And the day after tomorrow is Saturday, the day of the Battersbys' party. I still haven't described Penrod station to you."

Ignoring him, Tia walked from the room. But Ben was too fast for her. Grasping her arm, he flung her around to face him. She banged solidly into the hard wall of his chest. Her hands flew up, grasping at his shoulders to keep from falling. They landed around his neck, and suddenly Tia found herself mashed against the rigid length of his body.

His arms closed around her, her flesh subtly yielding as it met the solid strength of his. Tia gasped in shock. Nothing in life had prepared her for the impact of flesh meeting flesh. She had never imagined that a man's body could be so wonderfully arousing. She could feel the chaotic beating of his heart and wondered if hers was pounding as furiously. Heat radiated from the depths of his silver eyes, and too late Tia realized her danger. Naively innocent, she had never experienced desire before nor realized the power of a mere touch. Was it like that with all men and women?

Gazing into Tia's blue-green eyes, Ben wondered if her lips tasted as sweet as they looked. The way he felt now, he wouldn't object to being seduced. He would welcome it. Welcome the chance to prove that angels didn't exist, that they were mere flesh and blood with needs and desires like common folk. Yet there was an innocence about Tia, as if she had spent her life closed off from the world instead of associating with the dregs of society.

Ben couldn't have stopped what happened next if his life depended on it. Her mouth was too inviting, too evocative to resist. A gurgling sound escaped from Tia's throat as his lips settled over hers, gently at first, learning the lush contours with his tongue, then more forcefully as his blood heated and pounded through his veins. Tia was suffocating, drowning in a whirlpool of liquid fire, lost in a sea of swirling emotions. She had never been kissed before, not even by—Never! She was hot, she was cold. She was feeling things that confused her.

When she felt Ben's tongue slide between her teeth to explore the honeyed sweetness of her mouth, she stiffened, certain he was doing things he had no business doing. Then his hands began a sensuous foray to forbidden territory. Slipping down her back, his fingers curled around the soft mounds of her buttocks, drawing her tightly against the rising heat of his desire. The moan that escaped Tia's lips was a combination of protest and shock. Yet she seemed defenseless against Ben's potent power. The kiss deepened as Ben sought even closer intimacy, his tongue delving deeply into her mouth. But when his hands slid upward to cup her breasts, Tia suddenly found the strength to break the spell he had cast upon her senses.

Pushing against the hard wall of his chest, she broke free of his arms, panting and shaking her head in vigorous denial. She was feeling—oh God—she was feeling things she didn't know existed. And as she looked at Ben, who was smiling smugly, the tenuous hold on her temper snapped.

"Ye bleedin' idiot! What in the 'ell do ya think yer doin'? I told ya before I ain't no doxy."

Ben continued to smile, too pleased with Tia's initial response to him to realize that she was an untried girl unaccustomed to passion. "Reverting back to gutter language?" he taunted, clicking his tongue in marked reprimand. "Why are you so angry? You liked it well enough at first. Who are you trying to fool? Certainly not me. Obviously you're not as inexperienced in sexual matters as you'd like to pretend. This farce has gone far enough."

Tia paled. Arrogant bastard! she thought as she stared up at his handsome features. Evidently the man was accustomed to having women fall into his arms at the slightest provocation. She'd be damned if she'd add herself to his list of conquests. In a way she pitied Caroline Battersby. Pitied any woman unlucky enough to fall beneath Ben Penrod's roving eye.

"Gutter language is all you deserve," Tia said in perfect English. "I promised to help you

65

dupe the Battersbys, not warm your bed or play the whore. Keep your hands to yourself. Just remember, I'm your wife in name only. As soon as you've accomplished what you set out to do, I'll be out of your life forever."

"It can't be soon enough for me," Ben said tightly.

Bloody hell, how did things get out of control so fast? He fumed in silent anger. The little tart had a way of getting to him. Lord knows he didn't want her, or so he tried to tell himself. The kiss was just something that happened, so spontaneous that it took him by surprise. Bedding the little witch was the last thing in the world he wanted, wasn't it? Just because she felt so wonderful in his arms, her kisses so sweetly seductive, didn't mean he felt anything for her. He was a man, with a man's needs, and his body had acted instinctively to a warm, female body.

Whirling on her heel, Tia left the room. Her flushed face and tingling flesh left little doubt in her mind that Ben Penrod was a danger to her very existence. What if he found out who she really was? What would he do if he learned the truth about her? Preposterous, she scoffed, there was no possible way anyone would learn her secret.

The next day, the day before the Battersbys' party, Tia and Ben met one last time to go over the facts he had been drilling into her during the past week. She sat opposite him in the study, her mouth turned down sullenly as he issued an ominous warning about her foul language. Tia was so unpredictable that Ben never knew when she would lapse into language guaranteed to singe one's ears. Once would be all that was needed to rouse the Battersbys' suspicions.

"Listen to me carefully, Tia," he schooled patiently. "Keep your voice modulated and speak only when spoken to. Above all, don't speak when you're angry. Lord only knows what will come out of your mouth when your dander is up."

"Yes, master," Tia said, her words dripping with sarcasm. "Perhaps I should pretend to be deaf and dumb so I won't offend your hoity-toity friends."

Ben fixed her with an assessing look, as if actually mulling over her suggestion. After several seconds, he shook his head. "No, I don't think it would work. Battersby is no fool. Neither is Caroline. It would look suspicious to introduce a wife who could neither hear nor speak. Just do as I say and everything will work out as I predicted. Is there anything you're not sure of yet?"

"Tell me again about the sea voyage," Tia prompted. The sea fascinated her. She never tired of hearing about the voyage from New South Wales to England.

"It took nearly six months and was boring," Ben repeated, having told her about the trip many times over.

"And when it's summer here it is winter in New South Wales," Tia said wonderingly. "How strange."

"Much about Australia is strange," Ben agreed, "but 'tis a country like none other. Wildflowers grow in profusion and the outback is wild and untamed. It's only been within the last few years that men have conquered the Blue Mountains and migrated west. The town of Bathurst has grown tremendously since Robin and his wife went there to live. Some of the biggest sheep stations in Australia are located west of the mountains. Robin owns one of them."

"Didn't you say Robin Fletcher was once a convict?"

"Yes. He was convicted of poaching and transported when he was very young. We've been friends since the day we met aboard ship. You'd like his wife, Kate."

"And Casey O'Cain is Dare's wife," Tia said slowly, trying to keep everyone straight in her mind. "She was also a convict. And your father married an ex-convict. I'm surprised you didn't continue the tradition by marrying an ex-convict."

"I told you, I have no intention of marrying— ever. And keep your nasty thoughts away from Casey. She's a gem and has made Dare very happy. She was wrongly accused of murder and pardoned by the governor. She and Dare went through hell to be together. Yet Casey is every inch a lady. I don't know Father's new wife well, but from what I've seen, Maude will suit him just fine."

Tia fell silent. Obviously Ben loved his family well and was very protective of them. Too bad he is such a heartless, manipulative bastard, she mused in silent condemnation. How many women were there like Caroline who gave themselves to him with the intention of becoming his wife? she wondered. He was the kind of man who took and took and gave little except that which was physical. All promise but no substance, she thought disparagingly. She hoped his loving was worth the anguish his lady friends suffered when he left them without a word of apology. Like so many of the ton, Ben Penrod was a selfish, arrogant animal who took his pleasure where he would with little thought for his partners. He was no better than—

Suddenly Tia looked up, aware that Ben was staring at her. "What are you looking at?"

"I'm amazed at the change in you since I brought you here, a grubby little urchin with a foul mouth and no manners." His tone was hard and mocking.

"Think what you want," Tia said, lifting her chin defiantly, "but contrary to your beliefs, I am quite equal to your society friends."

Ben laughed harshly. "Somewhere along the line you've picked up refined speech, but it proves nothing. Except that one of your lovers taught you more than bed manners. If you belonged anywhere but on the streets, you wouldn't have been caught picking my pocket. Or wearing filthy rags."

Tia bristled angrily. "You have no right to judge me. You have no idea what my life is like or why I lived on the streets."

"No, but I'd like you to prove me wrong about you," Ben said softly. "Why don't you tell me? I'm willing to change my mind about you." He tossed her the challenge and it hung in midair between them, unclaimed.

Tia's mouth clamped tightly shut and her face grew hot under his abusive scrutiny. She'd be damned if she'd tell him anything. Let him speculate all he wanted.

Ben snorted, recognizing Tia's stubbornness and unwilling to deal with it at this time. There were more important things to consider. If the little brat didn't want to divulge her background, it mattered not at all to him. Once she served her purpose he'd be shed of her for good.

"I really don't care what you think about me," Tia said sullenly. "I just want to get this masquerade over with and get on with my life."

"In the slums?"

"I'm comfortable there. Are we finished?"

"Is there anything else you need to know about Australia?"

"My head is so full of facts it's swimming."

"Have your ball gowns arrived?" Tia nodded. "Wear the blue-green one tomorrow. I want everyone to be properly impressed. Can you do your own hair?"

"I'll manage," Tia said dryly. "You'll not be disappointed."

He wasn't.

When Tia appeared the next evening, Ben was thunderstruck. He had grown impatient waiting for her to appear and had just poured himself a second brandy when he sensed her presence in the room. Whirling, he saw her poised in the doorway, striking a pose meant to impress him. It did.

The taffeta gown was nearly the same striking shade as her blue-green eyes. The neckline was cut low, providing a perfect frame for the generous curves of her breasts. Though he tried to look elsewhere, Ben's eyes fastened hungrily on the sweet white mounds pushed upward above the shimmering material of her bodice. With great reluctance his eyes traveled downward, past an incredibly slim waist, over generously curved hips to the tips of her dainty slippers. Two puffed sleeves hung low on her arms, leaving her shoulders bare. She had chosen to let her silver hair hang loose over her shoulders in back, catching up the sides with a black ribbon and drawing it behind the trailing mass. In lieu of jewelry she had tied a matching ribbon around her neck. She was stunning. No one would guess that Tia was anything but a perfect lady in every sense of the word. Ben had difficulty now recalling the ragged urchin who had picked his pocket.

"Well?" Tia asked, arching a well-shaped brow. "Do I pass inspection?"

Deliberately quelling his lustful thoughts, Ben assumed a thoughtful pose, his chin held level in an attitude of frank appraisal. "You'll do." His voice was deliberately bland. He certainly didn't want Tia to think he was impressed, which he was. Despite her fancy trappings, she was still a guttersnipe who counted her friends among thieves, pickpockets, and prostitutes.

Jeevers waited at the door with Tia's wrap, a cape lined with fur that Ben had purchased in a moment of madness and included with the rest of her new wardrobe. Getting rid of the scheming Caroline was worth every penny he spent on Tia, he told himself in an effort to explain away his extravagance. Of course he had bought gifts before for women, some of them quite expensive, but he was always rewarded by the lady's passion. But for some unexplained reason he found a curious satisfaction watching Tia's face light with pleasure when she tried on her new clothes. She was like a child in many ways, and in other ways incredibly streetwise. She could be crude, outrageous, stubborn, argumentative—and so damn beautiful she put an angel to shame. Simple things pleased her, yet nothing about her was simple. Tia was complex and mysterious, and Ben decided he had problems enough without probing for answers she was unwilling to divulge.

What Ben assumed would be a small dinner party proved to be a gathering of some forty-odd people. Carriages lined both sides of the street in front of the large brick townhouse, and Ben spat out an oath as he and Tia paused on the wide stone steps before the door. Since his own house was nearby and the night balmy, he had chosen to walk. That suited Tia fine, for she had been cooped up for a week and welcomed the fresh air. But when she saw the number of carriages sitting outside the brilliantly lit townhouse, her stomach lurched dangerously and all her insecurities rose up to assail her.

What if she failed? What if she was thrown out on the street or put in jail for being an impostor? What if someone recognized her after all this time? Suddenly she balked, wildly resisting Ben as he led her by the elbow up the stairs.

"What's wrong, Tia? This is not the time to get cold feet. You'll do just fine."

"I—I can't. I can't go in there and pretend to be someone I'm not," Tia said, swallowing convulsively. "Why should I be put on display like a—a freak in a sideshow?"

His soft response bore a note of stern reproach. "Because I said so. Because if you don't go in there and convince everyone you're my wife, you'll never see the light of day again. Prison is a terrible place for a woman. You'll be at the mercy of every kind of pervert. If you back out now, I'll take you straight to the authorities."

Tia's expression grew mutinous as she stared at Ben. She knew he was unyielding and stubborn, but thus far he had given her no reason to believe he could be cruel as well. Would he really turn her over to the authorities if she didn't do as he said? Despite his threats, he didn't seem the type who enjoyed inflicting pain or punishment on women. She never doubted he was a womanizer and rake, a man whose ego was fed by his numerous conquests, but would he really carry out his threat? Tilting her chin defiantly, she decided to challenge him.

"Go ahead, call the police. I've had enough of your bullying. Find another woman to bail you out of your troubles, I'm leaving."

Stunned, Ben watched as Tia whirled and walked away rapidly. Was she testing him? Did she really intend to leave without fulfilling her end of their bargain? It certainly looked that way, for she was already halfway down the block. Incredible rage released Ben's frozen limbs as he sprinted after Tia. He caught up with her as she rounded a corner. Grasping her arm, he halted her flight with a backward jerk.

"You're not going anywhere except to the Battersbys' party or to prison. Which will it be."

"I'm not going to the party," Tia said sullenly.

Ben's mouth turned downward and storm clouds gathered in his gray eyes. "You leave me no choice," he said grimly as he began dragging her down the street. "If I'm not mistaken, we passed a policeman a few moments ago. Ah, yes, there he is," he announced smugly as the burly policeman strode into view beneath a street light.

"No, wait!" Tia cried, digging in her heels. "I've changed my mind." She didn't relish spending the night in jail. Or all the nights thereafter.

"Don't ever doubt me again, Tia," Ben said. His statement was emphatic, his eyes cool and probing. "Come along, we're already late."

"Ye bleedin' fool," Tia muttered beneath her breath. "If yer brains weren't in yer britches ye wouldn't be in this mess. I'll 'elp ya, but I ain't likin' it."

Ruing the day he met Tia, Ben implored the heavens for strength as he said, "One more outburst like that, brat, and I'll wash your mouth out with soap."

Chapter Four

Tia grit her teeth and allowed Ben to steer her toward the Battersby mansion. She glared at him hatefully but wisely held her tongue. The sooner she got this ordeal over with, the sooner she'd be free to disappear back into blessed obscurity.

"Don't embarrass me," Ben hissed when the door swung open at his knock. Judging from the buzz of voices coming from the rear of the house, the party was in full swing.

Tia merely smiled, refusing Ben the satisfaction of her assurance of good behavior. They followed the footman into the ballroom, and when he announced in a loud voice the arrival of Mr. and Mrs. Benjamin Penrod, Tia's knees began to quake. It wouldn't have been so bad if an instant hush hadn't fallen over the crowd of some forty people. As if on cue, everyone present turned and stared at them. Tia felt like a freak in a sideshow and would have bolted if Ben hadn't had a firm grip on her arm.

"Remember, just smile and let me do the talking," he advised from the side of his mouth as a beautiful brunette detached herself from a group of people and headed right for them. Tia's mouth widened until she thought her lips would crack. Then all thought slammed to a halt as Caroline Battersby stopped directly in front of them.

"I wasn't sure you would come," Caroline said to Ben as she slid an assessing glance at Tia.

"Whyever not?" Ben asked blandly. "Tia wasn't so far away that I couldn't bring her to London when I needed her."

"Obviously not," Caroline commented dryly. "Won't you introduce me to your 'wife'?"

Ben groaned inwardly, sliding a nervous glance at Tia. He prayed she was sufficiently intimidated by him and intelligent enough to play his game, for if she wasn't, he'd find himself saddled with a wife he neither loved nor wanted. Lord Battersby had enough clout to see him and Caroline properly wed should he doubt Ben's story. Lord, what a coil!

There was no help for it, Ben thought, turning to Tia. "My dear, I'd like you to meet Caroline Battersby. Caroline and her father are some of the new friends I've made in London." He turned to Caroline. "Caroline, this is my wife, Tia."

"Tia, what an interesting name," Caroline said, her dark eyes narrowing with malicious intent. "Have you and Ben been married long, Tia?"

"Three years," Ben interjected before Tia opened her mouth. "We married shortly before we left Australia."

"How—nice," Caroline said, openly skeptical. "Do you have children?" This question was also directed at Tia, but once again Ben chose to answer.

"No, no children."

Caroline slanted him an exasperated glare and tried again. "Tia," she asked pointedly, "were you born in Australia?"

Before either Ben or Tia could answer, Lord Battersby came up to join them. "So this is the wife you've kept hidden from your friends for nearly two years."

"This is Tia," Caroline said in a voice so sweet Tia felt her insides curdle. No wonder Ben didn't wish to be married to her. She struck Tia as manipulative, spoiled, and demanding.

Lord Battersby turned toward Tia, his eyes boldly condemning. "Haven't I seen you someplace before?" he asked coolly. "Perhaps at Madam Lila's?"

For a moment Tia looked puzzled. Who in the world was Madam Lila? She glanced at Ben, hoping for enlightenment, and was startled to find his face contorted into a mask of fury.

Ben nearly choked on Battersby's words. Madam Lila's! The most prestigious bordello in London. Surely Battersby gave him more credit than that. Ben had more sense than to enlist the aid of a whore who had likely serviced half the men in London.

"You, sir, are out of line," Ben sputtered angrily. Angry enough to give the impression that his wife had just been insulted. "As you can see by my wife's expression, she doesn't even know what or who Madam Lila is."

Battersby offered a grudging apology. "I'm sorry, Mrs. Penrod, I didn't mean to offend. It's just rather difficult to believe your 'husband' has kept you a secret all this time. Especially since you are so lovely. Where did you meet your husband?" he asked with keen interest. It was obvious that Battersby still didn't believe Ben's story.

"I—"

"We met in Australia," Ben offered before Tia could form a reply. "Tia's father is an immigrant and has settled in Bathurst."

Battersby frowned as he exchanged a meaningful glance with his daughter. Then he cleared his throat and tried again. "Tell me, Mrs. Penrod, where in England are your relatives located?"

"Tia's people are distant relatives in a small town in Kent," Ben replied without batting an eyelash. "You wouldn't know them." Tia couldn't help but admire his glib tongue. What a smooth operator, she thought with a hint of malice.

"Does your wife speak or is she mute?" Caroline asked with scathing sarcasm. "I'm beginning to think you've cut off her tongue to keep her from answering questions."

"No such thing," Ben said indignantly. "Tia is perfectly capable of speaking. It's just that she's incredibly shy and finds speaking to strangers painful. That's why she's remained in relative seclusion during our stay in England. She prefers it that way, don't you, dear?" He turned to Tia, offering her a doting smile so counterfeit it made her giggle. Tia would never consider herself shy. Her levity earned her a poke in the ribs.

"Did you say something?" Caroline asked as Tia struggled to contain her mirth.

"I—" Lord, don't let me giggle now "—I *am* shy," Tia acknowledged, dropping her eyes to hide the laughter brimming in their blue-green depths. "My husband spoke the truth when he said I much prefer remaining quietly in the background. I've been in Australia so long I've forgotten how to act in London society. Not that I ever knew," she stressed, "for I've always lived a quiet life in the country with my parents before they emigrated to Australia."

"How nice to know you can speak," Caroline said drolly. Something was definitely wrong here but she couldn't put her finger on it. Why would a woman as beautiful as Tia allow her husband to play stud to half the women in London? If they really were husband and wife. She still wasn't wholly convinced.

"Has your husband told you why you were summoned to London so quickly?" Battersby asked. He was having difficulty believing Ben was truly married and didn't care who he hurt in the process of discovering the truth. His daughter wanted Ben Penrod, and she'd damn well have him if it turned out he was lying or trying to hoodwink them.

"I say, is that necessary?" Ben asked harshly. "There is no need for crudity. Tia is aware of the kind of life I lead in London."

"You Australians have a rather liberal outlook on marriage," Caroline said. "Tell me, Tia, do you approve of your husband's—er—outside activity?"

Tia felt like punching Caroline in the nose. And she would have if she didn't fear Ben's reprisal. Not even a wife seemed to dull the edge of Caroline's desire for Ben Penrod. What kind of a man was Ben? she wondered, to inspire such devotion in a woman. *She* couldn't bear the despicable bully and failed to understand why Caroline wanted him so badly. Was there more to the man than met the eye? He was handsome, true, with a dark, devastating charm that most women seemed to crave. He was so tall, so very much a man, but so damn infuriating she couldn't wait to be rid of him.

"Did you hear me, Tia?"

"What? Oh, I'm sorry, what did you say?"

"I merely wanted to know if Ben's outside 'interests' had your full approval. If he were my husband, I certainly wouldn't allow him to—to—well, you know what I'm referring to."

"Actually, I don't," Tia said sweetly. Oh, how she enjoyed seeing both Ben and Caroline squirm.

"Shall I tell you?"

"Please do."

Suddenly Ben began coughing and choking. His face turned red and he glared at Tia with unrestrained horror. He didn't need his sins enumerated, he already knew them. Besides, it had grown so quiet in the room he was certain that everyone present was privy to their conversation. When he got Tia home he was going to beat her black and blue. She was supposed to smile sweetly and leave the answering of questions to him. Obviously she was bent on destroying him.

"I think," Ben began once he got his breathing under control, "that Tia knows all she needs to know. Perhaps we should leave."

"No!" Battersby intervened. "I insist you stay for dinner. This party, after all, is given in your honor."

"Then we'd be delighted to stay, wouldn't we, dear?" Ben said easily as he nudged Tia. He certainly didn't want to give the impression that he had anything to hide, or that he was nervous.

"Of—of course," Tia concurred, wishing she had never agreed to this harebrained scheme.

How could she possibly get through a formal dinner when she hadn't dined in genteel company for more years than she cared to recall? There hadn't been time for Ben to brief her on proper deportment during a formal dinner. She'd just have to rely on her instincts and the manners she had been taught as a child. What Tia hadn't counted on was Caroline Battersby's constant badgering.

Ben drew in a ragged breath when Caroline and Lord Battersby reluctantly took their leave to resume their duties as host and hostess. He felt rather than saw Tia quaking beside him and felt a moment of pity for her, until he recalled how she had deliberately goaded Caroline. She had sufficient cause to be frightened, for if their sham was unmasked due to her loose tongue, he'd damn well beat her when they returned home. He slid a glance in her direction and sputtered in outrage when he saw it wasn't fear that was causing her trembling but laughter.

Tia couldn't control the laughter that bubbled up from her throat. Part of it was due to nervous reaction, but a good share of it was caused by the very absurdness of the situation. It was comical in a way. Obviously, Ben Penrod was willing to go to any lengths to resist marriage—even to claim being wedded to a thief and pickpocket. Wouldn't it be hilarious to shock all the highborn gentry present? she thought, hiccuping in an abortive effort to smother a giggle.

"If you laugh, so help me I'll strangle you," Ben hissed in a threatening tone. His entire life was falling apart and the little tart he had rescued from the gutter treated it as a big joke. "If you don't convince everyone that you're my wife, you'll find yourself in Newgate so fast it will make your head spin."

Tia had just about all she could take of Ben's arrogant ways and opened her mouth to tell him he could shove it up his arse when a man and woman joined them.

"Ben Penrod, where have you been keeping this ravishing creature?"

Though outwardly calm, Ben felt his insides churning dangerously. It was obvious the evening was far from over, and he and Tia would be expected to make small talk with everyone in the room. He should have known the little witch wouldn't be up to it. But when push came to shove, he had no other choice but to enlist Tia's reluctant help.

Smiling blandly, Ben said, "Percy, how nice to see you again. You, too, Lady Fenmore." The Fenmores were among Ben's closest acquaintances in London, and he'd been invited to their home often for dinner and intimate gatherings. He introduced Tia and held his breath, fearful of what would come from her mouth next. To his relief she merely acknowledged the introduction with appropriate words.

"I can't believe Ben would keep something as important as a marriage from us," Lady Fenmore said with a hint of censure. "Naughty boy, why have you chosen to keep Tia from London society? She's lovely, Ben."

"I prefer to keep my private life private," Ben said smoothly. "Besides, as you just noted, Tia is lovely and unspoiled and I prefer to keep her that way."

Lovely and unspoiled? Tia snorted derisively, earning an inquiring glance from the Fenmores and a warning frown from Ben.

"Did you say something, my dear?" Percy asked.

"N—no," Tia stuttered, "just clearing my throat."

"Well, I can't blame your husband for keeping you all to himself, but now that he's introduced you to society I daresay you'll be swamped with invitations."

"My husband is correct," Lady Fenmore concurred. "I'm having a small gathering next week and would like both of you to attend. I'll send around an invitation."

Before either Ben or Tia could refuse, the Fenmores were gone, only to be replaced by other couples anxious to meet Tia and extend invitations. By the time dinner was announced, Tia felt as if she had been wrung inside out. She was tired of smiling, sick of being fawned over, and definitely disgusted by Ben's constant vigilance. He was so afraid of her doing or saying something to discredit him that she felt like a puppet on a string.

"See how easy it is when you keep your mouth shut?" Ben whispered as he led her into dinner. "You can be quite fetching when you make the effort. No one suspects you're a little tart that I literally plucked out of the gutter."

Tia went still, glaring at Ben with rage. "Bloody 'ell, ain't ye an ungrateful bastard!"

Ben blanched, glancing around to see if anyone had heard Tia's outburst. Fortunately, they had dawdled and most of the guests were already in the dining room. With a hard pull on her arm he snapped her around to face him.

"Keep your voice down! Do you want everyone to think I married a slut? I come from a wealthy family with strong ties in England, and I can't afford to drag our name in the mud. My grandfather was an earl, and Dare would have inherited the title had he wanted it. That gutter language was completely uncalled for."

"Far be it from me to shock your highborn friends," Tia said in perfect English. "But I'm only being myself. That's more than I can say for you. You're the one who's claiming to be something he isn't. You're dishonest and untruthful as well as being an arrogant bastard. Although I can't say I blame you for not wanting to marry Caroline. The woman is a bitch." Then, looking coyly up at Ben through a curtain of long golden lashes, she smiled sweetly and remarked, "Yer brains were swingin' atwixt yer legs when ye took up with that one."

Ben's face turned white beneath his tan. Good Lord, he had created a monster! Well-bred women didn't use foul language. He should have known from the beginning this hoax wouldn't work. Tia was a product of the streets, and no matter how much knowledge he drummed into her head she was unlikely to change. He might have transformed her from a filthy guttersnipe into a raving beauty, but some things never change. Whichever one of her lovers had taught her proper language had failed to instill in her the rudiments of being a lady. The best thing he could do now was get her out of here as quickly as possible and send around a note of apology to Caroline and her father.

"Why are you two dawdling? Dinner can't begin without the guests of honor."

Ben groaned inwardly as Caroline appeared at their side and grasped both their arms, making it impossible to effect a hasty exit without drawing undue attention.

"I've seated you on either side of me so we can become better acquainted." Caroline beamed, enjoying Ben's obvious discomfort.

Her intuition told her that Ben couldn't possibly be married, that he had dredged up a "bride" from somewhere, and she intended to find out the truth. All of London was aware of Ben's aversion to marriage, and Caroline had made up her mind long ago to become Ben's wife. Few men could compare with him in looks and expertise in bed, and she wanted him at her beck and call forever. Besides, he was wealthy enough to please her father.

Tia knew a moment of panic when she was seated at the table and noted the numerous and varied forks, knives, spoons, and dishes placed in front of her. She concentrated on them for a moment, surprised to find that she still remembered in which order they were to be used. She glanced around Caroline and saw Ben staring at her grave with apprehension. He must have noted her confusion and feared that her lack of manners was about to blow their little hoax. Being a man he'd never considered teaching her things like which fork to use or where to place a napkin.

When the first course was served and Tia managed to pick up the right fork, Ben breathed a sigh of relief. He had no idea how she managed *that*, but he had to give her credit. Despite her crude beginnings and gutter language, she was intelligent and quick. If she kept her mouth shut and continued to smile and nod as if she hadn't a brain in her head, they might still pull it off.

The food was delicious, and Tia didn't realize she was eating more than was considered ladylike until Caroline remarked snidely, "The way you're eating leads me to think your husband doesn't feed you. Lord knows you're skinny enough. If you ate like that all the time, you'd be fat as a cow."

About to shove a fork full of roast beef into her mouth, Tia paused. Food hadn't come easily these past three years, and whenever food was forthcoming she tended to gorge herself. Old habits were difficult to break. She could feel Ben glaring at her, having obviously heard Caroline's remark, and rather than surrender to Caroline's goading and Ben's displeasure, she deliberately placed the fork full of beef in her mouth, chewed slowly, and swallowed. Only then did she acknowledge Caroline's question with an answer that made Ben nearly choke on his food.

"My appetite has been rather healthy of late. Perhaps I'm increasing. Wouldn't that be wonderful?" She turned a smile on Ben so mischievous that it took him some moments to recover. And when he did it was to slaps on the back and hearty congratulations from those seated close to him. Tia was the only one to correctly interpret the fulminating glance he aimed in her direction. It didn't bode well for her, but she couldn't resist the temptation to throw Caroline into a dither.

"Just—wonderful," Caroline said tightly. "But I wonder how all this came about? To my knowledge Ben hasn't left London in ever so long. In fact," she said coyly, "he's rarely left my side for the past six months, and you don't look big enough to be more advanced in your pregnancy."

Bloody hell! Tia swore beneath her breath. The bitch was throwing her own affair with Ben in her face. Tia didn't know how much more of this she could take without venting her temper. And Lord only knew how she'd hold her tongue once her dander was up.

"But of course as beautiful as you are, you'd hardly be expected to pine away for your husband when there are other men willing to provide—company," Caroline hinted crudely. Her statement brought a gasp from those assembled around the dinner table.

"Caroline!" This from Ben who saw the storm clouds gathering in Tia's eyes and knew from experience what was coming next. "I'm afraid you've done it now. You've insulted my wife once too often." He slammed to his feet. "Come along, Tia, it's time we left.

Tia wasn't placated so easily and she knew exactly what Ben was trying to prevent. Only this time it wouldn't work. If anyone in the room was a whore, as Caroline hinted, it was Caroline Battersby.

"I ain't leavin', Ben, till I tell yer doxy exactly what I think of 'er. Bloody 'ell! Yer whore's got some nerve accusin' me of bein' a slut when ya been beddin' 'er fer months. I oughta kick her arse to kingdom come but I'm too much of a lady."

The food spewed from Ben's mouth.

After uttering those paradoxical words, Tia leaped from her chair and stormed out of the room. Aghast, Ben stared at her stiff little back, too enraged to speak. Then suddenly the humor of the situation brought his anger under control as he tried to soothe Caroline's ruffled feathers and explain away his "wife's" unladylike behavior and shocking use of profanity. He wanted to laugh, but all he could do was think of the alternative if he didn't convince the Battersbys that he and Tia were indeed husband and wife.

"Please excuse Tia, Caroline. Australian women are naturally outspoken and accustomed to speaking their minds. You must admit you've goaded her unmercifully tonight and earned her contempt."

"I had no idea a lady could use such vulgar language," Caroline sniffed, far from appeased.

She found it shocking that Ben's wife would use language fit only for the gutter. What in the world had ever possessed Ben to marry such a woman? No wonder he kept her hidden away. She must have had a generous dowry to capture a prize like Ben Penrod. At that moment she felt profound pity for Ben, but it didn't make her any less determined to keep him for herself.

"I'm sorry you had to find out for yourself how volatile Tia's temper can be. But I can't help feeling you deserved it."

Several heads nodded in agreement. Most had been privy to Caroline's constant taunting and felt that Tia had been justified in fighting back, even if her searing tirade had shocked everyone within hearing distance. Most Australians were half civilized anyway, and Londoners expected little better from them.

"I suggest you send the little guttersnipe back to the country," Caroline sniffed haughtily.

Ben's silver eyes went murky with anger. It was one thing for *him* to call Tia a guttersnipe but quite another for someone else to do so. Especially someone like Caroline Battersby. A protective side he never knew existed made him want to defend Tia and the life she was forced to live, for surely no young woman would choose such a vile existence of her own accord.

"Perhaps I *will* send Tia back to the country," Ben said cryptically. "Now if you'll all excuse me, I must find Tia and take her home."

To Ben's chagrin, Lord Battersby followed him to the door. "I have this strange feeling you're trying to hoodwink me, Penrod. I have ways of learning things, and you can be assured I'll be watching you and your wife carefully in the future. You've deliberately kept the fact of your marriage, if indeed you are married, from all your friends. I don't appreciate the way you've led Caroline on, and if I find out you're not married, you'll learn just how ruthless I can be."

Ben didn't have time to argue as he hurried out the door after Tia. He knew he'd probably made an enemy, but there was no help for it.

Nothing or no one could force him to marry Caroline Battersby. Or marry anyone, for that matter.

Tia rushed through the Battersby mansion as if the devil himself was after her. And he probably was, Tia thought, imagining all the painful ways Ben would vent his anger on her. He definitely wasn't a man to cross. She paused only long enough in her headlong flight to snatch her cape from a downstairs room before running out the door. It was lined in fur and likely to bring a good price. Enough to appease One-eyed Bertha for her long unannounced absence. And Tia definitely needed Bertha's protection if she wanted to coexist with the dregs of London's underworld.

Tia raced along the dark streets, suddenly aware that wearing women's finery was definitely a disadvantage where she was going. And she certainly didn't want to expose herself now as a woman. She had no idea how long she'd be forced to live incognito, and posing as a boy was far preferable to using her woman's body to exist. As she thought along those lines, her first prerogative was stealing a set of boy's clothing from someone's clothesline. But Tia's luck deserted her. She ran straight into a brick wall. A flesh-and-blood wall as unyielding as solid granite.

Realizing where Tia was headed, Ben had taken a shortcut through alleyways, intercepting her on one of the streets leading into the stews of London. His arms came around her in fierce possession. "You can't escape me."

Tia's gasp echoed loudly through the deserted streets. "How—how did you know where to find me?"

"It wasn't difficult. I know exactly how you think. You were going back to the gutter. Perhaps I should leave you there to your dubious fate."

"Perhaps you should," Tia shot back defiantly. "I've done as you asked."

"Not quite. I'm not through with you yet. Come along."

Where are we going?"

"Home. The street is no place to air our grievances, and Lord Battersby is no fool. If you conveniently 'disappear,' he'll become suspicious and start investigating."

"I won't be bullied, ye mule-headed jackass!" Tia exclaimed, digging in her heels when Ben grasped her wrist and began dragging her behind him. But her meager strength was no match for him, and she soon found herself running to keep up with his long strides.

Ben merely grit his teeth and continued grimly on his way, ignoring her scathing outbursts. He was beginning to expect foul language from Tia when anger made her lapse into her gutter ways. What else could he expect from a girl raised in the stews of London and accustomed to fending off all the vile creatures who inhabited those slums? It was to her credit that she wasn't already worn out from being used by countless men. In fact, he was astounded to find her beauty and youth still so fresh when one took into account the fact that she probably was quite proficient in bartering her body for food.

Tia was surprised to find they weren't all that far from Ben's house. She had run when she left the Battersby's mansion, but evidently not far enough. Ben dragged her into the house, slamming the door so hard behind him it nearly flew off the hinges. Evidently Jeevers knew when to absent himself, for he remained safely hidden in some remote part of the house. Without a word, Ben dragged Tia up the stairs, shoved her into his room, and took great pleasure in banging shut another door.

They stood facing one another, sparks flying, tempers clashing, eyes sending messages completely at odds with what they were feeling. "Whatever made you lose control with Caroline?" Ben asked tightly. "You knew what was at stake yet deliberately risked your freedom as well as mine."

"Yer a bleedin' idiot, Ben Penrod," Tia said with remarkable restraint. "I don't give a damn what ya say, I ain't gonna take insults from the likes of Caroline Battersby. Bloody 'ell, I don't see how ya can bed a barracuda like 'er."

Ben smiled with a cool, self-assured arrogance that set Tia's teeth on edge. "It wasn't difficult. Caroline is a beautiful woman and I thrive on the attention of beautiful women. It just so happened I let down my guard where she was concerned and was forced into a difficult situation. But you're going to help me out of that situation."

"Like 'ell!" Her eyes flew open and she glared at him in brilliant defiance.

Ben's eyes shot heavenward. If he was wise he'd let the little witch disappear from his life. But for some unexplained reason the thought caused him considerable discomfort. "Think, Tia, how it would look if you disappeared as suddenly as you appeared. You've got to stick around awhile now that I've introduced you to society."

"How long?"

"I—don't know. As long as it takes to convince Lord Battersby that I'm not trying to hoodwink him. You're much safer here with me anyway. What kind of future do you have on the streets?"

"You promised," Tia said, suddenly overwhelmed by the idea of spending days on end in Ben's company.

"I—need you," Ben said softly.

His last words were a husky murmur. Tia felt the texture of his voice flow over her like a physical caress. Untutored in the ways of men, she watched in fascination as his mouth slowly descended. Her response shocked her. She drew in a shaky little breath, held it—and parted her lips.

Chapter Five

Ben kissed Tia with a savage hunger that left no room for gentleness, kissed her with a fierceness that rocked her to her toes and made her insides quake. It was the first time she had ever kissed a man and it reduced her to mindlessness. She felt her wits melt away, leaving her confused and disoriented. What was happening to her? How could a rake and womanizer like Ben Penrod reduce her to a spineless ninny? And the heat! She felt the torrid warmth of his kiss flood her veins with liquid fire and melt her bones. She tensed when she felt her breasts swell against the abrasive heat of his palm.

He was pressing against her now, making

her aware of the powerful surge of his sex and how much he was enjoying the kiss. His fingers strayed to her nipples, toying with the hard little buds until they grew erect and throbbed with painful need. When Tia felt his tongue parting her lips, her natural instincts were to accept the hard thrust of his tongue and press closer. Ben was doing things to her—wonderful things—that made her feel totally female for the first time in her life.

An anguished groan escaped from deep inside Ben's throat. He knew Tia was experienced but he hadn't expected such overwhelming passion. He couldn't recall when he wanted a woman as badly as he wanted Tia. She might be a conniving little whore and pickpocket, but he couldn't help himself. At times she seemed so innocent, so naïve, and at other times streetwise and knowledgeable in the ways of men. She was a contradiction to all he knew about women, and that fact alone made him want to discover the real Tia. Sometimes she acted every inch a lady, yet he knew she was a product of the streets.

Ben deepened the kiss, thoroughly exploring her mouth with his tongue as his hands memorized the full contours of her sweetly fashioned body. It amazed him that he could have mistaken Tia for a boy. She was soft and womanly and as beautiful as an angel. Until she opened her mouth to speak. Obviously her mouth was made for kissing, not for conversation, for her speech was deplorably lacking in refinement. Although he had to admit that she could speak correctly and with amazing aplomb when the notion struck her, the problem lay in the fact that he never knew what was going to come out of her mouth next.

Tia heard Ben's groan and wondered if he was feeling the same things she was. Or was he so jaded that one woman was much like another? The thought of Ben doing these same things with countless other women brought Tia abruptly to her senses. Good God, what was she doing? If she didn't stop now, Ben surely would think her the whore he accused her of being. When Ben's nimble fingers slipped inside her bodice to cup a bare breast, Tia stiffened and pulled away.

Ben frowned, puzzled by Tia's abrupt withdrawal. What was wrong? he wondered. Had he done something to displease her? Did she consider him an inexperienced lover who didn't know what women liked? If so he would personally guarantee that he'd measure up to her other lovers.

"What's wrong, Tia? Are you afraid I won't give you pleasure? There's no reason why we can't enjoy one another while we're pretending to be husband and wife. I promise you won't be disappointed."

"Damn and blast! Yer a conceited ass, Ben Penrod! Can't ye get it through yer thick skull that I want nothin' to do with ye?"

"You could have fooled me," Ben said with lazy amusement. "You made a damn good show of *pretending* to want me."

"You made it difficult to do otherwise," Tia said with perfect diction. "You—you caught me by surprise, but you won't find me with my guard down again."

"We'll see," Ben said cryptically. "You've had so many lovers, I doubt one more will make a difference."

That was the last straw. Without warning Tia leaped at Ben, catching him in the eye with one doubled fist. Ben howled in shock and pain. His arm flew out in automatic response, flinging Tia aside. Stumbling backward, she fell on the bed, her curses turning the air blue. When Ben saw what he had done he was immediately contrite. He hadn't meant to strike Tia. He'd never in his life abused a woman and didn't intend to start now, despite Tia's constant tirades and uncalled for outbursts of foul language.

"Tia, did I hurt you?" Ben asked remorsefully.

"Ye bleedin' bully," Tia said sullenly. "Go pick on someone yer own size." Her hand cradled her cheek where his blow had landed. She had received much worse from One-eyed Bertha but wasn't about to admit it to Ben. Playing the part of injured innocence to the hilt, she refused to look at him.

"Tia, look at me. Let me see where you're hurt."

Glancing up at him through lowered lids, Tia suddenly began to giggle. Ben's handsome features were clearly outlined in the glow of lamplight, and Tia was delighted to see that his eye was already turning black. She might be small but she was strong enough to do visible injury to a big man like Ben Penrod.

"What in bloody hell is so damn funny?"

Tia's giggle grew into gales of laughter. "Look at yourself."

Ben turned to glance into the mirror. The startling sight of one eye swollen and turning black brought a fierce frown to his face. Then suddenly something strange happened. The humor of the situation transformed the frown into a smile, then into outright mirth as he joined Tia in laughter.

"I'll have a devil of a time explaining this," he said, kneading the swollen flesh around his eye. "Who would believe a mite like you could pack such a wallop?" Suddenly he grew serious. "The life you lived couldn't have been easy." The thought of Tia fending off human predators, fighting to survive, brought an unexpected pang somewhere in the chambers of Ben's heart. He had no way of knowing it, but Tia was slowly destroying the barriers he'd erected to protect his freewheeling way of life.

"I managed," Tia said quietly. She was still lying on the bed where she had fallen after Ben's blow, and when she tried to rise, Ben pushed her back down and settled beside her.

"I think it's time you told me more about yourself. I've deliberately shied away from probing questions because they seemed to bother you, but there is more to you than meets the eye. Who are you, Tia? What are you? How long have you been consorting with thieves and picking pockets for a living?"

"Long enough," Tia answered tersely. "It's not important that you know more than that. When I've fulfilled my part of the bargain we've struck, I'll disappear and you won't see me again."

That's what I'm afraid of, Ben thought but did not say. "Just tell me one thing. Have you always lived on the streets? Or do you have a family someplace wondering what happened to you?"

"No family! No one," Tia said emphatically.

"You've answered only half my question."

Tia was thoughtful a long time before answering. "I'm not a product of the street," she said, her expression wistful. "Long ago I had a real family but—I have no one now. NO ONE! Please, stop badgering me. I've told you all I can." She glared at him mutinously, and wisely Ben realized his line of questioning was only making Tia angry and providing no insight into her background.

"Very well, Tia, I'll desist for now, but sooner or later I'll learn the truth."

"The truth is often deceptive," Tia murmured mysteriously. "Please leave, Ben. Meeting your friends and posing as your wife has left me exhausted."

"I want your promise first that your foul outbursts before my friends will stop."

"Caroline deserved it."

"Nevertheless I won't have it said I married a vulgar tart. You'll just have to learn to control your temper."

"Your warning is unnecessary. I don't intend to stay around and be insulted by any more of your friends."

"I won't allow you to leave, Tia, not yet anyway." His next words were so low that Tia barely heard them. "I still need you."

The intensity of his silver gaze probed her relentlessly, and his words brought her breath slamming against her chest. My God, what was wrong with her? He had only to look at her and she melted. It was as if those mesmerizing gray eyes of his could penetrate the tough facade she had created and see into the most private part of her soul. What kind of a man was he?

Lord help her!

He was arrogant and overbearing.

He was tall, handsome, and so overwhelmingly male she couldn't trust herself around him.

He needed her . . .

She had to leave before she lost more than she bargained for.

He was bending over her, so close she could almost taste the intoxicating odor of his special scent. Slightly spicy, musky, yet clean and masculine. Her nose twitched, wanting to memorize the tantalizing aroma so that when she returned to the stews of London she could recall it to bolster her in her lonely hours.

"Tia . . ."

"Hmmm?"

"I want to make love to you."

Tia jolted nearly upright. "What!"

"Let me, Tia, let me love you. I've been obsessed with you from the moment I unmasked you. I'll give you more pleasure than you've known with any of your other lovers."

Tia gulped back the automatic approval that sprang to her lips. Oh, how she wanted to give in, to experience tenderness just one time in her life before returning to the cold reality of living on the streets. And despite Ben's size and intimidating manner, she knew instinctively that he would be a tender lover. But regardless of the kind of life she had chosen to live these past three years and all the cruel realities most young women her age knew nothing about, she realized that giving herself to a man who wanted her only for the pleasure she could bring him was wrong. That he could make her want him only added to her distress.

Grasping at the only defense at her disposal, Tia assumed the hardened facade that had seen her through many impossible situations. "I ain't yer whore!" she flung out crudely. "Ye never said nothin' bout beddin' ya. I agreed to 'elp ya squirm out of marriage to Caroline, not ease yer lust. Ain't Caroline enough fer ya?"

"Stop braying like a lamebrained jackass," Ben said, and then stopped her angry tirade in the only way guaranteed to shut her up. His mouth closed over hers, and Tia inhaled with sharp pleasure as all those feelings she'd been trying to suppress turned her blood to puddles of molten fire.

Ben was astounded by the sudden, almost painful surge of passion that Tia roused in him. Even at her most outrageous there was something earthy and compelling about her. She infuriated him, frustrated him, challenged him, and—Lord help him—delighted him. He wanted desperately to love her, to feel her tighten around him, to thrust into her again and again until he drove her to perfect climax. And perfect was exactly how he wanted it to be for Tia. More perfect than anything she had ever known with any of her other lovers.

A moan slipped past Tia's lips as Ben deepened the kiss. She wanted to clamp down on his tongue when he inserted it into her mouth but couldn't summon the energy to do so. She was suddenly boneless and spineless, like putty in his hands. She had always been aware of Ben's strength, but it was his violence now that both repelled and attracted her. Not that he was hurting her. The kind of violence she was experiencing now was the violence of his passion. She began to understand Caroline's determination to keep Ben for herself.

Abruptly his kisses gentled, as he sensed her surrender and took pleasure in it and the sweet giving taste of her. When she lay soft and compliant beneath him, he began slowly—oh so slowly—to undress her. His mistake was in underestimating Tia's staunch will and implacable resolve not to be used by any man. She had escaped from a life of submissive servitude once and she wouldn't be charmed out of her maidenhead now by a rogue in gentlemen's attire.

"Take yer bleedin' 'ands off me!"

"What!"

"Ya 'eard me. I ain't spreadin' my legs fer a randy devil like you." She made her words deliberately crude and explicit, hoping to dampen his ardor. It did, but not for the reason she thought.

"Who do you spread your legs for?" Ben inquired tightly. The thought of Tia allowing other men to love her sent his temper flaring out of control.

Tia smiled with wicked delight and said sweetly, "None of yer bleedin' business."

Sputtering in rage, Ben realized that his desire had fled with his rising temper. Without being aware of it, Tia had effectively diffused his amorous intentions. All he felt now was the pressing need to strangle the little witch. Flinging himself away from her, he leaped to his feet.

"Go to sleep, Tia, I've had about all I can take from you for one night. If I don't leave now I'll either make love to you or beat you,

106

and my inclination now leans strongly toward the latter." His silver eyes held a dangerous light as they slid accusingly over her slender curves.

Only when he was gone did Tia dare to breath again.

The following day invitations began to arrive. The Fenmores' came first, followed closely by notes from nearly everyone Tia had met at the party. When Ben announced his intention to accept on their behalf, Tia groaned in protest.

"How far do you intend to carry this farce?"

"As far as necessary. At least until the Battersbys are convinced I am no longer available to coerce into marriage."

"That's too vague. I want to leave now."

"Why? Aren't you comfortable here? Your quality of life is certainly much better than what you're accustomed to. Is there some reason you want to leave?" The smug smile he bestowed on her was blinding in its raw sensuality.

Tia's heart shied away from that question. She feared feeling something for this man. It was too dangerous. Not just for her but for Ben. To feel would invite hurt; to care was to court disappointment; to love—God help her— was forbidden her.

She defended her reasons with a question of her own. "Why do you want me to stay? There is no future for us."

It was a contest of wills, and if a small voice inside Ben whispered of some long-denied emotion, he forced himself to ignore it. He would never surrender to an emotion he had vigorously resisted for as long as he could remember.

"I need you," he said in a tone that implied his simple reply needed no further explanation. Then he was gone, leaving Tia to fret over Ben's curious reluctance to release her.

Against her better judgment, Tia attended the Fenmores' party with Ben. There seemed to be no escaping him. At night he locked her in the room and during the day when he had to go out he enlisted Jeevers' help to keep Tia from straying. Of course she could have eluded the intrepid servant easily enough, but some strange emotion compelled her to remain until her part of the bargain was fulfilled. Besides, every day she remained with Ben meant a day she wasn't going hungry, or trying to please One-eyed Bertha, or fending off vile creatures who liked young boys almost as much as they liked women.

Ben's last words to her before they left for the Fenmores' that night were "Behave yourself."

Tia behaved with remarkable restraint that evening. She smiled as if she hadn't a brain in her head, spoke only when spoken to, and offered little beyond inane nonsense. Evidently her beauty was enough to endear her to Ben's very proper friends, for Tia was somewhat startled to discover that most had forgiven her for her outrageous outburst at Caroline Battersby. Of course it helped tremendously that Caroline had chosen not to attend the Fenmores' gathering. But two nights later luck deserted Tia when both Caroline and her parents attended the soiree given by the Patersons.

"I see you've recovered from your—indisposition," Caroline said snidely as she sidled up to Tia and Ben.

Tia didn't have to ask to whom the statement was directed. "I wasn't indisposed," Tia replied blandly. "I didn't like the company." Tia started to say something else until Ben's warning poke in the ribs reminded her to hold her tongue.

"Father would like to speak with you, Ben," Caroline said, ignoring Tia's thinly veiled jibe. "I'll take you to him."

Ben frowned in consternation, wondering what the old buzzard wanted now. Deciding to honor the request, he nodded to Caroline and waited for her to lead him to her father. Tia made as if to follow.

"Just Ben," Caroline stressed, stopping Tia in her tracks.

Tia started to protest until Ben said, "Wait here for me, Tia, I won't be long."

Uncertain what to do next, Tia found a secluded alcove and sat down to await Ben's return. The wait stretched out into long anxious minutes of wondering what Lord Battersby could possibly want with Ben. At the end of forty-five minutes Tia began fidgeting nervously, wondering what was amiss. Then she spied Lord Battersby across the room conversing with friends and was seized with a cold fear.

Where was Ben? Had something happened to him? Then in a flash the answer came to her. Lord Battersby hadn't really wanted to see Ben, it was all Caroline's doing. She wanted to get Ben alone, and her reasons needed no explanation. Tia wondered if she should look for him or leave him to the tender ministrations of his former lover. Some unexplained emotion made her leave the alcove and walk from the room.

Ben had followed Caroline to a deserted room down the hall from where most of the guests were gathered. It never dawned on him that he wasn't going to meet with Lord Battersby until he discovered that the room was empty save for a bed and Caroline. He swung around to face Caroline, his eyebrows raised in question.

"What's the meaning of this, Caroline?"

"I wanted to talk to you—alone."

"There is nothing left for us to say. We enjoyed one another, but it's over. I may not be a model husband but I *am* married and therefore out of your reach."

"Father has considerable influence, and should you seek a divorce, I'm certain the courts would look favorably upon your suit."

"I don't want a divorce," Ben insisted. "Tia pleases me well." Suddenly Ben went still, realizing the startling truth of that statement.

"She's still a child," Caroline scoffed derisively. "If you've been married three years, she couldn't have been more than fifteen or sixteen at the time. I had no idea you liked children."

"Tia is older than she looks," Ben defended.

"Make love to me, Ben, for old time's sake," Caroline said with compelling urgency. She was convinced that once she had Ben in her bed again he would realize what he was missing and dump his young wife.

"Sorry, Caroline, not this time." He turned to leave.

"Ben, look at me!" A noise suggesting material being rent apart piqued Ben's curiosity and he turned to see what Caroline was up to.

Caroline had seized the neckline of her gown and ripped it down the front, exposing her generous breasts. "If you don't make love to me, I'll scream rape. Think of the consequences. Think of the gossip and what it will do to your family name. I'm not asking much, only that you love me."

Ben's mind worked furiously. He had no desire to make love to Caroline, but neither did he want his name dragged through the mud. Australia wasn't so distant that word of his escapade would never reach his family. Dare would kill him when he learned that Ben was accused of committing rape—if his father didn't do it first. And Ben certainly didn't intend to remain in England forever. Australia was his home, and he had always planned to return after he tired of the fast life in gay old London. But Ben's agile mind had already found a solution to his dilemma.

"Making love to you will be a pleasure, Caro, just like always." A ghost of a smile played over his lips. "Take off your clothes."

Caroline squealed in delight and began tossing aside her clothes. When she was naked she lay full length on the bed, beckoning to Ben with a crooked finger. Neither had the slightest notion that Tia, having grown worried about Ben's lengthy absence, had begun a search for them. One by one she opened each closed door in the Fenmore mansion, until she came to the room holding Ben and Caroline. She listened for a moment to the murmur of voices, then cautiously turned the knob until the door opened enough for her to peek inside. Her eyes opened wide as she stared at Caroline's nude body draped over the bed and of Ben bending over her. Then, on silent feet, she turned and fled. If she had stayed a moment longer she would have heard Ben laugh and tell Caroline that he was leaving. That he wanted nothing more to do with her. That she could cry rape all she wanted, but it would be difficult to convince anyone she had been raped when her assailant was gone and no evidence existed to convict Ben.

Ben found Tia exactly where he left her. He apologized profusely for leaving her for so long but didn't elaborate. When he suggested they leave, Tia did not object. If she was quiet and withdrawn on their ride home, Ben didn't notice; he was still fuming over Caroline's audacious behavior. When he finally seemed to remember Tia, they were but a few short blocks from his house.

"Thank you, Tia."

"For what?" Tia asked sullenly. She was glad he had given her time to think, for she had plans to make.

"For acting the lady tonight. You were quite impressive."

Tia opened her mouth to spit out a nasty retort but was forestalled by the sudden jolt of the coach in which they were riding.

"Wha—what's wrong?"

Ben leaned out the window to question the driver when the door was flung open and he found himself being yanked bodily from the coach. "What the hell! Is this a robbery?"

Two men brandishing clubs flanked him. The driver had already been clubbed and lay on the ground. The hour was late, the streets deserted. "It's the woman we want," one of the men barked as he motioned for his partner to drag Tia from the coach.

"Leave her out of this, she has nothing of value," Ben said. "Empty my pockets if you will, then go on your way."

His words made little impression as Tia was forcibly dragged from the coach, spouting threats and flinging curses that no lady would use.

"Whoeee, do ya hear that, Crebs? Are ye certain sure we've nabbed the right woman? I'd hate ta get me arse chewed fer snatchin' the wrong duckie."

"Ye'll get more than yer arse chewed if ye don't shut yer trap. Ye know our orders."

"Aye, take care of the nob and I'll handle this one."

Those were the last words he ever spoke. As he hustled the wildly struggling Tia away he bumped into Ben, who was waiting for just such an opportunity. Well aware of the danger that existed on the streets of London, Ben never left home without a weapon. It was the same in Australia, where bushrangers roamed the bush and mountains and often attacked without provocation. The knife was hidden in his boot, and he wasted no time in removing it when the thief jostled him. Since the man holding Tia was the closest, he was the first to feel the bite of cold steel. He went down clutching his stomach, freeing Tia instantly.

"Get back in the coach, Tia," Ben barked, turning his attention to the second assailant. But coward that he was, the man took in Ben's size, the dangerous glint in his eyes, and decided not to push his luck. His partner already lay dead or dying and he didn't relish joining him. If the rich man paying him tried to find him in order to wreak vengeance for failing in his mission, he could always disappear in the stews of London where he could remain forever and

114

never be found. He turned and ran.

Had he been alone, Ben wouldn't have hesitated to give chase. But he had Tia's safety to consider. By then the driver was stirring and Ben helped him to his feet and hustled him inside the coach with Tia. Then he hopped into the driver's box and set the horses in motion. Inside the coach, Tia was too stunned to move— or even speak. Obviously, those two men had wanted her and Ben would have lost his life if he hadn't been smart enough to carry a weapon. Perhaps next time he wouldn't be so lucky. Tia knew exactly what needed to be done. She must make absolutely certain there never was a next time.

It was only a short distance to Ben's lodgings, and before Tia could protest he lifted her out of the coach and carried her into the house. He didn't set her down until they were inside the bedroom she occupied.

"Are you all right? Those men didn't hurt you, did they?"

"No, I'm fine," Tia said somewhat breathlessly. "Thank you, Ben."

"I'm afraid a simple thank you won't work this time, Tia. I want answers and I want them now. Those men weren't thieves; they wanted you. Why, Tia? What did they want with you?"

Chapter Six

"I—don't know why anyone would want to kidnap me," Tia hedged. She didn't dare look at Ben for fear he'd recognize her lie for what it was.

"I don't believe you, Tia. Are you in some kind of trouble? I can't help you if you don't tell me."

"No one can help me," Tia said quietly. "Besides, I have no idea what those men wanted with me."

"Tia, look at me." Placing one finger beneath her chin, he raised her face so he could look into her eyes. Their gazes locked in silent struggle, each aware of something explosive and powerful building between them. Tia could feel his desire, she could see the heat in his gray eyes, and something inside her responded with a melting warmth.

He bent his head and took her mouth in a kiss that was meant to be domineering, but his intent became confused when her soft mouth parted beneath the force of his. She moaned softly as the kiss deepened. A flame flickered to life inside her, eroding her bones. The passion, once ignited, grew, and neither seemed capable of suppressing it.

Ben broke off the kiss, drew back, and stared at Tia curiously. What was it about this tiny, feisty woman that made him ache to possess her? She was lovely, true, but so were dozens of other women he'd known. Many of them intimately. At times she was a shameless hussy who spouted vile language, then, when he least expected it, she surprised him by acting demure and ladylike. There was a mystery about her that defied defining, yet she refused to divulge anything of her life beside the fact that she earned her keep by picking pockets. And Lord knows what else. The vile things she must have done to survive didn't even bear thinking about. Yet somehow none of that mattered. Lord help him, but he wanted her!

"Let me make love to you," Ben groaned, dragging her against him and letting her feel the hard thrust of his need. "You want it as much as I do."

"No—I'm not—I haven't done this before."

Ben's lips curled in a mocking grin. "There

117

is no need to lie, sweetheart. I know what you are and I don't care. I'm not without experience myself."

What good would it do to keep insisting she was a virgin? Tia reflected grimly. Ben had already made up his mind and obviously wasn't in the mood to hear the truth. To be perfectly honest with herself, Ben made her feel things she never knew existed, made her experience yearnings she'd only imagined. Would it be so terrible to feel loved and wanted one time in her life before she lost her identity and disappeared once again into the bowels of London where no one could find her?

Ben took Tia's silence for acquiescence as he swept her into his arms and carried her to the bed. "You won't be sorry, sweetheart, I swear. I want to make you happier than any man you've known before."

Leaning over her, he grasped the hem of her gown and pulled it up, his hand brushing her naked flesh, coming to rest on her upper thigh. Slowly he worked her gown to her waist. Her legs were long and slim and he stared at them in wonder. It was as if hers were the first pair of female legs he'd ever seen, yet he had seen many. But none of them as shapely as Tia's. He quickly stripped off her shoes and stockings, by now so aroused he fumbled like a green lad with his first woman. Then he pulled her to a sitting position so he could lift the gown from her shoulders and over her head.

Naked and defenseless, Tia tried to cover her breasts with her hands but Ben pushed them aside. "No, don't hide from me. I want to see all of you. You're beautiful, you know. Your breasts are perfect. Has no one told you how lovely you are?"

"I—no, no one," she gulped, so consumed by heat and flushed with the first real stirrings of her body that she was at a loss for words.

"Then the men you've bedded before are fools." Suddenly his face hardened and he grew thoughtful. "How many men have you shown your body to, Tia? You must have had to reveal yourself at various times in your life."

A tight coil of anger burst inside Tia. "Blast and damn, Ben, why must you spoil everything?" She pushed on his chest but he refused to budge. Instead, his body came down on hers, pinning her beneath him.

"It doesn't matter, sweetheart, nothing matters. Bloody hell, I don't know how I managed to keep my hands off you this long."

"I doubt you'll be nominated for sainthood," Tia bit out sarcastically.

"Shut up and kiss me."

When his mouth slanted over hers, Tia felt the heat building again. He held her head in place and kissed her face, her nose, her cheeks, telling her how much he needed her, how he loved the feel of her soft flesh, how he wanted to come inside her and thrust and thrust until he spilled his seed and she cried out in sweet ecstasy. Then he scrambled to his knees, undressing with growing impatience until he was as naked as she was.

Tia watched him, her eyes large and vivid as he shed his clothes and poised above her, magnificently naked. He was lean and sleek, his torso bulging with ropy muscles. His hips were slim, his flanks tapering to long legs as sturdy as oak trees. But it was his thick, fully aroused manhood that Tia's eyes came back to again and again.

"I hope I please you." A ghost of a smile hung on one corner of his mouth.

Tia gulped back a spurt of raw fear. In that instant she knew he would break her in two if he came into her, and she told him so.

Ben's grin widened, followed by outright laughter. "I've never split anyone in two yet. I'll admit you're tiny but I assure you women feel pain only once. And since that doesn't apply to you, I fully expect to bring you only pleasure."

He was covering her again, his male flesh against her, and he was kissing her wildly, finding her nipples and rolling them between his fingers, his tongue probing her mouth until it found hers. Then his fingers were between them, parting her flesh, teasing and massaging until she cried out with a need she couldn't explain. He raised her hips and she felt his sex pressing against her, prodding relentlessly, slipping inside her slowly, filling her—hurting her.

Tia whimpered as he stretched her to accommodate his great size. Ben mistook the sound for a moan of pleasure. "Patience, sweetheart, I want this to last a long time."

"Oh God, it hurts," Tia moaned, trying to escape the terrible pressure that grew worse the further Ben slid inside her.

"I know I'm big, sweetheart, but if you relax you'll enjoy it more."

Tia gnawed her lower lip, stifling the cries that came unbidden from her throat. If she had known it would hurt like this she'd never have allowed Ben to make love to her. Did women actually *like* this?

"Stop!"

"I—can't."

"You're killing me!"

Suddenly Ben went still. It couldn't be! Yet it was. His sex had butted against the barrier of Tia's maidenhead. "Tia, look at me! Why didn't you tell me?"

"Ye damn scurvy bastard, I did but ye didn't believe me. Now will ye stop?"

"No."

He thrust deep—deeper. Tia felt her maidenhead stretch against his sex. She cried out at the wrenching tear inside her. Gathering her in his arms, Ben tried to soothe her, kissing her gently, smoothing back her hair with his large hand, all the while holding himself still and deep inside her. Slowly the burning edge of pain subsided, replaced by a tingling ache that made her want to rotate her hips against him.

"I'm sorry, sweetheart, truly. Not sorry that I was the first to take you but sorry because I caused you pain. God, you're so small, can you feel me inside you? I've never felt anything so incredibly erotic." She rotated her hips experimentally. "Sweet Jesus, don't move or this will be over before we want it to."

Sweat popped out on his forehead as he fought for control. His harsh panting subsided, and then slowly he began to move. His breath whispered soft and warm against her mouth as he murmured, "Lift your hips, sweetheart."

Tia obeyed instantly, his hands drawing her up to meet his thrusts, and she moaned as she felt him embedded full and deep inside her. His face was contorted as if in pain, and he was heaving, delving deep, his breath sharp and raw. He could have climaxed immediately but deliberately paced himself in order to give Tia the maximum pleasure.

Then something began to happen to Tia. Her aching core became soft and yielding. Deep in the tender center of her a terrible, vibrating need filled her with raw, sweet agony. She couldn't help herself and cried out as he thrust into her again and again.

Then suddenly she was responding wildly, grinding her hips against his, inviting his violence, his passion, demanding all he had to give. And Ben gave it gladly, joyously, his restraint admirable as he withheld his own climax until he heard Tia's trembling gasp and felt her body stiffen beneath him. The end came in an explosion that caught Tia by surprise. Her body vibrated, then broke apart into thousands of tiny brilliant lights as she catapulted into an unexplored world of sexual delight. Ben threw back his head and cried out, and she felt his release, felt his wetness as he emptied himself inside her.

"Tia."

"Ummm?" How could she speak when waves of raw feeling were still pulsing through her veins?

"Did I hurt you?" Ben was lying on his side, staring down at her with a perplexed look on his face.

"Yes, at first. But later—I never felt anything so wonderful."

"Shy little thing, aren't you?" he chuckled, amused by her frank observation.

Tia flushed a becoming red. "Well, you asked."

"If I had known you were a virgin I would have taken it easier with you."

"I tried to tell you."

"So you did. But who would have thought . . . I think you owe me an explanation."

"We've had this conversation before and I'm growing weary of it."

"You're the most exasperating female I've ever known."

He rolled away from her and lifted himself

123

off the bed. She watched apprehensively as he went to the washstand, poured water into the bowl, and returned to the bed. When he parted her legs and gently began cleansing away evidence of their recent mating, Tia watched in fascination. The water in the bowl turned red, and she frowned, slanting Ben an inquiring look.

" 'Tis just your maiden's blood," he explained.

When he finished he stretched out full length beside her. He knew he should give her time to recuperate, that she'd likely be sore, but he felt himself swelling again, wanting her, needing her in a way that startled and puzzled him. He lowered his head and kissed her, then slid his mouth downward, exploring, slowly teasing her sensitive nipples with his tongue until her limbs grew heavy and her blood ran like thick honey in her veins.

"I want you again, Tia. I can't seem to get enough of you. I think you've bewitched me."

When his lips settled on a tender spot between her legs, Tia jerked nearly upright. "Ben!" Her hands flew down to push him away.

Reluctantly Ben moved up her body. She was so incredibly erotic. She exuded a potent steamy sexuality that made him want to love her in every way possible for a man to love a woman. But she was still so new to loving that he thought it best to initiate her slowly, savoring each nuance of her education as he went along.

Tia drew in a ragged sigh when Ben desisted.

She felt shame for reacting to his slow, intoxicating arousal, yet the feeling he evoked was so potent, so incredibly fantastic, she wanted it to go on forever. But she had learned the hard way that nothing was forever. Men were deceitful, arrogant, demanding, and cruel. All of them. And that included Ben Penrod. Just because she had given her body to him once didn't mean he owned her. No man owned her, except . . . No, no one!

"Go away, Ben, this shouldn't have happened."

His eyes flickered, narrowed, and his hand moved to cup the side of her face. "But it has. And it will again. Now."

His kiss was gentle at first, soft and slow, parting her lips so that his tongue could slide inside. His face was hard with passion, his eyes hot with it. But there was something more besides passion, something Tia couldn't define. Then, flinging out a curse, he rolled on top of her, pressing her into the mattress, his hands all over her as he parted her thighs with his knee. His hand slid between their bodies, between her legs, found the hot wetness there and stroked her. With experienced fingers he located the spot where his tongue had been moments before and massaged gently. Tia cried out, gasping and trembling, her body shuddering with its own pleasure. Then he was thrusting inside her, deep, so deep that the sheer enormity of him startled her and she waited for the pain.

125

But there was no pain. Only more pleasure. Pleasure so intense she convulsed with it again and again. She writhed beneath him, her mind separate from her body, a wanton, wild thing, mewling and panting, crying out his name. Spurred by her response, Ben clamored to join her, desperation driving him as he found his own release.

When Tia surfaced, Ben was leaning on his elbow, staring down at her. "I can't believe you've never done this before, you're so good at it. Your body is all passion and response."

Tia flushed and opened her mouth to fling out a scathing retort, but Ben forestalled her. "No, don't say it. I can't bear to hear street language coming from your sweet lips."

"How do you know what I was going to say?"

"I've grown accustomed to the unladylike phrases that come spilling from your mouth."

Tia glared at him with unfeigned disgust. "I suppose you know all about ladies."

"As a matter of fact, I do."

"I don't consider Caroline Battersby a lady."

"Caro is spoiled and can be quite bitchy at times, but no one would dispute the fact that she is a lady."

Tia sniffed disdainfully. "If she's such a lady, why are you so dead set against marrying her?"

"It's not just Caro. I'm not the marrying kind. There has never been a great love in my life, and I have no compelling need to produce an heir. My brother Dare has already provided my father with three grandchildren. Marriage is for idiots who don't know any better. Besides, I'd make a lousy husband."

"For once we're in perfect agreement," Tia muttered sleepily.

Ben couldn't help but grin at her rather pointed statement. Fascinated, he watched as her thickly lashed lids lowered over her incredible jewel-like eyes and she slid easily into sleep. He had to admit he had exhausted her. Too bad he couldn't say the same for himself. He'd never felt stronger in his life. He felt as if he could love Tia all night, nonstop, renewing himself each time he emptied his seed inside her. Usually once or twice was enough, but something about Tia made him a veritable sexual giant.

Bloody hell! Thoughts like that were dangerous.

Deciding to sort out all the foreign emotions assailing him at a later time, Ben rolled over and pulled Tia into his arms. Still hovering on the outer fringes of sleep, Tia merely sighed as her body melted into his, yielding when she knew it was wrong, fitting so perfectly it felt like home.

When Tia surfaced, the sun was shining and Ben was gone.

Tia lingered in bed as long as she dared. Hunger gnawed at her but she ignored it, unwilling to meet Ben so soon after her surrender. She wasn't certain what to expect from him. Would he laugh at her for succumbing to his subtle seduction? Or make fun of her because she was a virgin? She dawdled in her room as long as she dared, then went downstairs when hunger drove her to the dining room in time for lunch. Ben was waiting for her, looking supremely smug and disgustingly rested. Against her better judgment, her eyes met his, and there it was. The passion, hot, intense, and so sensual it went right to the melting core of her. He sent her a lopsided grin, and her heart slid down to her shoes.

"I hope you slept well."

Hardening her heart against his devastating charm, Tia merely nodded.

"I hope you're hungry. I had cook fix a special lunch."

She nodded again.

"Are you angry with me?"

"I—no, not really."

"Good." He seemed genuinely concerned and glad she wasn't angry. "I'll be good to you, Tia, I promise. You'll not be sorry. When I go back to Australia I'll make certain you're taken care of so that you won't have to steal for a living ever again."

"What!" Did Ben mean what she thought he meant?

"I want you to live with me as my mistress for as long as I remain in London. Besides, people will expect my wife to live with me."

"No," she said with stiff hauteur.

"You're refusing me?" Ben hadn't counted on that.

"Of course. I've never belonged to any man and don't intend to start now. Few people would envy my life, but at least I'm free."

"Bloody hell, Tia, you've nothing to lose by becoming my mistress," Ben contended, throwing down his napkin.

"Haven't I? This conversation bores me, Ben, and besides, I'm famished."

She calmly filled her plate and began eating. But truth to tell, she wasn't as calm as she appeared. Her heart was beating furiously against her breast, and the thought of falling asleep every night in Ben's arms gave her an unwelcome comfort. She couldn't afford such thoughts. There was no future for her and Ben and never would be. Not only was he dead set against marriage, but her own situation forbade any thought of a normal life most women craved. Any kind of relationship with Ben would lead to disaster.

Abruptly Ben rose, his face contorted with unexplained anger. He had no idea why the thought of Tia leaving him should cause such raw anguish. He only knew he wanted her with him for as long as he remained in London. He'd already introduced her as his wife and saw no reason now for her to quietly disappear. Lord help him, he still wanted her!

"You're not leaving, Tia, and that's final! We're to attend the Fishers' soiree tonight. Wear the white satin gown." So saying he strode from the room, his jerky steps effectively conveying his vexation.

Tia was subdued and thoughtful when she accompanied Ben that night to the Fishers' soiree. Despite Ben's words to the contrary, she knew her time with him was limited. It was much too dangerous to remain, for sooner or later she might be recognized. She already knew that men were on her trail, and it was only a matter of time before she'd be forced to return to the deplorable situation she'd escaped from three years ago.

The evening was pleasant, Ben attentive yet puzzled by her strange mood. He would have been shocked had he known that Tia was waging a war within herself. Deep in the chambers of her heart the urge existed to remain with Ben for as long as he wanted her, to be his mistress and savor the shallow love he offered. No— not love—never that. But she could pretend, couldn't she? She never expected to feel the things Ben made her feel or experience the wild ecstasy his loving brought her. Now that she had it, it was difficult to give up, knowing she would never experience it again. But it was for that very reason she must leave. She didn't dare lose her heart to the tender rogue.

When Ben suggested they leave, Tia agreed with alacrity. Her mouth hurt from smiling and she was still exhausted from lack of sleep the night before. This time the ride home was uneventful, though Ben was watchful and tense, relaxing only when the coach ground to a halt before his front door. He helped Tia from the coach, then turned to speak to the driver. Momentarily distracted, Tia glanced absently down the deserted street. From the corner of her eye she caught a movement in the shadows at the side of the house and turned her gaze in that direction.

To her horror she saw two men lurking there. When they saw her glance their way, they melted into the darkness, giving Tia the distinct impression that she and Ben were being spied upon. Dragging in a shaky breath, she hurried toward the house. Having paid the driver, Ben was close on her heels. He opened the door and she swept inside.

"Go on up, I'll join you in a moment," Ben drawled, slanting her a meaningful glance.

He watched her ascend the stairs, a thoughtful look on his face. He was so damn randy it took every ounce of self-control to refrain from bounding after her, tossing her on the bed, and thrusting into her again and again. But he had seen something as he spoke with the driver, something that needed investigating. If he wasn't mistaken, he and Tia were being watched, and he strongly suspected it was related to the two men who had accosted them the previous night. Tia was in danger, and sooner or later he'd wring the truth from her.

Tia paced the room in short, nervous steps.

She knew she'd eventually be forced to leave Ben's house, and the occurrences these past two nights only drove home the need. Not only was she in danger of losing her freedom, but she was placing Ben's life in jeopardy. If something happened to Ben because of her, she'd never forgive herself.

The door swung open and Ben entered the room. They stared at one another for what seemed an eternity before Ben spoke. "Did you see anyone lurking outside the house when we arrived home tonight?"

Perched on the horns of a dilemma, Tia didn't know what to answer. If she admitted spotting the two thugs, Ben would probably interrogate her until he broke down her defenses. And she couldn't allow that to happen.

"No, I saw no one."

He looked at her sharply. "Are you certain?"

"Of course, why would I lie?"

"Why indeed." He unbuttoned his shirt and pulled it out of his pants.

"What are you doing?"

One dark eyebrow arched upward. "Getting ready for bed."

"This isn't your room."

"You're mistaken, this *is* my room. Everything in it belongs to me, including you."

Tia tried another tactic. "I don't think this is a good idea."

"It's a wonderful idea." He unfastened his pants and slid them down his narrow hips.

Tia licked her suddenly dry lips and lost the ability to speak for all of two minutes. When her voice returned it lacked conviction.

"I—I'm too tired tonight. This isn't what I want."

"It's exactly what you want," Ben said with supreme arrogance. "Do you need help undressing?"

"No—I mean—yes—oh God, I don't know what I mean."

"Tia, don't fight it, I'm going to make love to you tonight. I've thought of nothing else since I left your bed this morning."

"Why? I'm sure there are other women more experienced than I am who would love to have you in their beds."

"Damned if I know why I want you. I haven't tried to analyze it yet."

He was naked now, every inch of his perfectly sculpted body exposed. He was hard and ready and advancing toward her with slow, measured steps. Tia backed away until the back of her knees collided with the edge of the bed. When she turned to retreat in another direction, Ben had his arms around her, dragging her against the unyielding wall of his chest, his lips seeking hers with demanding urgency. This time Tia wasn't about to give in so easily, brutally aware that each time he loved her made leaving all the more difficult.

She stiffened, immobile within the span of his tense arms. But Ben left no room for protest

133

as he began stripping off her clothing. He loved the way she was all feisty defiance one moment and shuddering surrender the next. He loved—everything about her. Even the way she tried to make him believe she didn't want him. In the end it made little difference what Tia wanted, for her body responded independently of her mind as she surrendered to the mastery of his touch. She tried not to feel the warming of her blood or the coil of searing flame rising up through her veins, but all was lost as her senses flew out the window.

The next thing she knew, Ben was stretched out on the bed, positioning her atop his loins as he thrust inside her. Of their own accord her hips began to churn, meeting each delving thrust as she tried to assuage the beautiful torment building inside her. Her excitement escalated and she rocked her hips, riding him with wanton abandon. Unable to contain the powerful surge of raw passion driving him, Ben brought them both to shattering climax. He cried out her name and was rewarded when he heard his own name whispered through her lips as softly as sweet summer rain.

Tia's mind was made up. She had to leave Ben and she had to do it now—immediately—before something dreadful happened to him. He had left the house early the next morning, and Tia decided the time couldn't be any better for her to quietly disappear from his life. She had served her purpose, in a capacity she hadn't reckoned with, and nothing good could come of her remaining with Ben. She would only cause trouble in his life, especially now since it seemed likely her presence had become known to the one person who had just cause to ruin both her life and Ben's.

Since she couldn't leave dressed like a woman, she searched Ben's closets, hoping to find something more suitable to wear. But his garments were so large she couldn't possibly wear them. She thought of asking Jeevers for something of his to wear but decided the very proper butler would become suspicious and detain her. At her wit's end, she climbed up to the attic and began rummaging in trunks she found stored there. Her luck took a turn for the better when she found a wardrobe of young boys' clothing neatly folded in one of the trunks. They were out of date and musty but all the better for her purposes. There were several caps from which to choose, and Tia picked one that slid down over her ears to cover her abundant blond tresses.

When she emerged from the attic some time later, not even Ben would have recognize her, Tia thought smugly. She was wrong, but since Ben wasn't there to challenge her, she ignored the niggling suspicion that of all people Ben would be the one most likely to identify her. Before she slipped out the door she entered the den and rifled through the desk, searching for coin. Ben already knew her for a thief and pick-pocket, so one more strike against her wouldn't matter much. Besides, One-eyed Bertha would likely backhand her if she didn't show up with some sort of appeasement along with her explanation of her long absence.

Fortunately, Ben always kept coin on hand for Jeevers should the need arise, and Tia quickly pocketed half of what was there. She turned to leave, then had second thoughts as she scooped up the remaining cache of coins and slipped stealthily from the room and out the front door. She looked back only once. Tears streaming down her face at a furious rate prevented her from seeing anything beyond the misty curtain of water.

She had experienced paradise once; if only it could last a lifetime.

Chapter Seven

Ben returned to the house in a jubilant mood. He had purchased a piece of jewelry for Tia and couldn't wait to present it to her. He was excessively pleased with himself, and with Tia, thinking he couldn't have found a more responsive mistress. She was everything a man wanted in a woman—and what made the whole thing extraordinary was the certain knowledge that he had been the first to introduce her to sensual pleasure. It truly amazed Ben that Tia had been a virgin, especially in view of the horrid conditions in which she'd lived. Assuming the identity of a boy was a stroke of genius, but he wasn't certain how much longer she could have continued with the charade.

Jeevers met Ben at the door. The butler's

long face and soulful look sent Ben's heart plummeting down to his shoes, and he knew immediately something was amiss.

"What is it, Jeevers? You may as well tell me."

"I'm sorry, sir, I had no idea . . . that is, I was busy and never for a moment thought she would—"

"Has something happened to Tia?" Ben's first thought was that the person or persons who were after her had succeeded in getting to her in his absence. He cursed his stupidity for leaving her unattended. "Is she hurt?" He asked the question almost hopefully, preferring an accident over her seizure by someone who would do her physical harm.

"She's gone, sir, just disappeared into thin air. I was in the back of the house and when I went to her room later to check on her, she didn't answer the door. A thorough search failed to produce her anywhere in the house."

"Perhaps she went shopping?" Ben suggested optimistically, though in his heart he knew shopping was the last place Tia would go.

"I don't think so," Jeevers said slowly. "Nothing is missing from her wardrobe, not one of the new dresses you purchased for her."

"She certainly didn't leave the house unclothed."

"I also checked your wardrobe, recalling that when you brought the young lady here she was dressed as a lad."

"And . . . ?"

"Everything is in place."

"Bloody hell!"

Taking the steps two at a time, Ben bolted up the stairs and into Tia's room. It was just as Jeevers said. Rummaging through the wardrobe, he noted that all her dresses were hung neatly inside.

"Tia!"

He went from room to room, calling her name, becoming angrier and more worried by the minute. After her near abduction, didn't she realize the danger of going out unattended? Why would she leave in the first place? Ben reflected, puzzled. He hadn't hurt her. In fact, he had given her pleasure. And received more pleasure than he could ever remember in return. The ungrateful little brat, he thought ungraciously. He had been so pleased with her he went out and bought her a gift, and she had disappeared the moment his back was turned.

Then a terrifying thought entered his brain and refused to be dislodged. What if those thugs had her? The mystery of why they wanted her still remained, but it did little to ease his fear— or rage. The unappreciative wretch! When he found her again he'd beat her to within an inch of her life. He'd blister her bottom until it was permanently red. He could picture it now. That pert little derriere bare and squirming as he upended her across his knees.

Bloody hell! He was growing hard just thinking about that perfect little bottom, and he could conjure up a dozen more pleasant things to do to her than beat her. But first he had to find her. Charging back down the stairs, Ben rushed past a startled Jeevers and out the door. He made his way unerringly toward the worst section of London, certain that Tia, had she left of her own accord, would head back to the life she felt comfortable with. Since he carried a pistol as well as the knife in his boot, and it was still daylight, he felt relatively safe.

Though Ben met with dozens of unsavory characters, was propositioned by several bed-raggled prostitutes and accosted by beggars, he saw neither hide nor hair of Tia. When he asked questions he received blank stares in reply. When he tried doling out coins for information, his reception was slightly more open, though he was astute enough not to trust any of the sly, grasping creatures he encountered. Unfortunately, no one seemed to have seen a young lad roaming the streets. Or if they had, Ben's description matched any of a dozen lads.

Ben walked the streets until long past midnight, until a heavy rain began to fall and he was forced to abandon his search. But he returned the following day, more determined than ever to find Tia. The terrifying thought of all the horrible things that could happen to her drove him nearly wild with worry. She was too beautiful, much too female to continue her masquerade as a boy. Sooner or later someone would unmask her and she would fall into the hands of men who would ravish her without mercy.

That horrendous thought made Ben cringe inside. Tia might be an exasperating brat, but she didn't deserve the kind of life she'd been living before their fateful meeting. How could she prefer so low an existence when he offered her so much more? he wondered crossly. Why had she left after he'd told her he would take care of her so she'd never have to steal for a living again? Hadn't he promised to see to her welfare when it came time for him to return to Australia? Did her leaving have anything to do with the men who had tried to abduct her?

Questions. All of them unanswered. He had had little sleep in the past two days and even less food, for he hadn't taken time to eat while out searching the slums for one slip of a girl who seemed to cease to exist. Had he imagined her? Was she a figment of his dreams? Unlikely, he snorted, recalling every mind-boggling detail of their love-making. She was like quicksilver in his arms, warm and wonderful and so responsive her passion seared a permanent brand across his mind and body.

When Ben returned home late that night, a message was waiting for him. Jeevers informed him it had been delivered by the captain of a ship recently returned from New South Wales. It was from Roy, Ben's father. Tired as he was, Ben tore open the envelope and devoured the

141

contents. Due to the length of time it took to travel from England to Australia, he had received blessed little correspondence from his family, and anything could have happened in his long absence.

Fortunately, no catastrophe had struck his family, but the news was nonetheless startling. Ben's father, Roy Penrod, urgently requested Ben to return to New South Wales as soon as possible. Roy, newly married to emancipist Maude Rawlins, wanted to take his bride on an extended honeymoon to England and Europe and even considered spending his remaining years in England. He was placing his prosperous sheep farm into Ben's keeping since his older son, Dare, had more than he could handle with his own extensive holdings and growing family to care for.

Ben was thunderstruck. It was the worst possible time to have to return to Australia. There was too much unfinished business to attend to. He didn't want to leave before he found Tia, yet in all conscience he couldn't disobey his father's wishes. He had been gone two years, after all, and he'd frittered away the time in frivolous pursuits while his father and Dare worked for their livelihood. If he was needed, then he'd leave as requested. At one point in his life Dare had spent time in London, just as Ben had, only Dare had returned with a wife. Ben hoped they didn't expect him to emulate his big brother, for they'd be sadly disappointed.

* * *

"So ye decided ta return, did ye? Did the law catch up with ya?"

One-eyed Bertha squinted at Tia through her good eye, noting the clean clothes and healthy glow on her cheeks, which had filled out considerably in the weeks she was gone.

"Ye finally got yerself a man, did ya?" she asked astutely. "Ye got that look about ya. I hope he was worth it. Why did ye come back?"

Tia flinched. Bertha was the only one outside of Ben who knew her identity, and Tia depended on the woman's goodwill, such as it was, to keep others from learning her secret. Thus far she had been able to appease the woman because she was the best pickpocket around and kept Bertha in coin. But Tia hadn't the slightest doubt that Bertha would sell her out if the price was right.

"I'm back, that's all ye need to know," Tia said sullenly.

Bertha's one eye blazed with malice. No one could accuse the ragged bag of bones of having a tender heart. No one knew exactly how Bertha had lost her eye, and few dared ask. Tall and gaunt, she was cunning and had a veritable army of beggars at her beck and call. She could bring down disaster on one of her clan at the drop of a hat while offering protection for the exchange of coin. She rarely bathed, and her hair stuck out every which way in tangled gray strands all over her head. Just looking at her would give a child nightmares for life.

Yet she had developed a fondness for Tia from the beginning, if one could accuse Bertha of harboring fondness in her petrified heart. But only as long as the blunt was forthcoming.

"Watch yer mouth, lad," Bertha warned, swinging around suddenly and catching Tia with the back of her hand. "Just remember, yer safe only as long as I say ye are. Many of me mates would be 'appy to learn yer a wench."

"I'm sorry," Tia muttered, picking herself up off the floor. She had to remember it wasn't Ben she was sassing now but Bertha. She knew that Ben would never really hurt her, but she had no such assurance about Bertha. "Wait till ye see what I brung ya." She dug the coins she stole from Ben from her pocket and held them out to the woman.

"Well, now, that's more like it. Sit yerself, lad, there's food laid out on that crate over yonder."

Bertha had taken up residence in a rat-infested warehouse, long deserted by its previous owners. She slept on a ragged pallet and held court amid decaying ruins and crumbling walls. It was cold in winter, hot in summer, and Tia had called it home for three miserable years. What made it all the more deplorable was the fact that she had recently sampled comfort. But comfort was not for her. Not now, not when she faced a far greater danger if she remained with Ben.

The next day One-eyed Bertha sent her out on the streets to ply her trade. But she couldn't bring herself to pick a single pocket, nor filch food from street vendors, nor steal coins from the tills of storekeepers. And she had Ben Penrod to thank for it. The only good thing that came from returning to the dubious company of thieves was the knowledge that she couldn't be found by her enemies. Or Ben, for that matter.

Ben . . .

The name brought back memories so exquisite they were more akin to pain than pleasure. The arrogant swine was so handsome that looking at him stole her breath away. His determination to avoid marriage had amazed her, but she had agreed to play his game because she truly believed he would send her to jail if she refused. Since then she had come to know him as a rascal and rogue whose devilish smile had charmed half the women in London. The other half clamored to occupy his bed. And to make matters worse, she had allowed him to seduce her. She should hate him, but God, it had been wonderful. No wonder Ben Penrod was much sought after in London. He was so good at making love.

Why had avoiding marriage become an obsession with Ben? Tia wondered. Not that she blamed him; she didn't think much of the institution herself.

That night Bertha was livid when Tia returned

without a farthing to acquit herself. If Tia hadn't been so fleet of foot, she would have found herself sprawled on the floor nursing a sore jaw. But by now she knew what to expect and had fled in haste rather than subject herself to Bertha's abuse. She roamed the streets that night, longing for the comfort of Ben's arms and cursing the fates that made her life so difficult.

The day after his father's message arrived calling him home to Australia, Ben arranged passage on the next ship due to depart for New South Wales. As luck would have it, the ship belonged to Jeremy Combs, a longtime friend married to an ex-convict who had been a servant in his home at the same time as Casey, Dare's wife. Jeremy's ship, the *Martha C*, was due to sail on the midnight tide, carrying a cargo of rum, tea, and spices. After they had greeted one another and exchanged information about their families, Ben booked passage.

"You can come aboard any time you like," Jeremy said, pleased to have a friend aboard to share his idle time with.

"There's something I must do first, Jeremy," Ben hedged. He was thinking of Tia and the fact that he still hadn't located her. He'd never forgive himself if he didn't find her and at least offer something to make her life easier. Hell, he was rich enough to give her enough money to go to France, or anywhere she desired. Far enough away so she couldn't be found by her enemies—though he still had no idea who they might be.

"Don't be late, mate."

"I'll be here, Jeremy, you can count on it. I'll send my baggage down with a servant."

Ben hurried home, where he instructed Jeevers to pack his trunks. Then he went back to the slums, still harboring hopes, albeit slim ones, of finding Tia. After two days of searching, of questioning countless nameless, faceless men and women, Ben began to fear that Tia was lost to him forever, and the thought gave him a curious pain. A pain he was certain he had never felt before nor was likely to feel again.

Only that morning, Ben had learned from Jeevers that the cache of coins he kept in the desk to take care of household matters was missing. At first he'd been relieved that Tia at least had some money to buy food, but then, after thinking about it, he had grown angry. Once a thief, always a thief, he thought disparagingly. The little witch was just waiting for the right time to make off with his money—though Lord knows it was little enough. Perhaps it was the notion that she could just up and leave so easily after the passionate night they shared that had made him so angry. When he found her—if he found her—she still deserved a beating.

Ben was so engrossed in his thoughts that he failed to notice the woman who had sidled up beside him. Only when she touched his arm did he whirl around to face her. The eye patch stood out on her thin, dirt-smudged face with startling effect. Ben knew instantly who she was. One-eyed Bertha. He had heard Tia mention the hag.

"Are ye the gent what's been askin' questions 'bout a lad?" Bertha asked in a high-pitched voice that set Ben's teeth on edge.

"Aye, do you have information for me?"

"Well, now, that depends, mate. Old Bertha's information don't come cheap."

Ben pulled a handful of silver coins from his pocket. "Will these do?"

Bertha's one eye lit up greedily. But she was wily enough to know there was more where that came from. "Ye can do better than that."

Ben pretended to consider Bertha's words. Then he dug in his pocket again and came up with a gold coin. Bertha reached for it, but Ben quickly placed it out of her reach. "Oh no you don't, how do I know your information is correct?"

"I know the 'lad' yer talkin' 'bout," Bertha hinted slyly. "He ain't like other 'lads,' if ye ken my meanin'." Ben knew exactly what she meant.

"Talk. Where can I find her? And you'd better not try to hoodwink me or you'll be sorry.

"The 'lad' beds down with me at night. I protect the little runt as best I can," Bertha whined obsequiously.

"I'll bet. Where do you live?"

Bertha gave him directions to the derelict warehouse. "The little bugger didn't come 'ome last night but 'tweren't my fault."

"Didn't come home? What do you mean?"

"I mean the ungrateful wretch took off last night and didn't return."

"If you've done something I'll—"

"Ain't done nothin'," Bertha said sullenly. "Just come ta the warehouse, I suspect hunger will bring the wretch 'ome tonight."

Then, before Ben could question her further, she seized the gold coin from his hand, turned, and fled. Since Ben already had the information he sought he did not give chase. He couldn't care less about One-eyed Bertha, or the money. There were only a few short hours left in which to find Tia, and at least he now knew she had been seen in her old stomping ground. And if One-eyed Bertha was right, Tia would return to the warehouse by nightfall. He only hoped it would be in time. And that her absence the previous night didn't mean she had encountered trouble or that the impetuous little witch hadn't run recklessly into a situation she wasn't prepared to handle.

Ben found the warehouse One-eyed Bertha spoke of easily enough and draped himself inconspicuously in a doorway across from the entrance to wait for Tia. When darkness fell with no sign of Tia, Ben began to worry. Time was growing short, and if he wasn't aboard the *Martha C* by midnight, it would sail without him. The next ship for Australia wasn't due to leave for several weeks, so he couldn't afford to dawdle past the time it took to reach the docks. It began to rain, a steady misty curtain that chilled him to the bone and filled him with cold fear for Tia's welfare.

When a chilling rain began to pelt her, Tia came to the inevitable conclusion that braving Bertha's abuse was preferable to spending another night in the open in the freezing rain. Her only other alternative was to return to Ben, and no matter how badly she wanted to, it was out of the question. Danger still existed. Danger to Ben and danger to herself, and that included her heart as well as her body. Losing her heart to Ben Penrod was perilous and futile. She had learned the hard way never to trust men.

Bowing her head against the sharp needles of rain and stinging wind, Tia made her way slowly through the deserted streets to the warehouse, which was the only refuge available to her at the moment. The fog was so dense that she was unaware of the coach following behind her, or of the man shivering in the doorway of a building adjacent to the warehouse. She was just happy to be within sight of warmth and comfort, dubious as it might be.

When the coach drew abreast of Tia, the door opened and two men leaped out. Their steps were cushioned by the sound of falling rain, and when they seized Tia from behind, she was totally unprepared for the attack. She managed one muffled squawk before a grimy hand stifled her outcry and she was dragged toward the waiting coach. But it was enough to alert the man huddled in the doorway. Cold and miserable, Ben had nearly given up hope when he spied the small hunched figure braving the wind and elements.

The ominous black coach had come out of the mists like a harbinger of doom, making the hairs rise on the back of Ben's neck. The moment it stopped beside Tia, he realized his danger. When he saw two men leap from the conveyance he acted swiftly, willing his thoroughly chilled limbs to answer his call for speed. The pistol stuck in his belt was already primed and loaded and leaped into his hand as if by magic.

The tableau unfolded as if in slow motion. One of the abductors turned, and took Ben's shot in the chest. The other man released Tia and attacked Ben. He was nearly as tall as Ben but not as muscular. But he had all the instincts of a veteran street fighter. Ben was fully up to the challenge, having braved the Blue Mountains and Australia's rugged outback in fine fettle. The fight was short but brutal. Both men suffered telling blows, but in the end the thug was no match for Ben, who fought not just for himself but for Tia's life. When the thug lay stretched out at his feet, Ben turned to Tia, his face a mask of rage.

"You bloody little wretch!" Ben bit out from

between clenched teeth. He was tired, hungry, cold, battered, and so damn mad he could spit nails. "Why did you run away?"

"I—I—I—" Her teeth were chattering from cold and fright and she was trembling from head to toe. Suddenly all the anger left Ben's big body. Glancing around, he spat out a curse when he saw the coach jerk into motion and bolt down the street. Evidently the driver didn't intend to suffer the same fate as his friends.

"Bloody hell, now what are we going to do? On a night like this, in this section of town, we're unlikely to find another hack for hire. And it's nearly midnight."

"M—m—midnight?" Tia stuttered, still unable to express her thanks or compose her thoughts. "What happens at midnight?"

"Come along," Ben said, grasping her wrist and dragging her behind him. "If we hurry we can just make it."

"Dammit, Ben, what are you talking about? Where are you taking me? I'm cold and wet and too tired to go three feet without collapsing."

Ben's answer was a muffled growl as he increased his pace, forcing Tia to run to keep up with him.

"I know you're angry, Ben, but I left for your own good."

"Did you steal my money for my own good?" Ben threw over his shoulder.

"Is that why you're angry? Because I took your money? I'll pay it back, I swear. Those few coins couldn't have meant that much to you."

"It wasn't the money, Tia, it was—Bloody hell, shut up and keep moving or we won't make it in time."

Tia dug in her heels. "Not until you tell me where you're taking me. If you're taking me to jail, I've a right to know."

Jail? If Ben wasn't in such a damn hurry to get to the *Martha C* before sailing time, he would have stopped and laughed. The last place he wanted Tia was in jail. Hell, he couldn't even bear to leave her behind in England. He didn't have time to figure it out yet and wasn't certain he wanted to, but the fact remained that Tia wasn't safe in London and leaving her behind was unthinkable.

His answer was a furious jerk on her wrist, forcing her to give up her questions in order to find the breath to follow. She was panting now, running and gasping and totally worn out. They were almost to the docks when Tia realized where they were going.

"What—are we doing here?" Tia gasped breathlessly.

Ben merely grunted. Then he saw it. The *Martha C*. She was strung with lights and he could see men scurrying to and fro on deck preparing to raise sail. The gangplank was still in place, waiting for the last passenger. Ben's relief was enormous as he pulled Tia up the gangplank. Jeremy met him as he stepped onto the deck.

"Another minute and you'd have been too late, mate." Jeremy grinned as he welcomed Ben aboard. "Who's the lad?"

"Can you take on another passenger, Jeremy?"

"There are no empty cabins, Ben," Jeremy said, eyeing Tia curiously.

"The brat can share my cabin."

Tia was too stunned to speak in her behalf or even utter a protest. What ship was this? Where was she bound? Why was Ben bringing her aboard?

"In that case, of course we can take on another passenger." Ben turned into the light and Jeremy got a good look at his face. He sucked in a shocked breath. "Good Lord, what happened to your face?"

Ben winced, suddenly aware of the pain, and he lifted his hand to his battered features. One eye was swollen nearly shut, his lip was split, and his nose felt as if it had been flattened. "You should see the other man," he said, grinning cheekily. Even that hurt and he groaned.

"There's water in your cabin, go on down and see to your injuries," Jeremy said. "Your trunks arrived earlier, they're in the last cabin at the end of the passageway. What about the lad? Does he have baggage?"

"No," Ben said, refusing to meet Jeremy's eyes. "The brat's clothing is packed in my trunks." Then he pushed Tia ahead of him toward their cabin.

"Where are you taking me?" Tia asked once

she found her voice. "I'm not leaving England."

"You'll damn well go where I take you," Ben said tightly. They were in the small cabin assigned them, facing each other, both defiant, both equally determined.

During the past few hours he had come to the startling realization that he couldn't leave Tia in London. Her life was in danger. And neither could he remain in England to take care of her, for he was needed back home. The only alternative, as he saw it, was taking Tia with him and keeping her safe until the mystery was solved.

"I'm leaving—now," Tia declared, flinging open the door. When Ben made no move to follow, she flashed him a smug grin and bounded up the ladder to the deck above. When she raced to where the gangplank should have been, she gawked in stunned silence at the ever widening expanse of sea and at London harbor growing smaller in the distance. While she and Ben were below arguing, the *Martha C* had slipped its moorings and sailed away on the tide.

"You'll like Australia," Ben said as he came up behind her.

"Blast and damn! Yer a bloody tyrant, Ben Penrod. I never said I wanted to go to that damn heathenish country."

"Would you rather I had left you to the mercy of whoever wants you so badly? Which, in case you had forgotten, you haven't bothered to tell me about. And if I were you, I'd watch my language. It wouldn't do for people to think I'd married a woman off the streets."

"Married! Yer—your daft. I'm not your wife, and we both know that's never likely to happen."

"This will be a long journey, Tia, and people aren't stupid. Soon the captain and other passengers will begin to wonder about you. Introducing you as my wife will make things much simpler in the long run." The notion had come to him suddenly, but the idea pleased him. "So far only Jeremy has seen you, and he'll say nothing about how you arrived aboard his ship."

"What about clothes?" Tia asked, surprised that he would want to claim her when obviously it would serve no purpose. She could pose as a lad here just as well as in London.

"I brought along all the things I bought for you in London," Ben said smugly. "I intended to give them to Casey, since most of them hadn't been worn yet."

Tia knew from previous snippets of conversation that Casey was Dare's wife and Ben thought her a paragon of beauty and virtue. "Obviously I have no choice but to go to Australia, but I do have some control over my actions," she said, pulling off her cap and tossing her golden mane of curls. "I will not be your mistress. I'll share the cabin if I must, but nothing short of force will make me—" she flushed "—make me allow you the use of my body. Had I wanted to be

some man's plaything I would have remained—
well, never mind, that part of my life is over
and done with. Once we reach Australia I'll find
a job and make a new life for myself. Without a man to complicate my existence. Perhaps
you're right," she allowed grudgingly. "Perhaps
going to Australia is the best possible thing I
could do."

Ben's mouth flopped open as he gaped at
Tia in wonder. Six months in the same cabin
with Tia and not make love to her? Ridiculous.
"We'll see, sweetheart, we'll see." Ben smiled
cryptically.

Chapter Eight

Ben was exasperated. Tia had thrown herself on the bed and promptly fallen asleep. She'd had little rest during the past two nights and had reached the end of her endurance. And the way Ben had pulled her through the deserted streets in the rain had nearly done her in. Oblivious of the wet clothing that clung to her like a second skin, and unwilling to argue with Ben about her role in his life, she had collapsed on the bed and immediately succumbed to sleep.

"Little witch," Ben muttered to himself as he gazed down at her. He couldn't let her sleep in wet clothes, so he began stripping off her shoes and stockings. Her soaked breeches and shirt followed, then the short chemise. By the time she was completely nude, Ben was shaking as if from ague.

Bloody hell! he thought wonderingly. How could such a little mite set up so wild a clamor in his blood? He'd seen many naked women before, some of them as lovely as Tia, but none of them affected him like the mysterious little witch now sharing his cabin. She slept so soundly she hadn't even been aware that he was stripping her. If he wasn't such a gentleman he'd throw himself atop her and thrust into her again and again until he purged her from his system. But a little voice inside him whispered that purging Tia from of his system wasn't going to be easy. In fact, it might be the most difficult thing he'd ever attempted.

Sighing regretfully, Ben stripped off his own soaked clothes and crawled into bed beside Tia, pulling the covers over both of them. Her chilled body felt like a block of ice next to his, and though he knew it would stretch his control to impossible lengths, he turned toward her and pulled her unresisting body into his arms. A soft moan whispered through Tia's blue lips and she snuggled deeper into Ben's arms, absorbing his warmth. Blissfully warm for the first time in two days, Tia slept heavily and deeply. Not so Ben. The torture of holding Tia's soft body close to his heart, so small, so vulnerable, was unbearable. Six months of this and he'd be a raving maniac long before they reached Australia.

Before Tia awoke the following morning, Ben went to see Captain Combs. He found him on the bridge.

"Did you sleep well, Ben?" Jeremy asked, somewhat startled by Ben's hollow-eyed look.

"Truth to tell, I didn't sleep at all," Ben admitted dryly.

"If the lad bothers you, perhaps I can find him a place with my first mate."

"Like hell," Ben growled, sending Jeremy such a fierce scowl the poor man didn't know what to think. "There's something you should know, and I hope you'll try to understand when I tell you."

Jeremy waited patiently for Ben to continue. "That 'lad' I brought aboard last night isn't a lad at all, she's my wife."

An arrested look came over Jeremy's plain features. He was well aware of Ben's aversion to marriage. He didn't believe Ben, not for one minute. But if that's what Ben wanted him to believe, who was he to dispute his claim? "Rather irregular, isn't it?" He had all he could do to suppress his laughter. Ben had always been a scamp and it looked as if he hadn't changed.

"I know this is hard to swallow, Jeremy, especially in view of the way I brought Tia aboard, but believe me when I say Tia belongs to me." Jeremy didn't doubt it for a moment. Most women would admit to anything, do anything in order to snare a rogue like Ben Penrod.

"I'm not questioning your integrity, Ben," Jeremy grinned. "If you say the lad—er—young lady is your wife, then that's good enough for me."

"I'd appreciate it if you said nothing to the other passengers about how Tia looked when I brought her aboard last night. It's a complicated story that I don't want to go into at this time."

"Certainly. When will I be introduced properly to your 'wife'?"

"As soon as she wakes up. She was quite exhausted last night when we finally got to sleep."

Jeremy nearly choked on the bubble of laughter caught in his throat. "Let her sleep, then, I'm sure she's earned her rest." Then he did break out in laughter. "I'm sorry, mate, but knowing you like I do I find this hilarious. Too bad Martha didn't sail with me this time, she enjoys a good laugh as much as I do."

Ben flushed, somewhat embarrassed to have told Jeremy such an outright lie about him and Tia, but oddly unwilling to name her as his mistress. Tia was now his responsibility. He had claimed that responsibility when he dragged her aboard the *Martha C* and forced her to accompany him to Australia. She had no friends in Australia, no visible means of supporting herself. Since it was his fault she was now on her way to a strange land, his honor forbade him to abandon her. Besides, he had taken Tia's innocence and owed her his protection.

Tia stretched languorously. She couldn't recall when she had slept so well. Vaguely she remembered strong arms holding her, a deep voice murmuring in her ear, and warmth. She had been so cold, until Ben's body provided warmth and comfort. Lord help her when she wasn't too exhausted to respond to his nearness! It was going to take all the self-control she possessed to keep Ben at arm's length and her own heart intact.

Just then Ben opened the door and stepped inside. He was carrying a tray of food that smelled delicious. "Time to get up, sleepyhead. I hope you're hungry."

"Famished," Tia said, sitting up so Ben could place the tray across her lap. Only then did she realize she was nude. She flushed, pulled the sheet to her chin, and bent him an austere look.

"I undressed you. Couldn't let you sleep in wet clothes, now, could I?"

"Of course not," Tia bit out tightly. "What else did you do?"

Ben looked startled. "Nothing. I may be a bastard, but I don't enjoy making love to women who are incapable of feeling or responding. When I make love to you I want you fully awake to enjoy it." He flashed her such a wicked grin that Tia had difficulty holding her temper.

"Like hell you will!"

Ben merely chuckled. "Hurry up and eat. After you're dressed I want to take my 'wife' topside to meet our fellow passengers."

"You're still spouting nonsense. I'm through with pretending to be your wife."

"How do you propose to explain our sharing a cabin?" Ben asked pointedly. "Would you rather be known as my whore?"

"Damn yer arrogant hide! Must ye always have everythin' yer way? Mayhap I'd rather be yer whore than yer wife."

"You little witch," Ben said from between clenched teeth. "There are many women who would envy your position."

"Like Caroline Battersby?"

"Well—yes, Caro would be ecstatic to share this cabin with me and be introduced as my wife."

"Then why didn't you marry the little conniver?"

"I don't want to marry anyone!"

"Good," Tia said smugly. "Neither do I."

"This pretense is strictly for your benefit. I certainly have nothing to gain by it."

Tia acquiesced with bad grace. "Very well, Ben, I'll go along with this farce, but only until we reach Australia. After that we each go our own way. Agreed?"

"I'd have it no other way, Tia," Ben concurred with supreme arrogance.

Jeremy Combs was quite pleasantly surprised

when he met Tia later. She looked stunning dressed in a flattering gown, her golden hair blowing about her beautiful face, her small but shapely body held proudly erect. But then he had expected nothing less from Ben Penrod. Tia and Ben were introduced to most of the other passengers, twenty in all, and were accepted as the married couple they portrayed. Each night Ben joined Tia in bed, but to his chagrin she steadfastly refused to be seduced. And Ben had no desire to force the little hellion. But, Lord, he didn't know how much longer he could stand the sweet torment of sleeping next to her, of feeling her warmth seep into his pores, of wanting her badly enough to offer—

Jesus! His thoughts these days appalled him. He was contemplating things that several weeks ago, before he met Tia, had filled him with revulsion. But as the journey passed from days into weeks, those thoughts kept returning, tempting him, teasing him—torturing him. Tia was driving him crazy, and the only solution he could think of was one he had avoided with an all-consuming passion, one that had patterned his adult life. He couldn't go on like this. Something had to give—something—something—

Tia's thoughts ran in the same direction as Ben's. The pretense of being his wife was wearing thin. She had the title but none of the benefits. If she didn't know exactly what those benefits included, it wouldn't have mattered so much. But she had tasted passion, drank deeply of Ben's special brand of loving, and wished desperately for the real marriage she and Ben were pretending. But no one knew better than she how impossible that dream was. Not just because Ben had an aversion to marriage but because her life was too complicated. Love was an emotion she could not allow herself to feel, for she wasn't meant to experience a man's love or return it.

Tia hastily made ready for bed, wanting to be asleep before Ben returned to the cabin. It was much easier than lying awake for hours, feeling the heat of his body, seeing the passion in his expressive silver eyes as they bore into hers with an intensity that melted her bones. Unfortunately, Ben arrived in the cabin before Tia crawled into bed.

"You're still up, good," Ben said. He had a strange look in his eyes, making Tia immediately wary. "There's something I want to ask you. I've been thinking about this a long time and feel it's the right thing to do."

Tia's eyes widened. She had no idea what Ben was talking about but instinctively knew she wouldn't like it. Neither did she have the slightest idea what this was costing Ben, or how many nights he had lain awake pondering his decision. Old ideas and habits were difficult to break, and it had taken much thought and struggling with his conscience to even get to this point.

"I'm tired, Ben. What is it you want to ask?"

165

Ben gulped. His mouth was dry and his throat felt as if it were clogged with layers of thick cotton. He had to swallow several times before words formed.

"Marry me, Tia. Captain Combs can perform the ceremony in our cabin so none of the other passengers will suspect."

A stunned silence prevailed as Tia digested his words. Ben was proposing? Ben? The man who vowed never to marry? Proud, arrogant Ben who used women shamelessly? Disbelief suffused Tia's delicate features, quickly followed by delight, which reluctantly gave way to utter hopelessness.

"I . . ."

"I've already asked Jeremy to marry us and he is willing. He'll be here in an hour."

"No. I can't—I mean I won't."

"You . . . won't?" Her strangled reply stunned Ben.

"I won't marry you, Ben."

"Dammit, Tia, what kind of brazen hussy are you? I took your innocence. I literally abducted you and dragged you aboard the *Martha C.* Would you rather be my whore?"

Tia bit her lower lip until she drew blood. "Admit it, you don't want to be married any more than I do."

"That's beside the point. I asked you, didn't I? What's the problem? Why won't you marry me?"

"You wouldn't understand," Tia said lamely.

"Try me."

"I don't want a husband. I don't want to belong to anyone."

"You never answered my question. Would you rather be my whore?"

"I—yes, dammit, I'll be your whore, if you forget all this silliness about marriage and don't mention it again."

Ben couldn't believe his ears. Never would he understand women. What made one woman go to any length to force him to the altar and another agree to become his mistress in order to avoid marriage? It was bloody humiliating, that's what it was. He had humbled himself because he felt guilt over Tia's plight and had gallantly offered marriage as a way out of her predicament. And what did he get in return? An outright refusal. It was too much. It was a good thing love wasn't involved, he told himself, refusing to acknowledge the strange jolt to his heart.

"Very well, Tia, have it your way. You can be my whore, but don't expect me to propose again. And don't try to deny me, for you won't get away with it. Blister it, Tia, I want you and I'm damn well going to have you!"

Quietly. "I want you too, Ben."

"What! What's the catch?"

"No catch, I'm just being honest with myself. It's just that—marriage is not for me."

Ben grinned owlishly. "Suits me, sweetheart, I was only thinking of you when I proposed."

167

That wasn't entirely true, but Tia didn't have to know how long he'd anguished over his offer.

"I appreciate your offer, Ben, truly, and I know how difficult it must have been for you."

"But . . ."

"But I don't want to talk about it any more. I'd rather—" She sent him a smoldering glance that made words unnecessary.

"No more arguments, Tia, I bow to your wishes. You can be my mistress, it's what I wanted all along anyway. Now, sweetheart, shut up and let me show you what mistresses do best."

Then he was kissing her, searing her with his heat, branding her with the passion he had suppressed all these weeks. "Take this damn thing off," he growled, pulling her nightgown over her head and tossing it aside.

Then he was ravaging her mouth again with seductive little nibbles, rubbing his lips against hers until they were so sensitive to his touch they ached. His lips were scorching hot, moist, hard. One large hand slid up her spine to cradle the back of her head, holding her in position to accommodate him while his lips and tongue worked their magic on her. He drew her up on tiptoe and she clung to him, her fingers digging into the hard strength of his shoulders.

One of his hands descended slowly, cupping and caressing her small bottom. Her bones were melting, her heart was banging furiously in her chest. Suddenly Tia became aware that his other hand was resting on her naked breast. A shaft of pure awareness rippled through her. Her nipple puckered instantly against the hard caress of his palm. Wanting to give Ben the same kind of pleasure he was bringing her, Tia inserted her hand between their bodies and grasped the rigid length of his shaft.

"Wait," he gasped, tearing at his clothes with indecent haste. "Let me get these blasted clothes off."

Tia backed off and watched as he quickly divested himself of every stitch of clothing. He was a big man, with massive shoulders and broad chest. He was dangerously handsome in a rough, wild way. His entire body was swarthy, as if hewn from mahogany, his features boldly masculine. Crinkling with naughty delight, her eyes drifted lower. His manhood was thick and fully aroused.

She wanted him.

The sheen of silver glinted in Ben's eyes as he stared at Tia. She was small but perfectly formed. Her breasts fit his hands like none other he could recall, and every luscious curve and valley was sculpted from the finest alabaster. Her hair tumbled down her back in a wild riot of pale golden silk, and an angel would envy her lovely face. His gaze slid downward, to where a nest of golden curls protected that secret place between her legs that gave him so much pleasure.

He wanted her.

"You're so bloody beautiful. I can't remember when I've wanted a woman as badly as I want you."

"You're beautiful too," Tia gulped breathlessly. When Ben turned his silver gaze on her, she went up in smoke.

Groaning from pure pleasure, Ben dragged Tia against his hardening body. The intimate contact released a heat wave in her loins that continued unabated as he kissed her again and thrust his tongue into her mouth. Then he was walking her toward the bed, and they fell together on the soft surface in a jumbled mass of arms and legs. Before she fully recovered, Ben's mouth found a breast and he suckled her, using his tongue to tease the rigid nipple while his hands drifted between her legs.

"You're so warm and wet, sweetheart," Ben groaned hoarsely. "I love the feel of you when you want me." He slipped a finger inside her, probing with smooth, gentle strokes, watching her face as she writhed and thrust into his deep caress.

"Ben, please . . ."

"Not yet, sweetheart."

"I—can't stand it."

Ben merely smiled as he slid down her body. "You wouldn't let me do this before."

Tia went rigid. She wasn't going to let him do it now, either. "Don't."

"You'll like it, I promise." Her protest was lost in a moan as Ben's mouth found her. Never had Tia felt so utterly defenseless, so completely open and vulnerable. The feeling intensified as Ben's tongue and lips explored her thoroughly, tasting, teasing . . . loving her in a way she never imagined before.

She felt touched to her very core, and when Ben's fingers located the tiny bud of sensitivity between her legs she exploded in a starburst of tingling awareness.

Then he was inside her, huge and pulsating, embedding himself so deeply that Tia felt every throbbing inch of him caress every throbbing inch of her. She was still spasming with pleasure when he began thrusting, taking her once again to that plateau of tingling sensation where pain and pleasure collided. She screamed, but didn't know it. She knew nothing but thrust and withdrawal and the sensual agony of blissful fulfillment. His loving made her feel . . .

God help her, but she felt loved.

Ben clung to the edge of rapture as long as he could, until he felt Tia's shuddering release, felt tiny ripples surround and throb against him, felt her body surrender totally to the mastery of his. Then he thrust one last time, deep—so deep Tia screamed in response—and emptied himself inside her. Her arms clung to him with such fervent ardor that Ben knew it would be a long time before he'd desire any other woman but Tia. Beyond forever. Her response made him feel . . .

God help him, but he felt loved.

Weighted with sweet languor, Tia slowly regained her senses.

"I've never felt the need to take a mistress before but I think I'm going to enjoy it now," Ben said, favoring Tia with a wicked grin.

A knock on the door forestalled Tia's answer. "Ben, Tia, it's Jeremy. I'm here to—well, you know."

"Go away, Jeremy, we've changed our minds," Ben called back.

"Are you sure, Ben? It's no trouble." Ben had explained the situation to Jeremy earlier and had received promise of a discreet ceremony.

Ben looked at Tia, his eyes glowing with a savage inner fire. "Are you sure, Tia?" Tia gulped and nodded her head. Ben shrugged and turned away. "We're sure, Jeremy. Thank you."

Agreeing to become Ben's mistress was not making Tia's life easy. They loved with a fervor that both shocked and delighted her. He was a generous lover, careful that she found her pleasure before he sought his own. He was demanding. He would not allow her to lie passive in his arms as she tried to do a time or two, hoping that passivity would salve her conscience for the terrible sin she was committing. But no matter how often she tried to condemn herself for letting Ben love her, she couldn't find it in her heart to feel regret. Ben was so easy to love, no wonder women came to him easily. Still, Tia saw no harm in letting Ben love her, as long as they both understood that it must end when the ship docked in New South Wales.

And they argued. Vocally, vigorously, with all the lusty display of two healthy animals who were happier fighting together than being apart. Their fellow passengers looked on them with indulgent tolerance, thinking them newlyweds whose passion for one another hadn't yet waned. Jeremy Combs was the only one whose thoughts turned in another direction. He had known Ben for several years, visiting the Penrods whenever his trade took him to Australia, and never had he seen the young man so utterly captivated by a woman. Whether Ben knew it or not, Jeremy thought the handsome rogue had finally met his match.

Even their arguments had sexual undertones, making most of the other passengers fully aware of the crackling tension between the two. Sparks flew, tempers clashed, but the attraction between them could be neither denied nor ignored. As if anyone could ignore Tia and Ben when their wills collided. It was like watching fireworks erupt.

Tia was resting in her cabin one afternoon when Jeremy cornered Ben for a private conversation on deck.

"Why don't you marry the chit, Ben?" Jeremy asked. "If ever two people belong together, it's you and Tia."

The corners of Ben's generous mouth turned

down in a scowl. "Believe it or not, Tia wouldn't have me."

"You—you mean she turned you down?" Jeremy sputtered, nearly speechless with shock. "I assumed you were the one who decided against it."

"Aye, can you believe it? 'Tis the last time I propose to any woman. I only offered marriage to ease her situation, but it seems Tia would rather be my mistress than my wife."

"Seems to me that's a damn shabby reason to offer marriage," Jeremy chided reprovingly. "Maybe Tia doesn't want a man who thinks marriage is for idiots. Maybe she thinks you'd make a lousy husband."

"For whatever reason, she wouldn't have me and that's final. I won't make the mistake of offering again."

"What happens when you reach New South Wales?"

"I—don't know," Ben said lamely. "Bloody hell! I know nothing about the witch. Her whole life is one big mystery."

"If I might make a suggestion," Jeremy offered, realizing he was treading on forbidden territory but certain that Ben and Tia belonged together. "There are still many long weeks left before we reach Australia. Perhaps now is a good time to press Tia for an explanation. It could be she's just too shy or ashamed of her former life to tell you."

"Tia shy? Ha!" Ben laughed harshly. "The little vixen is tougher than either of us. And from what I know of her, she has nothing to feel shame over." He flushed deeply as he recalled his shock at finding her still a virgin.

"Well, you'd be a fool to let her walk away," Jeremy advised. Then he excused himself, leaving Ben with much food for thought.

When Ben joined Tia in their cabin a short time later, his face wore such a determined look that Tia grew wary.

"Do you trust me, Tia?" Ben asked, bending her an inscrutable look.

Tia's eyes grew bleak. "As much as I trust any man."

"I think it's long past the time that you told me the truth about yourself."

"There's nothing to tell," Tia denied belligerently. "You already know all there is to know."

"I think not. What about those men who were trying to abduct you? I've been more than patient, waiting for you to tell me of your own accord. But obviously you have no intention of explaining."

"There is nothing you need to know, Ben, truly," Tia lied, keeping her eyes deliberately lowered.

Ben slipped a finger beneath her chin and raised her head. "Look at me, Tia." She lifted her eyes and was blinded by his silver gaze. "I won't let anyone hurt you. Why do you think I brought you with me?"

If Tia wanted to be honest with herself, she'd

admit that she had hoped Ben felt more than protectiveness toward her. Or pity for her plight. But that was an emotion she dare not hope for from a man. "You wanted me for your mistress," Tia said sullenly.

Ben rolled his eyes. "Bloody hell, Tia, if I wanted a mistress, any woman would do. I feel responsible for you. When I was called home I knew I couldn't leave you to face danger by yourself."

Tia's heart sank down to her shoes. It was just as she suspected. Ben enjoyed making love to her, but any woman would do as well. He felt only pity for her, and being a rogue and rake, bringing her with him to Australia piqued his sense of outrageous behavior. And being a gentleman, he felt the dubious need to protect her. The thought depressed her. And made her stubbornly determined to protect her background.

"Knowing everything about me would be utterly useless," Tia said. "Once we reach Australia you need not concern yourself with me."

"How do you intend to survive in a strange country? Pick pockets? Steal?"

Tia flashed him a withering glare. "I'll work. I'm young and strong and capable of providing for myself. Perhaps, when I save enough, I'll return to England."

"Work? Ha! Little you know about Australia. Work is provided by convicts who are assigned to settlers. They work for room and board until they are emancipated and settle on their own land."

A stunned look settled over Tia's features. If she couldn't work, what would she do?

"You could," Ben suggested crudely, "make your living with your body. Lord knows you're talented enough."

"Ye bloody arrogant ass!" Tia exploded, flying at him. Ben caught her easily, sobering as he held her at bay.

"Tia, I didn't mean to insult you, just show you how impossible it will be to make your own way in Australia. Why in the hell do you think I proposed? If you're still set on returning to England after we reach our destination, I'll arrange your passage and give you enough money to keep you from returning to the streets." His words sounded grand, but it was the last thing he intended to do. He said them merely to appease her.

"For services rendered? I don't need your money. I'm a survivor."

Quietly. "Why did you refuse my proposal?"

Tia closed her eyes against the sudden jolt of pain his words caused. "Because neither of us truly wanted it."

Ben let that pass. "You're the stubbornest, most confusing, irrational woman I've ever had the displeasure of meeting." And the most beautiful, passionate, tantalizing witch he'd ever met, he thought but did not say. Making love to Tia gave him more pleasure

than he knew existed. Life would be exception-
ally dull and boring without her. Lord, was he
growing maudlin again? Proposing once was
bad enough, but doing so twice was out of the
question. Wasn't it?

"You've called me those names before," Tia
said wearily.

"And we've had this conversation before," Ben
returned. "With the same results, I might add. I
end up learning no more about you than when
we first met."

"That's exactly how I want it," Tia replied
adamantly.

"It seems the only time we're not at each
other's throats is when we make love," Ben
said with growing frustration. Why must she
thwart him at every turn?

"I know," Tia murmured wistfully.

"Then let's do what we do best."

Grasping her waist, he pulled her roughly into his arms, slanting his mouth across
hers in a demanding kiss that quickly ignited
a flame inside her. His tongue against her
lips compelled her to open her mouth and
it delved inside, then retreated in a wildly
exciting rhythm. Heat clenched her belly and
a liquid tightness throbbed between her legs.
He had only to touch her and she evaporated
into scalding steam. Was there no cure for the
tumult Ben created inside her?

Only one, a little voice whispered. *Savor it
while you can.*

Chapter Nine

New South Wales, Australia, January 1819

After Ben's attempt to learn about her past, Tia appeared to withdraw into a shell. Ben had to goad her to even get an argument out of her, and that worried him. She was silent and uncommunicative, and adamantly rejected any attempt to discuss her past. In fact, the more Ben pried into her past, the deeper she withdrew into herself. What secrets was Tia protecting? Ben wondered. Why would keeping those secrets be so important now that they were thousands of miles from London?

Once Ben realized that questioning Tia was getting him nowhere, he gave up. She seemed much more agreeable when they were just enjoying one another's company. Or arguing about inconsequential things that had nothing to do with her past life. The feisty little witch's tongue was sharp and cutting whenever Ben's arrogance overstepped the bounds of what she thought he should know. The only time he got the best of her—if one could call it that—was in bed, making love. And once they finished, Ben was uncertain who had won, for afterwards he was left with an aching that lasted until the next time they made love. He could foresee a bleak future without Tia, and yet there seemed to be no solution to their problems.

For half of the six-month voyage, Ben and Tia had been at each other's throats, finding an anonymous safety in their frequent arguments. The other half they were passionate but wary lovers. It was January 1819 and a beautiful midsummer day when the *Martha C* arrived in Sydney Cove. Tia was more than anxious to debark from a journey that had lasted half a year.

Ben and Tia had just finished lunch and arrived topside to watch docking procedures. Ben's face wore an expression that bespoke his joy at being home again despite the wonderful time he had abroad, while Tia's features conveyed her anxiety and dread of the unpredictable future ahead of her in this wild land she knew nothing about. Ben noted her distress and tried to ease it.

"I predict you'll like Australia, Tia, 'tis a

wonderful place and so huge it will be years and years before man can tame it. Robin was one of the first to cross the Blue Mountains, which were thought impossible to breach, and is now magistrate of Bathurst. He was the first emancipist to be named magistrate."

His voice carried so much pride that Tia would have thought Robin was a brother to Ben instead of a mere friend.

"It amazes me that your family is so friendly with a man convicted of a crime and sentenced to transportation," Tia remarked.

"I'd hardly call poaching a serious crime," Ben scoffed. "Besides, Robin more than paid his debt to society when he lost his freedom and the land he fought so hard for and was resentenced for aiding an escaped convict. Thank God Governor Macquarie saw fit to emancipate him. Then he found Kate McKenzie and his life really became complicated."

Tia grinned despite herself. "Kate sounds like a woman after my own heart."

"You'll meet both her and Robin one day. And their daughter Molly."

"Perhaps," Tia said cryptically. She had no idea what the future held for her or how long she'd remain in Australia.

Ben chose to ignore her remark. "I hope Dare is here to meet us. He's probably met every English ship to arrive for the past few weeks."

"Dare is your brother," Tia said, having heard all about Dare and Casey and their hopeless but steadfast love. They now had three children, two boys and a girl, and lived near Parramatta on the Hawkesbury. Dare was a wealthy and prosperous landowner, grazier, and farmer.

"Aye, Dare is my big brother. He can be somewhat arrogant at times, but Casey has taken him down a peg or two. You'll like Casey, she's a red-headed virago who went through hell both before and after she fell in love with Dare. Both Robin and Dare found out the hard way that falling in love doesn't necessarily mean happiness follows quickly. It was the difficulties they went through in winning and keeping their women that made me realize the advantages of remaining free and unencumbered."

"I thought perhaps you had soured on marriage because some woman had broken your heart."

"Hardly," Ben said with a hint of mockery. "I've given my heart to no woman."

Tia mulled over his words in aching silence. She thought it highly unlikely that handsome, arrogant Ben Penrod would lose his heart easily or often. He was so adamant about avoiding marriage that he had built a protective wall around his heart. The only reason he had offered to marry her was because of the decency instilled in him by his father and because he pitied her and felt responsible for her. The best possible thing she could do for him was to quietly disappear from his life so he wouldn't have to feel guilt over her plight every time he looked at her.

"The gangplank is in place, Tia, shall we go down? It will be a great relief to set foot on solid ground again. It's been years since I've trod upon my adoptive country. I may have been born in England, but my heart belongs in Australia."

"Ben, wait," Tia said, placing a small hand on his arm. "Remember our bargain?" He looked puzzled. "We each agreed to go our own way at our journey's end."

"You can't possibly expect me to honor that agreement," Ben scowled, aghast that she should even suggest such a thing. "How will you survive? You have no money, nothing except your clothing."

"I thought you might provide me with a small loan until I found work."

"I've already explained that you'll find nothing suitable in Australia. Come along now, we can decide all that later."

Then he grasped her arm and strode down the gangplank with such unwarranted haste that Tia had difficulty keeping up with him. Her first step on solid ground brought a wave of dizziness that caused her to clutch convulsively at Ben in order to steady herself. Thank God he had stopped to look around before continuing on. In those few minutes Tia was able to regain her equilibrium and drink in the sights.

The first thing she noticed was the crescent of black sandy beach. Never had she seen black sand before, and it seemed strange indeed. There were several other ships docked in the cove, each carrying a different flag, and men working in the heat loading and unloading cargo. The mosquitoes were dreadful, even in full daylight, and she swatted at them as they buzzed around her. Ben seemed unperturbed by the pesky insects.

"Dare!"

Tia looked up to see Ben waving frantically at someone. Then she saw a man striding toward them, his face wreathed in smiles. He could have been Ben five or ten years earlier. The man was outrageously handsome, strongly built, and firmly muscled. As he drew up beside them, Tia noted the same distinctive gray eyes and black hair that made Ben so irresistible to women. She almost felt sorry for Casey O'Cain Penrod, for Tia instinctively knew that Dare was as subtly dangerous and determined as Ben. Perhaps more so.

"Well, little brother, you've finally decided to come home."

"Did you doubt it, after Father's letter?" Ben replied, embracing his brother and slapping him on the back in exuberant greeting.

"One would think you had enough of the social life after two years in London. One year of the social circuit was about all I could stomach. But then I was never considered the rake you are."

"That's not the way I heard it." Ben grinned

cheekily. "How is Father? And Maude? I can't imagine Father wanting to leave Australia."

" 'Tis for Maude's sake," Dare said solemnly. "He's just learned Maude has the wasting sickness and he wants to take her to a clinic in Switzerland where they specialize in that type of ailment."

Ben paled. "Nothing was mentioned in the letter about Maude's ailment."

"He promised Maude he would allow you to make up your own mind about returning home without using her illness as a lever," Dare said. "I've brought the gig. We'll talk on the way home. I've already arranged for your trunks to be transported to Penrod station later." Suddenly he seemed to notice Tia for the first time. She hovered in the background, unwilling to intrude or call attention to herself.

"Pardon me, miss, are you waiting for someone? Can I help you?"

Tia gulped convulsively, looking from Ben to Dare. What could she say, that she was Ben's mistress? That she'd slept with him for the past six months but now intended to go her own way?

"Tia is with me," Ben said with such fierce resolution that Dare swung startled silver eyes around to stare at his brother.

"You've brought your wh—woman with you from England?" Dare asked, his voice ripe with disgust. "Bloody hell, Ben, are you daft? What will Father say? I can see the past few years have done little to change your ways. Well, you'd best

185

find a place for her in Sydney, for she can't stay on at the farm. Think of the gossip."

Tia cringed inwardly. Dare's harsh words hammered in the fact that she was nothing but Ben's whore and unworthy of his family's regard.

Ben flinched beneath his brother's crude accusations. Dare had no right to condemn Tia, knowing nothing about her or her circumstances. Since when had Dare become such a pompous, self-righteous ass? Once one got to know her, Tia was a sweet girl, somewhat rough around the edges and often hoydenish, but basically innocent until he'd got his hands on her. For Dare to think Tia a whore was unconscionable and more than Ben could allow.

He opened his mouth to tell Dare exactly where Tia fit into his life and gulped back the words when he realized he'd be forced to introduce her as his mistress. He turned to gaze at Tia, searching her small white face for an answer to his dilemma. She looked frightened but proud, standing there with her chin raised and her blue-green eyes openly defiant. Tia might be his mistress, but he'd never met a woman to compare with her and he wasn't going to embarrass her now by telling Dare she meant nothing more to him than any other woman in his past. He'd lie first.

"I think you owe Tia an apology, Dare," Ben said quietly. "Tia is my wife." Dare's gasp was so loud it completely inundated Tia's.

Ben's blatant untruth shocked even himself. He hadn't meant to resort to outright deceit, but neither could he allow Dare and his family to regard Tia as his whore. Until he got this all straightened out he deemed it best for everyone to think Tia was his wife. But Tia's shocked gasp alerted him to the fact that he'd not only have his family to contend with but Tia as well. Convincing her to continue with the sham they had begun in England wasn't going to be an easy task.

"Ben, it isn't right . . ."

"It's going to be fine, sweetheart," Ben said, cutting her off in mid-sentence. "Dare will understand. He brought a wife home from England himself not too long ago." He glared at her, his silver gaze so intense she fell silent. But Ben could tell by her mutinous glare that she didn't like lying to his brother.

Dare finally found his voice. "Married? You? Bloody hell, Ben, you're the last person in the world I'd expect to see married. Not that I'm not happy about it. Just the opposite. I'm ecstatic. I didn't think I'd live to see the day my little brother, the confirmed bachelor who charmed women with a mere smile, would bring home a wife. And such a lovely one," Dare added, regarding Tia with such warm delight she couldn't help but offer him a shy smile in return. Now she knew exactly from whom Ben had learned his charm. She was willing to bet that Dare in his single days had been every bit the rogue that Ben was.

"Welcome to the family, Tia. I can't wait to introduce you to Casey and the children. They'll be as delighted to meet you as I am. I can't believe it. Ben married. You must be a special woman to bring my brother to heel."

Ben grit his teeth and wondered what devil had possessed him to introduce Tia as his wife. Now he had to warn Jeremy before he spoiled things by telling Dare the truth. Whenever Jeremy was in New South Wales he made a point of visiting Casey and Dare and Roy. Sometimes his wife Martha sailed with him, and Ben thanked God this wasn't one of those times. Martha would never have countenanced Ben's lie or refrained from setting everyone straight. But if he could get to Jeremy fast enough, he knew the man would honor his request.

"Take Tia to the gig, Dare, I need to speak to Jeremy before we leave," Ben said.

"Can't it wait? I'm sure Jeremy will come and visit before he leaves Sydney."

"No, this can't wait. I'll only be a few minutes." He turned and hurried off, leaving Dare with a stricken Tia. She had every reason to want to strangle Ben, and when they were alone she might just do that. How dare he place her in this untenable situation? How dare he assume she'd agree to the silly pretense of being his wife? What earthly good would it do, when in the end the truth would come out?

She was not Ben's wife and never would be.

"Are you from London, Tia?" Dare asked as he handed her into the gig.

"I—no, I lived in the country," Tia said, making up a story as she went along.

"Who are your family? I know many people in England from my visit there several years ago."

Damn Ben to hell and back, she cursed beneath her breath, for placing her in this awkward position. "You wouldn't know them," Tia said as Dare slid into the gig beside her. "We lived quietly in the country and weren't particularly rich or well-known."

"Where in the country?" Dare's pointed questions were making her extremely nervous. Did he suspect the truth?

"Kent," Tia replied, which wasn't far from the truth. At least she knew that part of the country well enough to talk about it intelligently.

"What was your name before you married?"

Tia squirmed uncomfortably. Dare's questions were becoming more alarming by the minute. She had no way of knowing he was merely curious, that he wasn't questioning Ben's sudden marriage. He knew Ben well enough to realize that his brother would never lie about something as sacred as marriage. Though Ben had vowed never to enter the state of matrimony himself, he held those vows in high regard so long as they applied to others. Fortunately, Ben returned at that moment, and she conveniently ignored Dare's query as Ben swung into the seat beside her and barged into the conversation.

"We'll answer all questions later, Dare," Ben said, having heard part of the conversation. "I want to point out places of interest to Tia as we pass through Sydney."

Dare took up the reins and set the gig into motion.

"I can't believe all the building that's gone on in my absence," Ben said, gazing around in wonder. "Macquarie has done wonders in the short time he's been governor."

"Tell that to the British government," Dare said with a hint of sarcasm. "They strongly object to the governor's public works expenditures. If you recall, some influential people in New South Wales want the emancipists to be given less and the big landowners more. Thank God Australia has already been established on firm economic foundation in such a manner that will not allow any great disparities to develop between groups of people.

"Macquarie has served well by holding a proper balance within the colony and giving it public facilities to function. The 'Rum Corps' is just a dim memory, relegated to history."

"Is that a bank?" Ben asked, pointing to a building that hadn't been erected when he left Sydney over two years ago.

"Aye, and next to it is a church. And over there—" his arm stretched to a point beyond Government House "—are convict barracks.

They've been a long time in coming but are desperately needed."

Everything looked strange to Tia. Some of the buildings still sported raw, unpainted wooden frames, and the roads were no more than ruts. Compared to London it was a crude assemblage of buildings that would fit in St. George Park.

"You should see the track to Bathurst now," Dare said. "Convicts have constructed quite a credible road. And shipbuilding is now being conducted on the Hawkesbury."

"What about the farmers? Are they being offered fair prices for their grain?" Ben asked, anxious to learn what improvements had been wrought in his prolonged absence.

"Since Macquarie caused storage facilities to be built, great strides have been made. Grains are now being sold at fair prices and farmers are no longer at the mercy of speculators."

"What about the emancipists? Are they being treated fairly?"

Dare frowned thoughtfully. "Nearly 400,000 acres of land have been granted, but only 70,000 of those to ex-convicts. Many are still badly in debt, and some small grants have fallen into the hands of capitalists. Some things never change. But Robin is doing his best as magistrate to help the situation."

"How are Robin and Kate? Still happy, I hope. Lord, she gave him a rough time."

"All's well." Dare grinned. "Robin and Kate couldn't be happier in Bathurst. Little Molly is thriving. She'll soon have a baby brother or sister."

Tia listened carefully to the conversation, not understanding most of it but interested enough to want to know everything about this wild land Ben had brought her to against her will.

"Did you know a commission has been appointed to investigate Governor Macquarie?" Dare asked as they left Sydney behind.

"I heard. There is much speculation in London about the replacement of Macquarie. Do you think it will happen?"

" 'Tis bound to. The British don't care what's happening half a world away, and since it's costing them money to provide for the colony, they will replace our governor rather than see him spend their money on public works. Lord only knows what the next governor will be like."

They rode in silence a few minutes, giving Tia time to adjust to the strange sights and sounds. Nothing had changed much since Dare and Ben had traveled the road with their father when they first settled in Parramatta. Though the road was now better than the early rutted track, thick bush and tall eucalyptus trees still grew in dense abundance on either side. A wild profusion of flowers, wattle, and brush stretched out as far as the eye could see.

Though only fifteen miles upriver from Sydney, Parramatta seemed much farther and took considerable time to reach due to the rough road and primitive method of travel. Since

Dare was one of the wealthier farmers, he now owned a gig, but not too long ago the trip had been accomplished by bullock and dray, or on foot. There were few horses in the colony. Suddenly the jungle cry of a kookaburra, laughing hysterically, startled Tia.

Ben bent Tia an indulgent smile. "You'll get used to all the strange sights and sounds," he said. "See those birds with the bright plumage in that tall gum tree?" Tia nodded, thinking she'd never seen such an arresting sight. "They're cockatoos and parrots. You'll more than likely see kangaroos, wallaby, wombats, many varieties of butterflies, grasshoppers, scorpions, snakes, and crocodiles lurking in the bush."

"Oh," Tia said, gaping in wonder. "Look. Are those orchids growing wild?"

"Aye," Dare replied. "And that brilliant tree growing beside the road is bottlebrush. They're in full bloom this time of year."

A gray kangaroo jumped out from the bush and hopped across the road in giant leaps. Tia clapped her hands and laughed delightedly. "Did you note the young joey in her pouch?" Ben asked, curiously anxious for Tia to like his homeland.

"No," Tia said, disappointed. "But I'll know what to look for next time."

The trip to Parramatta went surprisingly fast, so enthralled was Tia with her surroundings. She could understand Ben's love of Australia but wasn't certain she could ever appreciate this strange land the way he did. It was too different from London. She wondered how long it would be before she could return to the environment she was familiar with. As soon as she was able to speak with Ben privately, she intended to give him the broad side of her tongue for placing her in this awkward position.

They passed through Parramatta late that afternoon. The town had grown in leaps and bounds and now consisted of many buildings constructed of timber and brick erected by convict labor during the past several years. It was now possible to buy nearly everything one needed in Parramatta without having to travel to Sydney. Tia hoped to explore the town more thoroughly later. They continued on through the city, and after a time Ben said that they were on Penrod station.

It stretched west and south along the banks of the Hawkesbury River in an endless expanse of acreage mostly cleared of brush. They turned down a dusty road and came to a large, rambling house surrounded by dogleg fences, green paddocks, many outbuildings, convict barracks, and grazing sheep on the hillsides. A huge gum tree offered dappled shade to the rectangular two-story house, and chickens pecked at the dusty ground beneath its protective branches.

"We're home, Tia." Ben smiled and leapt from the gig with an eagerness that bespoke his pleasure and pride in his home. "It can't compare with the grand houses in London, but you'll find it comfortable."

"It—it's quite grand," Tia said, meaning it. She hadn't expected anything so fine in a country that still hadn't been fully explored.

Grasping her hand, Ben pulled her toward the door. "Come along, I expect Father will be waiting for us."

"He'll be waiting for *you*," Dare corrected, "but Tia will come as quite a surprise to him. A pleasant one, I might add."

The door flung open and Roy Penrod strode out to greet his youngest son. "Welcome home, Ben, I'm grateful you came in reply to my summons."

"I booked passage as soon as I received your letter," Ben said, embracing the older man. Roy's hair was nearly completely gray now, but he was still handsome in his late fifties, still robust and vigorous for his age. "Where is Maude?"

"Resting. Did Ben tell you that Maude is— ailing?"

"Aye, and I'm sorry. Why did you say nothing in your letter? What if I hadn't come straightaway? What if I'd decided to stay in London a few more months before answering your summons?"

"I trusted you to do the right thing," Roy said, smiling warmly. "I knew you wouldn't let me down. Besides, I promised Maude I wouldn't spoil your time in London by speaking of her illness. If you hadn't come, I would have booked passage to England anyway and left Dare to deal with Penrod station, though Lord knows he already has his hands full with his own farm and the land he bought from Kate and Robin."

Roy led the way into the house and Ben followed, dragging Tia behind him. Dare was close on their heels. When they were inside, Roy seemed to notice Tia for the first time. He slid an inquisitive glance at Ben, then frowned, waiting for an introduction. His first thought was that his unprincipled son had brought home a mistress, and that was something he wouldn't allow.

"Perhaps you should introduce me to your— friend, Ben," Roy said quietly. His tone was sternly disapproving as he studied Tia with gray eyes amazingly like those of both his sons.

"I think you should sit down, Father," Dare advised, nearly bursting with laughter.

"That bad?" Roy asked, choosing to stand as he waited for Ben's explanation. "What has the young rakehell done now? Have you gotten your doxy with child and brought her home to bear your baby? I don't suppose it ever occurred to you to marry the chit, did it, Ben?"

Ben burst into peals of raucous laughter. Tia wasn't nearly so amused. It was the second time today she had been called a whore, and it rankled to think that they weren't so far from the truth. No matter how one looked at it, she was

Ben's mistress. Her face turned a bright red and she opened her mouth to spew forth words to vindicate herself in plain street language when Ben realized what was about to happen.

"Please, Tia, let me explain," he said, ready to place a restraining hand over her mouth if need be. "Father, Tia is my wife. Tia, meet my father, Roy."

"Bloody hell, Ben, why didn't you warn me?" Roy blasted, looking at Tia with such a hound-dog look she couldn't help but smile. "Your wife! I can't begin to tell you how happy I am that you've finally married and settled down. Tia must be some woman to bring you this far. You must love her very much. Welcome to the family, Tia. Please forgive me for my— assumption that—that—"

"You're forgiven, Mr. Penrod," Tia said, sending Ben a fulminating look. She'd never forgive him for doing this terrible thing to his family. They were genuinely thrilled with Ben's "marriage," and when they learned the truth they probably would hate her. Lord, what a coil!

"I imagine you're tired," Roy said, still dazed by Ben showing up with a bride. "Go on up to your room and settle in. You can meet Maude at supper. Dare can bring Casey and the children over too. It will be wonderful to have the whole family together again. Too bad Robin, Kate, and little Molly aren't in town, for they'd be as thrilled to meet you as I am. Lord, won't they be surprised!"

197

"That's a wonderful idea, Father. I know Tia must be exhausted. We could both use a nap." He leered at Tia with such a devilish glint that both Roy and Dare burst out laughing.

"It must be wonderful to be young and in love," Dare sighed with an exaggerated intake of breath.

"You have no room for talk, big brother," Ben said. "You and Casey still act like a pair of newlyweds despite your years of marriage and three children. Though I must admit Casey is a special woman, deserving of all the love you lavish on her."

"True," Dare agreed, beaming. "And so is Tia or you wouldn't have married her. Go along with you, Ben, we'll have lots of time to talk tonight. See you later, Tia. Meeting you has been a pleasure. It does me good to learn my rakish brother has a heart after all."

Ben's room was spacious, with a view of the river to the south and hills to the west. The furniture was solid and comfortable, and Tia tried to keep from looking at the huge bed that dominated the room. She stood staring out the window for a few minutes, thinking of all the vile things she wanted to say to Ben.

"You'll like it here, Tia," Ben said, coming to stand behind her. His arms slid around her, hugging her close. She whirled in his embrace, her eyes dark with anger.

"How dare you! You had no right to introduce me as your wife! I feel like a complete fool. I hate

198

to imagine what your family will think once they learn the truth."

Ben frowned. He knew that what he'd done wasn't exactly ethical, but he couldn't bring himself to introduce Tia as his mistress. And his father would never allow her to live in the house with him without benefit of marriage. He couldn't have left her in Sydney to fend for herself, could he? Bringing Tia to Penrod station was the only thing he could do under the circumstances. If he had brought Tia home merely as a guest, they would be expected to occupy separate rooms for propriety's sake and he couldn't bear being in the same house with her and not making love to her. It wasn't as if he hadn't proposed, for God's sake.

"It doesn't matter what they think," Ben said with supreme arrogance. "I want you here, in my bed, and introducing you as my mistress just didn't appeal to me. Don't worry, sweetheart, we'll cross that bridge when we come to it."

Before she could protest, he dragged her hard against him, kissing her fervently and soundly. "Come to bed, I want to welcome you properly to my home."

"You're going to have to cross that bridge sooner than you think, Ben. I'm not staying."

"You're not leaving, Tia, I won't let you."

Chapter Ten

Hands on hips, Tia glared mutinously at Ben. "I don't enjoy playing your family for fools. I should leave now before this sham blows up in our faces."

"At least stay until Father and Maude leave," Ben cajoled. "I'd rather they not be told. I'll deal with it if and when they return to Australia."

"Your brother is no fool," Tia maintained. "What will he think when he learns I'm merely your m—mistress?" She stumbled over the word but knew that mistress was all she would ever be to Ben.

"You had your chance to become my wife and for reasons only you and God know decided against it. Once Father and Maude settle in Europe, Penrod station is mine and Dare has no say as to what goes on here. If I choose to have my mistress live with me, then that's how it will be."

"I—can't live a lie. You must tell them I'm not your wife. If you do it now, they won't be so shocked when I leave."

Ben flinched. Whenever Tia spoke of leaving a jolt of raw pain twisted his gut. Thank God he realized it was only lust he felt for the little witch. His damnable lust for Tia was the reason he couldn't let her go yet. He still wanted her, still felt the thrill of possession whenever he touched her, and he bloody well wasn't going to let her go off to God knows where on her own until he was good and ready.

"In my own good time, Tia. The time isn't right yet to tell my family the truth. Perhaps," he suggested slyly, "when you tell me the truth about yourself I might be willing to pass it on to my family and explain about our bogus marriage."

Tia's eyes grew round as saucers. Were they back to that subject again? Would Ben never tire of plying her with his infernal questions? Perhaps if she did tell him the truth he might be convinced to let her go. That notion certainly bore thinking about. Lost in a myriad of confused thoughts, she wasn't aware of Ben's avid scrutiny, or the way his silver eyes roved freely over her small, curvaceous form. It wasn't until he spoke that she realized what he intended.

"Take off your clothes, sweetheart, we've plenty of time before dinner." He peeled off his coat, pulled his shirt from his trousers, and slowly began to work the buttons from the buttonholes.

"Do you think everything can be solved in bed?" Tia snapped, exasperated by Ben's casual treatment of what she deemed a very serious problem.

"Maybe not solved, but it certainly makes us feel a helluva lot better," he said with a roguish grin.

Tia made an unladylike sound deep in her throat. "Have you ever thought about the consequences should I—become pregnant?" She sent him a blistering look that spoke volumes.

Ben paused, an arrested look on his face. "Pregnant?"

"I've known how babies are made for some time now," Tia said with a hint of sarcasm.

A child, Ben reflected, oddly pleased by the thought. Becoming a father had never been one of his goals. In fact, he had taken great pains in the past to keep his paramours from conceiving. As far as he knew, he had no bastards either here or in England. He was relieved when Dare had provided the family with heirs and felt no pressure or need to follow in his brother's footsteps. Truth to tell, having Tia bear his child was a rather intriguing thought. In fact, a tiny voice in his brain whispered, it was certainly one way of keeping her from leaving.

"You're not increasing, are you?" he asked, suddenly struck with the notion that Tia wouldn't have brought up the subject without good reason.

"No, thank God," Tia said with such heartfelt relief that Ben frowned with annoyance. Did Tia never want to have children, or was it just his children she didn't care for? "But that isn't to say it won't or can't happen."

"You can trust me to take care of you," Ben said quietly. "I'm not totally without honor. We'll cross that bridge when we come to it."

"Another bridge, Ben? What happens when the next bridge you come to ends abruptly in the middle of the water and you're forced to sink or swim?"

"Then I'll swim, of course," Ben returned smartly. He reached for Tia. It unsettled him to talk about something so remote it might never occur. Besides, he meant every word he said. If Tia should conceive while they were together, he'd take care of both her and their child. Perhaps it would make her feel differently about marrying him. Not that he had any intention of proposing again, he told himself. Once was enough, especially after the outcome of the first time.

"I know a perfect way to make you forget unpleasant things," he said, dragging her against the hard wall of his chest. "Newlyweds aren't supposed to think of serious things, they're expected to enjoy one another as often as possible. And I do enjoy you, Tia, enormously. You're such a passionate little thing I can't believe my good luck in finding you."

If Tia admitted the truth, she'd say exactly the same thing about Ben. If Ben hadn't taken her off the streets of London, she might be dead now. Terrible things were always happening to street people forced to live precariously among thieves, rapists, and the dregs of society. One-eyed Bertha might have taken it into her head to sell her to any one of her vile friends who produced sufficient coin. She could have been violated and slain with no one to mourn her passing.

And Ben had introduced her to a source of pleasure that Tia never knew existed. If not for him she felt she would have gone her entire life without tasting love—if what she and Ben did could be called love. Tia was astute enough to realize that Ben desired her and was merely sating his enormous appetite. She was an unknown quality, a mystery that piqued his sexual appetite, and her attraction would last only until his lust for her was appeased and she no longer amused him. Her pride demanded that she leave him before that happened.

Or before she lost her heart to him.

A nagging voice inside her told her it was already too late.

Then her thoughts halted abruptly as Ben kissed her, his mouth hot and hard against her own, his tongue nudging her lips apart to thrust inside. His hand was under her chin, holding her head in place as he ravaged her mouth at will, claiming her with all the male arrogance for which he was so well known. Tia tried to turn her head but he held her too tight, and then all resistance wilted beneath the fury of his kisses. Being kissed by Ben was like being swept into the vortex of a violent storm from which there was no escaping.

To Tia's horror she found she didn't want to escape from Ben.

Not now—not ever.

While engaged in kissing her, Ben had pushed down her bodice, pinning her arms to her sides and baring her breasts. The thatch of dark fur covering the massive expanse of his naked chest felt highly erotic against the sensitive peaks of her nipples. Moaning, Tia rubbed against him, his sharp intake of breath telling her how much he enjoyed her response.

"You'll never be able to convince me you don't want me," Ben said. His voice held a strange quality that defied defining. "And Lord knows I want you. You affect me like no other woman I know."

Lifting her high in his arms, he carried her to the bed. Tia offered no protest, knowing it would do her little good. Ben would have his way in the end, and she was truthful enough to admit she wanted him. Before he joined her on the bed he slowly stripped off his clothes. Tia watched with burning eyes, thinking him the most attractive man she'd ever seen. There wasn't an ounce of fat anywhere on his large frame. He was all hard flesh and bone, attractively packaged in corded muscle and sinew. When he turned to toss his clothes across a chair she admired the taut mounds of his buttocks and long, sturdy legs.

Then he was kneeling beside her, his eyes dark with desire, undressing her with the expertise of a man familiar with women's apparel. When she was completely nude he sat back on his heels to admire her. Tia quivered as he made slow, languid love to her with his eyes. Then he was touching her, her breasts, her nipples, pausing to stroke her stomach before sifting long fingers through the golden fleece between her legs. She jerked in response when his fingers found her, opened her, and slipped inside.

Ben watched her intently as his fingers slid in and out in a rhythm that set Tia's blood afire. She writhed against the pressure of his hand in order to ease the ache in her loins.

"I love watching you when I give you pleasure," Ben whispered against her lips. "Your face is so expressive; your eyes tell me you enjoy what I do to you. Pretending to be my wife has its advantages, wouldn't you say?"

Ben's insensitive remark brought her senses back under control and her temper flaring. "Dammit, Ben, yer an arse if ye think yer the only man who can give me pleasure. I suspect all men 'ave the same equipment and some even as knowledgeable as ye are when it comes to lovin'."

"Perhaps," Ben admitted, gnashing his teeth in frustration, "but you'll never learn whether your suspicions are correct. You belong to me, Tia, and I'll be damned if I'll let you go. And I don't appreciate your gutter language." No matter what he said, Tia's sharp tongue came back with a cutting reply. "Now shut up and let me love you."

Then he was pressing her down into the mattress, his body hot and hard, demanding her full attention as he thrust into her. Tia welcomed his entry with a hoarse cry, all thought suspended as her legs locked around his hips, urging him deep—deeper . . .

Deeply embedded, Ben paused, savoring the play of tiny muscles that closed around him, enjoying the searing heat of Tia's body in a way he had enjoyed no other woman.

"Ben . . ."

"Be patient, sweetheart, you'll get what you want. Have I ever let you down yet?"

His words failed to ease the raw torment building inside her as she surged against him. Ben groaned but remained perfectly still, bending his head to place nibbling kisses across her breasts. Then suddenly he was reversing their positions and Tia was straddling him, giving her all the freedom she craved. She arched her back, bringing him deeper inside her. But still Ben didn't move, not until Tia began a slow rocking back and forth. Suddenly Ben could stand no more as he cried out and grasped her hips, holding her in place while he thrust into her again and again. Tia rode him passionately, joyously, wildly. Ben grit his teeth and persevered.

Abruptly she stiffened and Ben felt explosive little tremors ripple through her body. His blood was thundering so furiously through his veins he gave his own passion full reign, thrusting again and again until his climax exploded upon him.

When Tia came to her senses, Ben was leaning over her, gazing at her with a wondering expression on his face. His eyes bespoke his puzzlement, as if not quite certain where his feelings lay in regard to Tia. But his emotions were too raw right now, too close to the edge to explore them fully.

"Go to sleep, Tia," he urged softly. "I'll awaken you in plenty of time for dinner."

Tia needed no further urging as she turned over and fell promptly asleep. Ben sighed, pulled her into his arms, and tried to remember all the reasons he vowed never to marry.

Dare and his family were already assembled in the parlor when Ben and Tia arrived downstairs. Tia had overslept and Ben hadn't awakened her until the last moment, so she hadn't been able to spend as much time as she would have liked to make herself presentable. Ben laughed at her frantic preparations, telling her she couldn't improve on her looks if she spent the next three hours trying. Tia assumed it was a compliment but, knowing Ben as she did, she couldn't be certain. She needn't have worried.

She looked charming and absurdly young wearing a teal green gown that hugged her narrow waist to perfection and displayed the pearly white tops of her breasts to the best advantage above the modest décolletage of her bodice. She . had attempted to pile her pale blond hair atop her head in an effort to appear older, and the results were a charming riot of curls with trailing ends that clung to her neck and forehead in springy spirals. Ben had never seen her lovelier, except perhaps when she was flushed from his loving, her eyes luminous with passion.

Tia was shy at first, still guilt-ridden over the sham she and Ben were engaged in. She wanted Ben's family to like her, yet thought it might be more appropriate if they didn't. Having their disregard would make it easier when she left and they finally learned she wasn't nor ever would be Ben's wife. But Casey Penrod made it difficult to remain aloof with her warm welcome. And the three adorable Penrod children captured her heart.

"Tia, I was speechless when Dare told me Ben had married," Casey said, laughing delightedly. Tia thought she was the loveliest woman she had ever seen with her flame-colored hair and vibrant personality. She looked much too young to be the mother of three children.

"Ha," Dare observed with a humorous chuckle, "it would be the first time you were at a loss for words. Your sharp tongue is constantly wagging in my direction."

"I daresay you deserve it, Dare Penrod," Casey shot back saucily. Her brilliant green eyes sparkled like emeralds, and it was obvious to Tia that Dare and Casey were well matched. And just as obvious that they loved one another dearly. The heated looks they exchanged were a sensual celebration of the close relationship they shared.

Then once again Tia found herself the center of their attention. "Tell me all about yourself, Tia," Casey said. "Ben never wrote a thing about you or hinted that he had fallen in love with an Englishwoman. He always was close-mouthed, but this is ridiculous. We're all ecstatic to see the young devil happily married and settled down. How and when did you meet?"

The room grew quiet as everyone waited for Tia to relate more personal details of her courtship and marriage. She slanted Ben a fulminating glance, licked her dry lips, and said, "We—sort of bumped into one another on the street."

"You must have made quite an impression on Ben," Dare ventured. "How long have you known him?"

"Not long, actually," Ben said, saving Tia from inventing more lies. "I knew the moment we met that Tia and I were meant to be together."

Tia gasped, preparing to fling an angry challenge at him but warned to silence by Ben's penetrating glance.

"How romantic," Maude said, her eyes suspiciously misty.

Never a vigorous woman, she had grown quite frail in the years since Ben had last seen her. Her years of servitude and hardships before she'd met Roy and been emancipated by Governor Macquarie had taken a toll on her health. Her once ruddy skin was now waxy and nearly transparent. Roy had fallen in love with Maude when she was in her middle forties and worked for Robin and Kate Fletcher at McKenzie station. Ben couldn't blame his father for wanting to take Maude to Switzerland for the best possible care, for she was a sweet woman whose life hadn't been easy.

"How long have you and Tia been married, Ben?" Casey asked with innocent curiosity. She had no idea her questions were fanning the flames of guilt in Tia's heart.

"We were married shortly before I received Father's letter summoning me home."

"I'll bet Tia's family hated to see her sail halfway around the world," Roy injected.

"I—" Tia looked helplessly at Ben, but this time he remained silent, waiting to hear what she had to say about her family. "My parents are both dead. I don't have any close relatives."

"I'm sorry, Tia," Roy said sincerely. "I didn't mean to pry or to open old wounds. Perhaps we

211

should all go in to dinner and save our questions for later."

At first Tia was too nervous to do more than pick at her food, but when no further questions concerning her "marriage" to Ben or her background were introduced, she finally relaxed and enjoyed the delicious meal. After six months of monotonous shipboard fare it tasted wonderful, and she feared she was making a pig of herself. Once Ben reached under the table for her hand and gave it a squeeze; she supposed to bolster her courage. Strangely enough, it helped.

After the meal, Tia devoted her full attention to nine-year-old Brandon, already a young man and the picture of his handsome father; adorable red-headed Lucy, nearly seven; and little Quin, a very vocal and energetic two-year-old. She would give anything to have children like this one day, Tia thought wistfully, and a loving husband who adored both her and their children. The possibility existed that she might bear Ben a child if she remained with him, but it hurt to think that they could never be a real family like Dare and Casey.

Maude excused herself first, quickly followed by Roy who joined her in their bedroom. Dare, Casey, and their children left a short time later. Tia lingered in the open doorway a few minutes after they left, listening to the strange night sounds of birds, animals, and insects. The air was soft and fragrant, the heavens ablaze with thousands of twinkling stars and the moon so full and bright that looking at it hurt her eyes. She could hear the river in the distance, gurgling as it sped along its course, and she gave a fleeting thought to the stench of London's sewers, its crowded waterfront and crush of humanity vying for space in the teeming city.

"Incredible, isn't it?" Ben said, coming to stand behind her.

"Yes," Tia agreed, quivering as his large hand warmed her shoulder. Had he always affected her thus? *Yes*, her conscience replied. *Why do you think it's so difficult to leave?*

Because you love him.

The thought was so stunning that she started violently, then began to shake.

"Are you cold, sweetheart?" Ben asked solicitously

"No." The sudden notion that she loved Ben frightened her. Love had no place in her life. Love was for women who could love freely and without reservation. She was not free to love or give herself to any man. Thank God Ben wasn't interested in marriage. "I was just thinking that—" She fell silent.

"Thinking what?" Ben prodded.

Tia worried her bottom lip. "That—I'm tired. You quite exhausted me this afternoon, and after our long journey I feel like I could sleep uninterrupted for days."

"You were quite impressive tonight, sweetheart," Ben said, his eyes glowing happily. "You've captured the hearts of my entire family.

213

They consider me lucky to have found you."

"You know how I feel about that," Tia said, turning and closing the door softly behind her. "I hate lying to them. I want to leave."

"To go where? To do what? Staying with me hurts nothing but your pride. Father told me he and Maude will sail to England on Jeremy's ship next week. After they're gone you can tell Dare and Casey that we're not married, if that's what you really want. Just don't think you can up and leave, because I won't let you go. You make a wonderful mistress."

"Is that all I am to you, Ben?" Tia didn't wait for his answer. She merely stared intently into his eyes for what seemed an eternity, then whirled and flounced away. Ben watched her stiff back and tantalizing slim ankles as she ascended the stairs. His eyes were bleak as he went into the study, shut the door quietly behind him, and proceeded to get roaring drunk.

Is that all I am to you, Ben?

Tia's words echoed in his head, obscuring everything but the challenge she'd flung at him. Bloody hell! She was a wonderful mistress. Warm, passionate, so responsive he had only to touch her and she went up in smoke. He'd bedded passionate women before but none who affected him as profoundly as Tia. Yet he understood nothing about her. At times she was a foul-mouthed little witch whose language scalded his ears. Then she shocked him by turning all soft and wanton in his arms, her speech refined, her manners above reproach. Who was the real Tia? What in bloody hell did she mean to him? He became drunk long before he solved the mystery surrounding Tia or untangled his feelings for her.

Tia awoke as daylight burst upon the land with an abruptness that startled her. Ben had explained that darkness arrived just as abruptly, like a dark curtain that fell without warning, but it would take some getting use to. Then she recalled that Ben hadn't come to bed all night. It bothered her more than she cared to admit. Had he decided to find a bed elsewhere? Had he tired of her? Or had he finally decided that there was merit in her suggestion that they give up this sham?

Ben chose that moment to stagger into the room, blurry-eyed and disheveled. A blue-black stubble shadowed his chin and he looked like hell.

"Tell Father I'll be down later," he mumbled, falling across the bed. Tia scrambled to get out of his way. But she couldn't escape the stench of his alcohol-laden breath. "Tell him my 'bride' has quite exhausted me." He grinned at her foolishly.

"You're drunk," she observed, wondering what had driven him to the bottle. Ordinarily he drank only moderately.

"Just slightly," he said dryly. But before Tia could question him as to the reason for his shameful state, he fell asleep, his snores driving her from the bed.

Roy was more than pleased with the way things had worked out for Ben. He had no second thoughts whatever about turning the farm over to Ben now that Ben was married and settled down. Roy might never return to Australia and felt he could rest easy knowing that the land he had worked so hard to maintain would prosper under Ben's capable handling. Just as Dare's land would be his children's heritage, so would Penrod station be left for Ben's children. He said as much to Ben in one of their private conversations in which Roy informed Ben he might never return. Once Maude was cured, if she was cured, he intended to take her on an extended honeymoon to all the places she'd never seen.

It had been on the tip of Ben's tongue to honor Tia's request and tell his father that he and Tia weren't married when Roy's words took all the wind out of his sails. He couldn't bring himself to disappoint his father, whom he loved dearly, or delay Roy's voyage abroad to seek medical help for Maude. Tia would just have to bide her time until Roy and Maude left Australia aboard the *Martha C.*

Meanwhile, Ben did some serious soul-searching. He greatly feared that Tia was becoming much too important to him. During the day he kept busy reacquainting himself with the farm and assuming all the responsibilities that had once belonged to Roy, but at night he wanted Tia with a fierce need that transcended his need for food and drink. He was obsessed with making love to her again and again, putting his brand on her for all time. It still rankled that Tia had turned down his proposal of marriage once and he vowed he'd not be so stupid again. Somehow, some way, he had to overcome his obsession and think of Tia as merely fulfilling a need that any other woman could fulfill.

His first step toward putting his life back in order was the most difficult thus far. After that first day at Penrod station, Ben abruptly stopped making love to Tia. Getting drunk that night had been the first indication that Tia was turning him inside out. Ben was a man who prided himself on the number and variety of women he bedded without becoming emotionally involved. He was nearly thirty years old and his heart had never been touched. He wasn't about to allow a little hoyden fresh from the streets of London to change his life. He liked his life just the way it was, thank you. Besides, Tia had stepped on his ego one time too many.

Tia reluctantly agreed to continue their charade until Roy and Maude left for England, but not a moment longer. When Ben stopped making love to her, she supposed he had given serious thought to what she had said about becoming pregnant. Obviously he didn't want any bastards, and that was fine with her, though the thought of having Ben's child wasn't at all alarming to her. In fact, it was oddly comforting. She pushed the thought from her mind. She had no idea that sleeping beside her night after night without touching her stretched Ben's control to the breaking point.

At the end of the second week after Tia arrived at Penrod station, she and Ben took Roy and Maude to Sydney Cove to board the *Martha C*. Jeremy Combs welcomed the older couple aboard, and while Tia helped them settle into their cabin, Jeremy spoke privately with Ben.

"I've kept your secret, mate, but I'm not sure it's the right thing to do," he said, frowning at Ben. "Roy seems quite fond of Tia and pleased with your marriage. Dammit, Ben, marry the girl! How long are you going to keep her as your mistress? Dare will have your hide when he learns the truth."

A dull red crept up Ben's neck. "She turned me down, remember? Don't worry, I'll straighten things out."

Just then Tia reappeared and bid Jeremy goodbye. Then she and Ben left the ship. They waved from shore as the ship slipped her moorings and her sails filled with wind. Roy and Maude had returned topside and were waving back in vigorous response. Ben seemed reluctant to move until the *Martha C* was a dark speck on the horizon. Then he grasped Tia's arm and turned her toward the gig parked a short distance away.

"We've plenty of time," Ben said, "would you like to do some shopping before we return home? The clothes I bought you in London aren't adequate for Australia. Can you sew?"

Tia shook her head. One didn't learn sewing while picking pockets. "No matter," Ben shrugged, "one of the servants can help."

"I don't need anything," Tia demurred. She didn't want to be indebted to Ben any more than she already was. "But I would appreciate it if you'd allow me to query the shop owners to see if anyone needs help. I want to earn enough money to buy passage back to England."

Ben was so incensed he literally tossed Tia into the gig before leaping up beside her. "Don't you ever listen to anything I say? It will be impossible to find work."

"I can try," Tia insisted stubbornly.

"I think not. When I'm good and ready to let you go I'll pay your passage myself." Why was he torturing himself like this? He should just let Tia go and be rid of her.

"I won't live in your house as your mistress. Hire me as your housekeeper and pay me a wage."

"What! Out of the question." He picked up the reins and set the gig into motion.

Tia fumed in simmering silence as they left Sydney behind. Why was Ben being so obstinate? Obviously he had tired of her, for he hadn't attempted to make love to her in days. Why did he even want her around?

"Keeping me here will serve no purpose," Tia said, giving vent to her thoughts. "You can't stop me from leaving, Ben."

Ben realized that Tia spoke the truth and searched his mind for a plausible reason to keep her in Australia, in his house, in his bed. Only one came to mind. Abruptly he stopped the gig and pulled off the road into a grove of tall eucalyptus.

What now? Tia wondered, alarmed by Ben's grim expression. It was almost as if he were waging some kind of war within himself. When he turned toward her, his eyes were dark with raw emotion. He opened his mouth and words came tumbling out. Startling words. Words he hadn't meant to utter but that spewed forth unbidden.

"Marry me, Tia. We can go back to Sydney now and be quietly married by the preacher."

Tia looked stricken. She wanted to marry Ben. More than anything she wanted to marry Ben. Though she had willed it otherwise, the unthinkable had happened. Somewhere along the way she had lost her heart to Ben Penrod. She had no right to love Ben, or any other man. Surely God was punishing her for forsaking her duty. It didn't matter that she'd had no say in the matter. Now she was being punished.

"I—can't marry you, Ben."

Ben's eyes grew so cold and remote that Tia shivered. "Can't or won't?"

"It's all the same. I can't and I won't."

"Damn you!" His voice was bitter as he picked up the reins and drove back onto the road.

Chapter Eleven

That night Ben moved out of the room he had been sharing with Tia. His last words before he strode out the door were, "I've created a monster. Obviously all you want from me is stud service."

Ben couldn't recall when he'd been so angry. Not only had he done something he swore he'd never do, but he did it twice. And Tia had wounded his pride by turning him down each time. What in bloody hell did she want from him? Did she enjoy seeing him grovel? Did she relish watching him make an ass of himself? If he was smart he'd pay her passage back to England and forget about the little witch.

If it was as easy as that, why couldn't he do it?

After seeing all the trials and tribulations that Dare and Robin had gone through to win their women, he had sworn never to marry. But despite his vow he had allowed himself to be manipulated and turned inside out by a young slip of a girl who harbored some vile secret she refused to divulge.

If he hadn't still wanted her with a need that bordered on desperation, he'd give her some money and bid her goodbye.

Tia lay awake a long time that night. Ben had every right to toss her out on her ear, yet he hadn't. Did he enjoy punishing her? Was that it? Knowing that she loved him and was unable to do anything about it was a special kind of torture. He knew she had no money of her own and couldn't leave without his help. Now she was trapped in a situation so painful that each day was a test of endurance. If she wasn't such a coward she'd take her chances on earning the price of the fare to England despite Ben's insistence that employment was unavailable. Another thing that held her back was the inescapable fact that returning to London was deliberately courting danger.

The impasse between Tia and Ben continued. Ben barely spoke to her in the days that followed. When Casey visited she sensed a sadness in Tia and wondered what Ben had done to cause the obvious rift that had suddenly loomed between them. She mentioned it to Dare, who suggested a party to celebrate Ben's marriage to

Tia. Casey thought it a wonderful idea and sent a message to Robin and Kate asking them to come to Parramatta for the affair. They broached the subject of the celebration on their next visit to Penrod station.

"It will be wonderful," Casey exclaimed, clapping her hands. "We haven't had a party in ever so long." Her green eyes glinted with excitement. "It will give all our neighbors an opportunity to meet Tia. I've already notified Robin and Kate."

Tia's heart constricted. Casey's enthusiasm and her intention to introduce her as Ben's wife was a bitter pill she couldn't swallow. She owed it to these good people to put an end to this charade once and for all. She glared at Ben in mute defiance, lifted her chin, and said, "I'm afraid a party to celebrate our 'marriage' is out of the question."

"Oh, Tia, please," Casey implored. "I don't know what is going on with you and Ben, but I know it can be mended. It's obvious that you two love one another deeply. A party will be just what the doctor ordered."

"No doctor in the world can cure something that never existed."

Casey looked puzzled, but Dare sent Ben a fulminating glance, beginning to understand where the trouble lay.

"Would you care to explain, Tia?" Dare asked.

Tia drew in a huge gulp of air and said, "Ben and I aren't married, nor have we ever been.

Thrill to the most sensual, adventure-filled Romances on the market today...

FROM  LOVE SPELL BOOKS

As a home subscriber to the Love Spell Romance Book Club, you'll enjoy the best in today's BRAND-NEW Time Travel, Futuristic, Legendary Lovers, Perfect Heroes and other genre romance fiction. For five years, Love Spell has brought you the award-winning, high-quality authors you know and love to read. Each Love Spell romance will sweep you away to a world of high adventure...and intimate romance. Discover for yourself all the passion and excitement millions of readers thrill to each and every month.

Save $5.00 Each Time You Buy!

Every other month, the Love Spell Romance Book Club brings you four brand-new titles from Love Spell Books. EACH PACKAGE WILL SAVE YOU AT LEAST $5.00 FROM THE BOOK-STORE PRICE! And you'll never miss a new title with our convenient home delivery service.

Here's how we do it: Each package will carry a FREE 10-DAY EXAMINATION privilege. At the end of that time, if you decide to keep your books, simply pay the low invoice price of $17.96, no shipping or handling charges added. HOME DELIVERY IS ALWAYS FREE. With today's top romance novels selling for $5.99 and higher, our price SAVES YOU AT LEAST $5.00 with each shipment.

AND YOUR FIRST TWO-BOOK SHIP-MENT IS TOTALLY FREE!

IT'S A BARGAIN YOU CAN'T BEAT! A SUPER $11.48 Value!

Love Spell ✦ A Division of Dorchester Publishing Co., Inc.

Get Two Books Totally
F R E E —
An $11.48 Value!

▼ Tear Here and Mail Your FREE Book Card Today! ▼

PLEASE RUSH
MY TWO FREE
BOOKS TO ME
RIGHT AWAY!

Love Spell Romance Book Club
P.O. Box 6613
Edison, NJ 08818-6613

It's all a lie, a sham. I—I'm sorry, truly, I never wanted to hurt anyone."

Dare looked furious as he rounded on Ben. "What in bloody hell does Tia mean, little brother? Your explanation better be good or I'm going to beat the hell out of you. Does your freedom mean so much to you that you'd take unfair advantage of an innocent young girl?"

"You don't know what in the hell you're talking about," Ben returned hotly. He could wring Tia's neck for opening a can of worms.

"I'll pass judgment when I hear the facts," Dare scowled. "But knowing your penchant for debauchery and womanizing, I'd venture to guess that none of this is Tia's fault. I could have sworn you're an honorable man. You've proved it on more than one occasion, if you recall." He was referring to the time that Ben had selflessly offered to marry Casey himself and keep her safe for Dare rather than allow another man to have her.

"It's true that I brought Tia to Australia against her will but—"

That's all Dare needed to know as he flew at Ben. Rarely if ever had he struck Ben, but this time he felt justified. Ben staggered beneath his brother's telling blow but made no move to defend himself. Dare was the hotheaded member of the family, and Ben knew that as soon as he vented his anger his temper would cool. Ben rubbed his chin as Dare eyed him narrowly, preparing to launch another punch. This time Tia intervened.

"Dare, don't, it's not Ben's fault! He *is* honorable. He offered to marry me, but I refused."

"Oh, Tia, why?" Casey asked, finally finding her tongue. From the difficulties she'd encountered before she and Dare had wed, she knew that things weren't always what they appeared to be and was more than willing to listen to Tia's explanation.

"It—it's personal." She gnawed at her bottom lip, suddenly aware that these wonderful people would keep her secret should she decide to divulge it. Did she dare?

Dare wasn't at all convinced. "Are you protecting Ben? We're all aware of Ben's aversion to marriage and that he's been living loose and free in London these past few years. What argument did he use to persuade you to leave England to become his mistress? Did he ruin you and then threaten to tell everyone he debauched you?"

"Bloody hell, Dare, you make me sound like a first-class swine," Ben snapped. His voice was bitter as he glared first at Tia, then at Dare. It hurt when his own brother accused him of being less than honorable. What a fine coil he had gotten himself into. And all because he was obsessed with a beautiful little hoyden who associated with thieves, cutpurses, and lowlife scum. "I did propose to Tia. Twice."

Dare blinked repeatedly. "Twice? My brother

proposed twice?" He was so stunned he expected lightning to strike.

"It's true," Tia contended. "It's my fault we didn't marry. I couldn't—I mean, I didn't want to marry Ben."

"You'd rather be Ben's mistress than his wife?" Casey asked, aghast. "I think you owe us an explanation, Tia. What possible reason could you have for refusing an honest proposal? Any fool can see you two love one another." Casey's words brought a sad little smile to Tia's lips. It was the second time Casey had suggested that Ben and Tia loved one another. Too bad it applied to only one of them.

"I'd be interested to hear that explanation myself," Ben observed dryly. His lips turned up in something short of a smile.

Tia met Ben's eyes with a flicker of lashes. "I'm—not good enough for Ben. He found me living among thieves and pickpockets. In fact, I picked his pocket the day we met."

"She was dressed as a young lad and gave me quite a start when I—er—accidentally discovered that beneath those rags was the body and face of an angel. And you should have heard her language." He rolled his eyes suggestively.

"But that's impossible!" Casey exclaimed. "Tia is much too refined to do all those things you said."

"If you had heard her curse you wouldn't say that," Ben insisted. "She turned the air blue with her foul street language. She was so good at it one would never guess it was just a facade she assumed to hide her sex. The one thing she never divulged was her reason for hiding among the lowlife of London, or why her life was in danger."

"Is all this true, Tia?" Dare asked guardedly.

"I—yes," Tia whispered.

The rigid lines of Dare's face relaxed into reluctant acceptance. He'd heard many strange tales before, but this was positively bizarre. "I'm sorry, Ben, I shouldn't have struck you."

"That's all right," Ben allowed. "I probably deserved it. You always did have a vile temper. I don't know how Casey has put up with you all these years."

"It wasn't easy," Casey said with a saucy grin, "but I know how to handle Dare. And I also know how to mend this situation. We'll have a quiet wedding at Penrod station."

"No!" Tia cried. Given the predictable unpredictability of her explosive nature, Ben was certain she was going to lapse into gutter language. He thought she showed remarkable restraint when she merely repeated, "No."

Dare and Casey exchanged meaningful glances while Ben merely shook his head. "I've proposed twice and I refused to so again. Tia has stomped on my pride for the last time. It's a foregone conclusion that she'll turn me down for the third time if I propose again, and I prefer to retain a measure of self-respect."

"Ben is right," Tia added, choking on the words. "I won't marry Ben under any circumstances." It was the most difficult, untrue sentence she'd ever uttered. And caused a wrenching pain in the region of her heart. Her life was a mess, and the best thing she could do for Ben and his family was to make certain they would never become involved in her problems. It was a vow she intended to keep.

"Are you certain about this?" Casey asked, trying to understand Tia but finding it difficult.

"Absolutely," Tia vowed, looking absurdly fierce.

"Then I think there is nothing more we can do here," Dare said, slicing Tia a stern look. "Perhaps Ben and Tia need to talk this out for themselves. I'm convinced there is a solution here someplace, but it's up to Ben and Tia to find it."

In short order Casey and Dare gathered their children and left. Ben and Tia stood glaring at one another. The brooding slant of Ben's mouth hinted at his anger. "I hope upsetting Dare and Casey made you happy."

"It was necessary. They had to know sooner or later. I'll pack up my things and leave tomorrow."

"Leave? Where will you go?"

"I don't know—anywhere. If you give me a small loan I'll find a place in town and look for work."

"We'll talk about it tomorrow," Ben hedged. "Good night, Tia." He turned his back and walked away. Arguing with Tia was senseless when he knew he'd never let her go no matter what she said or did. Even though he hadn't bedded her in days, he still remembered how magnificent it was, how absolutely wonderful she made him feel and how wildly her body responded to his touch.

Tia watched Ben walk away, her face set in obstinate lines. Instinctively she knew that Ben wasn't going to allow her to leave, and one part of her warmed at the thought of what his wanting to keep her meant. Yet another part of her—the practical side—knew she meant nothing more to him than a warm body. He may have proposed twice but he would never love her as she loved him.

The next day Ben was reluctant to leave the house. He feared—and rightly so—that Tia might attempt to leave once his back was turned. He was growing desperate, wanting her fiercely yet stubbornly refusing to indulge his body's demand. He feared making any woman indispensable to him, even Tia—particularly Tia. Admitting to Dare and Casey that he had proposed twice to Tia had seriously damaged his ego.

He gave a long, moaning sigh, realizing that he'd have to do something about his damnable lust for the little witch soon or go crazy. This was the first time in his life he could recall being unable to control his body's urges. What was it about Tia that made him a groveling idiot?

Have you never heard of love? a little voice whispered.

Ben stubbornly refused to consider the answer.

Tia was in the kitchen talking with the cook, a convict named Gert, when she became aware that someone was knocking on the door. No, knocking wasn't the right word, more like pounding. She had no idea that Ben was in the house and met him in the hallway just as he came out of the room he used as an office. She stood slightly behind him, hidden by his bulk when he opened the door, so she failed to see immediately who was causing such a loud racket.

"Can I help you?" Ben asked, leading Tia to believe he didn't know the caller.

"I'm looking for Ben Penrod."

Tia paled. That voice! It couldn't be! Dear God, please don't let it be.

"I'm Ben Penrod."

"Are you the Ben Penrod who recently returned from London?"

A jolt of warning sizzled along Ben's spine. Though he had never seen the man before, he disliked him immediately. Short, stout, and slightly balding, the man oozed wealth and power. His close-set eyes were the opaque blue of dirty water, and Ben perceived an innate cruelty about the taut line of his thin lips.

231

"Aye, I've recently returned from a trip abroad that included London. But I'm afraid you have me at a disadvantage; I can't recall having met you."

The moment the man was assured of Ben's identity his face darkened with inexplicable rage. "We've not met before but we have one thing in common. My name is Damian Fairfield. Lord Fairfield." He watched Ben's face closely for a reaction to his name, and when none was forthcoming, he grew even angrier.

Tia reeled as the world closed in on her, suffocating her, making her aware that her life would never be the same again. Was this how it was all going to end? She hadn't realized the world was such a small place. She had traveled halfway around the globe but it still wasn't far enough. After more than three years Damian had found her, and after spending a fortune finding her, he would punish her severely she felt sure.

Unable to see the startling effect Damian Fairfield had on Tia and completely unaware that the man's visit had anything to do with Tia, Ben replied, "I can't imagine what we might have in common, Lord Fairfield." He disliked the man more with each passing minute. He struck Ben as being egotistical, demanding, and driven by something maniacal.

Fairfield bent Ben a withering glance. "Then by all means let me come to the point, Penrod. I want my wife, though Lord knows the little bitch is nothing but a whore."

Ben failed to make the connection. "I beg your pardon."

"As well you should. Where is she? If you don't produce her immediately, I'll bring the law down on your head."

"I have no idea to whom you are referring."

"Are you suggesting that my wife isn't your whore, or that you didn't help her leave London? That's something I refuse to believe. The little slut isn't clever enough to flee to this remote country on her own. I won't press charges if you hand Tia over to me now."

Tia? Ben shook his head, thinking he hadn't heard correctly. This man was old enough to be Tia's father. Nay, grandfather! She wouldn't marry someone as old and repulsive as Lord Fairfield, would she? He swung around to confront Tia, searching her pale face for a hint of truth. And found it. Though her wide blue-green eyes were filled with terror and she was trembling from head to toe, the truth was evident in her expression, in her posture, and in her quiet acceptance of Lord Fairfield's claim.

"This man is your husband?" Ben asked harshly. His probing gaze raked her like sharp talons. Unable to speak, Tia winced and nodded.

"Why? Why in bloody hell didn't you tell me you were married?" His voice was brittle with bitterness and his gray eyes drove into her very soul, seeking, accusing, condemning. "You played me for a fool!"

"No! It wasn't like that," Tia said on a rising note of panic. "I didn't want to involve you in my problems."

"Those men who tried to abduct you in London, were they connected to your—husband?" He hurled the words at her like stones.

"Ah, you're referring to my henchmen," Fairfield interjected. "You foiled them both times, Penrod. It took three years and a small fortune to find Tia. I knew she wouldn't come back willingly, so I hired men to seize her."

Ben swung his gaze back to Tia, her pale face giving him pause. "Why didn't you tell me? I would have helped you."

"Would you?" Tia asked shakily. "How did I know you wouldn't return me to my husband?"

Husband. The word brought back memories of making love to Tia that first time and being surprised to find her a virgin. It also made him angry. Damn angry. What vile thing had Lord Fairfield done to his innocent young wife to cause her to run away before the marriage was consummated? Tia couldn't have been more than fifteen at the time and hardly aware of what was going on.

"This is all very touching," Fairfield spat, "but if you don't mind, I'll leave now and take my wife with me. She's shirked her duty all these years and it's high time she got on with doing what women are supposed to do. And that's not playing whore to a sheep farmer whose hands smell of dung. I want heirs, and in order to have them I need my lawful wife." He reached for Tia. She shrank against the wall, realizing that nothing outside of a miracle would save her now from becoming Damian's wife in every sense of the word. And she was fresh out of miracles.

Ben had been so stunned by Fairfield's surprising claim that he merely watched while Tia's husband closed a meaty fist around her slender wrist and dragged her out the door. "I'll deal with you later," he promised, jerking her brutally. She stumbled past Ben, sadly aware of the terrible wrong she had done him by failing to divulge her secret. She realized that it was much too late to lament over something that could not be undone, but it didn't stop her from suffering regret. Fairfield was a proud man, his family name an old and honored one. She had known from the beginning that divorce was out of the question.

Suddenly Ben came out of his stupor. Tia was nearly out the door when he seized her waist and yanked her from Fairfield's cruel grasp.

"What's the meaning of this?" Fairfield demanded. "I have every right to claim what's mine."

"Tia isn't yours," Ben said quietly. Too quietly. Those who knew him stayed well out of his way when his voice grew dangerously low and his gray eyes turned the color of stone.

"What do you mean? I married Tia and have the papers to prove it."

"The marriage was never consummated."

"I won't ask how you know that, for it's obvious the little whore is your mistress. But as soon as I get Tia back to the ship I'll remedy that unfortunate situation."

"Over my dead body."

"Ben," Tia began, fearing for Ben's safety. She knew from experience just how ruthless Damian could be. "Damian is right. I'm his wife, and it's best for everyone if I go along with him without a fuss."

"No."

"Listen to Tia, Penrod. I'm a man with far-reaching powers. Even as far-reaching as this godforsaken land you call home. I could easily ruin you if you force my hand."

"You're welcome to try," Ben grit from between clenched teeth. "No one is taking Tia from my house. Especially not you. How do I know you won't mistreat her? Something made her run away, and until I find out what it was she's not going anywhere with you."

"If you force me to leave without my wife, I'll bring the law back with me."

His threat was not an idle one. Ben knew that should the law become involved it would be on Fairfield's side. But the delay would afford him some much needed time to think of a way to help Tia out of her predicament. First he needed

236

to find out more about this marriage and Tia's reason for escaping it. She had gone to desperate lengths to keep from discharging her wifely duties to Damian Fairfield, and the thought of handing her over to her husband was repugnant to Ben.

"Tia is not leaving," Ben reiterated. "If you aren't off my property in five minutes, I'll have my men escort you. Good day, Lord Fairfield."

Fairfield's ruddy face grew even redder as he sputtered and gestured wildly in impotent rage. "You won't get away with this, Penrod. I'll be back, and when I do I'll make the little whore sorry she ever left my protection. I was appalled when I discovered how she's been earning her living these past years. You're just another one of her many lovers. I know the vile things that go on in the stews of London. She's whored for the last time!"

Furious, Ben slammed the door in his face. Cowering in the corner, Tia turned stricken eyes on Ben. "I'm sorry this had to happen, Ben." Her voice was strangely flat, her eyes dull with grief. "I never meant for you to find out. I was safe from Damian hidden in London's underground; that's why I chose to remain there."

"I think it's time you told me the truth," Ben said with remarkable restraint. Tia nodded. "Upstairs, away from prying ears." He waited for her to precede him, then followed her up the stairs. She paused before her room and when Ben nodded, she quickly went inside. Ben was hard on her heels. He closed the door softly behind him.

"Sit down, Tia. I suspect this is going to be a rather involved story. Begin at the beginning, please."

Tia perched gingerly on the edge of the bed, wringing her hands while she gathered her thoughts. She was amazed at the incredible restraint and patience that Ben had shown thus far. She had lied to him, defied him at every turn, shown her worst traits, and wounded his pride. She fully expected him to hand her over to Damian without reservation, happy to wash his hands of her. She didn't dare lie to him now, not when he had challenged Damian on her behalf, especially since he knew that Damian was in the right and likely to make trouble.

"Damian has been my guardian since my parents died when I was ten years old. I was promised to Damian's only son and heir since birth. Our two families were old friends. The terms of my father's will placed me and my inheritance in Damian's hands when they perished of a contagious fever. I suppose all would have gone as planned had fate not intervened. Life under the Fairfield roof was dull and uneventful during those early years.

"Then Grant Fairfield, who had always been a sickly lad, died, dashing Damian's hopes of obtaining an heir for his title and my fortune to enrich his coffers. Siring another heir on his wife's frail body seemed unlikely, and without an heir the title would fall to a distant branch of the family. Weakened from a long string of miscarriages, Eliza Fairfield obligingly died when she suffered yet another miscarriage. That's when Damian's thoughts turned to me and my inheritance. After having the use of it all those years, he couldn't afford to let my fortune slip through his hands."

"Bloody hell," Ben muttered ominously.

"At first I was merely a bothersome child Damian was expected to feed and clothe and keep out of harm's way until I was of an age to marry his son. But after Grant died he looked at me in a new light. I was no longer a shapeless child but a young girl blossoming into womanhood. The thought of gaining a young virgin and her fortune made Damian view me quite differently. Since I was young enough and strong enough to bear him several healthy children, Damian told me he had magnanimously decided to make me his wife.

"I was horrified. I didn't want to marry an old man. At fifteen I had dreams of finding a man who would love me for myself. Besides, I was aware of the deplorable way in which Damian treated his poor sickly wife, forcing himself on her again and again in an effort to beget an heir. I wanted no part of him."

"So you ran away," Ben said slowly.

"I only wish it could have been before the ceremony, but I was given no opportunity. It wasn't until Damian sent me upstairs to await him after the wedding guests departed that I was able to escape. I climbed out a second-floor window."

"Sweet Jesus, you could have been killed!"

"But I wasn't. And I never looked back. Not once. I found my way to the slums of London, where One-eyed Bertha found me and took me under her wing. She taught me to pick pockets and beg. Many a time she boxed my ears for not bringing home enough blunt, but I survived."

Tia's courage amazed Ben, and something inside the deepest chambers of his heart melted. "Did Bertha know you weren't a lad?"

"She knew, but she liked me. Nonetheless, sooner or later she would have given away my secret in exchange for the right amount of coin."

"She already has."

"What?"

"How do you think I knew where to find you? Why didn't you tell me this before?"

"I didn't want to involve you in my problems."

"You involved me the moment you chose me for your victim on that deserted street. I'd like to turn you over my knee and blister your bottom but I'd probably end up making love to you. Bloody hell, Tia, what am I going to do with you?"

"Nothing. Damian will take me back to London and force me to bear his heirs. Because of my inheritance he'll never divorce me. No matter what I've done, as long as I'm alive I'm the only woman capable of bearing him a legitimate heir. He'll punish me, but not in ways that show. I've already resigned myself to suffer his abuse. Perhaps I'll be fortunate and bear him a son right away and he'll leave me alone after that."

"Not bloody likely," Ben snarled. Nothing outside death could persuade him to leave Tia alone if she were his wife. "I'll kill him."

Tia blanched. She thought Ben perfectly capable of killing. But why would he bother? After all she'd done to him, she wouldn't blame him if he wanted nothing more to do with her. "Damian isn't worth going to jail or being hanged for."

"Are you saying you want to go with Fairfield?"

"I—no, I don't want to go with Damian but I have no choice. I've spent three years avoiding the man, suffered all kinds of hardships and deprivations. How can you even think I want to be a wife to Damian?"

A lone tear glistened at the end of a long golden lash. When it dropped off and rolled down Tia's cheek, Ben felt his restraint evaporate. "I won't let him take you, sweetheart."

"You can't stop him," Tia sniffed, trying desperately to contain the tears spilling from the corners of her eyes.

"I'll think of something. We have a day or two in which to find a solution. It will take at least that long for Fairfield to tell his story to the authorities and return. I could hide you in a nearby aborigine village where I have loyal friends who would guard you with their lives."

Tia shook her head. "It's useless, Ben. I know Damian; he'd find me no matter where you took me. You've too much to lose by helping me. Damian wasn't lying. He's rich and powerful and could destroy you. That's what I was afraid of from the beginning. Someday you'll find a woman who is free to accept your proposal. Marry her and be happy."

"Bloody hell, Tia, haven't I sworn never to propose again? I haven't changed my mind."

Tia smiled through a veil of tears. It was just like Ben to resist marriage even now when it was unlikely she'd ever be free to accept another proposal from him.

"Ben Penrod, yer an arrogant, stubborn arse. Yer brother aughta knock some sense in yer 'ead."

"And you, my bewitching little baggage, are a foul-mouthed brat who tempts me beyond redemption. I don't care if you're another man's wife. I don't care if the law says you belong to someone else. As far as I'm concerned, you belong to me. I've never stopped wanting you, not since the first time I saw your luscious little bottom upended over my knee. I made you mine, and you're damn well going to stay mine."

Chapter Twelve

Tia looked at Ben through an opulent curtain of golden lashes. "Why? Why should it matter?"

Ben's expression grew fierce. "Damned if I know. Except that just thinking about another man touching you drives me insane. Call it jealousy, call it possessiveness, call it obsession, but I've never felt this way before."

"Would you call it love?" Tia ventured softly.

"I—" Bewildered, he settled down beside her on the bed, searching her face with the same rapt regard in which he was searching his heart. "Love is an emotion I'm unfamiliar with. I know I want you. Not just today but tomorrow and all the days after that. Isn't that enough?"

A disturbingly poignant smile curved Tia's

lips. Ben's admission was the closest he'd ever come to telling her he cared for her. He was so mule stubborn the word love wasn't even in his vocabulary. "It could have been a beginning for us," she observed wistfully, "instead of the end. Oh, God, Ben, love me. Love me one last time before Damian returns to claim me."

"Loving you is easy; explaining my feelings is difficult. Besides, loving you gives me great pleasure." His words brought a fresh flow of tears coursing down her cheeks. "Don't cry, sweetheart, I'll think of something."

Emotion weakened her voice until it was a mere whisper. "I love you, Ben."

The quiet strength of her words shook Ben's emotions, leaving him too stunned to form a coherent reply. How could Tia love him after the underhanded way he had treated her? Perhaps she was just grateful to him for promising to help her escape from a deplorable situation. Though Lord knows he had no idea what he was going to do to extricate her from Damian's clutches. He offered no verbal reply to Tia's whispered declaration of love, preferring instead to show her how much he cared for her.

Tia tried not to show disappointment over Ben's failure to respond in words to her startling revelation. She should have known he had given all he had to give when he said he cared for her. Then her thoughts skidded to a halt as his mouth covered hers. His kiss was gentle at first, then turning hard and fierce at the thought of losing Tia to another man.

Her lips savored his, her nostrils were filled with his scent, and her ears heard only the harsh rasp of his breathing as his mouth rained teasing kisses on her lips, eyes, and nose. She was hardly aware that he was undressing her until she felt the cool air tease her bare skin.

His lips abandoned hers to glide over the slope of her bare shoulder, capturing the rosy peak of her breast. His hands ran the length of her exquisite body, seeking out each sensitive point, leaving her flesh trembling beneath his intimate touch. She closed her eyes and succumbed to the dizzying sensations that coursed through her, painfully aware that this final time with Ben would have to last forever.

He left her, rose to his knees, and stripped. Tia's breathing grew ragged as she watched his powerful body emerge from his clothes. He let her look her fill, until his body swelled and throbbed and the need to touch her grew so fierce he ached with it. Then he was atop her, pressing her into the soft surface of the mattress, surrounding her with the hard molten heat of him.

He covered one pertly aroused nipple with his mouth, laved the small sensitive bud with his tongue, nipped it with his teeth, while his hands gently caressed the flesh of her stomach, tangling in the downy golden hair at the apex of her thighs and parting the quivering moist flesh of her inner lips. Shivers of blistering heat jolted through her as his fingers thrust inside her and his thumb rotated the bud of desire he found there.

A sweet, delicious agony built inside her, making her writhe and arch against his hand. Suddenly she yearned to give him the same kind of pleasure he was giving her. Her hand drifted over his neck, savoring the smooth, hot texture of his skin, discovering the bones and sinews of his shoulders. Then her hands moved downward, brushing through the inky swatch of hair on his chest, over ropy muscles and ribs and narrow, taut waist. Boldly she pressed on and saw his eyes grow dark with pleasure as she grasped the rigid length of his shaft. When Ben gasped, her hand stilled.

"No, sweetheart, don't stop. I don't think I could bear it."

With renewed vigor her fingers explored the hardness of him, the incredible length, the power and fragility of the rigid pillar of strength. She heard his breath quicken and watched his eyes close with the intensity of sensation. Suddenly he removed her hand. "Enough! I was wrong. If you don't stop now I won't be able to bring you the pleasure you deserve."

Ben laced his fingers through hers, stretching her arms out on either side of her. His chest brushed her breasts as he leaned over her, his lips caressing each outstretched arm, from shoulder to elbow to the pulse beating erratically at the underside of her wrists. The hairs of his chest teased her swollen nipples, and the powerful length of his manhood felt like satin-covered steel brushing against her abdomen. His heat, his scent, engulfed her. Cupping her breasts, his mouth adored them. Crested waves of raw pleasure spiraled through Tia as she moved restlessly against him, tightening her thighs to contain the turbulent pressure building inside her. Her breasts ached. Her heart raced. She burned. Her blood felt hot and thick as sun-warmed honey.

"Open your legs, sweetheart."

His hands moved beneath her, cupping the soft mounds of her buttocks as he lifted and opened her. His eyes sparkled like diamonds as he lowered his head and tasted her. Tia jerked in response, her body vibrating in tune to his relentless probing. She couldn't imagine any other man but Ben doing this to her. She'd die before she'd allow Damian—Oh, God—Ben's fingers were stroking the tiny center of her need while his tongue lashed into her again and again.

Tia screamed. And screamed again.

Then Ben was inside her, filling her, intensifying her climax by thrusting into her as lightning bolts sizzled from his body to hers and back again. His muscles were tautly drawn, his face a mask of tortured pleasure as he drove into her, seeking the ultimate depths of intimacy.

"Tia," he groaned at the end, thrusting deep inside her and holding himself there while wild tremors quaked through his body. Tia felt his seed warm her insides and gasped with pleasure. Her arms clutched his back and her legs held him captive, reluctant to emerge from the ecstasy of their fierce mating. Deep in her heart she knew it was the last time she and Ben would ever be together like this, and she wanted it to last as long as possible.

Ben couldn't believe what he had just experienced with Tia. It seemed unbelievable that Ben Penrod, connoisseur of women, jaded rake, experienced lover, had just been reduced to a quivering mass of flesh and bone by a young, inexperienced girl barely out of the schoolroom. Tia had him in such a state of heightened awareness that her mere touch turned him to cinder and one smoldering look from her incredible blue-green eyes destroyed his control. What did one call that deeply intense emotional response he experienced with Tia? he wondered. If it was love he wasn't certain he'd survive that foreign emotion.

"Hold me, Ben," Tia murmured as Ben eased out of her and settled down beside her. Her eyes were wide and frightened. The appalling thought of leaving Ben was like a knife piercing her heart.

Dragging her into his arms, Ben kissed away her tears, feeling nearly as bereft as she did. The minutes and hours were slipping away too fast; he had yet to find a solution to Tia's dilemma and was assailed by the fearful suspicion that no solution existed.

In lieu of words, they made love again, this time more gently, without the wild tempest of need that had driven them the first time. They slept, awoke near dawn, and made love again. There was no need to communicate verbally. What could they say that hadn't already been said? Damian would return to claim Tia, and there was nothing Ben could do about it except let her go. Tia knew it, Ben knew it, but neither accepted it.

Damian did not return the following day. The tension was unbearable as Ben and Tia awaited the terrible separation that neither of them wanted. Tia never mentioned love again, deeming it hopeless. She would have rejoiced to learn that although Ben had failed to utter the words, his heart had opened to that emotion he had fought so long. Most disheartening was the knowledge that hours of scheming and careful thought had uncovered no way to keep Damian from claiming Tia. They went to bed that night and made love with almost frantic fervor, knowing that when they awoke the next day Damian was sure to return to Penrod station. Both knew it, neither mentioned it.

It was mid-afternoon when Damian arrived. He wasn't alone. Two constables accompanied him. Ben knew both of them. One was a man named Riker and the other Clemons.

"I told you I'd return, Penrod," Damian sneered as he shoved Ben aside and stormed into the house. "This time I brought the law. Where is she? Where's my wife?"

Tia waited in the parlor, unwilling to face her husband immediately. When she heard her name spoken she cringed inwardly and waited for Ben to bring Damian to her. She didn't have long to wait. Damian charged into the room without invitation, both constables and Ben hard on his heels. Her knees shaking, Tia turned to face him squarely.

"So there you are," Damian blasted. "You won't escape me this time, I've brought the law to back me up."

Constable Riker gazed at Tia, his face suffused with pity. "Is this man your husband, ma'am? He has produced a marriage license, but I'd like to hear what you have to say before passing judgment."

Panic-stricken, Tia looked at Ben imploringly. The expression on his face was one of such abject misery that Tia knew immediately her plea for help was futile. She was Damian's wife and according to English law she belonged to him.

"Yes," Tia said with quiet dignity. "Much to my regret, Damian Fairfield is my husband."

Damian's small eyes narrowed menacingly as he glared at Tia. "Are you ready to leave?"

"No, I'll never be ready."

"For God's sake, Fairfield, can't you see Tia wants nothing to do with you?" Ben cried, clenching his fists until his nails drew blood on his palms.

"It makes no difference what Tia wants. The only way to gain the heirs I need is to force Tia to perform her wifely duties. There isn't a man alive that doesn't want heirs, nor a law that will deny me my right."

"Can't you do anything?" Ben appealed to the constables. "The man will abuse her. I know his type, they take pleasure inflicting pain on those weaker than themselves."

"Don't listen to him," Damian spat. "He's used my wife shamelessly. The woman is a whore, but I've decided to forgive her and take her back to England with me. Who could blame me if I keep her confined in order to put an end to her sluttish behavior? Once she's borne several of my children she'll settle down."

Tia shuddered.

Neither constable believed the terrible things Damian said about Tia—she looked so young and innocent—but she *was* in another man's home, posing as his wife, and the law *was* on the side of the wronged husband.

"Lord Fairfield has sufficient proof that this woman—Lady Fairfield—is his wife. It's his right to take her wherever he pleases," Riker advised. His companion nodded agreement. "We are here to see that you don't interfere with the law, Mr. Penrod, not to pass judgment. We have great respect for your family and suggest you don't do anything that will cause them embarrassment."

"Ben—Mr. Penrod—won't cause trouble," Tia said, sending Ben a warning glance "I'm ready to leave with Damian. I'll get my belongings."

"Hurry," Damian called to her departing back. "I've purchased passage aboard the *Southern Star* for our return to England and the captain has graciously given permission for us to occupy the cabin until we sail three days hence."

The rigid line of Tia's back and the proud tilt of her head gave little indication of the anguish she was suffering. But Ben knew. Her jerky movements, her uneven steps, her shallow breathing, gave every indication of her unwillingness to become Damian's wife, her terror of being subjected to his abuse, her horror of bearing his children. And there wasn't one damn thing he could do about it.

Tia was back almost instantly, carrying only a small case with some personal belongings and wearing a warm cloak. Summer had changed into fall and the air was chill with the promise of winter.

"Is that all you have?" Damian asked sharply. Tia merely shrugged. "No matter, I'll buy whatever else you need. Obviously Penrod was a stingy lover." He grasped her arm and pulled her roughly toward the door. Tia stumbled and nearly fell.

"See here, Fairfield, there's no need for roughness," Ben charged. Stormclouds gathered in his face, and had Damian known Ben better he would have had the good sense to heed the warning.

"Tia is no longer your affair."

"Until you leave my property, everything that takes place on it is my affair."

"There is no need to mistreat the lady, Lord Fairfield," Constable Riker said, trying to diffuse a potentially explosive situation. He had known the Penrods for several years, and every one of them was hotheaded to a fault. Including Dare's wife, fiery, flame-haired Casey.

Astutely Damian realized that using unnecessary force with Tia was causing the constables to view him in an unfavorable light and immediately changed his attitude. He could afford to be generous and forgiving before others, for soon he'd have Tia to himself and could punish her to his heart's content for making a fool of him on their wedding day. Searching for her over the years had cost him a small fortune; she'd experience soon enough the extent of his anger. Tia would be a proper wife to him if he had to beat her into submission daily. Who would have thought the docile child bride he had taken would turn out to be a stubborn, willful chit with more courage than brains?

"I wouldn't think of doing my wife bodily harm," Damian said, smiling ingratiatingly. "I'm not a violent man."

Ben groaned, wanting to tear the bloated little bastard limb from limb. The thought of him lay-ing fat, sweaty hands on Tia's smooth, unblemished flesh made him break out in cold sweat. Tia may have resigned herself to the fact that she belonged to Fairfield, but he hadn't. Somehow, some way, he'd release Tia from the insufferable worm who had married her when she was too young to protest.

"Don't worry, Tia, I'll kill the bastard if he hurts you." Grief and helpless fury hung heavy in his voice.

Tia turned once and looked at him, memorizing for all time the bronze hue of his sun-kissed skin, the way his black hair clung boyishly to the back of his neck, his gray eyes with their unique silver glow. Then Damian was lifting her into the dray while the constables climbed in beside her. Neither man liked what they were doing, but both had sworn to uphold the law.

His face set in harsh lines, Ben watched Tia ride out of sight and out of his life. Letting her go was the most difficult thing he'd ever done. And it hurt. Knowing it was forever nearly killed him. Nothing would ever be the same again. How could he stand idly by and let Tia be taken away from him? He raised his head, opened his mouth, and let loose a hoarse cry that gave vent to all the bitter frustration he felt at being unable to help Tia when she needed him most. *No, by God,* he flung out, shaking his fist to emphasize his words. *No one was going to take Tia from him!*

An hour later Ben burst into Dare's house

with the fury of a fierce summer storm.

"What in the hell is this all about, Ben?" Dare asked when Ben located him in one of the outbuildings. Casey was hard on his heels, having followed Ben when he burst into the house looking for Dare.

"She's gone, Dare. That slimy bastard came and got her. He's taking her back to England."

"Who's gone? What are you babbling about?"

"I think he's talking about Tia," Casey offered, trying to make sense out of Ben's agitated words. She had never seen Ben like this before. He was utterly devastated. His eyes were bleak, his face a mask of grief and disbelief.

"Come into the house, Ben, where we can discuss this intelligently."

"There's no time," Ben lamented. "I don't even know why I'm here, except maybe to ask the advice of my big brother. And even then I don't know if I'll follow it. Dammit, Dare, I'm desperate. I can't let him take Tia, yet there isn't a damn thing I can do about it."

"Who in the hell are you talking about?" Dare asked, exasperated. "It would help if you told me who took Tia away and why."

"Her husband," Ben said, choking on the word. "Lord Damian Fairfield."

"Bloody hell!" Dare looked visibly shaken. "You took a married woman away from her husband? Why did you tell me you proposed to Tia when you knew all along marriage was impossible?"

Casey's green eyes grew wide with distress, but she held her tongue, waiting for Ben to explain.

"I didn't know," Ben insisted. "Not until Damian Fairfield showed up on my doorstep. For some reason Tia kept that little gem of information from me. She ran away from her husband on their wedding day."

"This sounds like a long story, Ben. I suggest we go back to the house before you begin to tell it. Besides, the walk will allow you time to cool off."

"I don't want to cool off," Ben persisted. "I want to take Tia away from that bastard. She told me the whole story, Dare, and I don't want that swine touching her." Nevertheless, he allowed Dare to turn him toward the house.

Once inside they sought Dare's den where they could speak in private. "Very well, Ben, let's hear it," Dare said when they were all seated.

Ben launched into a tale so incredible that Casey found it difficult to believe. Yet she didn't doubt Ben's veracity nor Tia's version of her self-serving husband. "Tia is the bravest woman I know," she said, meaning every word. "I don't know if I'd have the courage to live like she did."

Dare sent her a glance so intimate and filled with love that Ben turned away. "Bravery is a common thread that binds all the women loved by Penrod men. Of course," he said somewhat sternly as he turned his gaze on Ben, "I'm assuming that Ben loves Tia." It was more of a question

256

than a statement and demanded an answer.

Ben frowned, turning thoughtful. "I'm not certain I know what love feels like, but I sure as hell know how much it hurts to lose someone you care about."

"That's the poorest admission of love I've ever heard," chided Casey.

"I've never felt like this about any other woman," Ben admitted solemnly. "Will that do?"

Casey smiled. " 'Tis love, Ben, you're just too damn stubborn to admit it."

"Now that Ben's feelings have been fully explored, let's get down to the facts," Dare said. Practical and dangerous, Dare was the brother who had faced many enemies during his lifetime and emerged victorious. He had won Casey against all odds and knew how Ben felt about losing the woman he loved. "The law is with Lord Fairfield. He has every right to claim his wife. Most people will consider him a saint and praise his generosity for forgiving his wife her indiscretions."

"The man is old enough to be her father. He's brutal and sadistic. He'll beat Tia into submission." The lines of Ben's face deepened, his mouth hardened into a thin white line, and his gray eyes turned so cold that Casey shivered. Never had she seen Ben so determined. His resemblance to Dare at that moment was uncanny.

"He's Tia's husband," Dare reminded him. "Are you certain Tia wishes to be rescued from her legal husband? Obviously he's a rich man who can offer her much."

"Tia hates Fairfield. He'll make her life a living hell. I'll kill him if he lays a hand on her," Ben threatened ominously.

Dare sighed. He had felt the same way when Lieutenant Potter took Casey. "What are you going to do?"

"I'm going to Sydney before the *Southern Star* sails and bring Tia back to Penrod station."

"I don't think that's wise," Dare advised. It's what he would do in the same circumstances, but his position as the older and wiser brother persuaded him to offer a word of warning to his hotheaded sibling. "You could end up behind bars—or worse, depending on Fairfield's mood. Legally he's in the right, you know."

"I'll take Tia to Bathurst," Ben persevered. "Or south. Settlements are springing up all over Australia. New territory is being opened and Tia and I could quietly disappear."

"And leave Penrod station?"

Ben hesitated. Never did he think anything would be more important to him than Penrod station. "We'll be able to return once Fairfield leaves Australia. He won't remain here forever; he's too fond of his luxuries."

"Perhaps," Dare allowed, unconvinced.

"I'm going to Sydney, Dare."

"What can I do to help?"

"Nothing. I guess I just wanted someone to talk to."

"Will you wait till morning?" Casey asked.

"No, I'm leaving immediately. No telling what that bastard is liable to do to Tia once he gets her alone."

"Be careful, Ben," Casey cautioned.

Ben hugged her, then turned to his brother. They embraced warmly. "Take care of Penrod station if—if I'm unable to return for any reason."

"Don't worry, brother," Dare assured him, "Penrod station won't suffer in your absence no matter how long you're away. But please don't do anything rash. Without you Tia has no hope of obtaining her freedom."

Tia spoke little during the ride to Sydney. Her mind was in turmoil, her thoughts dark and forbidding. She had pretended compliance with Damian's wishes for Ben's sake. She knew that if she offered resistance Ben would disregard danger to himself and fly to her aid. Not only was he likely to do something reckless and dangerous, but he could end up in jail for foolishly trying to defend her. But Tia had no intention of allowing Damian to take her back to England. And she'd kill either herself or him before she'd allow him to bed her. Bearing his child was so repugnant that just thinking about it made her skin crawl.

Though the constables tried to be friendly, Tia preferred not to make small talk, and when it became obvious that she wished to remain silent, they gave up trying to draw her into conversation. Tia had plans to make. Plans that included escaping Damian and remaining hidden until he returned to England. She knew he wouldn't keep looking for her forever, for Australia wasn't a place Damian would be happy in for any length of time. Sooner or later he would grow tired of so crude a settlement and get himself back to London. Without her, she hoped.

It was dark when they dropped the constables off and continued on to Sydney Cove. The *Southern Star* was the only English ship in the harbor.

"So, Tia, we're finally alone," Damian sneered, jumping to the ground and pulling Tia after him. "Now you'll pay for those long years of anguish you caused me. I could already have my heir if you had been a dutiful wife instead of a willful little whore."

"I'm not a whore," Tia denied defiantly.

"What do you call what you did with that dirty sheep farmer?"

"I love Ben. And he's not a dirty sheep farmer. He's more man than you'll ever be."

"You think so? I'm sure you'll find I'm man enough to plant my seed inside you, even though the field has been thoroughly plowed before I arrived."

Curving an arm around her narrow waist, he dragged her up the gangplank. No one but the watch was on hand to greet them, and if he noted Tia's obvious reluctance he said nothing.

Damian led her straightaway to their cabin, one of the largest set aside for passengers. If the best was available, Damian demanded it, Tia thought sullenly. He opened the door and flung her inside with such force that she stumbled against the desk, bruising her hip. Damian slammed and locked the door behind him, pocketing the key. He smiled with such malice that Tia shuddered, fearing that he intended to begin her punishment immediately.

"I'll scream," Tia cried, backing away.

"The watch has been amply compensated to turn a deaf ear. And since the crew are ashore and no other passengers have boarded yet, your cries will only earn severe punishment."

His lip twisted cruelly as he slowly began unbuttoning his jacket. He tore it off and flung it aside.

"What are you going to do?"

"Consummate our marriage, my dear. It's time, don't you think? All you need do is open your legs and pretend you're playing whore to Ben Penrod. Of course I may have to beat you in order to work myself up to my best performance." He pulled his belt from his pants. "If we're fortunate, my seed will produce fruit immediately."

Desperate, Tia said the only thing she could think of that could make him change his mind. "I might already be carrying Ben's child! Do you want another man's bastard inheriting your title and wealth?"

Damian grew livid and his normally ruddy coloring changed to a deep mottled red. "You faithless little slut!" Drawing back, he backhanded her, all his anger and frustration loosed in the strength of his vicious blow. The bitter taste of blood flooded Tia's mouth as she flew backward, hitting the bulkhead with a resounding smack. Then she crumbled to the floor, glaring up at Damian through glazed eyes.

"Go ahead, beat me," Tia dared, "it won't change a thing. I'll still hate you and I still might be carrying Ben's child."

Damian took a menacing step toward her, then thought better of it. Though he itched to inflict severe punishment, he didn't want to do Tia serious harm until she had borne him a son. In contrast to his dead wife, she was strong and healthy and he needed to keep her that way until she had served her purpose. There were other ways to inflict punishment without adversely affecting her ability to conceive. He turned abruptly, his face a mask of fury.

"You'll live to regret your affront to my good name and my good graces. You've whored for the last time. You'll remain healthy only so long as you keep producing my children. But once you've lost that ability you can expect to suffer severely for your sins."

"Bedding you will be punishment enough," Tia shot back recklessly.

"I'll wait until you have definite proof that you are or are not carrying a bastard inside your soft belly. If you are, we'll get rid of it so I can start sowing my own seed. If you're not increasing now, you can expect to be very soon."

Then he calmly unlocked the door and exited the cabin, careful to secure the latch behind him.

After Damian left, Tia stared at the closed door with something akin to horror. She had escaped Damian this time but realized that sooner or later she'd be made to pay for all the damage she'd done to his ego and his purse. She prayed she wasn't carrying Ben's child, for Damian would find a way to rid her of it and that would be murder. She'd rather die herself than kill Ben's child. Picking herself up off the deck, she gingerly explored her bruised cheek. It was swollen and tender, and she imagined it was already turning black and blue. She was right. Not only was her cheek discolored but her eye was beginning to blacken.

She perched on the narrow bunk, afraid to give in to sleep, fearing that Damian would return and do Lord knows what to her. Toward dawn, exhaustion overtook her and she slumped over, finally succumbing to her body's demand for rest. She awoke the following morning feeling as if she hadn't slept at all. Fortunately, Damian hadn't returned.

Tia gazed around the small cabin, suddenly noticing Damian's trunk sitting in the corner. Desperation drove her as she quickly threw open the lid, having no clear idea what she was looking for. Anything—anything at all to help her escape. At first she found nothing. But then she happened to notice a small pouch lying beneath a layer of clothing. She gasped with pleasure when she found it contained a small hoard of gold coins. She wasn't certain how, but perhaps it would aid her in her escape. She quickly stuffed the pouch in her bodice and snapped shut the lid of the trunk. She had just returned to the bunk when the key rattled in the door and the panel flew open.

Tia leaped to her feet, girding herself to do battle with Damian, and came face to face with a lad who was nearly as shocked to see her as she was to see him.

"Yer pardon, m'lady, I thought the cabin was empty," the boy apologized sheepishly. "I come ta make certain all is in order before the passengers arrive. 'Tis part of me job."

"Who are you? How did you get in?"

"Me name is Tom, I'm the cabin boy. The key was in the lock so I let meself in." Suddenly he realized what that meant and stared goggled-eyed at Tia. "Were ye locked in, m'lady?" His eyes grew even wider when he noticed Tia's bruised and swollen face. "Blimey, m'lady, who did that to ye?"

Tia's hand flew to her face, realizing how she must look. Shame nearly made her explain her injury with a deliberate lie, but a spark of sympathy in the lad's eyes convinced her that telling the truth was a wiser choice. "My husband struck me."

"The bleedin' bully!" The lad had his own opinion of a man who would strike a defenseless woman and didn't mind voicing it. Even as young as he was, he'd seen and experienced brutality at the hands of ruthless men and knew exactly how it felt. "Why did yer 'usband lock ya in yer cabin?"

"It's a long story," Tia said. Her mind worked furiously, eagerly seizing the opportunity she had been praying for. "I need help, will you help me?"

The boy scratched his thatch of rust-colored hair and screwed up his face until he looked like a wizened monkey. "Don't know if I can, m'lady. What would ye 'ave me do?"

"Help me escape. My husband is brutal. I can take the beatings, but . . ." She let the sentence dangle, instilling the boy with visions of all the terrible ways a brutish man could hurt a delicate woman. Still, she was asking him to place his own life in danger.

"I—don't know, m'lady." His slight hesitation gave Tia cause for hope.

Grateful for having had the foresight to search Damian's trunk, Tia reached in her bodice and removed the small pouch she had secreted there. Extracting a shiny gold coin and holding it up before the lad, she hoped it would pave her way to freedom. When the boy's eyes grew as large as saucers, she knew she had won him over.

"This is yours if you help me. And I'll add

265

another to it if I leave the ship without being discovered."

"Blimey!" Tom's fear dissolved when he saw the size of Tia's generosity. Two gold coins would keep him and his mother and young sister in food and shelter for several years. And he wouldn't have to go to sea again, that was the best part. He could remain home and see to their safety. He'd have to serve aboard a ship ten years to earn the equivalent of two gold coins. "How can I 'elp ye?"

"My husband is likely to return at any moment, so it's imperative that I leave immediately. But I'll need a set of boy's clothing. Do you have an extra set?"

"Aye. They're worn but clean. Should I bring 'em to ye?"

"Yes, please hurry."

The lad scooted off, returning within minutes carrying a pair of gray canvas pants, a white shirt baggy enough to conceal her breasts, and a heavy jacket. He even offered her a pair of leather boots with worn heels and scuffed toes and a woolen cap that looked as if it would completely cover her head. When Tia reached for them, he held out his hand, just in case she'd decided to withhold his reward. Tia dropped one gold coin in his outstretched palm.

"Wait outside the door while I change," she said, eager to be gone before Damian returned.

It took scant minutes to don Tom's clothing. The last thing Tia did was pull the wool cap down as far as it would go, jamming it over her forehead until her eyebrows all but disappeared. Then she joined Tom in the companionway. "Check the deck," she instructed as Tom scrambled up the ladder.

He poked his head out, looked around, and quickly withdrew. "All's clear. The watch is lookin' toward the bow so ye'll 'ave no trouble gettin' past 'im. He won't bother with ye anyways, he'll think yer me goin' ashore on an errand fer the cap'n. Good luck, m'lady."

Tia smiled, then gave him not just the second promised gold coin but added a third. "Blimey!" Tom's eyes bugged out, but before he found his tongue to thank her properly, Tia scooted up the ladder and ambled nonchalantly toward the gangplank, remembering to strut like a young lad. By now she was good at it, having posed many years as a half-grown boy. But she wasn't out of the woods yet. Anything could happen before she left the ship.

But fortune smiled on Tia. No one challenged her. She kept her head down and her step lively as she scooted down the gangplank and plunged into the crowd milling about the dock.

Chapter Thirteen

Her chin tucked against her chest, her eyes lowered, Tia maintained a brisk pace as she walked toward town. Drawing attention to herself was the last thing she wanted to do. She knew she had to disappear quietly and remain hidden until Damian gave up his search for her. He was a man who held a grudge but not one given to denying himself the pleasures of life. And Australia certainly didn't offer much pleasure for a sophisticated man like Damian Fairfield. She had to trust in providence to grant her wish that Damian would return to England after a few weeks of fruitless searching. But disappearing wasn't as easy as it sounded, Tia thought glumly.

Her first inclination was to return to Parramatta and seek Ben's protection. But she was astute enough to realize that Ben could offer scant protection against a law that favored Damian. So she reluctantly abandoned that line of thought and concentrated on her other options—which were blessed few. Then her thoughts led her to something Ben had told her. About bushrangers. They lived in the bush and were virtually impossible to locate and rout. They were escaped convicts who had chosen a life of crime over serving out their sentence in servitude. They engaged in daring bailups, robbing unsuspecting travelers as they journeyed between cities. If they could hide for years in the bush, living off the land, then she could certainly survive for a few short weeks.

Her mind made up, Tia realized there were certain things she needed to purchase for survival. Thank God she'd had the foresight to lift Damian's coins. She gulped back a giggle, imagining how Damian would rant and rave when he found out he'd been robbed of his small hoard of gold. Losing his blunt would rile him nearly as much as her disappearance.

Lifting her head a fraction, Tia noted that she had entered a street containing several stores where goods were sold. People hurried by, showing no interest in the solitary lad as they went about their own business. The day was cold and clear, and the promise of a warm hearth once their tasks were completed hastened their steps. She chose a store at random,

silently praying that the shopkeeper wouldn't
grow inquisitive when she produced a gold coin
to pay for her purchases. Glancing nervously
over her shoulder, she entered the shop. And
collided head on with a customer just leaving.
His arms were full of bundles which scattered
in every direction.

"Watch where you're going, you little guttersnipe!" His face livid, he whirled and cuffed
Tia's ears.

Her ears ringing, Tia staggered, then froze
when she lifted her eyes to the man. What rotten luck! Of all the people in Sydney, why did
she have to bump into Damian? "Beggin' yer
pardon, yer worship," Tia whined obsequiously, disguising her voice and using the cock-
ney twang she had developed years earlier. She
ducked, bent to retrieve Damian's packages,
placed them in his arms and stepped aside to
allow him to pass.

Disdaining an answer, Damian brushed by,
carefully avoiding contact with any part of the
urchin. He'd come across many such on the
streets of London and either kicked them aside
or called the constable like a good citizen to
take the miscreants off the streets. Besides, he
had other things to think about. Keeping his
sluttish wife in line was one of them. Originally
he had decided not to beat Tia, but the longer he
thought about how she had willingly lain with
a sheep farmer after years of avoiding the bed
of her legal husband, the angrier he became.

When he returned to the ship he intended to administer a beating she'd remember the rest of her life. A beating that would discourage further disobedience. By the time their ship reached England, she would be fully recovered from her beating and he would know whether or not she was carrying a bastard. If she wasn't, he'd see that she would soon be pregnant with his child.

Tremors shook Tia's slender form as she watched Damian stride briskly down the street. When he reached the ship he'd learn that she had fled once again. She didn't have much time. Fortunately, it would take Damian at least a full day to trace her steps and he wouldn't expect her to disappear into the dangerous bush. He'd expect her to return to Penrod station, and that was exactly why she couldn't.

"Can I help you, son?"

Tia started violently. The shopkeeper, having served his previous customer, now turned his attention to Tia. "Er—aye, sir, I'm on an errand fer me cap'n." It sounded logical and the best excuse she could think of for having a gold coin in her possession.

"Your captain?"

"I'm off the *Southern Star*, sir."

"A mite young, aren't you?"

"No sir, not fer a cabin boy, I ain't."

"What is it you need, lad?"

Looking around, Tia chose a wicked-looking knife in a sheath that strapped around the waist,

271

a small pistol and a box of shells, some boys' underwear, socks, comb, brush, soap, matches, and blanket. When she added some foodstuffs, the shopkeeper looked at her curiously.

"What in hell does a ship's captain want with food?"

"Oh, the food ain't fer the cap'n, sir." Tia grinned engagingly. " 'Tis fer me. Ship's fare gets mighty borin'. The cap'n is right fond of me and gave me permission ta buy what I wanted." To reinforce her words she placed a generous amount of peppermint candy on the growing pile of supplies on the counter. But when she added a pot and fry pan to her purchases, the shopkeeper became even more suspicious.

"Aren't there any cooking utensils aboard the *Southern Star*?"

"Those are fer me mum, sir. I promised I'd bring her back somethin' from Australia. And she needs pots."

"Seems to me you could find something more appropriate for your mother. Something she'd treasure. A pot hardly seems the type of gift . . ."

"Me mum will be pleased," Tia insisted stubbornly.

The shopkeeper scratched his balding head and shrugged. "Oh, well, if that's what you want." He began totaling the cost. When he finished, Tia handed him one gold coin. "Gold is it?" He bit down on the shiny surface, expressed satisfaction, and counted out Tia's change. Then he placed all her purchases in a swag. Tia nodded, shouldered the bag, and held her breath as she left the store, remembering to add a boyish swagger to her step. The storekeeper was already suspicious and she knew he was debating whether or not to call the authorities to verify her story about being from the *Southern Star*.

Instead of going west toward Parramatta, she struck out toward the south, unaware that the storekeeper stood in the doorway, watching her until she could no longer be seen.

Damian's step was light as he boarded the *Southern Star*. After locking Tia in his cabin he had spent the night in the new hotel with a very accommodating young whore. Only recently transported to the penal colony, she was still relatively clean and treated him like a virile man, not like a lecherous old fool the way his wife did. The woman had so inflated his ego that he was now filled with himself and eager to relate to Tia every lurid detail of his invigorating night with a whore. Afterwards he would beat her until she pleaded for mercy, until she begged him to plant a child in her belly.

The key was still in the lock when Damian reached the cabin in which he had left Tia. His face was drawn into a sneer when he flung open the door. The sneer quickly turned to a look of utter shock when he realized the cabin was empty, then changed to stark rage.

"No!" he screamed, his face red with fury.

"Not again. I'll kill the bitch when I find her. Then I'll marry someone appreciative of me, someone eager to bear my children." Whirling on his heel, he went in search of the captain.

"I'm sorry, Lord Fairfield, I have no idea what could have happened to your wife," Captain Waring said. Damian deliberately failed to mention that he had locked Tia inside the cabin. "Barker was on watch earlier today, perhaps you should question him. Your wife may have gone ashore to purchase a few incidentals for the voyage, you know how women are."

"Indeed I do," Damian said bitterly.

Seaman Barker had seen nothing, except Tom the cabin boy going ashore earlier that day. And he wouldn't have noticed that much if he hadn't caught a fleeting glimpse of him walking down the gangplank. And then all he saw was his narrow back as he disappeared into the crowd milling about the harbor.

Damian's attention sharpened. "The cabin boy, you say?"

"Aye, sir, young Tom."

"How old is he?"

"I ain't sure, twelve, fourteen, mayhap."

Damian turned sharply, a preposterous idea beginning to form in his mind. An idea that became more conceivable the longer he thought about it.

Damian found Tom in the galley, helping the grizzled cook stow supplies. The first thing Damian noticed was that Tom and Tia were both about the same height with slender builds. The second was the distinct feeling that he had seen someone recently dressed in clothing nearly identical to what young Tom wore. But he discounted that, realizing that Tom wore the same kind of duds as half the lads in New South Wales.

Tom saw Damian standing behind him and blanched. He knew it was Lord Fairfield because he had seen the man speaking with Captain Waring on the day his lordship booked passage.

"Do you know why I'm here?" Damian asked, scowling fiercely at Tom.

"N—naw, sir, should I?"

"Did you let my wife out of her locked cabin?"

Aware that his life depended on his agile mind, Tom scratched his head and looked somewhat addled. "She was locked in 'er cabin?"

"That's what I said. For her own protection, you understand."

"No one would have hurt 'er aboard Cap'n Waring's ship," Tom countered indignantly.

"That's besides the point." Damian was quickly losing patience with Tom's deliberate avoidance of the subject. "Did you or didn't you let Lady Fairfield out of her cabin?"

"Mayhap," Tom admitted sullenly. "But I swear I didn't know anyone was inside the cabin when I unlocked it."

"You meddling little bastard!" Before Tom

could sidestep the blow, Damian backhanded him, sending him flying across the deck.

"'Ere now, you had no cause ta do that," cook said, helping Tom gain his feet. Everyone aboard the *Southern Star* liked young Tom, including the captain.

"The little bugger interfered with something between me and my wife. I'll kill the bloody brat." He grasped Tom's shirtfront, shaking him until his teeth rattled. "Where did she go?" Suddenly another thought struck Damian. "Did you go ashore earlier today?" Was it Tia he had bumped into as he came out of the store?

"Naw, Tom ain't been ashore in two days," cook threw in, thinking to help Tom's cause. He had no idea he was causing more damage than good. "He's been in the galley helpin' me."

"So," Damian accused, "you gave my wife a set of your clothes and that's how she sneaked ashore without being seen."

"I didn't give 'er nothin'," Tom denied. It was the truth. Lady Fairfield had paid handsomely for his old clothing, he had given nothing away for free.

"How did she get your clothes?"

"I don't know." He shrugged expansively. "Didn't ye hear cook just say I was helpin' him these last two days? Besides, I ain't sure me duds are missin'."

Enraged, Damian began shaking Tom again, but this time cook intervened. "If ya got somethin' against Tom, m'lord, let the cap'n decide the punishment. It's his ship and he's mighty fond of young Tom."

"Never mind," Damian grit out, sliding Tom a quelling look. "I know the brat is lying. If I'm not mistaken I saw my wife in town wearing Tom's clothing—or clothing nearly like Tom's. I know of nowhere else she could get such an outfit on short notice. Kindly tell the captain that if I'm not back before the ship sails to put my trunks off and I'll collect them later. I won't be leaving until I've located my wayward wife—or her body," he added meaningfully.

Damian searched the town thoroughly. He hired two thugs and spent several fruitless hours asking questions. Unfortunately, he was unable to question the shopkeeper who owned the shop where he had bumped into the young "lad" he suspected now was Tia. The man had just left for Bathurst to deliver a load of supplies and wouldn't be back for several days. Damian had hit a dead end. Only then did he realize he had missed the obvious. There was only one place Tia would go. Back to her lover. Back to Penrod station. Damian left immediately, bringing his two thugs with him.

As luck would have it, Ben's trip to Sydney had been delayed. He had left as planned, but after traveling no more than a third of the way, his horse stepped in a wombat hole and broke his leg. Ben realized he had been insane to attempt this trip at night and suffered a pang of guilt as he put a pistol to the poor animal's head and put him out of his misery. He had no choice but to return to Penrod station for a new mount. It took the remaining hours of the night and part of the following morning to reach his home on foot. By then he was dead tired, and sheer exhaustion forced him to seek his bed for a few hours of rest.

Ben awoke at midday, refreshed and ready to take on Lord Fairfield and the whole world, if need be. After eating a hasty meal, he hurried out the door to the stable. Three riders were entering the yard. Hoping it had something to do with Tia, he waited for them to approach. He started violently when he recognized Fairfield, accompanied by two men who looked like hirelings. Tia was not with them, and icy fingers danced along Ben's spine.

Fairfield reined in alongside Ben and leaped from his mount with the vigor of a much younger man. Tracking down and punishing Tia had given him renewed purpose in life. Where once he was content to beat her and force his children on her, he now sought a more permanent type of punishment. There wasn't a court in the land that would convict him of slaying his unfaithful wife.

"Where is she, Penrod?"

Ben's blood ran cold. "Are you referring to Tia? If *you* don't know where she is, how in the hell do you expect me to? She left with you, remember?"

"Of course I'm talking about Tia. Where are you hiding her?"

"Isn't she with you?"

"You know she isn't. I locked her in our cabin aboard the *Southern Star* and the cabin boy let her out."

"Did you hurt her?"

"I did nothing to her she didn't ask for," Damian said cryptically. "If you don't produce her immediately, I'll bring the law back. Only this time I'll insist on your incarceration."

"Damn you, Fairfield! I have no idea where Tia is. I assumed she was with you. I was just now leaving for Sydney to try to convince you to let her go. She doesn't love you. She doesn't want to be your wife. Let her be. Tell everyone in England she's dead and marry someone who will be more than happy to give you children for what you can offer in return."

"This has gone on so long it's now a matter of principle. I won't allow the little bitch to get the best of me. Will you hand her over peaceably or must I order my men to use force? I assure you that when I find her it won't be pleasant."

"I'm telling the truth. Tia isn't at Penrod station. She's not stupid, Fairfield. She knows this is the first place you'd look. If Tia has left you, you'll have to look elsewhere. I thank God she got away before the *Southern Star* sailed and it was too late."

"I don't believe you," Damian sneered.

"You're welcome to search," Ben invited. He knew the man wouldn't be satisfied until he had poked into every nook and cranny of Penrod station.

Damian nodded to his two companions, who dismounted and sidled past Ben into the house. "I think I'll join them," Damian said, flashing Ben an impudent grin. He fully expected to find Tia cowering in one of the bedrooms.

Damian and his hirelings searched the house thoroughly from corner to corner, from room to room, every place imaginable where a person might hide. With angry reluctance Damian finally admitted that Tia was not to be found on Penrod station.

"If Tia does come here, I expect you to bring her to me," Damian flung over his shoulder as he mounted and prepared to ride away. "I'll be staying in Sydney at the hotel."

"Like hell!" Ben shouted back. "You'll never get your hands on Tia if I have anything to say about it."

His words were lost to the wind as the three men spurred their mounts. The tattoo of hooves pounding against the dry ground reverberated in Ben's head, the words a litany of fear and hope. *Tia's gone, Tia's gone.* It echoed and reechoed through the chambers of his brain. The terrible fear of all the unspeakable things a woman alone in a penal colony could encounter overshadowed the surge of hope he'd felt when he learned she had escaped from Damian.

Tia's escape altered Ben's immediate plans to go to Sydney. It occurred to him that Tia had nowhere to go and would likely turn up at Penrod station once Fairfield had come and gone. She might even be nearby watching, waiting for the opportune time. Once she presented herself, he'd take her to Bathurst, or anywhere, as long as it was as far away from Damian Fairfield as they could get.

Tia was amazed at how simple it was to merely walk away from Sydney. If keeping herself hidden from Damian proved as easy, she'd have no worries. She had secreted herself as deep into the bush as she dare go without becoming hopelessly lost and had spent the past few days trying to keep warm beside her meager fire and scrounging for food.

Having fended for herself in the slums of London, she had the courage to survive on her own and she seldom went hungry. She used her staples sparingly, killed a few unsuspecting small animals, and once almost succeeded in snaring a wallaby. Since it was fall, fruit and berries were out of season, although once while digging beneath rotted leaves she found some fruit that still looked edible. She had no idea what kind of fruit it was, or if it was poisonous, but she took a small bite and found it delicious. And since it produced no ill effects, she later ate it all.

Tia was quite proud of her accomplishments;

providing for herself was something few women dared. If and when her staples ran out she could always sneak back to Sydney and replenish her supply. After a week in the bush with no complications, Tia began to relax. She had just lit a fire one evening from her hoard of dry wood with one of the sulfur matches she'd purchased and was measuring tea into a billy can when a snapping twig startled her. Jumping to her feet, she peered into the gloom. Tall eucalyptus, stately gum, and huge bottle trees combined with black wattle to cast eerie silhouettes against the purple sky.

Inhaling a shaky breath, Tia chided herself for being so jumpy. It wasn't like her to start at every little noise. Quite possibly it was just a gray kangaroo or small night animal searching for food. She hoped it wasn't a stray dingo that might have turned vicious from lack of food. Her hand slid to the comforting weight of the pistol stuck in her belt.

Poised on the balls of her feet, her body tense, Tia strained her ears for the sound she'd heard. Nothing. All was quiet. Obviously, being alone had done strange things to her mind. For all she knew, she was alone out here in this vast wilderness with nothing but birds and animals for company. She hoped it stayed that way, at least until Damian returned to London. She turned back to the fire, hunkering down on her heels to measure out the tea.

"Are ye wantin' company?"

The tea spun out of Tia's hands as she knocked over the billy can, and the water it held made the fire crackle and sputter. She leaped to her feet, her heart thundering in her chest as several men materialized silently from the shadows. The man who'd spoken stood slightly behind her, having moved into position with the stealth of a wraith.

" 'Ere now, that's good tea yer wastin'." The man bent to scoop the spilled tea leaves back into the billy can.

"Who in bloody 'ell are ye?" Tia reverted easily into street language, remembering to lower the tone of her voice as she spoke. She didn't dare let these men know she was a woman.

"I was just gonna ask ye the very same question."

"Me name's Tom."

"I'm Walls. Me mates are Dawes, Leon, Stiles, Cress, and old Gimpy. We call him that 'cause he's lame."

Six of them! Tia gulped nervously. What was she going to do now?

"Are ye alone, lad?"

"Aye." Her dry mouth made speech extremely difficult.

"The lad don't look like no bushranger ta me," Cress offered. "Pretty, ain't he?"

Walls, who appeared to be the leader, made a disgusted sound deep in his throat. "Leave the lad alone, leastways till ye know if he's willin'." Tia's eyes grew round. "Cat got yer tongue, lad?

Tell us what yer doin' hidin' in the bush."

"I—I jumped ship," Tia stuttered. "The cap'n was a cruel man, I couldn't take it no more. I knew he'd send out a search party when he found me missin' so I run off. He'll have a devil of a time findin' another cabin boy."

Walls studied her slim form for several excruciating minutes. Tia kept her head lowered, her eyes downcast, waiting for the verdict. He either accepted her story or saw through her disguise.

Suddenly he seemed to reach a decision. "We're in the same boat, mate, we're all hidin' from someone. Ye might as well join us."

"Oh, no, I wouldn't want ta trouble ya."

"Ain't no trouble, we insist."

Trapped!

Chapter Fourteen

Tia walked between Walls and Gimpy as they trudged deeper and deeper into the forest. She'd really gotten herself into a fine mess this time. When Walls finally called a halt, she had no idea where she was or in which direction Sydney lay. Her back ached from carrying her swag slung over one shoulder, and her legs shook from exhaustion.

It was obvious to Tia that Walls and the others were familiar with this place. The small clearing beneath towering eucalyptus trees looked as if it had been deliberately hacked out of the wilderness. The swags lying about the area confirmed Tia's suspicion that this was some sort of campsite, and she surmised that the bushrangers she'd had the misfortune to fall in with used this spot as a gathering place. Dropping her swag, Tia slid down the trunk of a tree she was leaning against and rested her head atop her knees.

"Can ya cook, Tom?" Walls asked hopefully. "Ain't none of us worth a tinker's damn at cookin'."

Afraid to admit she knew little about cooking over an open fire, Tia nodded her head.

"There's flour and salted beef in the swag over yonder beneath that tree. We ain't had decent damper since old Pockets got captured. He was the only one of us that could cook."

Tia looked at him stupidly. "Damper? I—I ain't never cooked damper. Ain't never tasted it either. What is it?"

Walls looked at her incredulously. "Ye can't make damper? Everyone in Australia knows how ta make damper."

"I ain't been in Australia long," Tia shot back. "I'm a cabin boy, remember? This is my first time out of England."

"'Tis easy, mate, ye just mix salt, flour, and water and cook it in hot ashes," Gimpy instructed. "Damper with either salted beef or fresh-killed wallaby makes a feast fit fer a king. Make sure we have plenty of billy tea ta drink and ye'll hear no complaints."

Tia did an admirable job preparing a meal for the seven of them. The damper was simple to prepare and tasted wonderful. The salted beef, recently purloined in a bailup, was somewhat tough and stringy but palatable. When the men had served themselves, Tia helped herself to a generous portion and sat on the ground to eat, her back supported by a tree. She ate with gusto, shoveling the food in noisily. She ignored the bushrangers when they laughed at her and made jokes about her lusty appetite. Once she had eaten her fill, she set her tin dish aside and hugged her legs, resting her head on her knees. She was tired, too tired to make the effort to gather up the plates and stow the leftovers. The other men seemed just as indolent, lounging on the ground after they finished their meal. Some had already rolled up in their blankets.

Unconsciously Tia's mind wandered back to Penrod station, wondering what Ben was doing and if he missed her. Had Damian returned to Penrod station looking for her? If so, Ben must know by now that she was missing. Would he even care? Or was he happy to be rid of her. He had seemed devastated when Damian took her away, but knowing Ben as she did, she supposed he would find someone to replace her soon enough.

She could picture him now, standing so tall and broad, his tanned flesh drawn taut across his cheekbones. She loved the way his eyes looked while they made love, like pure silver glistening in sunlight. He made her feel something she thought no man would ever make her feel. After knowing Damian, Tia had no use for men. Living on the streets and seeing

287

firsthand how cruel men could be had made her distrustful of the opposite sex. She had scoffed at love, decided that the emotion was vastly overrated and not for her. But Ben had changed all that.

Without a doubt Ben was a roguish devil, who attracted women in droves. But his aura went far beyond mere sensuality—though Lord knows he had that in abundance. What she felt for Ben went beyond sexual attraction, beyond intimacy. She felt it in her heart and in her soul. She touched her fingertips to her lips and remembered how wonderful it felt when he kissed her. How fervently she responded. How his touch made her flesh burn and her bones ache with a need she'd never imagined.

She fell asleep in that position, her head filled with Ben, her mind consumed with the love that had grown in her heart despite the insurmountable barriers between them. When Walls made to kick her awake so she might complete her tasks, Gimpy stopped him, performing the chores himself. Gimpy had a soft spot in his heart for youngsters and thought "young Tom" a brave lad for striking out on his own in a wild country like Australia.

Tia slept undisturbed. Someone had thrown a blanket over her hunched shoulders and she slumbered deeply until the still, dark hours just after midnight. It wasn't the rustle of dried leaves that awoke her, or even the shallow breathing that rasped harshly in her ear. It was the hand that fell on her thigh and inched slowly along the inner curve that finally pulled her from sleep. Her eyes flew open and met the hot, dark gaze of Cress. His hand had almost reached the vee between her legs when she grabbed his wrist and flung it aside.

"Ye bleedin' idiot, what in the 'ell are ye doing?"

"Quiet," Cress hissed. His gaze turning nervously to the other sleepers, he was relieved to see that none of them had stirred. "Ye know bloody well what I want, ye've been on a ship long enough. I was a sailor once, and there's only one reason a pretty lad like you would be signed on." His hand settled suggestively on her buttocks and squeezed. "Ye've a soft arse, lad, as soft as a woman's. Give me what I want and ye won't be sorry."

Still groggy from sleep, Tia's mind went blank. What did Cress want from her? Had he somehow seen through her disguise?

Cress, taking her silence for acquiescence, chuckled and brought his hand back to her inner thigh. "That's more like it. Don't worry, mate, I'll treat ye real good."

His vile insinuation jerked Tia wide awake. She had lived too long among creatures of the street not to know what he was talking about and on more than one occasion had been protected by One-eyed Bertha from men like Cress. Thinking she was a young lad, they tried to work their perverted wiles on her. Bertha had given her a lecture the first time it happened on how nature sometimes played tricks and made men who desired the same sex, particularly young boys whose cheeks were as fresh and downy as a maid's. It could happen to women, too, she had gone on to explain. That mind-boggling thought had made Tia sick to her stomach. This time Bertha wasn't around to protect her. Tia had only her wits to rely on.

"Ye bleedin' pervert, keep yer filthy 'ands off me!" Tia screeched at the top of her lungs. Kicking Cress away, she rolled out of his reach and leaped to her feet. By now the other men were beginning to stir.

"I warned ye ta shut up!" Cress snarled, grasping her jacket and slamming her against the tree. The breath left her in a whoosh. When her breath returned, she drew in a lungful of air and opened her mouth to lash out with another scathing insult. But Cress clapped one hand across her mouth and the other at the base of her throat. "Ye get me in trouble and I'll choke the breath out of ya."

Tia's words gurgled to a halt as Cress's hand tightened. But it was too late. Her angry outburst had succeeded in awakening the other men. Gimpy was the first to reach her. His thin gray hair flew around his face in wild disarray as he thrust his bearded face at Cress.

"What in 'ell do ye think yer doin', Cress? Take yer 'ands off the lad."

"I ain't hurtin' the brat," Cress snarled. "He's

a whiner and a tease. He's been invitin' me with sly looks all day."

"N—no," Tia gasped when Cress let go her throat. "He's lyin'. He tried to—to—"

Walls finally arrived, disgruntled at being awoken in the middle of the night. "I told you, Cress, if the lad wasn't willin' yer not ta bugger him."

"He's willin'," Cress said sullenly.

"No, I'm not! He's a perverted bastard, I want nothin' ta do with him." Tia was shaking now, distraught, shocked, and so damn angry she could spit nails.

"Ye heard Tom," Walls said, providing the final say in the matter. "The lad ain't one of yer kind, let him be. Now go on back to sleep. All of ye."

Slanting Tia a fulminating glance, Cress slunk back to his blanket. One by one the others left until no one remained but Gimpy.

"Keep away from that one," Gimpy warned. "He's a buggerin' bastard and a mean one. He ain't gonna leave ye alone until he gets what he wants from ya. A pretty lad like ye are too much of a temptation fer a man like Cress." So saying he turned and limped back to his bedroll.

Tia watched him go, her eyes wild and frightened, her hand massaging the spot where Cress's fingers had left a red indentation on her delicate skin. Her sleep for the night was ended. Hours later she watched the sky lighten from black to purple to mauve, then suddenly burst into full

291

daylight. The day was cold, a light frost dusted the ground and crunched under her shoes as she sought a private spot away from the men to perform her more personal tasks. When she returned, the other men were stirring and she began preparing breakfast while Leon started the fire. While they ate she chose a place apart to take her own meal, secretly studying each man in turn.

Walls was the leader by dint of brains and brawn. He looked to be in his thirties, was big and unkempt, and wore a hodgepodge of clothing stolen from various sources. As with the others, his hair was shaggy and he wore a beard. Tia thought he looked wily and dangerous and a man easily aroused to anger.

Leon was the youngest, barely older than she was. He was blond, lean, wiry, and looked as if he wouldn't harm a fly. But looks were often deceiving.

Stiles was a grizzled, hard-bitten man of middle years. His face wore a permanent scowl and his lips rarely smiled. Tia decided she wouldn't like to tangle with him under any circumstances.

Dawes rarely spoke, appeared confused most of the time, and seemed content to follow the others. Next to Gimpy, he was the oldest. He was also the fattest.

Tia shuddered when her eyes came full circle to Cress. He was small and athletic with sly features and pale darting eyes that never seemed to light on anything. He looked like a man who would hold a grudge and kill with little provocation.

Tia was least afraid of Gimpy, though she sensed that he was a man who could turn dangerous at the blink of an eye. Of medium height and weight, he was over fifty with sparse gray hair and a thin beard. His limp had resulted from a broken leg that hadn't been set properly.

Tia knew that she had fallen in with a desperate group of men. Discovery could bring about her death—or worse.

Damian returned to Sydney in a state of rage. Tia had done it to him again! When he found her—and he didn't doubt for a moment that he would—she'd pay dearly for disrupting his life and causing him to miss his ship. Tia had put him through hell these last few years after she had made him an object of ridicule by running off after their wedding. For years he had no idea whether she was dead or alive and was forbidden by law from taking another wife. When his hired investigators finally caught up with her, she had latched on to a goddamn sheep farmer and taken herself off to Australia. She couldn't bear his children from long distance, so he'd been forced to go after her, certain this time she'd not escape him. But he had been wrong. The wily little bitch was probably sitting somewhere in the Australian bush right now laughing at him.

Damian collected his trunk from the *Southern Star* and checked into the only hotel in Sydney. That's when he found that the sack of gold coins he had stashed in his clothing was missing. His curses turned the air blue as he realized that Tia now had the means to remain in hiding for as long as was necessary. His money would provide food and clothing and whatever else she needed to survive. He now knew with a certainty that Tia had bribed the cabin boy aboard the *Southern Star*. And probably had purchased food and supplies from the shop where he had bumped into her. Having had Tia within his grasp and not realizing it was what really rankled.

The wretched little slut!

When Damian went back to the shop, the proprietor had returned from Bathurst. It took only a nudge from one of Damian's hirelings to make the shopkeeper recall the lad from the *Southern Star* who had paid for his purchases with a gold coin. He had seen damn few gold coins in New South Wales.

"Did the lad tell you where sh—he was going?" Damian asked sharply.

"Back to the *Southern Star*, I would assume."

"Did he tell you that?"

The shopkeeper scratched his head as he searched his brain. "Don't think so. Like I said, I just assumed—"

"In which direction did he go after he left your shop?"

"Strange that you should ask. The lad didn't look like he was returning to Sydney Cove and his ship. I thought it odd at the time but figured it was none of my business."

"Which direction, man?"

"South. He definitely headed south. I watched till I could no longer see him, and he sure didn't look like he was going to change his direction."

Satisfied, Damian purchased bush clothing from the shopkeeper, a pistol, knife, and sufficient food and sundry supplies to last him and his two hirelings many days. He was going after Tia.

And God help her when he found her!

Ben was in a quandary. On the one hand he desperately wanted to leave Penrod station immediately and look for Tia. On the other he thought he should wait a few days in case Tia turned up on his doorstep. One day passed, then two. He paced; he chafed; he grew impatient and withdrawn. Dare came and tried to calm him down, but nothing helped. Three days and still Tia did not appear. Four days and Ben was nearly desperate to leave. On the fifth day, Robin and Kate Fletcher arrived with their daughter Molly, expecting to attend a celebration. Kate was heavily pregnant and radiant. Robin looked prosperous, calm, and confident. Marrying Kate had added a new dimension to his life.

Expecting to greet a man head over heels in love, Robin was shocked to find Ben highly distraught and consumed with anxiety. Then Robin recalled Ben's staunch vow never to marry and assumed that Ben was having second thoughts about finally succumbing to an emotion he had avoided for many years.

"Welcome to the brotherhood, Ben," Robin teased relentlessly. It did his heart good to see Ben in the same position he and Dare had once been in. "Don't fret, mate, vows mean nothing when you fall in love. Where is this paragon Casey told us about?"

Ben could do little more than stare at Robin, having forgotten that Casey had invited the Fletchers to celebrate his marriage to Tia. So much had happened since then that he didn't know where to begin.

"What's the matter, Ben, cat got your tongue?" Kate teased. "I'm anxious to meet your bride."

Kate regarded Ben through incredible violet eyes that never ceased to amaze him. He couldn't blame Robin for falling hard for dark-haired, feisty Kate despite her vile temper and sharp tongue. She had tamed irrepressible Robin just as Casey had tamed his arrogant brother.

"Ben, what's wrong? Has something happened?"

"Come inside," Ben said tightly. "Since you're here you might as well know everything."

Kate followed Ben inside, exchanging a worried look with Robin as he picked up their daughter and followed. Ben sat them down and produced an intense hour of revelations which Robin and Kate found difficult to understand. And even more impossible to believe.

"Bloody hell, Ben, this tops everything. Nothing either Dare or I experienced compares with what Tia has put you through."

"I wouldn't say that," Ben replied, recalling how Kate had become lost in the Blue Mountains returning from Bathurst where she had found Robin in bed with another woman. And how everyone thought Casey was dead when in reality she had left New South Wales and turned up in England where Dare eventually found her. "It's situations like this I've been trying to avoid all my life."

"So what are you going to do?" Compassion darkened Kate's expressive violet eyes to a deep purple.

"I've got to find Tia before Fairfield does. Someone in Sydney must have seen her."

"Good luck," Robin offered. "Would you like me to come with you? I haven't had an adventure since—well, since Molly was born."

Ben smiled. "Thanks, mate, but I'm going alone. Kate needs you here. Will you stay at Penrod station?"

"No, Dare has already offered to put us up, and since Molly enjoys the children, I think we'll take him up on the offer. Will you be leaving soon?"

297

Ben nodded solemnly. "Tomorrow. I can't wait any longer. I have a feeling Tia needs me."

Consuming thoughts of Tia rode Ben all the way to Sydney. A desperate longing stirred within him that had little to do with physical desire—although desire for Tia raged inside him like an inferno. He saw her lying beside him in bed, her beautiful golden hair spread about her like shimmering moonbeams, her incredible blue-green eyes soft and hazy in the aftermath of love, her skin flushed.

Ben flexed his muscles, recalling how the soft velvet texture of her skin felt against the hairy roughness of his, how wonderfully sweet her flesh tasted to his tongue, how her curves fit his body as if they were made for one another. Tia might be small but she was all woman; small, firm breasts, slender waist and hips that curved gently into surprisingly long, shapely limbs. Piercing the hot tightness of her sheath was like sliding into heaven. Just thinking about her made Ben's flesh tingle and swell, and he shook his head to clear it of thoughts that interfered with his mission. Thinking about Tia gave him great pleasure, but finding her would bring him greater satisfaction. Keeping her with him on Penrod station would bring him a sense of fulfillment beyond that which was sexual.

Bloody hell! Was that he talking?

Since when did a woman come to mean so much to him? *Him!* Ben Penrod, the man his family had despaired of ever marrying. He hardly recognized himself. And he wasn't certain he liked the change. Sure, he wanted Tia, he'd be a fool to deny it. He'd always been a lusty devil, and Tia had piqued his fancy ever since he pulled off her dirty cap and discovered a woman beneath the filthy assortment of rags that disguised her lush curves. He had been intrigued enough to propose twice—and been turned down both times. Even though he was now aware of the circumstances that had made Tia refuse his proposals, it didn't hurt his pride any less. It would be a cold day in hell before he proposed again to a woman, he reflected.

Even Tia? a little voice inside his brain asked.

He refused to acknowledge the answer. He wasn't heartless, just cautious. He'd cross that bridge when he came to it.

Ben reached Sydney only to learn that Lord Fairfield and his two hirelings had already left. The clerk at the hotel didn't seem to know where they had gone but he did volunteer the information that his lordship was dressed in bush clothing and carried a small arsenal with him and had hired an aborigine tracker. The clerk also mentioned the name of the store that had delivered Fairfield's supplies to the hotel.

A surge of hope shot through Ben. Had Fairfield somehow learned where Tia had disappeared to? Then Ben's elation was tempered with a sobering thought. What would happen if Fairfield found Tia before he did? He feared the man was angry enough to do something unspeakable to his wife. Thanking the clerk, Ben hurried off to the mercantile, intending to question the shopkeeper about Fairfield's destination. Since he knew the man, he prayed he'd be cooperative. He was.

"His lordship was asking about a young lad who came in the store a couple weeks ago, mate," the storekeeper said. "The lad said he was from the *Southern Star* and paid for his purchases with a gold coin. What's this all about?"

"It's a long story, Perkins, but suffice it to say that Fairfield means the 'lad' harm. Do you have any idea where he went?"

"I wouldn't have told Lord Fairfield anything if I'd known the lad's life was in danger," Perkins maintained. "But I'll tell you what I told him. The lad bought supplies and headed south."

"South. Thanks, Perkins."

"I hope you find him first, mate."

"So do I, Perkins," Ben said fervently. "So do I."

Each day that Tia remained with the bushrangers earned her greater acceptance from the gang. Though Cress still eyed her with perverted lust, outwardly he treated her with surly indifference. At least in front of Walls and the others. Whenever he found her alone he goaded her with crude remarks and snide innuendoes. For the most part she kept her mouth shut. She became surprisingly proficient at cooking over a campfire and for all purposes became an integral part of the gang. She even took part in a daring bailup on the road from Sydney. Though she kept well in the background and was much relieved when the man and his family weren't harmed. After stealing their valuables, they allowed the family to go on their way.

The next bailup took place without Tia. She had invented an excuse to remain in camp while the others left to rob unsuspecting victims. After that it was taken for granted that she'd remain in camp to protect their possessions from being carried off by other bushrangers or the law. She had no idea what she would have done had another gang of bushrangers invaded their campsite in her companions' absence.

As the days passed, Tia began to think about returning to Sydney. She hoped that by now Damian had become discouraged and left Australia on the next ship bound for England. She had no idea she had so damaged Damian's pride that he had vowed to search forever for the woman who had deserted him on their wedding night. Meanwhile, most of the bushrangers had grown quite fond of Tia, particularly Gimpy. Except for Cress, whose smoldering eyes often settled on her with bitter resentment, the men treated her kindly enough. They thought her a plucky youngster who could curse with the best of them, was a passable cook, and seemed to know exactly how and when to avoid a nasty confrontation.

One day when the men had decided to go on a little walkabout to steal a cow from one of the small farms surrounding Sydney, Tia again voiced her desire to remain in camp. Since her presence wouldn't be missed, Walls offered no objection, privately thinking the lad was too small anyway to offer much help should they need it. Cress sent her a deprecating sneer but said nothing. When they left, Tia hunkered down by the fire, warming herself with a cup of tea and thinking that if she was going to leave, now was the time to do so. She was so certain Damian had left Sydney that she didn't give a thought to what would happen if she encountered him. What she did think about was her future. Would Ben still want her if she went back to him?

Marriage to Ben was still out of the question, even if he would have her. As long as Damian lived, she was not legally free to marry another. Remaining with Ben as his mistress was an equally painful thought. Everyone would know she was his kept woman, someone with whom he could slake his lust. How could she show her face knowing that everyone would consider her Ben's whore? She would lose Dare and Casey's friendship and earn their contempt. True, she would still have Ben, but for how long? One day, despite his denial, he'd find a woman to marry. Someone he could love and cherish for the rest of his life. What would happen to her when that happened?

Of one thing she was certain, Tia thought dismally: she couldn't remain in the bush with the bushrangers. Nor could she return to London. Perhaps America . . . So engrossed was she in her thoughts that she failed to hear the snapping of dry twigs. Suddenly a hand dug painfully into her shoulder, exerting cruel pressure and wrenching a cry from Tia's lips. Her feet left the ground as she was lifted bodily and slammed against a tree. Hurt and dazed, she looked into Damian's face and saw death.

"I've waited a long time for this," Damian snarled. His crazed expression sent sharp tendrils of fear curling along her spine. "Have you convinced your lawless companions you're a lad, or have you become their whore?"

"How—how did you find me?" Tia asked, finally finding her tongue.

"I have my ways. Anything is possible if you have enough money."

On the fringes of her awareness, Tia noted the two hired thugs and the aborigine tracker lurking in the background.

"You won't escape me again, Tia, not ever again. I need a wife who is docile and submissive. I now know you're not that woman. It's a pity you won't leave the bush alive. So young . . ." His sentence trailed off but Tia understood perfectly. "I'll grieve for a while, but by the time I arrive in London I'll be ready to take another wife."

"You're going to kill me," Tia whispered, her

303

tongue sliding around the constriction in her throat.

"You always were astute, even as a child. My spineless son wouldn't have been able to handle you properly had he lived to marry you. He was too much like his weak mother."

"No, please, I'll—I'll do as you say. I'll be a good wife." She'd promise him anything in order to live, even if she never meant to honor her promises.

"It's too late, Tia, much too late. It will truly pain me to report that you were slain by bushrangers and your body partly consumed by wild animals. No one will doubt me, and I'll be able to leave this untamed, uncivilized country behind."

Tia blanched. She'd give her right arm to see Ben one last time before death claimed her. She'd tell him she loved him, that he made her glad she was a woman instead of the boy she pretended to be. And she'd tell him she wished she could have had his child. Giving a child to the man she loved would have been life's greatest accomplishment.

Too late . . .

Chapter Fifteen

Tia's heart pumped furiously when Damian grasped her arm and dragged her away from the crude campsite. The aborigine tracker, sensing trouble, melted into the dense forest while Damian's two henchmen stood by awaiting orders. They were being paid enough blunt to ensure their compliance with any vile plan that Damian might have hatched for his recalcitrant wife.

"No! I'm not going anywhere with you," Tia cried, resisting with all her might the pull Damian was exerting on her arm. "Can't you just pretend I'm dead? You can remarry, do whatever you want, I promise not to intrude on your life."

"What? Leave you alive and chance having

you pop up at a most inconvenient time? Never! If I sire an heir on another woman, you might take it into your head to return and accuse me of bigamy and declare my heir a bastard."

"No, I wouldn't do that. Can't you understand? I never want to see you again. You can keep my money, it means nothing to me. I—I want my life. I'll even remain in Australia so you'll never see me again."

"Did you enjoy whoring for Ben Penrod?" Damian sneered. "What will happen when he tires of you and marries a decent woman? Perhaps then you'll have second thoughts about your legal husband and all that could have been yours."

"No, never!" Tia cried. Did Ben care enough about her to keep her with him forever?

"My way is best, Tia," Damian insisted. Despite Tia's resistance, he had dragged her nearly to the edge of the clearing. A few more steps and she would be lost from view of the camp and at the mercy of Damian and his two henchmen. Digging in her heels, she exerted more force, causing Damian to stop and shower her with curses.

When Damian's two henchmen made to help, he waved them away. "I don't need help. No little whore is going to best me." Drawing back his arm, he slammed his fist into Tia's face. A gurgling cry escaped her lips as she slid to her knees, supported only by Damian's cruel grasp. "That's only a sample of what you'll receive if you don't come along quietly. You've put me through so much needless anguish all these years I want to make you suffer before I snuff out your miserable life."

Stunned, Tia held her aching jaw and blinked back tears. Sensing victory, Damian renewed his efforts to drag her away from the bushranger camp.

" 'Ere now, what the 'ell is goin' on 'ere? Who are ye and what are ye doin' ta young Tom?" Walls and his followers had burst into camp while Tia and Damian struggled and his henchmen stood by watching.

Damian froze, fear racing up his spine. He had hoped to escape with Tia before the bushrangers returned to their campsite. Now facing them, he was thankful he didn't have to deal with them alone. If he couldn't bluff his way out of this predicament, they could always shoot their way out. There were only six bushrangers, after all.

Suddenly Tia gained her wits, and working around her painful jaw, cried, " 'Elp me! The bugger wants ta carry me back ta Sydney so the cap'n can flog me fer jumpin' ship."

Walls scowled menacingly at Damian. "Tom ain't goin' nowhere with ye." He moved closer. His men surged around him, prepared to defend one of their own, for they now considered Tia one of them.

"Now see here," Damian foolishly blustered, "this is none of your concern. What I do with T—"

His sentence was abruptly cut off when Walls reached out a dirty hand and grasped Damian by the throat. "This has everythin' ta do with me. Tom is our mate and his enemies are our enemies."

Damian gulped convulsively as the grim-faced men closed in on him. He signaled frantically for his two hirelings to brandish their weapons to extricate him from this threatening situation. But when he turned his head to look in their direction he was stunned to see that the sniveling cowards had disappeared. Both thugs had silently melted into the forest and fled at the first sign of trouble. Though willing enough to help capture a defenseless woman, neither was keen about tangling with six grizzly men.

"Cowardly bastards!" Damian screamed, enraged by their desertion. "Come back here and earn your money." His words were met with jeering laughter from the bushrangers.

"Ye ain't so brave now, are ye?" Walls taunted. "Leave now before I change me mind and set me mates on ye fer abusin' young Tom."

On hands and knees, Tia scrambled away from Damian. The company of bushrangers was far preferable to the fate Damian had planned for her. Damian saw what she was up to and made a grab for her. He missed and then made the mistake of reaching for the pistol attached to his belt. Tia cried out a warning and Cress alertly spun around, knowing one of them would die if Damian was allowed to fire. His knife was in his hand instantly, and left his hand even faster. It found its mark in Damian's throat.

A surprised look passed over Damian's features as he sank to his knees. Moments before he hit the ground he directed his gaze at Tia, opened his mouth, and rasped out, "You bi—" He was dead before he finished the sentence.

Accustomed to violence from her time on the streets of London, Tia was nevertheless appalled by Damian's death. She had never wished him ill, or wanted him dead; she had just preferred that they never meet again. She understood that his need for an heir drove him to do the things he did, and her desertion on their wedding night was the final blow that changed him into a vengeful, vindictive man. But fate had made this their last meeting. He would never bother her again. Never would she fear being discovered and returned to her legal husband. She was now a widow and free to live her life as she pleased.

Free to love Ben, if he still wanted her.

"Is—is he dead?" Tia asked in a strangled voice.

"Aye," Walls grunted, nudging Damian with his toe. "Cress rarely misses. Ye ain't squeamish, are ya? Cress did ye a favor, mate."

"Aye," Cress agreed, sidling closer. "The lad owes me." His lascivious grin left little doubt in Tia's mind how Cress expected to be paid, and she shuddered. She might be free of Damian, but she still had the bushrangers to deal with.

Especially Cress, who lusted after the young lad he thought she was.

"Don't press the lad, Cress, he ain't like us who lives with the constant threat of death. Likely this is the first killin' he's ever witnessed. Ain't that so, lad?"

Tia nodded her head vigorously, turning away from the sight of Damian's body now grotesque in death.

"What about the others?" Dawes asked, motioning in the direction in which Damian's henchmen disappeared. "Should we go after them?"

Walls shook his head. "Let 'em go. They ain't likely ta come back. They're merely paid thugs, no better than us." He turned to Tia. "You all right, lad?"

"Aye," Tia said jerkily. "But what about— him?" She sliced her hand to where Damian lay sprawled on the blood-soaked ground.

"Dawes, Stiles, get rid of the body," Walls ordered crisply.

Tia turned her head as the two men dragged Damian's limp form away from the campsite. She tried not to look at the spot where he had lain, but her eyes kept returning, wincing at the dark, damp area that marked the place where his blood had soaked the ground and he had breathed his last.

Ben knew he was close to a bushranger campsite. His tracking skills were excellent, and signs had led him to believe he'd soon encounter the gang. He worried constantly about what he would find if they had found Tia and discovered she was a woman. He hastened his steps, then came to an abrupt halt when he heard sounds that indicated someone was crashing headlong through the forest. He stepped behind the trunk of a huge eucalyptus and watched as two burly men rushed past, slapping away roots and brush that hindered their speed. Every few seconds they peered back over their shoulders as if the devil himself were after them. Ben saw no one.

Ben waited until the men were out of sight and he was certain no one was in pursuit before revealing himself. He had no idea if the men were bushrangers. It made little difference. All he cared about was Tia and finding her before serious harm came to her. Squaring his shoulders, he plunged onward. When the sound of voices drifted to him through the stillness of the forest, he became wary and cautious, gliding from tree to tree until he came upon a scene right out of hell.

He recognized Damian immediately. The man was surrounded by seven bushrangers. No, six, Ben corrected, for the seventh, no more than a lad, lay sprawled on the ground rubbing his cheek. Then suddenly Ben's blood ran cold as he recognized Tia nursing a bruised cheek. Had Damian hit her? he wondered, wanting to throw caution to the wind and lunge at Tia's husband. Or had she been harmed by one of the bushrangers? Before Ben could intervene, angry voices erupted and he watched in frozen horror as one of the men drew a knife from his belt and flung it at Damian. It pierced his jugular neatly and Damian fell, dead before he hit the ground.

There didn't seem to be any overt threat toward Tia, so Ben remained hidden for the time being, his mind working furiously. He feared that the same fate that had befallen Damian awaited him if he tried to take Tia away from the bushrangers by force. There were six of them and only one of him. Indications led Ben to believe that the bushrangers assumed Tia was a young lad and had absorbed her into their midst. There existed a code of sorts even between thieves and cutthroats, and they would feel obligated to protect her from him just as they did from Damian. Unless he could convince them he was one of them.

Tense and alert, Ben watched and waited until Damian's body was dragged from the campsite and Tia had retreated to huddle beneath a tree. Then he came to a decision. Never had Tia looked so forlorn, so utterly alone. His heart went out to her and he had to physically restrain himself from rushing to her side and telling her he'd die before he'd let anything bad happen to her.

Ben had never been in love before; never in his wildest dreams did he think he'd come so close to making a commitment to a woman, and it frightened him. As he boldly prepared to walk into the den of thieves, the thought uppermost in his mind was that he wanted Tia to belong only to him.

Forever.

Resting her head against her knees and hugging her legs, Tia was shaking uncontrollably, though she tried to hide it from the bushrangers. It wouldn't do to act too much a coward even if she felt like one. She had lived on the edge of violence for three years on the streets of London, but somehow what she had experienced here in the wilds of Australia far surpassed those dark days. She had gotten herself out of countless scrapes and close calls then; somehow she would do so again. Only one man had ever bested her.

Ben.

She had picked the wrong man to rob that day in London. Ben had changed her life forever when he brought her home with him. She loved Ben Penrod. Yet Tia knew that Ben wasn't the kind to commit to one woman for life. No matter how much he denied it, the thought of marriage repelled him, and he'd resent her forever if he broke his vow to remain a bachelor. Even if she got back to civilization safely, Tia was astute enough to realize that marriage to Ben was just a dream. She'd never place him in a position that would obligate him to propose.

Tia sighed, gazing aimlessly into the dense forest surrounding her. Suddenly a wallaby jumped from behind a bush, startling her, and two bushrangers took off after it, hoping to bring back fresh meat for dinner. Tia turned her eyes away but something drew them back. Something . . . A man. He stepped into the clearing. Tall and broad, his shoulders blocked out the sunlight filtering through the trees. For the space of a heartbeat he looked directly at Tia, his gray eyes flashing a warning.

Ben.

Tia's heart pounded, her stomach churned, and she had to literally bite her tongue to keep from crying out his name. He moved so stealthily it was several minutes before he was noticed. Only two men remained in camp, Walls and Gimpy. Two were disposing of Damian's body and the other two had sprinted off after the wallaby. Gimpy saw Ben first and nudged Walls, who whirled to face the intruder—their second of the day.

"Lookin' fer someone, mate?" Walls asked, noting that Ben carried no weapon. As a precaution Ben had removed his pistol and hidden it along with his swag behind a bush. He had then secreted his knife in his boot. He didn't want to present a threat to these desperate men. Not if he hoped to get out alive with Tia. "Are ye friend or foe?"

Though Ben's hands remained relaxed at his sides, his body was tense, alert. "Friend.

I've been trampin' through the woods since I escaped from a work gang. I sure could use a bite to eat." It was true. The pace he had set for himself allowed little time for food or rest. He looked tired, and his clothes by now were in no better condition than those of the bushrangers he faced.

"Escape from a work gang, did ye?" Walls chuckled, recalling his own experience with the law. "What's yer name, mate?"

"Me friends call me Ben," Ben said, knowing his name meant nothing to these men. He'd been gone from Penrod station and New South Wales for many years. "I ain't been in New South Wales long, and I tell you, mate, the work gang ain't to my likin'. So when the guard's back was turned I walked away."

"If me mates return with that wallaby they're chasin' there'll be plenty of food ta go around. Yer welcome ta share it," Walls allowed.

Just then Dawes and Stiles returned from their grisly task of dumping Damian's body. They nodded at Walls, indicating they had fulfilled their duty, and stared at Ben distrustfully.

"He's one of us," Walls said, having come to a favorable decision about Ben.

"Where ya from, mate?" Dawes questioned. Suspicious by nature, he wasn't entirely convinced about Ben.

"London," Ben said.

"What's yer crime?" Stiles inquired.

"Murder."

"Blimy. Ain't he a cool one," Dawes commented dryly. He thought the flinty-eyed stranger entirely capable of murder.

Tia held her breath, watching beneath lowered lids as Ben ingratiated himself with the bushrangers. Unlike Damian, he hadn't attempted to rile them. Nor had he expressed undue interest in the young "lad" sitting by himself. Walls had no sooner introduced the men already in camp than Cress and Leon returned with the wallaby. Gimpy let out a hoot and prepared to dress out the animal for the meat. Walls cast a speculative glance at Tia and stopped him.

"Let Tom do it. It will do the lad good ta get his mind off his—troubles." Then he turned to Ben. "The lad's name is Tom. He's a newcomer, but we've grown fond of him. Ain't that right, Tom?"

Tia started violently when she realized that Walls was addressing her. Unable to slide her tongue around the constriction in her throat, she merely nodded.

"Well, hop to it, lad, we're all fairly starvin'. Ben, here, more than the others." Tia slid her eyes to Ben, acknowledging him with a curt nod. "Don't mind the boy," Walls said, "he's a mite shy but he's all right."

Tia rose somewhat shakily to her feet and stared at the wallaby, having no idea how to dress it. Sensing her predicament, Ben offered to lend a hand. "I'll help the boy. 'Tis no more than fittin' that I should work for me meal. Can I borrow a knife from one of ye?" He wasn't about to let on to the fact that he had a concealed weapon.

Suddenly a knife came whizzing through the air, settling in the dirt between his feet. Ben didn't flinch a muscle. "Take mine," Cress said, leering owlishly. "See that ye return it when yer done." Ben nodded, picked up the knife, and joined Tia beside the carcass of the wallaby. They both squatted on their haunches, and Tia watched as Ben set to work skinning the animal with a skill that amazed her.

Once the bushrangers' attention was focused elsewhere, Ben's gray eyes probed Tia with tender concern, lingering on her bruised cheek. "Have you been harmed?" he asked beneath his breath. "What happened to your face?"

"Damian hit me," Tia admitted in a low voice. "But the bushrangers haven't hurt me. They think I'm a cabin boy who jumped ship in Sydney to escape a cruel captain."

"Why did they kill Damian?"

"You saw?"

"Aye, but too late to intervene."

"He tried to drag me away when I didn't want to go. I told them Damain was sent by the ship's captain to bring me back for punishment. Only I didn't wish him dead, even though he was planning on killing me and leaving my body in the forest. If he had left quietly they wouldn't have killed him."

"What's all the whisperin' about?"

Suddenly Cress loomed above them, scowling at Ben, his face fierce with jealousy. "If yer thinkin' of buggerin' the lad, forget it, I got first dibs."

Tia's complexion grew mottled and she made a gurgling sound deep in her throat, while Ben's response was to jump to his feet and face Cress squarely. His gray eyes were cold as ice, his features hard, his mouth thin with rage. "I don't abuse boys, Cress, nor do I have perverted appetites. I have no interest in Tom except as a friend. My tastes run to women. Do ye have a problem with that?"

Cress took one look at Ben's brawny biceps, the immense breadth of his shoulders, and the challenge in his eyes and immediately backed down. Without his knife he hadn't a chance against someone the size of Ben. "No offense, mate, I was just statin' a fact. I ain't touched the boy, but if he changes his mind I'm 'avin' him first."

He turned on his heel and joined Walls and the others, who had looked on in amusement at the exchange. They cared little about Cress' sexual preferences as long as he didn't bugger any of them or someone like Tom who was unwilling. If Tom decided to submit to Cress' perverted desires, they'd conveniently look the other way.

"Has that bastard been badgering you?" Ben asked. The words were forced from between his teeth in an angry hiss.

"It—it hasn't been all that bad," Tia declared, refusing to look Ben in the eye. "Walls and the others haven't let him touch me."

"But he tried," Ben ground out. He wanted to tear the man limb from limb. Tia didn't answer, fearing that Ben would do something rash and place both their lives in danger.

"Why are you here?" Tia asked, "You knew I could take care of myself."

"The only thing I knew was that you were gone and Damian was determined to find you. He turned up at Penrod station, you know, demanding that I return you. He assumed you were there. I wasn't going to let him take you back to England to bear his children."

"I knew Damian would look for me at Penrod station, that's why I deliberately set out in another direction."

"You little fool! Don't you know how dangerous it is for you in the bush? You could have been—"

"Ain't that wallaby skinned yet?" Gimpy complained in a loud voice.

"Bloody hell," Ben cursed beneath his breath. "Finished," he called out in a loud voice. To Tia, he whispered, "We'll talk later. Don't do or say anything that will make them suspicious. They're all desperate men."

Tia nodded and walked to the firepit to begin cooking the wallaby and making damper. Ben strolled over to the men and joined in the conversation. When Walls invited him to remain with them for the night, or longer, if he wished, Ben pretended to mull over the offer before accepting.

"I'll stay fer the time bein'," he said slowly, "but I'm thinkin' of headin' back to Sydney soon and stowin' aboard a ship sailin' back to England. This Australia ain't fer me. If I do it in the dead of night mayhap I won't be recognized."

"We're movin' on, too," Walls revealed. "Our campsite was invaded earlier today before you arrived and two of the men got away. We can't take the chance of them alertin' the law to our whereabouts so we voted ta move on." The others nodded agreement.

"Were there more than two men?" Ben asked, pretending innocence.

"Aye," Cress said with a sly grin, "but the other man ain't in no condition ta tell anyone where we're located, if ye get me meanin'."

"Where ya goin'?" Ben asked.

"I hear tell the Blue Mountains has caves and places where men could hide," Walls said. "Traffic across the mountains promises good pickin's, and there's some rich ranchers settlin' on the vast acres west of the mountains. Sure ya don't want ta join us?"

"Positive, I don't like Australia," Ben said, repeating his earlier reason.

"I ain't goin' either," Tia injected after listening carefully to the conversation. "I wanna go back ta London ta me mum. She needs me."

"Aw, Tom, what do ya wanna go back there for?" Walls said. "Yer a better cook than Gimpy and bloody good company. Besides, how ye plannin' ta get ta England, swim?"

"A ship can only remain in port a short time. I ain't wanted by the law, so once my cap'n sets sail, I can hire on another ship as cabin boy."

"Got it all figured out, ain't ye?" Cress sneered crossly. He had plans for the boy and hated to have them foiled.

"As much as I can," Tia said, raising her chin belligerently. "When I joined ye I never planned on stayin' with ye forever."

"I'll see that the lad gets to Sydney safely," Ben offered blandly. "I'll be headin' that way meself."

"I'll bet ye'll take care of him *real* good," mumbled Cress in an insinuating tone that made Ben want to lunge at him.

"If Tom wants ta leave he can leave," Walls decided. Ben let out a ragged breath, hardly able to believe his good fortune. He never expected it to be so easy to get Tia back to safety. And most of it was due to her own quick thinking. He knew of no other woman who could survive a dangerous situation like the one she had gotten herself into. It rankled to think that she probably didn't even need him to rescue her, she could do it all on her own!

That night Tia made her bed as usual a little ways off from the others. Ben noted the position of her bedroll and deliberately placed his halfway between her and the bushrangers. Then he forced himself to remain awake during the long night. He trusted none of the bushrangers, and Cress least of all. The man was filled with perverted lust for "Tom," and since this was likely to be the last night Tia would be with the group, Ben expected Cress to make his move. He was right.

It was the wee hours of the morning when Cress rose from his bedroll and crept toward Tia. Exhausted, Tia heard nothing, sleeping blissfully unaware. But Ben was prepared. Cress loomed above Tia, striking swift as a fox as he placed a hand over her mouth. Tia awoke instantly, unable to cry out or even struggle beneath Cress' restraining body. Cress never knew what hit him as he went limp and collapsed atop Tia. His hand on Tia's mouth was replaced by Ben's as a precaution.

Seized by terror, Tia struggled madly. Then she became aware of a gentle voice soothing her, reassuring her, and she knew in an instant that once again Ben had come to her rescue. She grew quiet. Only then did Ben remove his hand from her mouth, replacing it with his lips.

"I've wanted to do that since I saw you yesterday," he said quietly when he finally ended the kiss. "Bloody hell, woman, you do have a way of getting yourself into the most appalling situations."

"Oh, Ben, thank God you came," Tia said on a trembling sigh.

"I've not the slightest doubt that you could have extricated yourself without me," he said sourly.

Tia thought so too but wisely refrained from voicing her opinion. Instead, she said, "What are we going to do now?"

"Drag Cress into the woods and get the hell out of here. Do you have any rope?"

"In my swag," Tia said, pushing Cress away with her foot. She rummaged in her bag and pulled out a length of rope, handing it to Ben.

"Grab his legs and help me carry him. I don't want to alert the others."

Together they carried Cress deep into the forest. Tia was panting when Ben called a halt, pulled off his kerchief, and stuffed it into Cress' mouth. Then he tied him to a tree.

"If he's lucky his mates will find him. If not, wild animals will find him first."

Tia shuddered. "Now what?"

"Now we go home. Come on." He grasped her hand and pulled her forward. He made one stop to retrieve his pistol and swag from where he had hidden them before entering the bushranger camp.

"What about the bushrangers?" Tia gasped, nearly out of breath from the pace Ben set.

"I doubt any of them are experienced trackers," Ben reasoned, "and besides, they couldn't care less about us. They're heading for the Blue Mountains with or without us. We'll be at Penrod station before you know it. I left my horse in Sydney. We'll pick him up first, rent you a mount, and be home in three days."

Home. The word sounded wonderful to Tia. But would it really be her home?

Chapter Sixteen

Unerringly Ben led Tia through the forest, his intimate knowledge of Australian bush country standing him in good stead as he found them a concealed site next to a shallow billabong to spend the night. Tia collapsed in exhaustion while Ben scouted the site. She breathed a sigh of relief when he announced that they would be safe here for the night. When she looked longingly at the sparkling water in the billabong, Ben suggested she bathe while he prepared them something to eat. The suggestion earned him a brilliant smile as Tia eagerly began stripping, uncaring that Ben watched in avid appreciation. It had been too long since she had bathed all over, and nothing was going to interfere with that pleasure. Not even being ogled by Ben Penrod.

Ben watched Tia slowly peel away the layers of clothes hiding her sweet curves as long as he could stand it. He turned away before her last piece of clothing dropped to the ground. He wanted her, desperately. He wanted to tear off his own clothes and join her in the water. He wanted to make sweet, tender love to her until she grew dizzy with passion and cried out his name in ecstasy. He wanted—Bloody hell! he thought grumpily, where were his brains? Tia was tired, she didn't need him pawing her after the ordeal she had just been through. Her husband was dead; she had seen him murdered and needed time to come to grips with her feelings.

But that didn't stop him from desiring her. It had been like that between him and Tia from the first time he saw her. Suddenly he heard a splash and without thinking turned his head toward the billabong. He saw Tia partially submerged in the water, her head thrown back and her blond hair tumbling over her shoulders, her glistening breasts, fully revealed in the waning light, beaded with drops of water. His loins filled, his heart pounded, and his suddenly dry mouth made swallowing painful. Zombie-like, he dropped the bedrolls he was spreading out for the night and walked with slow, measured steps to the water's edge. The only thing that would have stopped him at that moment was if the ground had opened and swallowed him.

Smiling to herself, Tia let the cold water slide over her tingling breasts. Ice could have formed over the billabong and it still wouldn't have stopped her from wading intrepidly into the water. But it did make her aware of the way in which her taut nipples drew up into tight little buds and goosebumps rose on her chilled flesh. She turned toward shore and saw Ben standing several feet away in the shallows, his powerful form splendidly naked, his gray eyes dark with desire. Mesmerized, she watched in mute appreciation as the muscles on his long, corded legs tensed and propelled him toward her.

Ben's need was evident in the bold thrust of his manhood rising from the dark forest at the apex of his thighs. Not even the shock of cold water on his sex seemed to diminish the hard, throbbing length as he slowly advanced toward Tia. Tia swallowed but the lump in her throat remained. Seeing Ben like that made her recall their last night together, the night before Damian showed up to claim her.

Ben hadn't admitted he loved her, just that he loved making love to her. He cared for her, desired her, and even confessed that he'd never felt about another woman like he did her. But it wasn't enough. She wanted his total commitment. Even now, when she knew she couldn't resist Ben Penrod, didn't even want to, Tia wished that life was simple and that Ben wasn't so adamantly opposed to marriage. While she was wed to Damian, marriage to Ben was out of the question, but not now, not with Damian dead and all obstacles removed.

Ben was close enough to touch her now, close enough for Tia to feel his warm breath on her face. The heat of his body penetrated the icy chill of the water, surrounding and enveloping her with a pervasive warmth.

"Tia." Her name flowed from his tongue like warm honey.

He reached out with one bronze finger and drew a line from her right shoulder to the tightly drawn nipple of her right breast. Tia shuddered, the imaginary line forming a burning brand across her sensitive flesh. When he grasped both her shoulders and drew her against his hard body, she swore their combined heat turned the water around them to steam.

"Ben." Incapable of coherent speech, Tia melted against him, not just for the comfort his arms offered, but to assuage the terrible need inside her to know Ben's love again. When Damian had taken her away she feared she'd never see Ben again, never know his special brand of love.

His arms closed around her, his body hard, hot, the hairs on his chest brushing against Tia's breasts with devastating effect. Tia didn't even try to resist the treacherous weakness that overcame her whenever she was in Ben's arms. She succumbed to it, gladly, willingly, with utter abandon.

Then he was kissing her. A touch of fire.

Her cheeks, her forehead, her chin—finally her mouth. Tia moaned and kissed him back, no longer chilled by the icy water. Then he was lifting her, carrying her dripping body from the water into the cold night air. Tia shivered, partly from cold but mostly from anticipation, and from the urgency that drove them both.

Her trembling increased. "Are you cold, sweetheart?" Tia nodded. Her teeth were chattering, making speech all but impossible. "I'll fix that," Ben said, grinning down at her.

He carried her to the bedroll and lay down beside her, pulling the blanket over both of them. The wildness that had possessed him escalated as his big body surrounded and enveloped her and the rough surface of his hands warmed her. Soon Tia was burning, her skin so sensitive his touch turned her to flame. His lips found her breasts, the taut peaks growing warm and pliant beneath the heated moisture of his mouth. His rough tongue drew wet circles around the erect buds, bathing them gently, then continuing downward to the cup of her navel and beyond to the nest of honey-colored curls at the base of her belly.

Tia grasped his broad shoulders and moaned. "I want to kiss you all over," Ben whispered urgently. "You're mine now, Tia, all mine."

Tia's breath caught on a sob as Ben's fingers separated her and penetrated the silky moistness. After a few experimental thrusts he lowered his head and replaced his fingers with his mouth. Then his tongue found her and drove her to a wild frenzy of pleasure. She tried to make sense out of his words but she couldn't breathe, much less think. His clever mouth took her from one peak to another, each progressively higher. Just before she tumbled over the abyss he thrust his fingers into her again and sent her into a world of sensual delight so violent she pierced his shoulders with her nails and cried out.

He gave her only a moment's respite to float gently back to reality. When she looked up at him, his glittering eyes were dark and mysteriously bright, his mouth glistening with the moisture of her pleasure. He dropped his face, and Tia, realizing what he intended, cried out, "No, I can stand no more!"

Ben merely grinned. This time his mouth was rougher—his tongue, his lips, his teeth driving Tia to a fine frenzy of renewed ecstasy. Her nails bit into his flesh as furious pleasure overtook her again. But before her climax commenced, Ben hoisted himself on his knees and thrust into her, magnifying the exquisite sensations that rippled through her tight sheath and throughout her body. Tremor after tremor coursed through her until she whirled into oblivion.

Ben threw back his head and roared as his own climax began. His body tensed and exploded as his seed erupted violently in hot spurts of life-giving fluid.

They fell together in a heap, arms and legs entwined, breath mingled, the blanket beneath them wet with their sweat. Both knew they had just experienced something extraordinary, something few people knew in their lifetime, and a quietness overtook them as they contemplated the violence of their passion and what it meant in terms of their future.

"Are you asleep?" Ben asked when his breathing returned to normal.

"No," Tia replied, wishing they could remain like this forever, with nothing or no one to mar their happiness.

"Are you hungry?"

Tia considered telling him she wasn't hungry, but her growling stomach made its wishes known. Ben chuckled and swatted her delightfully rounded bottom. "Stay where you are, I'll fix us something to eat."

"I'll help," Tia said, looking for her clothes as she started to rise. Ben pushed her back down.

"No, don't get up, I'm not ready for you to get dressed yet." His roguish grin spoke more eloquently than verbal explanations.

"You're insatiable," Tia said, pulling the blanket up to her chin.

"And you're more passionate, more tantalizing than any woman I've ever known."

"And you've known many," Tia remarked sourly.

"A few," Ben admitted wryly.

"None you've wanted to marry."

"Absolutely none."

His words served to reinforce Tia's belief that

Ben had no intention of proposing to her again. The last time he had asked her to marry him and she'd refused, he said it would be the last time he proposed to any woman. Did he mean it? Things had changed since she was forced to turn down his proposal, and she no longer had a husband to worry about. But would Ben feel the same way? Or now that she was available, would he decide he no longer wanted a wife?

She watched in mute contemplation as Ben shrugged into his pants, built a fire, and fixed a hasty meal of damper, boiled beef, and billy tea. The flames cast his torso in shimmering bronze, emphasizing the impressive width of his shoulders and lean strength of his waist and hips. He was the most beautiful man she had ever seen, and she loved him.

They ate in silence. Ben's eyes never left Tia's face, unless it was to drift downward to where the bold thrust of her breasts were barely concealed by the blanket. Once she had eaten her fill, he removed the plate from her hand, stomped out the fire, removed his pants, and crawled into the bedroll beside her. His upper body was cold—though he had hardly seemed aware of the chill while he was preparing their food—and Tia recoiled from the contact of his icy flesh with hers. But he soon warmed and her skin began to tingle—this time not from cold. Definitely not from cold.

"I want you again, sweetheart," he whispered against her mouth. His breath was warm, his voice fraught with longing. "I can't seem to get enough of you. When Damian took you away I thought I'd lost you forever. That's when I decided to follow and take you by force, if need be."

"You were going to take me away from Damian? By force?"

"If that's what it took." Ben's voice was grim with determination. "I was ready to leave for Sydney when Damian showed up at my door with the news that you were gone. It seems, my impetuous little vixen, that you had taken matters into your own hands."

"I knew what Damian had planned for me and would rather die than return with him to England. I couldn't accept him as my legal husband after you—after we—I just couldn't be intimate like that with another man."

Her words sent a jolt of pure joy surging through Ben's veins. But it also gave him the eerie feeling that fate was laughing at him.

"Bloody hell, sweetheart, I feel the same way. I couldn't bear the thought of Damian—or any other man—touching you in the same way I did. I never thought I'd contemplate killing another man like I did Damian. I'm not normally a violent man."

"I'm a widow now." Her words seemed to have a sobering effect on Ben.

"The hell with Damian. He got what he deserved. And you're where you belong, in my arms. You're a feisty little vixen whose

333

foul mouth and gutter language pops up at the most inconvenient times, but I've managed to tame you. Now shut up and let me love you like you deserve."

"Foul mouth, did ye say?" Tia asked, slipping effortlessly into street language. "Ye bloody well better take back those words or ye'll find yerself sittin' on yer fancy arse nursin' a sore jaw."

Ben looked startled for a moment, then burst into raucous laughter. After a moment his laughter died away and all mirth fled as his gray eyes grew smoky with desire and he lowered his head. The moment his lips grazed hers, Tia began a slow spiral into a spinning world of exploding passion, fierce desire, intense pleasure—and love. Above all, love, even if it was only one-sided.

They reached Sydney the next day. While Tia replenished her woefully lacking wardrobe at the local mercantile, Ben visited Government House to report Lord Fairfield's death at the hands of bushrangers. One of the local magistrates was sailing for England in a few days and promised to notify the proper authorities who would see that his extensive estate was disbursed legally. Under Ben's prompting, the official informed him that according to English law if the estate wasn't entailed the bulk of the estate would fall to Fairfield's widow. At the very least the widow would be entitled to her dowry, which in Tia's case was quite generous. All this Ben related to Tia when he checked them into separate rooms at the new hotel for the night, since it was too late to return to Penrod station that day.

"I want nothing from Damian's estate," Tia said as they sat over dinner in the hotel dining room.

"Are you sure?" Ben probed. "Think about it before you decide. You could be a rich woman."

Tia stared at him but did not reply. She wondered what he was thinking. Did he want her to return to England to claim Damian's estate and leave him free? Nothing so far had been said about marriage; Ben had even rented them separate rooms for the night. She wondered about that and suddenly blurted out, "Why did you rent us two room?"

"For appearances," Ben revealed.

"I've been living with you for months, and appearances didn't seem to bother you then."

Ben flushed. "It's different in town. What we do at Penrod station is nobody's business."

"I see," Tia said, not understanding at all. His somewhat ambiguous statement only confused her.

"Just because I rented us two rooms doesn't mean we'll use both of them," he continued blandly. "Are you finished with your dinner?"

Tia nodded as a surge of raw heat warmed her veins. It rankled to think that all Ben had to do was beckon and she fell willingly into his arms. When had she lost her own identity, her will, her pride? The answer stunned her. When she met Ben, of course. He had her exactly where he wanted her, in his bed, and he had accomplished it neatly without benefit of marriage. Obviously he no longer felt the need to marry Tia and intended to remain faithful to his vow to remain single. Still, knowing all this, she followed Ben from the dining room and into his room. Later, after he had made tender love to her, she tried to imagine life without Ben. The picture she conjured up was dull, unrewarding, and bleak as hell.

The following day they set out for Penrod station, and Tia was surprised at how happy she was to see the sheep farm. If someone had told her when she was living on the streets of London that she'd be content living on a remote sheep farm in an untamed country, she would have laughed in their face. She suspected her contentment had to do with Ben Penrod and not with the location. Was her happiness soon to be shattered?

"I'll send word to Dare and Robin," Ben said soon after they arrived. "They were all very concerned about you."

"Robin? Your friend? Is he in Parramatta?"

"Didn't I tell you? Robin, Kate, and little Molly arrived the day after Damian took you away. I told them everything. They came to celebrate a wedding."

"They must have been disappointed to learn the bride was married to another man," Tia said with a sly grin.

Ben ignored her droll remark. "Kate is very close to delivering their second child. Robin wanted her to be with friends for the birth."

"Are they here? At Penrod station?"

"No, they're staying with Dare and Casey. Why don't you get settled and I'll ride over to Dare's place and tell them the good news in person? They'll probably all ride back with me to make sure you're all right."

Tia smiled. She adored being part of a close-knit family like the Penrods but knew that sooner or later her bubble was bound to burst. "I could use a hot bath."

"Perhaps I'll stay and scrub your back."

Tia correctly interpreted his wolfish grin, realizing she'd likely end up flat on her back if Ben remained to help her bathe. "If your family is as concerned as you say, you'd best go immediately. Besides, I can scrub my own back. Been doing it for years."

Disappointed yet realizing that Tia was right, he drew her into his arms, planting an exuberant kiss on her tempting red lips. His kiss deepened and Tia opened her mouth to his tongue as his hands slid around to grasp the firm mounds of her buttocks. While his tongue teased and taunted, he held her firmly against the hot thrust of his shaft, letting her feel the heat and hardness of him probing urgently against her stomach and between her legs. Abruptly she pulled away, panting, her blue eyes wide and dilated.

"Bloody 'ell, Ben Penrod, get yer arse outta 'ere before it's too bloody late and I end up on me back with me toes curled up!"

For a moment Ben looked startled, then he chuckled, finally ending up laughing uproariously. Just when he thought he'd tamed the little wildcat, she changed before his eyes into the street creature she had been when he first found her. Life with Tia would never be dull, he saw, nor would he ever take her for granted. Her mouth could drip honeyed words in the king's finest English, but at the drop of a hat she could spout curses and foul language fit only for the streets. Street urchin, refined lady, which was Tia Fairfield? Both or neither? Did it even matter? For better or for worse she was his. They didn't need legal words to bind their union. Or fancy phrases of undying love. What he and Tia had went deeper than mere words and phrases.

"You win, you little vixen," Ben laughed, slapping Tia on the behind as she turned away. "Have your bath now, but tonight belongs to me."

Three hours later Ben returned to Penrod station. With him were Dare, Casey, Robin, and Kate. Just as Ben predicted, nothing would do but for them to accompany him to Penrod station to welcome Tia back. And since Robin and Kate had yet to meet Tia, they were anxious to see the woman who had so captured Ben's fancy. The children had remained behind with servants, since Casey had decided that three active children underfoot would be too much of a distraction at this time.

Tia was nowhere in sight when they arrived. Exhausted from the ride from Sydney and a delicious soak in a hot bath, she stretched out on the bed to rest a few minutes. That was over two hours ago. When Ben found her asleep he decided not to awaken her. Instead, the new arrivals sat in the parlor with Ben, discussing Tia and her unusual circumstances.

First Ben related to them everything that had transpired up to the time he walked into the bushranger campsite.

"Bloody hell, mate, you could have been killed," Robin chided. "You should have taken someone with you. Big John and Lizzy accompanied us here, and you know what a good man Big John is to have around when you need him."

"Has Big John been keeping out of trouble?" Ben asked, aware of Big John's past with the law and his years as a bushranger.

"He's behaved so well I'm hoping to get his sentence remitted. Lizzy's sentence has already been remitted, and they want to marry. They hope to settle on their sixty combined government acres west of Bathurst."

"Who would have believed it?" Casey mused. "Lizzy and Big John. I hope she realizes she has a good man. He saved both Kate and me once and has been a good friend all these years. I'm glad he's finally found happiness."

"Now that Tia's husband is dead, that leaves her free to marry," Dare said, broaching a subject that had been delicately avoided by the group thus far. He was aware of his brother's aversion to marriage and wanted the subject out in the open.

"Aye, I suppose it does," Ben admitted grudgingly.

"Well?" Casey interjected, "when is the wedding?"

Tia paused outside the parlor door. She had awakened just moments ago to the sound of voices drifting up the stairs from the parlor. She had straightened her clothes and arrived at the parlor door in time to hear Casey ask about the wedding. She listened intently for Ben's answer, her body tense, her heart pounding with dread. Tia grew panicky when she realized she was about to hear the truth about Ben's feelings for her.

"Tia and I don't need a wedding to make us happy," Ben declared with firm conviction.

"You proposed once," Dare reminded him.

"Actually, I proposed three times," Ben revealed sheepishly.

Robin hooted with glee. "I knew it would happen one day. Love has a way of intruding when we least expect it." He slanted Kate a fond glance. "Kate and Molly certainly have changed me."

"I didn't say I was going to ask Tia to marry

me," Ben denied. "She has already said she doesn't want to return to England to claim her husband's estate, so I see no reason why we just can't go on as we are."

"Did Tia say she doesn't want to marry you?" Kate asked, offering her opinion on the subject. "I don't know Tia, but I'm willing to bet she'd accept your proposal. From what Casey tells me, Tia's a very practical woman who seems to know what she wants."

"Aye," agreed Dare, disappointed and disgruntled by his younger brother's inflexible attitude. "As head of the family, I demand you do the right thing by Tia. You've already destroyed her reputation by keeping her on Penrod station with you despite the fact that she was married to another man."

"Now hold on, Dare, I had no idea Tia was married when I brought her to Australia. And if you recall, I said I offered marriage, more than once. Now it no longer seems necessary, or even appropriate."

"Are you trying to say you don't love Tia?" Casey asked softly. Leave it to Casey to get to the heart of the matter.

Ben flushed. "I never said that."

"Then you do love her," Casey crowed triumphantly.

"I'm not sure how love feels, but I care deeply for Tia."

"Deeply enough to marry her?" Dare asked. He was growing angry now, angry enough to beat some sense into his obstinate brother. Robin was ready to join him.

"I—Bloody hell, Dare, are you ordering me to marry Tia?"

"I hoped it wouldn't come to that. You're an honorable man, Ben, Father raised both of us to recognize right from wrong. Forget your damn pride, forget that circumstances forced Tia to turn down your previous proposals and remember that she has no one but you and our family to depend upon."

"I'd never abandon Tia!" Ben declared hotly.

"Then marry her."

Absolute silence cloaked the room as four pairs of eyes probed Ben mercilessly.

"Very well, I'll arrange for the wedding immediately," he acquiesced with as much grace as he could muster.

Dare's stern features immediately softened. He knew he could depend on Ben to recognize his responsibility. Casey clapped her hands in unfeigned delight, and Robin and Kate exchanged looks that effectively conveyed their approval. But Tia, poised outside the parlor door, had other ideas. She wanted no part of a man who considered marriage only as a last resort. Hiding her disappointment behind a bright smile, she sailed into the parlor to greet their guests. Her sizzling anger she would save for Ben when they were alone.

The company didn't stay long. Only long enough for Tia to meet Robin and a very pregnant Kate, whom she liked immediately, and to satisfy their concern over her state of health. They left before dinner, having promised the children they would return in time for their evening meal. Dare sent Ben a searching look before he departed, and Ben's imperceptible nod left little doubt in Tia's mind what Dare was trying to convey.

"Alone at last." Ben grinned, turning toward Tia. "What did you think of Robin and Kate?"

"I liked them," Tia said truthfully. "They seem to be everything you said."

"Wait till you see little Molly, she's adorable."

"Do you like children?" Tia asked. She couldn't recall Ben ever voicing his opinion on children.

"I love children, when they belong to others," Ben said thoughtfully. "Since I never gave a thought to marriage I never considered having any of my own." He looked at Tia sharply, recalling Dare's ultimatum. "But I wouldn't be averse to having children if I ever married."

Tia said nothing. The silence deepened.

"Tia, I—we need to talk."

"I'm tired, Ben, can it wait? I want to go to bed."

"Bed? Aren't you hungry? You must have had a nice long nap this afternoon."

"Very well, Ben, first supper, then talk, if you feel there's a need."

"You won't be sorry, sweetheart," Ben promised. His smile set her heart atremble. Ben always was a charming rogue who set many a female heart aflutter. But she had to get a grip on herself. She didn't want a man who had to be reminded that offering marriage was the honorable thing to do.

Tia hurried through supper, barely tasting the food. When she pushed her plate aside, Ben rose and ushered her into the parlor, closing the door behind them. Though the servants were in another part of the house, he didn't want bothersome interruptions.

"What's so important, Ben?" Tia asked when they were seated side by side on the sofa.

Ben took her hand in his large, tanned fingers, turned it over, and placed a kiss in the center of her palm. "I want us to be married, Tia, soon."

"Why?"

Ben looked puzzled. "Why? Because—because—bloody hell, why do most men want to get married?"

"Do you love me?"

"I've told you often enough that I care for you. I love to make love to you, isn't that enough? I was the first to take you and hope to be the last. I want you with me forever."

The words came easily to his lips. And with shocking clarity he realized he meant every single one. He wasn't lying; without Tia life would be dull and meaningless. He didn't need Dare or Robin ordering him to marry Tia. He suddenly, achingly, wanted it more than he'd ever wanted anything in his life. Wanted it with a fierce need that took his breath away. It no longer mattered that he had proposed to Tia three times, or twenty times, he'd do it again and again until she belonged exclusively to him. He was just about to tell her this startling revelation when Tia's face screwed up into a fierce scowl.

"Ye bloody liar!" she screeched. "Ye don't want ta marry me, or any woman. Ye want me on me back with me legs open ta accommodate ye, but that's all. I heard what yer brother told ya, and I ain't gonna marry ya. Ye don't know the meanin' of love. Ye don't even know yer arse from a hole in the ground!"

Ben's mouth dropped open in mute protest. Tia's outburst had robbed him of coherent speech and left him floundering. Women! Never would he understand them. Least of all Tia.

Chapter Seventeen

"You heard?" was all Ben could think of to say.

"I heard, and I don't want a man who needs his brother telling him who to marry."

"It might have been like that at first but—"

"You want me to believe that all of a sudden you really want to marry me?"

"Well—aye, I guess you could say that." It sounded lame, but that's exactly how it was. "If you recall, I've proposed to you more than once since we've met."

"I don't know what precipitated those earlier proposals, but I no longer feel it's what you truly want. Dare's ultimatum left little room for refusal."

"Bloody hell! I'm my own man, Tia. Do you think Dare could order me to do something if it's not what I really want to do?" What did he have to do or say to persuade her?

That gave Tia pause for thought. Finally she said, "Yes, I think you care enough about Dare and Robin's opinion to influence your thinking and alter your decision about anything."

"You don't know me at all, do you, sweetheart?" Ben said with a hint of censure.

Tia's expression softened and she said slowly, "I know you too well, Ben."

That seemed to make Ben angry, as he grasped her arm and pulled her against the hard length of his body. "I should have left you on the streets with the dregs of society where I found you. But no, I had to bring you home with me and let you complicate my life. I even broke a solemn vow. I did something I swore I'd never do, I proposed. More than once, God help me. What do you want me to do, grovel at your feet?"

I want you to love me! Tia's heart cried out.

When those cherished words did not come, Tia turned away.

"Don't turn away from me, Tia, look at me. Can't you see how much I want you? When we make love the world shakes beneath our feet. No other man will be able to do that for you. I'm going to ask you one last time. Marry me, Tia."

Please tell me you love me, came Tia's silent plea.

"I care about you deeply, more than any other woman I've ever known. I sincerely believe I can make you happy."

"I want you to love me as much as I love you."

"Would I propose if I didn't love you?"

"What kind of answer is that?" Tia challenged, still convinced that Ben was merely pleasing Dare by proposing.

"Maybe you'll believe me if I show you how much I care."

With one lithe motion he swept her off her feet. Tia squealed and clung to him, throwing her arms around his neck and holding tight. He flung open the door, entered the hallway, and took the stairs two at a time. He carried her into his bedroom and set her on her feet, still holding her tightly within the circle of his arms.

"I'm going to love you, sweetheart, and when I'm finished you'll no longer doubt my feelings."

His desire for her surged and awakened in him a need that hadn't existed before. A need to convince the little wildcat that no other man had the power to move her like he did. A need that bordered on brutality—and Ben wasn't a brutal man. Tia recognized the change in him, was frightened by it and tried to pull away. Driven by an angry passion he did not understand, Ben took her arm and roughly jerked her to him. Tia's mouth opened in wordless protest and his mouth came forcefully down on hers.

His teeth nipped hurtfully at her soft bottom lip, released it, and deepened the kiss, his hard lips brutal in their invasion of her trembling mouth. Tia recognized his fierce aggression, felt his hunger, and her fright escalated. This wasn't Ben, the gentle lover who never failed to move her with his tender loving. This Ben was rough, and hard, and almost brutal in his passion.

"Ben, stop! You frighten me."

But her fright was of short duration. As it always did, her body betrayed her where Ben was concerned. She began to respond to his ardor as her blood warmed and her limbs grew leaden. Abruptly his mouth lifted and he looked into her eyes. Tia could not decipher his look—a mixture of harshness and helplessness. Then he lowered his head and kissed her again, his tongue penetrating deeply. She touched his tongue with her own and felt him shudder.

"Take off your clothes," Ben growled, placing a shaking hand at her neckline as if he meant to rip her clothing from her.

His words unleashed her temper. "Like hell! I'll take off my clothes only if I want to."

"You want to," Ben said, exerting force at the offending neckline.

"Wait, this dress is new!" She had just purchased it as well as several others yesterday in Sydney. Her fingers shook as she hastily undid the buttons. The dress fell from her shoulders and Ben pushed it and the chemise beneath aside, freeing her breasts.

His warm palm lifted a soft, bare breast, weighing it in his hand as his lips went unerringly to her throat. Tia's pulse jumped as his teeth grazed the sensitive spot below her ear and his fingers toyed with a swollen nipple.

"I—I don't like you like this, Ben," Tia complained.

Ben's answer was to hungrily kiss a molten path to her breasts. Slipping to his knees before her, his hot, open mouth enclosed an erect nipple. Then he pulled her dress and chemise completely free of her body, lifting her from the puddle of cloth at her feet. Possessively he gripped her bare buttocks, holding her close as he suckled her. Tia winced from the pleasure she felt.

Suddenly he lifted his head and gazed deeply into her eyes. "How *do* you like me, Tia? Evidently you don't like me as a husband, so I'll be your lover. After tonight you'll realize no other lover can please you like I do."

Then he lowered his wet mouth to her other breast, tugging at the nipple, moving his tongue back and forth. She gasped when his mouth opened wider to take even more of her breast inside. He sucked greedily, devouring her, thrilling her even as she tried to stifle her response.

Feeling himself growing painfully hard beneath the confines of his tight pants, Ben stood and shed his garments, every last one of them. Tia tried not to stare at his erection, but it looked so obscenely huge springing from the dark forest at the juncture of his thighs that

350

her eyes were riveted to that spot.

"Touch me," Ben said, aware of where Tia's gaze was directed.

When Tia hesitated, he reached out, grasped her hand, and drew it forward. His hand guided her as her fingers clasped him, surprised at the velvet softness covering the throbbing hardness underneath. Slowly he moved her hand, teaching her the rhythm. When he removed his hand, Tia, mesmerized by the delicate strength beneath her fingertips, continued stroking. Until Ben stiffened, groaned, and flung her hand away.

"Now it's your turn," he said, sweeping her off her feet and positioning her in the center of the bed. Shuddering, he reached for her, stroking his big hands down the length of her body. "You're beautiful." His mouth lowered to hers then and he kissed her deeply, his open lips devouring her. Then abruptly his lips left hers and moved aggressively down her shivering body.

"Oh, God, Ben, don't do this to me," Tia begged as he kissed her naked flesh hungrily, feasting on her as if she were a tender morsel and he a starving man. Tia shuddered with excitement when he reached her bare belly. His tongue on her quivering flesh sent all thought of further protest fleeing.

Ben's hot lips moved down, down until they found the moist golden curls between her thighs. His hands urged her legs open and his brown fingers stroked the soft insides of her thighs until they parted to allow him total access. Then he was between her legs, his hands beneath her rounded buttocks, bringing her up to meet his mouth. She felt his breath on her, warm and teasing, then his lips and tongue, probing, stroking, finding the tiny nub of pleasure amidst the golden curls.

Tia truly was frightened now. Frightened by the depth of her wild abandon. Frightened by the raw jolts of pure love she felt for this man. Frightened that he would take his mouth away and leave her. She needn't have worried. His tongue stroked harder, his mouth sank deeper, he loved and lashed as Tia's jerking pelvis rose up to meet his mouth. Then it began. The fierce spiraling into eternity that only his mouth could bring.

Though his own release was dangerously close, Ben stayed with her, giving her all she needed, all she begged for, loving her with hot, wild intimacy until the final tremors left her body.

"Now it's my turn, sweetheart," he gasped raggedly, kissing her again. His tongue skimmed along her teeth, then penetrated deeply as he ground his mouth against hers. She tasted herself on his lips and it was highly arousing. He slipped his fingers between her legs and found her flesh swollen and moist from his kisses, ready for him—waiting for him . . .

Eager for him.

Suddenly he shifted her atop him. "Ride me, sweetheart. Do whatever you want."

For a moment Tia looked confused. But when Ben lifted her and slid deftly inside her tight sheath, the strangeness of the position no longer seemed awkward. It was wonderful, it *felt* wonderful. She rocked experimentally and was rewarded when Ben grasped her hips tightly and slid even deeper inside. She felt him fill her, larger, harder, heavier than she remembered from their previous couplings, and she threw back her head, grasped his shoulders, and rode him wildly. She felt as if she could go on like this forever—never wanted it to end.

But unfortunately it didn't take long.

A look of total shock came over Tia's face when she realized she was going to climax again. Ben realized it almost at the same moment Tia did and began thrusting furiously. Within moments they were moving together in perfect harmony, each reaching for that final pinnacle of ecstasy. With deep, quick strokes, Ben's gyrating hips and thrusting pelvis drove them both toward total release. It came with a burst of shimmering stars, taking them to that place where lovers dwell.

The peaceful quiet was broken by the sound of twittering birds and the sudden emergence of daylight. Tia awoke abruptly, startled to find Ben in bed with her. Then it all came back to her. Dare's insistence that they wed and Ben's compliance, and the nearly explosive loving that had followed. She knew that Ben had been trying to prove something last night, and he had. He'd proved that she could never love any man but Ben Penrod. He hadn't proved that he loved her, only that he was a virile, passionate man who enjoyed making love to an attractive woman.

Ben cranked open one eye, watching the myriad of conflicting emotions flicker across Tia's expressive face. He had set out last night to prove to Tia that he wanted her with him always, and in his estimation he had done an admirable job of convincing her. Though she was slightly reluctant at first, his uninhibited loving had swept her reticence aside and she had responded with unrestrained passion. Didn't she realize he loved her? Saying the words were difficult for a man who had never intended to fall in love and marry, so he had attempted to demonstrate the depth of his feelings by loving her so thoroughly she'd never want to leave him.

"What are you thinking?"

Tia started violently, unaware that the sheet had fallen around her waist, leaving two rounded breasts just inches from Ben's mouth. Ben's eyes roamed freely over the ripe curves. He moistened his lips, ready to taste the luscious fruits bobbing before him so enticingly, when Tia said, "I've decided to book passage to England and claim Damian's estate."

"You've what! Bloody hell, **Tia**, have you lost your mind? Didn't last night mean anything to you? Why do you continue to resist? I want to marry you. I—" he swallowed convulsively, the word he wanted to say stuck in his throat. "I—"

"Don't say anything you don't mean, Ben," Tia advised. She hated it when he lied. "I understand how you feel. I know how much you want to please your brother and do what's right, but it's not necessary. I'll have my dowry back and part or all of Damian's estate. You don't have to worry about me ending up on the streets again. I don't need a man to protect me, I've managed just fine all these years."

"You're incredible," Ben said, meaning it. "But you're not leaving. I'm finally ready to make a commitment, and you're damn well going to stay until you agree to become my wife."

As he lay there with her soft, warm body pressed to his, Ben's thoughts grew troubled. What if Tia didn't love him enough to marry him? What if she didn't love him at all? No, that's crazy, he told himself. She couldn't respond to him the way she did if she didn't love him. She was just too damn stubborn to realize that she had altered his thinking about marriage. He was finally prepared to commit to one woman. Dare's ultimatum had nothing to do with his decision. Even if it took forever, he'd persuade Tia that they belonged together.

"I won't be your mistress," Tia said, lifting her chin belligerently. "I'll consider your proposal."

Ben flashed a roguish grin. "You'll stay?" If he could have her in his bed every night, love her as she deserved, he believed his powers of persuasion would be strong enough to convince Tia that he truly did want her for his wife.

Love.

Love was the final frontier; an unknown mystery he had thus far managed to avoid. He opened his mouth, ready to utter those intimate words totally foreign to his nature, when Tia's answer threw him into a state of confusion.

"I'll stay, for the time being, but you must promise not to try to seduce me. I can't think properly when you're making love to me. Marriage is forever; this time I want the choice to be mine."

Ben looked thunderstruck. He had been counting on having Tia in his bed. "I'm not sure that's possible." His eyes lingered on her bare breasts.

Tia noted the direction of his gaze. She pulled the sheet up to her neck. "I mean it, Ben. If you truly care about me you'll prove it by agreeing to my terms."

"How do *you* feel about *me*?

"I love you. That's why I can't marry you. At least not yet."

"What if I told you I loved you?" he asked quietly.

"Do you?"

"I—I can't think of another explanation for the way I feel about you."

"Are you looking for another explanation?"

"Perhaps I did once, but no longer."

"I want to believe you, Ben, but it's difficult after the conversation I heard between you and Dare."

"Forget that damn conversation. I have. I told you before that Dare couldn't force me into anything I didn't want to do."

"I can't forget."

"How can I prove to you I'm serious?"

Tia searched Ben's face, seeing all those qualities she loved so well. "Give me time to make a decision without pressuring me."

Ben dragged in a shaky sigh. It was going to be extremely difficult to keep his hands off Tia, and he wasn't certain he could do it, but he'd give it a try. Especially if it meant keeping Tia at Penrod station. This was her home now, she belonged here, and he never intended to let her leave despite her misgivings about his love. One day soon she wouldn't need to hear fancy words as proof of just how much he loved her.

The family was all gathered around the table. Even the children were seated with the adults for the happy occasion. Casey was hostess. Ben and Tia had been invited to join them for a celebration of sorts since they were all together except Roy and Maude for the first time in years.

Big John and Lizzy had been asked to join them, and Tia couldn't help but stare at the huge giant who looked so fierce but obviously had hidden qualities admired by the entire family.

Ben related some of the history involving Casey, Dare, Robin, and Kate, and it amazed Tia that those two couples had ended up in wedded bliss. Big John had once been a bushranger who at one time saved Casey and had been a guardian angel to the family ever since. He proved his worth by rescuing Kate years later. He had been instrumental in bringing the two couples together at different times in their lives.

The conversation was lighthearted and brisk, but from time to time Tia sensed their eyes on her, as if waiting for something to happen— someone to say something. She knew exactly what was expected and realized that their disappointment would be keen when she and Ben failed to live up to their expectations.

Finally Dare could stand it no longer. Looking at Ben squarely, he asked, "Have you two set a date for the wedding?"

Ben flushed, aware of what Dare would think when he revealed there wasn't going to be a wedding. Not yet, anyway. Taking pity on him, Tia rushed into the void. "There isn't going to be a wedding."

Dare's expression grew fierce. "No wedding? Bloody hell, Ben, where are your brains? Maybe you need some sense knocked into you."

"It's my decision," Tia said with quiet dignity.

Casey frowned and exchanged puzzled glances with Kate. Robin lent encouragement to Dare's suggestion. "I'll help you knock some sense into the lad."

Always practical, Kate advised, "Let Tia explain."

"There's nothing to explain. I've simply decided I'm not ready to make a commitment." She slid Ben a look that needed no interpreting.

"You're not leaving, are you?" Casey asked. For once in her life she was at a total loss for words. She could have sworn that Tia loved Ben. And Ben loved Tia, he was just too darn stubborn to admit it.

"Tia is remaining at Penrod station for the time being as my guest," Ben interjected.

"Your 'guest'?" Dare asked, lifting his dark eyebrows. His emphasis on the word left little doubt as to what it implied. He assumed that Ben was keeping Tia on as his mistress, and it didn't sit well with him. Apparently he didn't know Ben as well as he'd thought.

"My *guest*," Ben stressed. "Tia is obligated to me in no way, and I expect nothing from her."

Although no one understood what was going on between Tia and Ben, Ben's words eased Dare's mind somewhat.

"If Tia needs a place to stay, we'll make room for her here," Casey said, offering an alternate solution.

"You're already bursting at the seams," Ben said. "Tia will remain at Penrod station and that's final." His tone left no room for argument.

Tia could feel the family's disappointment and wished she could have explained to them exactly how she felt. But at this point she wasn't sure that marriage was the right thing to do. Lord knows she wanted to marry Ben. She adored the Penrod children and little Molly Fletcher, and would give anything to have Ben's child. She loved Ben enough for both of them, but feared that wasn't enough. She wanted to believe with all her heart that Ben loved her and fervently prayed that the next few weeks would bring her enlightenment and peace of mind.

That night it started to rain. And the following days brought a torrential deluge of drenching rain that slowly swelled the banks of the Hawkesbury.

Ben had known that living with Tia in the same house would be difficult, but he didn't realize how close to torture it would be, wanting her fiercely yet struggling to keep his promise not to make love to her. He knew he could easily seduce Tia into his bed, but to do so would damage his honor.

The constant rain wasn't helping matters any. Since he was forced to remain inside much of the time, he spent more hours with Tia, wanting her, needing her . . .

Loving her . . .

Tia was impressed with Ben's restraint. She knew what he was suffering, for she felt exactly the same. The long hours spent in one another's company were pure hell. Wanting him, needing him . . .

Loving him . . .

Tia was almost convinced that Ben truly did love her and was on the verge of telling him so when he invited her to ride into Parramatta one day during a two-day break in the almost constant rain. She accepted eagerly. She hadn't been feeling well for over a week and she thought an outing was just what she needed to perk up her spirits. In fact, the bouts of nausea, which at first had bothered her only in the morning, seemed inclined to strike at any time of the day now, and she was truly worried.

Jostling along in the wagon beside Ben, Tia felt miserable. The constant jolting had stirred up her queasy stomach and she feared she would embarrass herself in front of Ben. Fortunately the trip to Parramatta was a short one.

Ben noted Tia's reserve and was puzzled by it. Usually animated and buoyant, she was much too quiet. In fact, he had noted of late a definite reticence on her part. She looked peaked and appeared to have lost weight. A terrible fear set his heart to pounding. Was Tia sick?

"Why so quiet, sweetheart?" Ben asked after a long silence. "It's not like you. You're not sick, are you?"

Tia swallowed the bile rising in her throat and attempted a weak smile. Upsetting Ben was the last thing she wanted to do, especially since there was nothing really wrong with her. "I'm fine, Ben, just weary of this infernal rain. It feels good to be outside again and I'm savoring it."

"We're all tired of the rain, but I fear it's here to stay for a while." He cast a wary eye at the river winding alongside the road and another at the heavily overcast sky. "If it doesn't stop soon we may have a flood in the making. The Hawkesbury hasn't left its banks in several years, and most of us who live along its route have forgotten the devastation left in the wake of a flood. I think as a precaution I'll start the men sandbagging the banks when we return to Penrod station."

"Is it that serious?" Tia asked, alarmed.

"The last time I saw the river this high was shortly after Kate and Robin were married, but we were able to prevent a disaster that time. I don't want to alarm you, sweetheart, but if this rain continues, danger does exist for all the farms along the Hawkesbury."

The seriousness of the situation left them both in deep thought, and Tia's nagging illness was all but forgotten. When they drove down the main street of Parramatta, the muddy thoroughfare was clogged with people enjoying the brief respite from the rain as they scurried from store to store conducting their business. Ben parked the wagon in front of the store offering farm supplies and feed and hopped down from the unsprung seat. Before Tia could follow he was at her side, lifting her from the seat and splashing across a murky brown puddle to set her down on the narrow boardwalk. He seemed reluctant to remove his arms once she was on her feet.

"You have no idea how good it feels to have you in my arms again," he murmured into her ear as he clung to her waist with almost frantic urgency. "I don't know how much longer I can honor my promise."

Tia flushed, realizing that passersby were staring at them with unfeigned curiosity. "Ben, please, let me go. We'll talk about this later."

To Ben her words held special meaning. It meant that soon Tia would be his in every sense of the word. She would be in his arms, in his bed, and a part of his life forever. "I'm holding you to your promise, love." Ben grinned as he reluctantly released her and stepped away. "Tonight." His tone spoke eloquently of his need, of his plans for the night, and Tia felt a tingle of excitement travel up her spine.

"Ben! Ben Penrod!" Ben and Tia both turned their heads at the same time. The flame-haired beauty who had eyes only for Ben was rushing down the boardwalk in their direction.

Suddenly Ben's perplexed frown turned into a smile of welcome. "Megan? My God, it is you! Megan Mitchell. I thought you were still in Ireland visiting relatives."

"I arrived home two days ago," Megan gushed. She looked up at Ben through wide, adoring eyes the color of gleaming emeralds. "I wanted to come out to Penrod station immediately but the infernal rain interfered with my plans. When did you return from London? Aren't you glad to see me?"

"One question at a time," Ben laughed. He had nearly forgotten what an engaging girl Megan had been. Only she was no longer a girl. She was a woman, a very beautiful woman. When they were both nineteen he had a crush on her and would have seduced her if his father and brother hadn't urged him into going abroad and seeing a little of the world first.

"Tell me first if you missed me," Megan said. Tia tapped her foot impatiently while Megan flirted outrageously with Ben.

"Of course," Ben lied, too much of a gentleman to admit he had forgotten Megan the moment he reached London and discovered all the opportunities the intriguing city held for a virile young man.

"I've never forgotten you, Ben," Megan revealed, looking up at him through a smoky fringe of incredibly thick lashes. Tia thought ungraciously that the young woman had perfected the art of flirting to a fine degree and considered Ben a fool for acting like a besotted oaf.

When she had first met Ben he had been in trouble over a woman and she'd thought him a womanizer and scoundrel. Since that time there had been no other woman in Ben's life, but that didn't mean a leopard could change his spots. Once a womanizer, always a womanizer. If his behavior with little Miss Megan Mitchell was any indication, it appeared as though Ben was reverting back to his true character, and just exactly where did that leave her?

Suddenly Megan deigned to glance in Tia's direction, a sour look on her face. "Is that the woman?"

Startled, Ben frowned and looked at Tia. "Are you referring to Tia?"

"Is that her name?" Megan asked.

"Aye, Tia Fairfield. She's my house guest. Tia, this is Megan Mitchell. Megan and I are old friends."

"So I gathered," Tia remarked dryly.

"House guest," snorted Megan, her tone conveying her disdain. "That's not what the townspeople say. I wanted to come out to Penrod station and see for myself if the gossip is true. You've saved me the trouble."

Ben frowned. "Gossip? What kind of gossip?"

"We're all adults, Ben. Rumor has it that you passed Tia off for a time as your wife and then her husband showed up to claim her. No one seems to know what happened after that except that she's back with you again, this time as your mistress. If I had come home sooner, you'd have no need for a mistress," Megan hinted, sending Ben a smoldering look that told him Megan had gained experience as well as maturity in Ireland. She had come a long way from the green girl he'd known.

Tia gasped.

Ben winced.

Megan merely smiled.

"I'm afraid your source of gossip is faulty," Ben said. "Tia is a widow and we plan to marry soon."

Megan's face fell. "You're going to marry her? I thought—that is, I hoped we could renew our relationship. If you recall, we were once quite—close."

"We were young, Megan, a lot has happened since then. I'm going to marry Tia."

Tia stepped forward, finally finding her voice. "You forget, Ben, I haven't accepted your proposal yet." Turning on her heel, she stormed down the boardwalk.

Chapter Eighteen

When Ben would have given chase, Megan placed a fluttering hand on his arm and said, "Let her go. We haven't talked in ever so long and we've so much to catch up on. Tia sounds like a spoiled little girl to me."

"You're right," Ben agreed, thinking that Tia *was* acting like a spoiled brat. He'd offered her his love, his life, all his worldly goods, and she'd turned up her nose at his honest proposal. He wasn't going to indulge her now by running after her like a besotted youth. Groveling didn't become him. "Join me for a cup of tea and you can tell me all about Ireland." There, Ben thought triumphantly, that ought to show Tia she couldn't lead him around by the nose.

Megan smiled beguilingly, took his arm, and

led him off toward the nearest food shop: Being with Ben again was just like old times. She had every confidence that she could make him forget his mistress.

Tia looked back only once before entering the mercantile a short distance down the block. She was sorry she had. Ben and Megan, arm in arm like a pair of intimate friends, strolled down the street. Then she entered the store and they were lost from sight. Not that it mattered. She was grateful she had found out about Ben's fickle nature before she made the supreme mistake of marrying him.

Tia walked aimlessly around the store, fingering merchandise she had no intention of buying. Ben had given her money before they left Penrod station, but she'd be damned if she'd spend any of it. She'd have plenty of money of her own once she went to England to claim it. The air inside the store was dank and stale, pungent with the mingled odors of musty bolts of cloth, spices, spoiled food, and leather. The combined smells churned violently inside her stomach, making her feel ill and weak. Staggering against a counter, Tia fought desperately to maintain her equilibrium. Fainting was foreign to her nature, and she closed her eyes and swallowed, fearing she'd either pass out or spew out her guts.

"My dear, are you ill?"

Tia opened her eyes slowly. An attractive woman in her mid-twenties was staring at her with concern.

"I—I'm not sure."

"Do you need help?"

"Perhaps a breath of air."

"Of course, let me help you." Taking her arm, the woman slowly led Tia out of the stifling atmosphere of the store. Tia took several deep breaths and swallowed convulsively. "Do you feel better now?"

"I—yes, thank you," Tia returned shakily.

The woman's brow furrowed. "You don't look better. You're still very pale. Perhaps you should see a doctor."

Tia gave the suggestion serious thought. She hadn't been feeling well of late, perhaps she had caught something during her stay in the bush with the bushrangers. As if sensing her need and aware of her indecision, the woman said, "I'm Mary Proctor, Dr. Proctor's wife. My husband's office is just a few steps away. He'd be more than happy to treat you."

"I haven't been feeling well lately," Tia admitted, "but I don't know if I need a doctor."

"Why don't you let my husband decide that."

Mary's concern convinced Tia. "Very well, it can't hurt to consult a doctor. My name is Tia Fairfield."

"Come along, Tia, Dan will soon have you right as rain. He's an excellent doctor."

Dan Proctor was everything a doctor should be. Kind, concerned, caring, and very professional.

Once hopeful of winning Kate's hand, Dan

Proctor had eventually realized that Kate's heart belonged to Robin Fletcher. Soon afterward he had married pretty Mary, the daughter of a settler. It was a good match and he often blessed his lucky stars for placid, loving Mary whose temperament was the exact opposite of fiery, independent Kate.

Dr. Proctor greeted Tia, asked her several pertinent questions, then said, "Your symptoms are classic, Miss Fairfield, but an examination is needed to be absolutely certain."

"Mrs. Fairfield," Tia amended. "What kind of an examination?"

Dr. Proctor explained in simple terms what he intended to do. When he noted the rise in color in Tia's cheeks, he said, "There's nothing to be embarrassed about, but if it would make you feel more comfortable, Mary will accompany you into the examining room. She often serves as my nurse."

The examination, though embarrassing, didn't last long, and Tia had to admit that Mary's presence was comforting. Shortly afterward she sat across the desk from Dan Proctor, her face screwed up into a mask of concern. Had he found some rare disease that she knew nothing about?

"Well, young lady, you'll be happy to know that you are in excellent physical condition."

"What? You mean I went through that examination for nothing?"

Dr. Proctor smiled indulgently. "Not exactly for nothing. You're expecting a child, Mrs. Fairfield. You must have had some idea you were pregnant."

Tia shook her head in mute denial. A missed period or two had never concerned her before. It came as such a shock, she was utterly speechless. The only words she could utter were, "W—when?"

"To the best of my knowledge you'll produce a child in slightly under seven months. That makes you two months into your pregnancy."

"No, I can't be! That's not possible."

Dr. Proctor looked troubled. "I fear there is nothing we can do about it. I'm certain you'll feel better about this once you've had time to think about it."

Dan Proctor had lived in Parramatta a long time and there was nothing in the area he didn't know about. He knew that Tia was living with Ben Penrod and suspected he was the father of her child. If Tia's husband were alive, Proctor could understand her reluctance to bear Ben an illegitimate child. But if she was a widow, marriage to the child's father should present no problem.

"You don't understand, doctor," Tia said on a shuddering sigh. "I'm sure you're aware of who I am and that I've—been living at Penrod station." Dan nodded but said nothing, unwilling to pass judgment. "My husband is dead but I'm not certain marriage would be the right thing to do just now."

"If there is nothing preventing your marriage to the baby's father, then you must think of the child and his future." He wanted to say more but didn't feel qualified to tell a virtual stranger what to do. Perhaps he should speak with Ben Penrod. He'd known the young man for years, well enough to offer him some advice.

Tia rose to leave. "Thank you, doctor, I'll take your advice into consideration." She opened her reticule and paid him with a portion of the coins Ben had given her, then left the office in a daze.

Tia was waiting at the wagon when Ben emerged from the hardware store. Once Tia was out of sight he had offered Megan a flimsy excuse to cut short their reunion and hurried off to conduct his business. He was surprised to see Tia waiting for him in the wagon without any packages.

"Did you see nothing that takes your fancy?" he asked as he hauled himself up beside her. Tia seemed not to hear him. "Tia, did you hear me?" Nothing. She seemed distant and preoccupied. "Bloody hell, Tia, if you're angry about Megan . . ."

"What?" It suddenly dawned on Tia what Ben was saying. Right now Megan was the very least of her worries. "I—I wasn't listening."

"That's obvious. Are you ill? Perhaps you should see Dan Proctor while we're in town. You've been looking peaked lately, not at all like yourself. Megan is an old friend and—"

Tia frowned. "I don't blame you for being

attracted to Megan, she's very beautiful."

Ben fell silent, wondering what it would take to make Tia jealous as he set the bullock into motion with a flick of the reins. It started to rain as they lumbered down the track from Parramatta. Ben pulled a canvas over Tia's head and urged the bullock forward. The river looked ominous as it licked at the banks, and Ben realized that serious flooding was no longer a threat but a distinct probability. The Hawkesbury looked nearly at crest stage and immediate precautions were necessary. As soon as they arrived back at Penrod station he'd set the men to placing sandbags along the eroding bank. The workers had been filling sandbags for days now, readying them should the need arise.

Suddenly the wagon ground to a halt. The rain was falling in solid sheets now, drenching and chilling them. The canvas that covered Tia was next to useless as the wind lifted it and drove water underneath, soaking her to the skin. Ben didn't even have the meager protection of the canvas.

"Why are we stopping?" Tia cried above the din of rolling thunder. "We can't be far from Penrod station."

"We're stuck," Ben yelled back. He jumped from the wagon and unhitched the bullock, slapping him on the rump and allowing the animal to make his own way out of the mud. Then he turned to Tia and held out his arms. She slipped easily into his embrace and he carried her to ground only slightly dryer than the muddy track. When she began to shiver violently, Ben cursed and realized he had to find them shelter soon or have a very sick woman on his hands.

It took a few minutes to get his bearings, but when he did Ben realized they were on Penrod land and within a short distance of a shack used by sheep herders in inclement weather. It was normally stocked with wood, beds, and blankets. He grasped Tia's arm and propelled her away from the track toward a hill looming in the distance. Tia struggled along until her feet no longer had the strength to free themselves from the sucking mud. Then Ben, whose boots were much sturdier, swept Tia into his arms and carried her through the wind-driven rain toward a destination not yet discernible through the drenching downpour.

Turning her face into his shoulder, Tia didn't have the breath to ask where they were going. But she didn't need to ask. Deep in her heart she knew that Ben would let no harm come to her. She trusted him implicitly, except when it came to her heart.

Tia didn't see the hut, nestled as it was against the side of the hill, until Ben stood before the door. It was unlatched and he shoved it open with his foot. Rain preceded them inside as the door swung open and Ben carried her into the dank, dark interior of the hut. He set her on her feet and slammed shut the door. Water sloughed off their drenched clothing and puddled around their feet. The din on the tin roof nearly drowned out the roar of thunder as the wind drove rain against the hut in angry, lashing torrents.

"Are you all right?" Ben frowned with concern as Tia sagged against him. "I thought we'd be home long before the rain began. I shouldn't have taken you out today."

"I'm fine." Never had she seen such a violent storm. "I hope the bullock gets home all right."

Ben smiled. They were both drenched to the skin and shivering and she was worrying about the bullock. "He's a tough animal. He'll find his way back to the barn."

"When do you suppose the rain will stop?"

"I wish I knew," Ben said in a voice that conveyed his worry. "But enough talk. You're shivering. Get out of those wet clothes before you catch your death. I'll get a fire going in the hearth. There's a blanket on the bunk, use it while your clothes are drying." He set to work immediately, giving Tia no time to protest. Tia hesitated only a moment before shrugging out of her clothes and wrapping the blanket around her violently shivering body.

Tia was seated on the bunk, still shaking from cold, when Ben finished his task and began stripping off his own wet clothes. Unable to look away, Tia watched through lowered lids as Ben's bronzed flesh emerged from the sodden mass of his clothes. In the split second before he reached for the blanket, Tia caught a fleeting glimpse of back and shoulders corded with muscles, lean hips, tapered thighs, and the taut mounds of his buttocks flexing involuntarily against the cold. He glanced over his shoulder and their eyes met. Hers were glazed with shimmering desire; his were silver mirrors into his soul, reflecting his need—his passion . . . his love. Unable to withstand the sizzling heat of his steady regard, Tia looked away first.

"You're still shivering," Ben said when he was decently covered by the blanket. Pulling another blanket from the cot, he spread it before the newly lit fire. "Come here." He held out his hand.

Trustingly Tia placed her hand in his, allowing Ben to pull her forward. He sat down on the blanket and pulled Tia into his lap. His arms went around her and she felt his incredible heat seep into her pores, warming her blood to the consistency of warm honey. Within minutes she had stopped shivering, though her flesh was still icy to the touch.

"This is where you belong, sweetheart. I don't ever want to let you go. You don't know the torture you've put me through these past weeks. It's downright humiliating having my proposals turned down time after time. You've stripped me of my pride, my self-respect, and made a mockery of my desire to avoid marriage. Yet I find myself returning time and again for more of the same brutal treatment from you. When will you believe I love you and want us to be together forever?"

"What about Megan?"

"Who?" He had already forgotten pretty little Megan Mitchell, the old flame he had flirted with to make Tia jealous.

Tia gave an exasperated snort. "You'll never change, Ben Penrod. Once a womanizer, always a womanizer."

"Megan means nothing to me, Tia. I was only trying to make you jealous." He grinned delightedly. "Looks like I succeeded."

"Like hell!" Tia bristled. "I don't care what you do with Megan, or a dozen like her."

"That's just it, I don't want anything to do with them. You're the only woman I want."

Tia closed her eyes. If only she could believe him. She wanted to tell him about the baby, to watch his face when he learned he was going to be a father.

She wanted to marry Ben and live happily ever after.

"Are you asleep?" Just then a particularly savage gust of wind rattled the single canvas-shuttered window in the hut, and Tia snuggled closer in Ben's arms. The rain beat furiously against the outside walls, sending a fine spray through the cracks to mist them with dampness.

"How could anyone sleep with the racket going on outside? Do you think the river will flood? It certainly looked ominous."

"It doesn't look good," Ben admitted. He didn't want to alarm Tia but neither did he want to lie to her. "Forget the river for now, there's nothing we can do about it until we get back to Penrod station. Just relax and let my arms warm you."

His arms were doing more than merely warming her. They were comforting her, relaxing her, making her believe she was loved and cherished. She was hardly aware that he had lowered the blanket from her breasts until she felt the moist warmth of his mouth close over one nipple and suckle gently. Tia sighed with exquisite pleasure as Ben's mouth moved from one nipple to the other, nipping and teasing with his teeth, then sucking vigorously until Tia cried out.

"Ben, you promised!" Tia gasped when the sensation became too intense to endure.

"I lied." He'd been without Tia too long to allow her feeble protests to stop him now. He shifted her in his lap so that she was draped across him. Then he was kissing her, tasting her lips before urging them apart with his tongue so he might explore deeper.

His lips left her mouth to press random kisses over her cheeks, her eyes, her chin, the soft rounded tops of her breasts. At the same time he was kissing her his hands slid beneath the blanket, raising it inch by inch as his fingertips brushed along ankle, knee, and thigh. Her flesh was soft and supple and Ben wanted to push her legs apart and thrust into her again and again until he spilled his seed. But he gritted his teeth and persevered, wanting to give Tia the kind of pleasure she deserved.

378

When his hand reached the moist triangle at the apex of her thighs, he urged her legs apart. Hesitating but a moment, Tia spread her legs, allowing Ben unlimited access. He startled her when he sought her hand and placed her fingers against herself.

"Feel how ready you are for me, sweetheart? You want me as much as I want you." He released her hand and she removed it immediately, but his remained. "Tell me you want me. Tell me you love me."

He stroked her with gentle insistence, his hand warm and coaxing against her swollen flesh. When the blankets covering them interfered with his loving, he removed them and tossed them aside. The blazing fire had warmed the tiny room and its occupants until clothing and blankets were no longer necessary nor desirable. Tia gasped when the length of his hot flesh branded her with his desire. She gasped again when his fingers slid inside her.

"Tell me, Tia, tell me you want me."

His fingers slid deeper—deeper still as he caressed her intimately. She felt as if her insides were afire, as if a river of molten lava flowed through her veins. Desperately she tried to close her legs, but Ben was nibbling at her breasts and she found it impossible to control her response to his loving. He knew exactly where and how to touch her to bring her the most pleasure.

"Bloody 'ell!" Tia cried, falling unconsciously into street language. "Yer a bloomin' bastard,

Ben Penrod. Ye know I can't 'elp meself where yer concerned. What do ye want from me?"

"You, Tia, only you."

"Then take me, damn you! I want you, I've always wanted you, and you damn well know it."

Her words gave Ben renewed hope as he rotated his fingers inside Tia. Tia rewarded him with a trembling sigh as she arched her back and brought his mouth back to her breasts. His thumb found the tiny nub of her pleasure and he used a gentle massage to bring her even greater pleasure as he suckled her. He increased the rhythm of his fingers, urging her toward climax with erotic love words.

"Ben, I—I can't stand it! Please . . ."

"Relax, sweetheart, let yourself go, don't hold back. I want to watch your face while I'm making love to you. There are many ways to give pleasure and I want to teach you every one of them."

Tia was panting now, shaking her head from side to side and rotating her hips as Ben's fingers slid back and forth inside her. Pressure built until Tia thought she was going to explode. Then she did. Her body rocked and trembled while Ben worked diligently over her, refusing to remove his fingers until the last shudder left her body and she lay limp in his lap. The tempest raging outside wasn't nearly as violent as the tempest Ben had created inside her body.

Sated, Tia closed her eyes. "Don't go to sleep,

Tia," Ben said, jerking her from the edge of sleep. She opened her mouth to protest and Ben quickly covered it with his own. With one agile motion he slid her beneath him. Then he was arousing her again, pressing her down, surrounding her in a purely dominant way. His tanned hands were holding her face while he kissed her and kissed her, slowly at first, then with scalding fervor. Tia found herself responding anew to this fresh assault upon her senses.

Suddenly Tia wanted to touch Ben, to arouse him in the same way he was arousing her. Taking a deep breath she slid her hands over the heated flesh of his shoulders, back, and waist, continuing downward in wanton abandon to his taut buttocks. Her touch was like wildfire, spreading flame along his skin and causing tiny shocks of electricity along his spine. When Tia's warm palm closed around his fully aroused member, Ben jerked in response.

"I love it when you touch me," he groaned in helpless surrender. "Spread your legs, sweetheart, I want to be inside you so bad it's like an ache in my loins."

Tia's legs parted and Ben fit himself in the cradle of her thighs. He paused a moment to enjoy the sight of her swollen flesh open and ready for him before loosing a groan and sliding inside full and deep. "I've never felt anything so wonderful."

"Nor I."

"Put your legs over my shoulders." She did as

he bid and felt him deeper than he'd ever been before. "I love you, Tia." He thrust strongly, vigorously, pushing himself all the way inside, withdrawing, then thrusting again.

The pleasure was so intense that Tia was beyond speech, beyond coherent thought. She could only feel. And at that moment she felt ready and willing to accept Ben's love. Even ready to tell him about their child. Then her thoughts scattered as Ben drove her toward a second climax more powerful than the first. He was only moments behind her.

Tia was hardly aware of the storm raging against the window and walls of the hut, or of the rain splashing down in solid sheets of gray. She was tired, so tired. Too tired to tell Ben about their baby just yet. Her eyes closed and she sighed as Ben pulled the blanket around them and positioned her more closely against the warmth of his body. Within minutes they were sound asleep, unaware when the rain finally stopped and a weak sun peeped out from the clouds for the first time in days.

Ben awoke first, recognized the absence of pounding rain on the roof, and arose. The fire had died down and he reached for his clothes, noting that they had dried while they slept. He turned back to awaken Tia and found her staring at him. He smiled in response, dropped down to his knees, and kissed her on the mouth.

"The rain has stopped."

Tia sighed; she was still warm and flushed

from Ben's love-making and hated to leave their cozy nest. There were so many things she wanted to tell him, so much that needed to be said. She reached for him but he slipped easily from her grasp.

"As much as I'd enjoy lingering here with you, it's imperative that we leave as soon as possible. It's time for the men to shore up the river bank with sandbags. We'll need all the protection we can get when the river crests. Come on, sweetheart, up with you."

Ben's logic put all thought of further conversation to rest as Tia reluctantly rose and quickly dressed. Telling him about their baby would keep a while longer. She smiled a secret smile, touching the place where his child rested. She hoped he'd be as thrilled about it as she was.

Ben watched her closely. "What's that supposed to mean?"

"What?"

"That smile. Like a cat just offered a saucer of cream. I hope I put that smile on your face."

"Women are supposed to have secrets," Tia teased. "You'll learn soon enough. I'm ready now, shall we leave? How far must we walk?"

"Not far, this shack is less than two miles from the house."

"Ben . . ."

"Aye?" He cocked an eyebrow, waiting for her to continue.

"Nothing, it can wait."

*   *   *

The muddy track made walking difficult. They followed the river most of the way, and Ben remarked more than once that he hadn't seen the Hawkesbury this high in years. It did look ominous as the rain-swollen water lapped at the bank on either side. In low-lying places it was already ankle deep where it had left the bank. Churned by the wind and rain, it rushed along at a furious pace, carrying tree branches, brush, and debris with it. Angry whirlpools formed and swirled dangerously while white foam formed along the edges. Though Tia had learned to swim and did a fair job of it, this turbulent, murky water frightened her. She breathed a sigh of relief when the sturdy two-story house came into view.

Casey came out to meet them. "Thank God you're safe! I was preparing to send Big John out to look for you."

Kate came out on the porch to stand beside Casey. "I told Casey you'd find someplace to weather the storm."

Ben looked from Casey to Kate, surprised to find them at Penrod station. "Are Dare and Robin with you? What are you all doing at Penrod station?"

"We arrived with the children shortly after you left for town," Casey explained. "Big John came with us. Dare thought we'd be safer here since Penrod station is on higher ground. He and Robin are supervising the placing of sandbags. He expects the river to crest within twenty-four hours."

"My thoughts exactly," Ben replied. "I want to start my own men shoring up the river bank immediately. We'll work through the night if necessary."

"Big John has already seen to it," Casey informed him. "Since you weren't here, he took it on himself to supervise the operation. I hope you don't mind."

"Mind? I'm grateful. I'll get out there immediately and lend a hand. It's going to take every available hand working day and night to complete the job."

During the night a light rain began to fall. Nothing like the downpour of the previous day but still worrisome as the water inched upward over the river bank. Ben didn't return to the house that night. Tia slept fitfully, listening to the steady beat of the rain and fretting over Ben's safety. She arose early the next morning and went to the kitchen to help cook prepare breakfast for the extra people. Casey wandered in a few minutes later followed by Kate. Kate looked weary, moving sluggishly as she dragged her bulk around the kitchen.

Tia couldn't help but ask, "Are you well, Kate? You don't expect the baby any time soon, do you?" Lord, she hoped not. The way the river was rising, it was doubtful the doctor could get here in time.

Kate smiled wanly. "I'm fine, Tia. Molly was fretful all night and I didn't sleep well. According to the doctor I still have three or four weeks to go before delivery." Tia thought she looked big enough to give birth at any moment.

Ben rushed inside, drenched to the skin, his face ashen, his eyes sunken in their sockets. "The river is rising. I don't know if the sandbags will hold or not."

"What can we do?" Tia asked, alarmed.

"Move upstairs. Take enough food and water for several days with you." Even as he spoke, water began seeping under the door, soaking their feet and the carpets. "Hurry!"

"What about you and the men?"

"As soon as I change into dry clothes I'm going back to join the men. I'll send Big John to help move some of the more valuable furnishings upstairs. The house is sturdy, it has stood through many a flood and will survive this one too. Keep the children safe."

"Ben," Kate asked worriedly, "what about Robin and Dare?"

"They've been through this before and know when to abandon the farm and seek higher ground. Try not to worry, Kate, they can take care of themselves." He certainly didn't relish the thought of Kate going into labor at a time like this.

Chapter Nineteen

By mid-afternoon the water was ankle deep throughout the lower floor of the house. Big John carried load after load of valuables, food, and water to the upper floor and then went to the barn and stable to see to the animals. Ben was keeping watch at the makeshift dike the men had built from sandbags. He expected the river to crest later that day or early the next at the latest. Casey was with her children in one bedroom, keeping them calm, while Kate had taken little Molly into another bedroom for a nap. Only Tia was moving about inside the house, peering out the window at intervals and worrying about Ben. He hadn't returned to the house since early morning.

Though Tia had been cautioned against venturing from the upper floor, she ignored Ben's warning and crept down the stairs, noting that the water completely covered the floor now and was slowly rising. Sloshing through the ankle-deep muddy water, Tia cautiously opened the front door, hoping to catch a glimpse of Ben. He was nowhere in sight, but Big John was walking toward the barn and she hailed him. If Ben wasn't available to answer her questions, perhaps Big John knew what was going on. Her impulsive nature led her out the door and into the yard. Big John waited for her, frowning in disapproval when he saw water swirling around her ankles and tugging at her skirts.

Upstairs, little Molly was restless. Active, bright, and impetuous, the child saw her mother sleeping peacefully beside her and decided to test her wings. She rose from the bed and walked into the hall. No one stirred. She peeked into the room across the hall and saw her cousins sprawled on the bed sound asleep. Casey was slumped in a chair, dozing. Molly walked to the staircase, peering down at the dark, churning water below. Curiosity got the best of the child, and when she saw the partially open door, the lure of the unknown was too great. She slowly descended the stairs. Like most children, Molly loved to play in water, and this was more water than she had ever seen in her short life.

Their heads bent in earnest conversation, neither Tia nor Big John saw Molly splash through the yard in gleeful enjoyment. Though the water lapped at her knees, she wasn't afraid. Very little frightened the intrepid little girl; she was too much like her mother.

Having gained little information from Big John, Tia waded back to the house, her brow furrowed in consternation when she noted that the front door stood wide open. She could have sworn she had closed it, then realized that the force of the water could have pushed it open if it hadn't been latched properly. Tia had no idea what made her turn around and gaze toward the river before she entered the house. It was as if some compelling force had ordered her to do so. What she saw turned the blood flowing through her veins to ice water.

A short distance away, at a place where the river had been fortified by sandbags, stood little Molly Fletcher. She had waded through the water and climbed up the bank of sandbags, where she stood staring down in avid fascination at the swirling water below.

Tia gasped in horror, and for a moment her legs refused to obey her brain. Big John had already turned back to the barn, and no one else was near enough to reach the child before—before . . . Dear God, no! Willing her legs into motion, Tia raced toward the river. Water and mud tugged at her legs and skirts, hindering her progress. Too slow! her brain warned. Any moment Molly could tumble into the river. She couldn't let that happen! Calling out to the child wasn't an option Tia considered.

She realized she might startle Molly and make her lose her balance. Hopefully, she'd reach the little girl before something terrible happened. Tia's hopes crashed at her feet as she watched Molly totter, grasp at the air, then tumble head over heels down the embankment toward the rushing water.

Only then did Tia cry out, "Molly!" Over and over she screamed the child's name.

Tia reached the bank, gasping for breath and nearly beside herself with fear. Frantically she searched the bank, praying that Molly hadn't fallen all the way into the water. She saw a jagged piece of material from Molly's dress clinging to a branch and cried out in dismay. Then she saw her. Molly was bobbing in the water a few feet offshore, her white little face turned toward Tia in abject terror as the current caught her and carried her away.

Tia screamed, then reacted instinctively. She breathed deeply and dove headlong into the boiling river. Not once did she consider her own safety, or the fact that she was pregnant. She thought only of innocent little Molly who would surely drown if nothing was done to save her. And of Kate who was in no condition to suffer the loss of a beloved child.

Big John heard Tia scream and came sloshing out of the barn. Glancing toward the river, he caught a fleeting glimpse of someone or something hurtling into the water. Rushing to the river bank, he watched in frozen horror as Tia fought desperately to remain above water as the current carried her down river. When he saw little Molly floundering in midstream, he cursed the fact that he had never learned to swim. All he could do was watch helplessly as Tia and Molly were carried along by the strong current.

Big John ran along the shore, keeping up as best he could, waiting to pull them out if either Molly or Tia were tossed anywhere near shore. Tia was swimming now, trying desperately to reach Molly, who disappeared from time to time beneath the murky surface only to bob up again after a heart-stopping interval. Suddenly Molly went under and Tia dove after her, fearing the little girl wouldn't resurface. The water was dark; branches and brush tore at her hair and clothing. Rocks and debris stung her flesh and the swirling current flung her about like a rag doll.

Panic-stricken, Tia realized she must surface soon or perish. She thought of little Molly, so bright, so loved, and willed herself to even greater endurance. Her head was throbbing, her lungs bursting, and her body starving for air. In the split second before she was forced to push herself to the surface, soft, feathery tendrils brushed across her face. In a purely reflexive action she reached out desperately and shot to the surface. Molly's head bobbed up beside her, her long auburn hair clasped in Tia's hand.

Tia gasped for breath, coughing and sputtering as she cleared her throat of muddy water. She was tired, so tired she barely had the strength to grasp Molly snugly in her arms as the current carried them down river. She glanced into Molly's white face, fearing the child hadn't survived the watery ordeal, and was rewarded by a tiny gasp and faint breath as water spewed out of the little girl's mouth and nose.

"Breathe, Molly, breathe," Tia urged as she squeezed the child's tiny chest.

Tia glanced toward shore, gratified to see Big John running along the bank in an effort to keep up with them. His mouth was open and he was yelling something, but the roar of the rushing water drowned out his words. With sinking heart Tia realized suddenly that Big John couldn't swim, and her hopes plummeted. She was growing weaker and couldn't tread water much longer.

Suddenly something bumped against her back and she cried out in pain, nearly dropping Molly. Turning her head, she saw a floating mass of branches, brush, and debris. The entire mass was wedged against a tree that had fallen into the river. Though the mass of brush threatened to break loose at any moment, Tia used her free hand to anchor herself more firmly. Until it broke loose it offered a slim hope of survival for her and little Molly.

Ben paused in his backbreaking work to gaze a moment at the rising river. He knew that the crest stage was near, and if the water level didn't rise more than a foot or two the damage wouldn't be too severe. Earlier that morning he had led some of his workers a short distance down river to shore up the bank. They had done all they could to protect the bank directly in front of the house, and Ben hoped that sandbagging further down river could save some of his crops. Suddenly, from the corner of his eye he caught a glimpse of someone running along the bank, waving his arms and yelling something he couldn't make out. As the man drew closer, Ben recognized Big John.

Ben's blood ran cold. He realized that something must be desperately wrong at the house to bring Big John running and gesturing wildly. Could Kate have gone into labor? Big John was pointing toward the river now, and Ben frowned as he gazed across the swirling black water. It looked forbidding and cold and bleak as death. Then he saw them. He made a soft, wretched sound deep in his throat. Then Big John reached him and gasped out a brief, nearly incoherent explanation.

"Tia, hang on!" Ben called, cupping his hand to his mouth. She didn't hear him. But miracle of miracles, she saw him, and hope surged anew.

Willing his frenzied mind to think clearly, Ben sent one of the men racing back to the barn for a rope. But even as the man sped off, Ben knew he wouldn't make it back in time. The tree that had snagged Tia and Molly was already beginning to edge out into the swift current. If that happened, the mass of brush and debris would break apart and Tia and Molly would be swept down river and beyond mortal help. There was only one thing to do, and Ben didn't hesitate.

"I'm going after them," Ben said as he stripped off his boots and jacket.

Big John looked stricken. "I can't swim but I'll help. Tell me what to do."

Ben thought a moment, then said, "Wade out as far as you can without being swept away by the current. I'll need help bringing them to shore."

Big John nodded, fearing that Ben would be caught up in the current and become as helpless as Tia and Molly. He watched in apprehension and dread as Ben dove into the water.

Ben swam strongly, his powerful arms cutting cleanly through the swirling water. Big John watching on shore suffered a moment of fright when a whirlpool dragged Ben under, but he quickly resurfaced and continued. He'd had little sleep in the past twenty-four hours, but seeing Tia and Molly in danger of losing their lives sent a jolt of adrenalin surging through his veins. He loved Tia too much to lose her now. And little Molly was the beloved daughter of his best friend. Their lives meant too much to him to let them die without making a superhuman effort to save them.

Tia had watched in growing alarm as Ben dove into the river and swam toward them. When the whirlpool pulled him beneath the surface, she sobbed aloud, angry at him for sacrificing his life for them, yet loving him for trying to save them. Then he bobbed to the surface and struck out again with strong, steady strokes. Molly was whimpering now, thrashing around and trying to pull out of Tia's arms. Tia wasn't certain how much longer she could hold on to the child.

"Hang on, sweetheart!"

Tia heard Ben's words float to her over the roar of water, and a tiny spark of hope ignited in her breast. Could he possibly reach them in time? Miraculously, he drew closer, closer still, battling the current all the way, undaunted, determined.

He was gasping for breath when he reached them. His face was streaming water, his hair plastered to his head, and his gray eyes dark with exhaustion. Yet there was no mistaking the exhilaration he felt at having reached her and Molly. But Tia knew that only half the battle was won. There was no way he could get them both safely to shore in one trip. In that instant she made her decision.

"Sweetheart." Water sputtered from Ben's mouth. He was treading water beside Tia, afraid to anchor himself to the tree lest it give way beneath his weight. "Thank God. Can you hang on to me while I drag you and Molly back to shore?"

Brutally realistic, Tia shook her head. "It will never work, Ben." Her near total exhaustion was evident in her trembling voice. "You can't take both of us at once. Take Molly first. I can hang on until you come back for me." Her eyes were pleading as Ben shook his head in vigorous denial.

"Tia, no . . ."

"Please, Ben, please." She thrust Molly at him, and Ben had no choice but to take the child. Her drawn white face and wide staring eyes filled him with alarm, and the painful truth hit him in the gut with the force of a sledgehammer. Molly couldn't survive much longer. He had to get her to safety. If he tried to take them all back at once, there was a good chance none of them would survive.

It nearly destroyed him to leave Tia behind, but she was better able to cling to the tree than little Molly who hung limply in his arms. "I'll be back, sweetheart," he promised as he hugged Molly to his chest and struck out for shore. "I love you." His words floated to her on a sudden gust of wind that tore at the tree, making her position even more precarious.

Tia clung to the tree with the tremendous will that was so much a part of her character. She had Ben's baby to live for, and the life she'd always dreamed about with the man she loved. Anxiety furrowed her brow as she watched Ben struggle through the rushing current, falter once, then swim on. He seemed almost superhuman as he fought the current and wind, adroitly dodging floating debris that jostled him. A cry of jubilation escaped her lips when she saw Big John wade into the turbulent water and pluck Molly from Ben's arms.

At that point Tia's hopes for her own survival rose considerably. Perhaps it wasn't too farfetched to believe that Ben could work another miracle and rescue her from a watery grave. Then abruptly the tree broke loose and went hurtling into the current. The mass of twigs and brush that supported Tia disintegrated, leaving Tia floundering in midstream. Then she too joined the current in its headlong rush down river.

Ben's legs were shaking and his arms trembling as he thrust Molly into Big John's arms. "Have one of the men rush her up to the house. She needs immediate attention." His words were terse, his face grim. He prayed he had the necessary strength to return to Tia and bring her back safely. He'd either do it or die trying.

Filling his lungs with air, Ben turned to dive back into the water. He raised his arm to signal Tia that he was on his way, and saw an empty space where Tia had been only a moment before. He felt screams of stark terror gather at the back of his throat when he realized that the tree had given way and Tia was once more at the mercy of the fierce current.

"No! Oh, God, no!" His cry was picked up by the wind and scattered over the water like ashes. He couldn't even see Tia, had no idea where the current had flung her. Wading back to shore, he ran along the bank, followed closely by Big John who by now realized what had happened.

Then he saw her, bobbing helplessly in the swift current. Ben realized immediately that if he went into the water he would never catch up with her. All he could do was race along the bank and keep her in sight. Tia was swiftly approaching a place where the river narrowed, forming a billabong where he had swum as a child. Suddenly he recalled the eucalyptus tree that grew horizontally from the bank, its branches reaching out halfway across the river. He and Dare had used it as a diving board, and he remembered the sturdy trunk as being able to withstand the combined weight of several men. God willing, it still stood.

The tree was still there, anchored to the bank like a tenacious sentinel of the ages. He had reached the spot with only moments to spare when he saw Tia tumbling toward him. Scampering out on a huge limb just barely skimming the swollen, rushing water, he reached the end and leaned over, waiting to grasp Tia as she rushed by. To his horror, Ben leaned over a bit too far, lost his balance, and fell into the river.

Tia had seen the overhanging branch before she reached it and realized it was her last hope for survival. She no longer had the strength to fight the current. Then she saw Ben poised at the end of the tree, his arms stretched out to pluck her from the river, and for the span of a heartbeat she thought her ordeal had ended. She knew seconds before it happened that he was going to fall; she saw his body stretch beyond its limits, totter, then spill into the river. Fortunately, he had the presence of mind to cling to the branch.

Oh, God, I'm going to die! Tia thought as she saw Ben struggling to pull himself out of the water. Her next thought was a vigorous denial. *No, I'm going to live! I need to live!* She hadn't survived three years in the stews of London to die an ignominious death in a swollen river in Australia. She was under the tree now; it was so close to the water she could reach up and touch it.

With the last of her waning strength, she reached out both arms and grasped the thick branch. The rough bark dug grooves into her tender skin but she didn't feel them. All she felt was the powerful tug of the current on her legs and skirts. Then suddenly she felt Ben's arm around her waist, holding her against him, defying the current that threatened them both.

"I won't let you go, sweetheart," Ben promised as his fingers closed around her ribcage. She felt small and vulnerable beneath the strength of his hand. He was amazed that she had the presence of mind to function coherently in the face of such adversity. In her own typical, courageous manner she had more or less saved herself from a watery death. She turned and stared into his eyes with such perfect stillness and anticipation that tears formed in Ben's eyes.

"I know you won't," she whispered from between drawn white lips.

Then Big John was there, his long legs straddling the tree, his huge hands reaching out to them. Ben lifted Tia into Big John's arms, then scrambled up on his own when Big John slowly backed away toward shore with Tia in tow. Within minutes all three were standing on the bank. Ben rushed to take Tia into his arms, hugging her fiercely, his mouth stretched into a tight, thin line across his face.

"You foolish, brave little idiot," he said against her lips. "Why? Why did you do such a thing? I could have lost you."

Tia's limbs felt heavy, her body drugged as she stared into Ben's eyes. She blinked, then blinked again. Were those tears streaming down his face? Was Ben crying over her? Did he care so much about her that the thought of losing her brought him such terrible anguish?

"Molly," Tia managed to gasp out. "I did it for Molly." Those were her last words as her legs gave way completely and she slid into a world of darkness.

"Is she all right?" Big John asked anxiously.

Tia's face was white, her lips blue from cold, and she hung limply in his arms, but her heartbeat was slow and steady. "She's just fainted," Ben said. "I'll take her back to the house. Keep the men working, I feel certain the crest stage is near." Sweeping Tia into his arms, he carried her back to the house. "I'll return as soon as I know Tia will be all right."

Tia opened her eyes, stretched, and groaned. Every bone in her body ached. She felt bruised and battered, as if she had fought the biggest battle of her life. Then she remembered. She *had* fought a battle, one that had nearly taken her life from her. But she had survived. Immediately her hands went to her stomach. Had her child survived? She felt no pain, no twinges of distress, nothing to indicate she was going to lose her child. Evidently the babe inside her womb was protected enough to survive the buffeting Tia had taken from the swollen, turbulent river.

Tia glanced out the window and saw the murky light of dusk. Had she slept nearly the entire day? Where was everyone? Had Molly survived her near drowning? Where was Ben? As if in answer to her question the door was flung open and Ben strode inside, carrying a lamp.

"You're awake." His voice trembled with relief. Casey had told him Tia would awaken once her body had had time to rest, but he was

401

still frightened for her. "How do you feel?"

"Like I've been dragged behind a horse."

"You're badly bruised, sweetheart, and I doubt there's a place on you that's not black and blue, but you're alive and that's what's important."

"Thank you for rescuing me."

Ben snorted derisively. "I didn't. Once again you managed to save yourself. You're a resourceful little wench, and I thank God for your courage and determination. If you hadn't reached out for that tree when you did you would have been swept to your death."

"I couldn't have hung on to that tree for long without your support," Tia said. "And you did save Molly. How is she? Did she recover?"

"Another few minutes in the water would have spelled doom for the child," Ben revealed, "but thanks to your courage she is alive and will recover completely. Whatever possessed you to jump into the river? It could have meant your death."

"I—I know," Tia said on a trembling sigh. "But I couldn't just stand by and do nothing. No one else was nearby, it was up to me to save her. I did what I had to do."

"You did what few others would attempt, and I love you all the more for it. But if you had perished, I don't know if I could have gone on without you. Bloody hell, Tia, I love you!"

Tia stared at him, as if seeing him for the first time. His face was white beneath his tan, and she could have sworn there were lines around his eyes that hadn't existed before. His exhaustion was apparent, but what really drove home the depth of his feeling was the expression in his gray eyes. Raw anguish, terrible anxiety, tenderness, and—and, yes, love. Love was there for all the world to see. And she no longer doubted it.

"Ben—"

"No, sweetheart, whatever you're going to say will keep. You need rest and I must return to the river. It will be over soon and then we'll have the rest of our lives together." He kissed her gently on the mouth and left.

"Be careful!"

He turned and flashed that unnerving smile. "Don't worry about me, sweetheart, I'm sure if I get into trouble you'll come to my rescue." Then he was gone.

Tia smiled a secret smile as she watched Ben let himself out of her room. She supposed she could wait to tell him about their child, but the way she felt about it now she wanted to shout it to the world. Thinking about the baby growing inside her made her think about little Molly, and suddenly she had to see for herself if the child was all right. She didn't think Ben would lie to her—unless he thought it best that she not know the truth right now.

Getting out of bed was the most difficult thing Tia had done in a long time. Jumping into the raging river had been easy; bracing her aching, bruised bones into an upright position took much more courage and fortitude. She hurt in places she didn't even know existed. Dragging herself out of bed and to the door, she eased it open and stepped into the hall. A light shone under Kate's door, and Tia moved slowly and painfully to that beckoning beacon. She eased the door open and saw Kate hovering over Molly, who lay white and limp on the bed. A cry of distress slipped past Tia's lips.

Kate spun around, saw Tia, and smiled in warm welcome. "Molly's fine, Tia, thanks to you. Robin and I can never thank you enough."

"She looks so—so helpless," Tia said in a small voice.

"She's exhausted, and so should you be. Why aren't you in bed?"

"I had to see for myself that Molly's all right."

"You're the most courageous woman I've ever known."

"Anyone would have done what I did."

"No, not anyone, just you. Ben is very lucky to have you. Someday, when you and Ben have your own child, you'll know just how precious that little being is to you."

"Sooner than you think," Tia said softly. She bent over to smooth the hair from Molly's forehead and wasn't aware of Kate's confused look.

"Tia! Are you—are you and Ben . . ."

Tia smiled. "Aye, I'm carrying Ben's child. I just recently found out."

"Dear sweet Jesus," Kate said, stunned. "You

knew you were pregnant and still you jumped in that river? What if—what if—are you sure you're all right? No pain, no—no bleeding?"

"Except for bruises, scrapes, and stiffness, I feel fine. My body aches but that's only natural. I don't think I've done any serious harm to my child."

"Does Ben know?"

"I haven't had the opportunity to tell him. I—I haven't even told him I'd marry him."

Kate laughed delightedly. "Serves him right. For years he taunted Dare and Robin about being leg shackled to a wife and vowed to remain a bachelor all of his life. But don't you think it's time to put him out of his misery? I know he wants to marry you and would have long ago if you had agreed to it. He loves you, Tia."

"I know. I guess I've always known. And I love him. It was always my intention to marry Ben one day. The baby is rushing that day forward a little."

Just then Molly shifted and opened her eyes. She saw Tia and spread her arms. Tia uttered a cry and gathered the little girl close to her heart. In that split second she knew that what she had done was right even if it had cost her the life of her unborn child. Then abruptly Molly went limp in Tia's arms. Alarmed, Tia looked at Kate, who told her the child had fallen asleep again. Satisfied, Tia turned to leave, but was stopped dead in her tracks when Kate doubled over and cried out in obvious distress.

"Kate, what is it? Is it the baby?"

Kate's eyes dropped to her feet where a puddle of water spread around her feet. Her face was ashen, her lips tightly drawn. She merely nodded.

"I'll get Casey."

"Robin," Kate gasped, placing a restraining hand on Tia's arm. "I want Robin. He was with me when Molly was born and he promised he'd be here when this child arrived."

Tia's eyes grew wide. She knew exactly how Kate felt. When her time arrived she'd want Ben with her too. "I'll have him summoned immediately. The baby won't arrive for hours, and Dare's farm isn't so far away."

"Tia, thank you, thank you for everything."

Chapter Twenty

As it turned out it wasn't necessary to send for Robin. Both Robin and Dare burst through the front door while Casey and Tia were discussing how best to summon the men.

"The danger is past," Dare crowed jubilantly as he sprinted up the stairs. "Where is everyone? The river has crested and the sandbags held."

Casey and Tia appeared at the head of the stairs. "It's truly over?" Casey asked, hugging Dare. "What about the house and crops?"

"The house is awash in six inches of water, about the same as Penrod station, but damage is minimal. As for the crops, those closest to the river are ruined but the fields farther away have been spared. The animals were driven to high ground days ago and most are safe."

"Thank God." Casey's grateful sigh was muffled against Dare's shoulder as he wrapped powerful arms around her and held her close. Soon their three children were clamoring to greet their father and for a few minutes bedlam reigned while Tia and Robin looked on.

Suddenly Robin frowned and asked, "Where are Kate and Molly?"

Casey and Tia exchanged glances that made Robin's blood run cold. "What is it? Has something happened? Bloody hell, will someone tell me what's wrong!"

Casey placed a comforting hand on Robin's arm. "Kate's in labor, Robin. We were about to send someone for you when you and Dare arrived."

Relief surged through Robin. "Has someone gone for the doctor?"

"I doubt he'll arrive in time," Dare said, ever practical. "The roads are knee deep in mud and probably impassable."

"I'll do the best I can, Robin," Casey assured him. "I've had three children, after all, and Kate is a strong woman. We anticipate no problems."

"We weren't expecting the child for several weeks yet," Robin worried. "Of course I know you'll do your best for Kate, but I can't help remembering the pain she suffered with Molly."

Dare stifled a grin. "If I recall correctly, you vowed never to put Kate through this again."

Robin flushed and admitted, "So I did, but Kate had other ideas. And Kate usually gets her way."

"Go to her, Robin, she needs you now," Casey urged.

Before Robin could move past them to go to Kate, Ben entered the house, surprised to see that Robin and Dare had arrived ahead of him. Once the river crested he expected them at Penrod station to see to their families, but they had appeared so quickly he worried that something was wrong.

"Dare, Robin, what's amiss? The river has crested, the rain has ceased, and the sandbags have kept most of the water from the fields. How have things fared at your place, Dare?"

"All's well, little brother." Dare grinned. "Little damage has been done." Gray eyes raked Ben's disheveled appearance from head to toe. "You look like hell."

"You would too if you'd recently had a swim in a raging river swollen by floodwaters. Tia and Molly's ordeal was more harrowing than mine, yet they look none the less for wear. Which says a lot for the so-called weaker sex."

Hearing Ben's cryptic words, Robin whirled, his face a mask of shock and fear. "What about Molly? Bloody hell, Ben, what happened that you're not telling me?" Then he turned to Tia, noticing for the first time the bruises and scratches marring her flawless skin. Her paleness, enhanced by dark smudges beneath

409

her eyes, lent mute evidence to her ordeal. "Will someone explain!"

Ben shifted uncomfortably. "I'm sorry, Robin, I thought you knew. Molly is fine, or she was when I left the house earlier. She fell into the river and Tia jumped in after her. It was the bravest thing I've ever witnessed another human do."

"Sweet Jesus," Dare muttered reverently, looking at Tia with renewed respect. "How did it happen?"

Beyond coherent speech, Robin merely stared at Tia, amazed that such a tiny thing could survive the raging current and save his child at the same time.

As concisely as possible, Ben related the events in the river, deliberately diminishing his own involvement while heaping praise upon Tia's Herculean effort to save little Molly. All eyes turned to Tia, but it was Robin who expressed what they all felt in their hearts.

"I can't thank you enough for what you did for my family, Tia. As long as I'm alive you'll never want for a friend, or for anything else you might need. And if Ben doesn't treat you right, you have only to mention it and I'll set him straight."

"I did what I had to do," Tia said, embarrassed by all the fuss made over her heroic deed. "Casey would have done the same had she been the one to see Molly topple into the river."

"Nevertheless, you're a brave woman and Ben is lucky to have found you."

"I'm lucky to have found Ben," Tia returned, her eyes shining.

The conversation was interrupted by a moaning sound coming from behind a closed door a short distance down the hallway. "Kate!" Robin cried, leaping into action. "I'm coming, love."

Dare watched Robin in wry amusement. He recalled his own nervousness when Lucy was born. Since he wasn't around for the birth of his first son, it was all new to him. But by the time his third child made his appearance, he felt quite capable of handling it in a rational manner. Robin, however, seemed as anxious and worried as he'd been at Molly's birth. Dare glanced at Ben and wondered how his younger brother would react when it came time for him to await the birth of his first child. He'd probably fall apart at the seams, Dare predicted, noting how pale Ben had become when Kate's moans reached them.

Casey took charge immediately. Childbirth was never easy, but she was prepared to do whatever was necessary to ensure a healthy child and mother. "Dare, you and Ben make yourselves useful. See if you can find some dry wood and light the stove. We'll need plenty of clean hot water. Tia, keep the children occupied, I don't want them underfoot."

"My wife the boss." Dare rolled his eyes and smiled indulgently at Casey. His love for her seemed to grow each day, his obsession with the red-haired, green-eyed vixen he had married still vitally alive and exquisitely satisfying. Sending her a look filled with passionate promise, he moved with alacrity to do her bidding.

Ben lagged behind, hoping for a word with Tia once Casey and Dare had departed. "Tia, wait," he said when she would have turned and followed Casey. "Are you all right? I expected you to be abed recovering from your ordeal."

Tia smiled reassuringly. "It will take more than a few bruises to keep me in bed. Dare is right, you're the one who looks terrible." Her saucy answer put Ben's fears to rest but didn't solve his need to be alone with the woman he loved.

"I'll feel much better when we're alone and I can tell you properly just how much you mean to me and how frightened I was when I saw you in the river. Soon, sweetheart, soon we'll be alone again and we'll talk about marriage. This time I won't take no for an answer."

He pulled her into his arms, dragging his lips over hers, cherishing every part of her mouth with every part of his. Suddenly the sun streamed through the tattered gray clouds, caressing the gently rolling fields with long, lazy fingers of light that filtered through the windows, encompassing the couple in a nimbus of gold. It was as if God were blessing their union. Tia returned Ben's kiss enthusiastically, and Ben would have picked her up and carried her into the bedroom if Dare hadn't called from below, "Are you coming, little brother? Tia is in no shape to fend off your advances."

Grinning sheepishly, Ben released Tia, giving her a quick kiss, then bounding off after Dare.

Hours later Kate still hadn't delivered, and Ben and Dare sat at a table drinking strong tea and listening to Kate's moans drifting down the hallway. Both were tired beyond belief, yet aware that Kate was suffering in a way neither could comprehend. Tia was putting the children to bed, and Robin hadn't left his wife's side since her ordeal began. Casey was acting the midwife and busy preparing for the impending delivery. Dr. Proctor had been sent for, but it was doubtful he would arrive in time.

"Bloody hell, is it always like this?" Ben asked, raking long fingers through crisp dark hair.

"You remind me of Robin when Molly was born," Dare observed dryly. "He vowed he'd never put Kate through the ordeal of childbirth again."

"What happened?" Ben wasn't merely curious but interested, for he assumed that he and Tia would one day have children of their own.

"I suspect Kate had something to say about the decision. Just like Casey, she probably decided one child wasn't enough. Both Kate and Casey are strong women with minds of their own, and I suspect Tia is the same. We've been extremely lucky in our women, little brother."

Just then another anguished moan could be heard coming from behind the door and Ben slammed down his fist, coming to a sudden decision. "I'm not going to put Tia through this. I don't need children to be happy. All I need is Tia."

Highly amused, Dare chuckled. "Most men want at least one child. It has something to do with male ego and the notion that creating another human in their own image somehow enhances their masculinity."

"Masculinity be damned! I don't need a child for those reasons. I don't want a child for *any* reason. Tia is all I need to make me happy."

Dare knew Ben well enough to realize that his words were prompted by exhaustion, the fear of almost having lost Tia, and being made to listen to Kate's travail. He surmised that Tia would change his mind once they were wed. Women had a way of working their wiles on men in subtle ways. But Tia, having paused at the door in time to hear Ben's last outburst, thought only of the child growing in her stomach and Ben's vehement denial of fatherhood. She wanted to turn and flee to the privacy of her room where she could mull over her options now that she had heard Ben's startling opinion about having children. But then she recalled her reason for venturing down the hall, squared her narrow shoulders and stepped into the room.

Dare saw her first and jumped to his feet. "Is Kate all right?"

Tia smiled wanly. "Kate is fine. I just came to tell you that delivery is very near."

Even as she spoke a muted scream floated down the hall and into the room. All three rushed to the doorway, to stare out and listen. The scream was followed by a surprisingly strong wail, and smiles broke out all around. Robin came bursting from Kate's room, his expression weary but radiantly happy. "I have a son! A big, strapping boy the image of his father." His chest seemed to swell before their eyes. "Kate came through in fine fettle." Then he turned and raced back into Kate's room.

"Thank God," Dare said, his relief evident. "Now that all's well I'm off to bed. I don't know when I've been so exhausted."

"Damn good idea," Ben agreed, clasping Tia around the waist and urging her toward their room.

Tia followed reluctantly. Ben's words about children still echoed hollowly in her ears. Why couldn't he be as happy as she was about her pregnancy?

"Finally," Ben said once the door was closed behind them. "I think I suffered right along with Kate. I don't ever want to put you through that ordeal."

Tia said nothing as Ben started stripping off his damp clothes. "I'm soaked to the skin, sweetheart, will you dry my back for me?" he asked.

He handed her a towel lying nearby and presented his back. Tia took the towel and stroked vigorously over the hard planes of his shoulders and upper torso. Abruptly he turned and presented his front. Obediently Tia began rubbing the muscular chest covered with dark, curly hair. He looked tough, lean, and sinewy. Her eyes froze on his long, lean torso. He was a bronze figure of a man, strong and powerful, and she loved him beyond rhyme or reason.

"When you look at me like that, Tia, I want to throw you on the bed and make violent love to you."

Tia flushed and raised her eyes. "I don't think . . ."

He dropped his pants. "Dry me, sweetheart."

Tia's breath grew labored. With slow, hesitant strokes she guided the towel lower, lower still. When she reached his loins his hands clasped hers, halting their downward course. "Here, sweetheart, stop here." He grasped the towel from her hands and flung it aside. Her fingers touched naked swollen flesh. Ben moaned, instantly hard.

Gripping her hand, he molded it around his erection. He lowered his head, and his warm lips brushed the sensitive, aching corners of her mouth, her eyes, the tip of her nose. The stress of her recent brush with death was evident in the hollows beneath her eyes and the paleness of her skin. Ben knew he should let her rest but he couldn't help himself. He had nearly lost her and he desperately needed her in his arms, claiming her in the most basic way.

Tia's eyes glowed darkly and she licked her lips. She held her breath and moved her hand slowly against Ben's turgid flesh, creating a friction that nearly sent him blindly, hopelessly into explosion.

"Jesus!"

He flung her hand away, pulling her into his arms and holding her close as he struggled for composure. His breath was ragged, his chest heaved; his teeth were clenched in agony as he fought valiantly for control of his body.

"You make me wild, sweetheart, but I'm fine now." His hands moved to her neckline and the tiny row of buttons fastening her bodice. "I want you naked."

Tia started to protest but the thought dissipated when his fingers slowly released the buttons and pushed the bodice from her shoulders. He frowned at the bruises marring her delicate skin and proceeded to kiss every one of them. Enthralled by the feel of his warm lips on her flesh, Tia didn't realize that Ben had undressed her completely until his hands drifted down to clasp her bottom and press her against the hard length of his arousal. When he swung her into his arms and carried her to the bed, Tia finally found her tongue.

"Ben, wait, there is something we need to discuss."

"Now? Can't it wait?"

"No, this has to be said."

"Save it for later, sweetheart, I won't be able to think properly until I've made love to you. I need you, Tia, now, always—forever. I love you."

Will you love our child? The silent plea reverberated inside her brain.

His eyes drifted down the naked length of her. "You're incredibly lovely, Tia. You've more spunk and courage in that tiny frame than a woman twice your size. It frightens me to think I nearly lost you." He slid down beside her, pulling her into the curve of his body. Then he filled his hands with her breasts, gently teasing the nipples with his thumb. "You've grown larger, sweetheart. I've always thought your breasts were perfect, but now they're beyond perfection."

Tia stiffened, realizing this was the opening she needed to tell Ben about the baby. But when his mouth burned a moist path to her breasts and took first one nipple and then the other into his mouth and suckled, all coherent thought fled. She could only feel and respond, guided by some intangible force so strong she couldn't fight it. Incredible warmth was spreading through her swollen breasts and the insides of her thighs, and she sighed and squirmed as he continued to kiss and nip at her nipples and stroke between her legs. He licked and tasted and slipped long tanned fingers into her silken heat.

Tia's groan of pleasure spurred Ben on as he turned her gently on her stomach and urged her onto her knees. Tia's head swiveled, unsure what was happening. "Don't be frightened, sweetheart, this is but another way to love."

He moved into place behind her as Tia rested on her knees and elbows, feeling absurdly vulnerable and exposed in this ridiculous position. Then she felt his hard flesh probing for the opening. Grasping her hips, he thrust into her, deep—so deep Tia felt him touch her soul.

"Ben, oh, God!" She thrust backward against him.

Then he was moving, thrusting, his hips grinding against the softness of her buttocks. She felt his warm lips on her neck, her shoulders, her back, as the pressure inside her built. When he reached around her to stroke the tiny bud of her pleasure, her climax came quickly, bursting from within and shattering into brilliant shards of sublime ecstasy. She waited for Ben to follow her to completion and was surprised when he turned her over and paused. He waited patiently for her to float back to reality, holding and stroking her gently and whispering erotic words meant to soothe and arouse. Tia's eyes widened when he leaned over her and began leisurely arousing her again.

"Ben, you didn't—"

"Don't worry about me, sweetheart, just concentrate on what I'm doing."

Moving down her body, he pushed her legs apart and knelt between them. He flashed her a wicked smile and lowered his head. Tia

419

jerked violently when his mouth found her. His tongue worked its magic and soon Tia was soaring toward another climax. Moments before she exploded, Ben slid upward and thrust into her. His strong strokes drove them both beyond human endurance, and this time he was with Tia all the way. When Tia's contractions began, his own climax pushed wave after wave of incredible pleasure though his body. His cry of completion joined Tia's shriek of joy.

It was several minutes before either of them could speak. Ben was the first to express his feelings. "I can't imagine a greater happiness than making love to you for the rest of my life. Just the two of us, Tia, together—always."

Tia's heart swelled with joy, then just as swiftly contracted with regret. Did Ben mean what she thought he meant? Were children something he could easily do without? Would he be angry when he learned she was pregnant?

"I'm going to take care of you, sweetheart. I slipped up this time, but next time and all the others that follow I'll use precautions. I don't want you to suffer because of me. You're so tiny, I'd never forgive myself if you perished bearing a child of mine. I hope you feel the same."

Tia gulped back the lump forming in her throat. "Don't you want children, Ben?"

Thinking to make his decision less painful to her, Ben replied, "Not especially. I have nieces and nephews aplenty, I don't need a child of my own to prove my masculinity. You're all I'll ever need, Tia. All I want. We'll be married as soon as we can get to town to the preacher."

Ben didn't want children! The thought sent Tia into a tailspin. It changed everything. She needed time to think. Time to decide what to do. Would Ben hold it against her if she went into this marriage already pregnant? After all, she hadn't gotten that way on her own. But she definitely wasn't going to tell him now, not when he was so adamantly opposed to children. Perhaps she could think of some way to change his mind. Yes, Tia decided, sliding into sleep. She'd wait for a more propitious time to tell Ben about their child.

"What was it you wanted to tell me?" Ben asked, suddenly recalling that Tia had something important to discuss with him.

"N—nothing. I'm too tired to think right now."

Ben's expression grew puzzled, then lightened as he watched Tia drift off to sleep. He smiled, cuddled her close, and soon followed her into blessed slumber.

Cleanup after the flood followed immediately. Dare, Casey, and their children left the next day for their own farm. Robin and Kate remained with Molly and the new baby, whom they named Marcus Roy. Kate was still too weak to be moved, and Molly hadn't fully recovered from her ordeal in the river. Within days the house

421

was swept clean of mud and debris and life was slowly returning to normal. Robin voiced his need to return to Bathurst and their home, but until Kate recovered enough to travel, he made himself useful to Ben at Penrod station. It was while they were driving stray sheep down from the nearby hills that Ben received the shock of his life.

They had stopped to rest beneath a shade tree when Robin asked, "When are you and Tia getting married?"

"Soon," Ben replied. The cleanup from the flood had taken nearly every hour of every day, but he assumed the roads were passable by now since it hadn't rained in days. He also spent every night in Tia's bed and had kept his word about using precautions. "I'll speak to Tia about it tonight. Our work here is progressing well enough for me to leave."

"If I were you I'd not waste any time," Robin said cryptically.

Ben regarded him curiously. "What's that supposed to mean? You know I intend to marry Tia. I always intended to marry her."

Robin faced him squarely. "Before or after your child is born?"

"I don't intend on having children," Ben shrugged, "so it's a moot question."

For a moment Robin looked stunned. Could he have misunderstood Kate? She had told him that Tia was carrying Ben's child, that Tia had admitted it the night little Molly almost drowned. Then another thought struck him. Hadn't Tia told Ben? If not, why? Having a man's child wasn't something that could be kept secret forever. He decided to give fate a nudge.

"What are Tia's thoughts on the subject?"

"Tia wants what I want."

"Did you ask her?"

"Of course." He paused thoughtfully. "Well, not exactly. I did convey my opinion on the subject, though."

Robin groaned. "You bloody fool! Have you learned nothing from me and Dare?"

"What in the hell are you talking about?"

"It's too late to make decisions about children."

"How can it be too late? I'm already using precautions and—" Ben's words faltered. A confused look came over his face and he grew quiet. "Christ! Are you trying to tell me that Tia is— that she's expecting my child?"

Robin nodded sagely. "Has Tia said nothing?"

"Nothing. And in a way I don't blame her, not after I spouted off about not wanting children. Why am I the last to know? Me, the father! I suppose everyone else knows I'm going to be a father," he said with bitter emphasis.

"Not everyone. Tia told Kate and Kate saw no harm in telling me. We both naturally assumed that Tia had told you by now. By God, Ben, if you give that wonderful girl any trouble over this I'll beat you to a bloody pulp. Having children is a natural culmination of love and one of life's greatest joys. Only selfish fools don't want children."

When he showed no inclination to stop talking, Ben interrupted. "It's not that I wouldn't welcome any children Tia gave me, it's just that I fear she isn't strong enough to bear them safely. It would kill me to lose Tia in childbirth. She's such a tiny little thing and I'm so big. What if—"

"It's too late for suppositions or recriminations, Ben. Nature has a way of taking care of things. If I were you, I'd find Tia and make things right with her."

"Right you are, mate," Ben agreed, still stunned over the news that he was going to be a father. He ought to wring Tia's delectable little neck for telling everyone but him about her pregnancy. Then a terrible thought brought a gasp to his lips. Tia had jumped into the river knowing full well she carried a child!

Tia glanced out the window for the hundredth time. She had seen blessed little of Ben these past few days, and when he joined her at night he made sizzling love to her, then fell immediately to sleep. He was always gone the next morning before she awoke. The pressing problem that plagued her had yet to be resolved, and she could wait no longer. When he returned tonight she intended to broach the subject of her pregnancy. If he still didn't want children, she'd leave. Damian had left her an heiress, and she didn't need Ben's support.

She needed his love.

Then she saw him riding into the yard and her thoughts scattered.

Ben stabled his horse and took off at a brisk pace for the house. His face was grim, his expression determined as he strode through the door. Tia was waiting for him.

"Ben."

"Tia."

They spoke at the same time. Ben searched Tia's face before his gaze slid down her body, pausing briefly at the slight mound of her stomach. Why hadn't he noticed it before? And her breasts. He recalled remarking on their newly rounded contours. He started to speak, saw the servants moving about in another room, and thought better of it. Grasping her wrist, he pulled her toward the stairs.

"Ben, what is it? Where are you taking me?"

"We need to talk, in private."

When he reached their room he slammed the door and turned to glare at her. A bitter taste of apprehension came to her mouth. Did he know? Was he angry? His face might have been granite, so tightly was it set. His eyes drifted down to her stomach. "Why didn't you tell me?" He met her gaze. It was unrelenting, sparing her nothing as he cocked a questioning eyebrow. "Were you intending to tell me at all?"

"You don't want children," Tia cried, growing alarmed. "You told me so yourself."

He spat out a wretched sound. Turbulent, mindless emotions spun through his head. Not want Tia's children? What an incredible idiot he must have been. "I was only thinking of you when I said that. I didn't want you to suffer like Kate, or perish like some women do. Perhaps I was selfish to want you all to myself, but it wasn't because I don't like children. Look at you, you're so tiny, you'd suffer unbearably bringing a child of mine into the world."

"You don't know that," Tia said, seeing things more clearly. "Besides, it's too late. Your child will be born in six and a half months."

"I should have taken precautions from the beginning," Ben lamented, imagining all kinds of terrible things that could happen to Tia during childbirth. "Why did you wait so long to tell me? What were you going to do if I had rejected you because you were pregnant?"

Tia bowed her head. Her words were so low that Ben had to bend to hear them. "I was going to leave and raise your child without you." Then she lifted her head and looked him straight in the eye. "I still could."

"Like hell!" Ben thundered. "If you're having my child, I'm going to be right beside you raising him. And keeping you out of trouble. You have a penchant for getting yourself into the worst messes I've ever seen. Someone has to look after you."

Tia drew in a shuddering breath. "You mean it? You don't mind that you're going to be a father?"

"Not as long as you're the mother. Frankly, sweetheart, I'm thrilled. But don't tell Dare or Robin. I'd never hear the end of it. I can just hear them now, 'Confirmed bachelor falls in love, weds, and becomes father after swearing never to do any of the above mentioned.' Bloody hell, they'll have a field day with it."

Tia flew into Ben's arms. "Oh, Ben, I don't think I've ever loved you more than at this moment. I was so afraid that you didn't want our child."

"And I feared losing you. I still do. I won't rest easy until this child is in your arms. Promise me, promise me you'll take care of yourself. You're so brave, sweetheart, as brave and bold and wild as this raw new land our children will be a part of."

"I promise, Ben, so long as you keep loving me."

Ben grinned in wicked delight as he unfastened the buttons on her bodice. "Loving you is easy."

"Will you love me when my stomach is out to here?" She extended both arms in front of her to form a circle.

"Even then."

Chapter Twenty-One

The weather was cooperating beautifully. It was Tia's wedding day. A warm, benevolent sun beamed blessings down upon Penrod station as Tia prepared for the most important day of her life. After learning about their child, Ben had insisted upon an immediate wedding. Still, it was nearly two weeks before arrangements could be made with the preacher to come to Penrod station to marry them. The Penrods were a prominent family and had many friends in high places. The house was nearly bursting at the seams with neighbors and friends and dignitaries. Tia was somewhat awed to learn that Governor Macquarie had been invited, and though he couldn't attend due to pressing business, he had appointed a magistrate to represent him.

Dare had offered to give the bride away, and Casey warmly accepted Tia's request to be matron of honor. Robin stood as best man, and Kate, still recuperating from the birth of her child, provided her expertise as manager to supervise the many details of the wedding and reception. It never ceased to amaze Tia, who had spent her entire life virtually friendless except for the somewhat dubious protection of One-eyed Bertha, that she was blessed now with such a wonderful family and caring friends. And Ben. Was there ever a woman blessed with a man as loving, sensitive, good-natured, and handsome as Ben Penrod? She thought not.

Sitting before the mirror while Casey arranged Tia's pale hair atop her head in an attractive style, Tia counted every one of her blessings and thanked God. She wasn't aware of the tiny, wistful smile curving the corners of her lips until Casey said, "Why so pensive, Tia? This should be the happiest day of your life."

Tia's eyes crinkled at the corners and her smile widened. "I've never been happier. I had no idea that men like Ben existed. I love him so much." Her hands fluttered to her stomach. "Ben told me he wasn't the marrying kind so often, I never imagined I'd be his wife one day."

Casey laughed delightedly. "Ben's words were all bluff. I knew that one day he'd meet a woman he couldn't resist. He protested much too vigorously to be taken seriously. The difference between Ben and Dare is subtle, but I wouldn't be truthful if I didn't say Ben is much more open than Dare. Dare can be dark and moody and implacable, while Ben is sunny-natured, warm, humorous, and generous. Did you know that Ben once offered to marry me to keep me safe for Dare? That sunny, giving nature comes natural to Ben, while Dare has to work to achieve it.

"Robin, though unrelated by blood, is more like Dare than Ben. They are all handsome, sensual men, but I do think you got the prize of the lot, though don't ever tell Dare I said so. To me Dare is the most wonderful man to walk the earth."

"That's how I feel about Ben. He'll make a wonderful father."

"If he's anything like Dare, he will. I imagine the men's ears must be ringing after all this talk about our loves. And now it's time to put your dress on. Dare will be here for you at any moment."

Casey went to the bed and lifted the dress that Tia was to wear at her wedding. Originally Tia had thought to wear one of the better dresses in her meager wardrobe, but when Ben went into town to visit the preacher he purchased a lovely cream lace creation that nearly took her breath away. Fashioned with long sleeves and a snug waist, it bared her shoulders, and the tops of her creamy breasts rose temptingly above the sweetheart neckline. The dress was even more beautiful than the one Damian had bought Tia for her wedding day long ago. Instead of a veil, which wasn't readily available in Parramatta, she wore a wreath of flowers atop her pale blond tresses.

"You look like a dream," Casey said, meaning every word. "Ben is a lucky man."

Ben paced nervously. How in bloody hell did he ever come to such dire straights? Marriage! The thought frightened the daylights out of him. Proposing to Tia and actually succumbing to the state of matrimony were two very different situations. He knew that Tia was the only woman in the world for him. He loved her beyond reason, beyond life itself.

But marriage? It was so—so confining!

He didn't even want to consider life without Tia. She was having his child. She loved him. He'd fought tooth and nail for her.

Marriage. It was so—so intimidating.

In a few minutes he'd promise to spend the rest of his life with the woman he loved. Protect her, care for her, raise their children in a loving home provided by him.

Marriage. It was so—so frightening.

How many times had he actually proposed to Tia before she finally consented to become his wife? He'd lost count long ago. If he didn't truly want to marry Tia, he would have never proposed in the first place. Once he met

Tia, his pledge to avoid marriage scattered like ashes before the wind. He wanted her with an all-consuming passion that ruled his life and drove him inexorably toward the unknown; the ultimate challenge to virile manhood.

Marriage. It was so—so permanent!

He was ready.

"What's the matter, little brother, are you having second thoughts?" Dare asked. He had watched Ben pace from one end of the room to the other for over twenty minutes and he couldn't resist the jibe.

"Not where Tia is concerned."

"It's permitted, you know. I suspect that every man who ever stood in your place got cold feet at the last minute."

"Did you?"

"If you recall, I married Mercy McKenzie before I married Casey, and a more reluctant bridegroom never existed. By the time I married Casey I was more than ready. I'd thought she was dead. Then I found her again in England and was overjoyed. By then our son was over a year old."

"I remember Robin's wedding day," Ben chuckled. "He and Kate were more or less forced into the marriage by Kate's father. It was William McKenzie's deathbed wish that they wed. I wish I could have been privy to the fireworks following the wedding, but I'd bet on Robin any day."

"I'm placing my money on Kate," Dare said

with a grin. The reminiscence had done exactly what Dare hoped it would. Ben seemed much more at ease now. "Do you still have doubts about this marriage?"

Ben's gray eyes twinkled merrily. "It wasn't the marriage I doubted, it was my ability to be the kind of husband Tia needs. She deserves the best, Dare. Her life hasn't been easy."

"She *has* the best, little brother." Dare clapped Ben on the shoulder. Their eyes, so alike, met and held in a rare moment of perfect understanding that only close brothers enjoyed.

"It's time, Ben, Dare." Robin burst into the room, excitement coloring his words. "The guests are all seated, the preacher is waiting, and the weather is cooperating beautifully. Ben, the resolute bachelor and rake, is going to join us lesser mortals on one of the most glorious autumn days ever seen in New South Wales."

Dare and Ben exchanged amused glances.

"I'll get Tia," Dare said, leaving Ben to Robin's dubious care. Robin had been teasing Ben mercilessly since the day he learned that Ben was going to be a father.

"Shall we join the preacher?" Robin asked, noting Ben's sudden pallor. "Look, mate, I meant no harm by my teasing. Knowing that the world is going to lose one of its staunchest bachelors just tickled my perverse sense of humor. Pay me no heed. Tia is a wonderful woman, and you're a lucky man."

"I'm ready, Robin," Ben said, suddenly eager to have the ceremony over with, their guests gone, and Tia all to himself. "Your teasing was no more than a minor annoyance. I just hope Tia and I are as happy as you and Kate and Dare and Casey. You may not be aware of it, but you've both set good examples. And believe it or not, I'm ready to accept full responsibility for a wife and family. It's remarkable," he mused thoughtfully, "how true love conquers even the most reluctant bachelor."

Tia stood poised at the top of the stairs, her trembling hand resting on Dare's arm. He looked so handsome, Tia thought, smiling at her brother-in-law-to-be. So dark, so mysterious, so calm and stalwart. And so like Ben.

"Are you ready, Tia?"

Tia dragged in a shuddering sigh. "I've been ready for a long time."

Dare smiled, patted her tiny hand clutching his arm, and started down the steps. They reached the foot of the stairs and paused at the parlor entrance. Heads swiveled in her direction and Tia's legs began to tremble. Dare recognized her nervousness and whispered encouragingly, "These are all our friends. Ben is looking at you, smile."

The moment Ben saw Tia standing in the open doorway with his brother, every doubt he ever harbored about marriage fled. This was the woman he loved, the woman he wanted to spend the rest of his life with. The most beautiful woman he'd ever seen. She gazed at him across the distance and lit up the room with her radiant smile. Surrounded by long, thick lashes, her eyes looked like exotic jewels set against her creamy white skin. Suddenly everyone else in the room ceased to exist as Tia walked slowly toward Ben.

"My God, she'd absolutely gorgeous," Ben whispered reverently to no one in particular. She looked a vision of seductive innocence in cream lace as she floated lightly across the carpeted floor. Sunlight streaming through the windows surrounded her in a contrasting nimbus of purity and beauty. Ben was captivated, charmed, infatuated anew by the woman he was about to make his wife.

Then Dare was placing Tia's small, icy fingers into Ben's large tanned hand and fading into the background. The rest of the brief ceremony was a blur. Ben supposed he made the correct responses at the proper time, as did Tia, for soon the preacher was pronouncing them husband and wife and giving Ben permission to kiss the bride. Ben had no difficulty understanding what was expected of him, for he drew Tia into his arms and kissed her with such overwhelming enthusiasm the entire company of guests began clapping. Embarrassed, he broke off the kiss, but refused to take his arm from around Tia's slim waist while the guests crowded around offering hearty congratulations.

*   *   *

The reception seemed to drag on forever. Everyone was having such a good time that no one seemed inclined to leave. The ceremony had taken place at noon, and by seven o'clock Ben was eagerly looking forward to having his bride all to himself. Earlier he had arranged for a bottle of wine to be placed in their bedroom and a light supper served after everyone had left. Robin, Kate, and their two children intended to accompany Dare and Casey home where they'd spend a few days before returning to their own prosperous farm in Bathurst. During their lengthy visit, Big John's sentence had been remitted and he and Lizzy expressed their desire to be wed in Bathurst, where they intended to make their home.

"I can't take much more of this, sweetheart," Ben said as he guided Tia to a deserted corner of the room. "I want to be alone with you."

"And I want to be alone with you, but we can't desert our guests."

"You want to bet? Come on." He took her hand, pulling her through the milling crowd toward the stairs.

"Are you leaving us so soon, little brother?" A hint of laughter lurked in Dare's voice.

"Bloody hell!" Ben hissed beneath his breath. Leave it to Dare to bring attention to them. Forcing a smile to his lips, he turned toward the guests. "Please stay and enjoy yourselves as long as you like. My wife and I are going to retire."

"Ben!" Tia groaned, her face turning beet red. "What will they think?"

"They'll think I'm anxious to be alone with my wife, and they're right. I want you now, naked, in my arms, in my bed." His last words were for her ears only, but it wasn't difficult to decipher his meaning, for Tia's flaming face gave mute testimony to his impatient need.

"Good night, little brother," Dare said, toasting them with his glass. "Take care of your lovely wife, I'll see to your guests." Amidst laughter and good-natured ribbing, they escaped upstairs to the welcome privacy of their room. Tia's face was still flaming when Ben closed and locked the door.

"I don't trust them," he said, propping a chair beneath the knob for added protection. "Both Dare and Robin have a twisted sense of humor."

"That was terribly rude," Tia said, suddenly shy. She didn't know how to act as a wife, it was still too new.

Ben grinned. "Serves them right for not leaving when they should. Forget them, sweetheart, and concentrate on your husband. This is the first time I've made love to a wife who is my own."

"Ben!" Tia gasped, aghast. "You're outrageous!"

"Aye, and you're going to have to grow accustomed to it. But seriously, sweetheart, you're the only woman I've wanted to make love to since the day we met. The only woman I *have* made love to since we met. Doesn't that tell you how much I've changed since my wild days in London?"

"Do you mean it? What if you become bored with me?"

"Bored!" A low, rumbling laugh thundered along the broad wall of his chest. "Perturbed perhaps, furious probably, but bored? Never. How can I become bored with an extraordinary little vixen who manages to get herself in and out of wild escapades at the drop of a hat? A talented, seductive little wench who puts on a great show of acting tough and speaking in shocking gutter language. You didn't fool me for a minute, sweetheart. Inside you're sweet and fine and gentle. You're a damnable provoking female and you're all mine."

His sultry, smoky gaze caressed her, claimed for his own every luscious inch of her seductive body. The body that nurtured his child. And she willingly, eagerly surrendered herself to the powerful mastery of those incredible silver eyes. She went into his arms.

They kissed hungrily. How delicious it felt with his tempting wife in his arms, Ben thought distractedly. His wife. The word that once frightened him now gave new meaning to his life. Her soft lips melted beneath his kisses like warm honey.

He was married.

She made him feel every inch a man—wild, passionate, able to conquer the world.

He was married.

A low rumble echoed in his chest when Tia's eager hands descended across his belly to trace the band of his trousers. Tremors of tormented rapture danced down his spine.

"Vixen," he growled. "Turn around, let me act the ladies' maid."

"Only if you'll allow me to act the valet."

With slow, sensual delight they undressed one another. Soon they were gasping for breath as their hands roamed everywhere, lingering at the sensitive places that gave them the most pleasure. His lips glided over the slope of her bare shoulder, capturing the rosy peak of her breast. He suckled hungrily.

"Make love to me, Ben!" Tia cried, eager to feel him deep inside her.

"Patience, sweetheart." Her body was his and they both knew it. He carried her to the bed, slipping into the turned-down sheets beside her. "I thought we'd eat first."

"I'm not hungry for food." Her desire was so strong it sizzled like lightning bolts from her body to his. Ben groaned, his own body already afire. Without further words he shoved her legs apart and slid between them. He frowned when Tia resisted.

"No, I want to ride you." Her erotic words had the desired effect as they drove Ben nearly over the edge. Grinding his teeth in a supreme effort to stem his rush toward ecstasy, he rolled over on his back and flung Tia atop him. Grasping her buttocks, he raised her hips and slid full and deep inside her. He was huge; Tia closed her eyes, bit her lip, and moaned in an agony of delight. He suckled her nipples and teased between her legs with strong brown fingers as she stroked them both toward climax.

It was a wild coming together—fanning their passion like a roaring tornado, destroying everything in its path, churning, whirling, bringing them to the most perfect ecstasy they had ever experienced. Ben was numb, dazed, and fantastically content.

He was married.

He loved it.

Epilogue

Tia paused to look out the window overlooking the Hawkesbury River. It was calm and placid this summer day in 1829, a far cry from the churning tempest in which she had nearly lost her life ten years ago. A wistful smile curved her full lips when she thought about that day when she finally realized just how much Ben truly loved her.

Her smile widened when she saw Ben striding from the barn toward the house. Their ten-year-old son, Chris, was hard on his father's heels. Tall for his age, Chris was neither dark-haired like his father nor blond like his mother. Instead, his hair was the color of an autumn sunset. He was a strong, handsome lad, big for his age like Ben must have been, and wise beyond his years.

The front door opened and Tia saw their seven-year-old daughter, Tricia, walk sedately onto the porch to await her father and brother. Very much aware of her femininity, doll-like Tricia was tiny like her mother with coal black hair and large gray eyes. One day she was going to be a stunner.

Just then a small whirlwind burst past Tia to join Tricia on the porch. Three-year-old Polly rarely walked when she could run. Active, affectionate, and precocious, blond, blue-eyed Polly was the charmer of the family. Unable to wait for her father to reach her, she ran out on plump, churning legs to meet him. Ben scooped the child into his arms and lifted her high in the air. Squealing in delight, Polly wound dimpled arms around Ben's neck and planted wet, smacking kisses all over his face. Tia could hear their laughter all the way into the parlor.

When Ben and the children entered the house a few seconds later, Tia was waiting to greet them. Ben's eyes lit up at the sight of her. She had aged little in ten years, seeming to grow lovelier with each passing day. Three children and maturity had rounded her figure in subtle ways, though she still remained slim and supple.

Tia smiled warmly at her family, thinking no woman was ever so blessed. Ben was a wonderful father and husband, still handsome and virile, showing little sign of aging, still wanting her with the same intensity he had ten years ago. In Tia's opinion, all the Penrod men were amazing specimens of vitality and youthfulness no matter what their age. Dare, older than Ben by a few years, looked ten years younger than his age. The brothers had remained close throughout the years, and the Penrod cousins saw each other frequently, enjoying close family ties. Dare and Casey were more deeply in love than ever, if that were possible.

Roy had returned from abroad shortly after Tia and Ben's wedding. His wife had died of tuberculosis in Switzerland, and Roy had returned to spend his remaining years in the bosom of his family. He derived great pleasure from his grandchildren. He lived at Penrod station, still handsome and vigorous at sixty-five.

Robin, Kate, and their two children still resided in Bathurst on their large and prosperous farm. A magistrate of some renown, Robin had made a name for himself as the first emancipist to be appointed magistrate by Governor Macquarie. They visited Parramatta often, dividing their visits between Dare's farm and Penrod station. In return, the Penrods often ventured to Bathurst, since the roads had improved dramatically in ten years.

Big John and Lizzy had married shortly after their return to Bathurst ten years ago. In quick succession they had produced several children,

443

five at last count. Big John was still a gentle giant but had gained respect in the community by helping those in need and working with emancipists to make their lives easier. His farm was prospering.

Ben set Polly on her feet and the child went scampering off. The two older children, having specific chores to perform, also left. Ben watched the children depart, his eyes soft with love and pride. He turned to Tia, and his heart swelled to bursting. He couldn't imagine life without her. And to think he was the man who had scorned marriage. He had no cause for regrets, but did Tia? He thought not but still couldn't help but ask, "Are you sorry, sweetheart?" His strange question startled Tia.

"About what?"

"About being away from London all these years. About having to live in an untamed country with little of the amenities of a big city. About never claiming your inheritance from Damian. About—marrying me."

"Ye bleedin' idiot! Are ye daft, Ben Penrod? Yer a dimwitted arse if ye think I'd return ta London after all these years. I ain't never regretted marryin' ye, even if ye do ask stupid questions sometimes."

Ben's mouth dropped open. It had been years since he heard Tia use vulgar street language. He stared at her. Her blue eyes twinkled merrily and her mouth twitched at the corners, straining from the effort of maintaining a straight face.

Their eyes met in perfect understanding and they fell into each other's arms, giggling hysterically.

In another part of the house their laughter reached the ears of Chris and Tricia. The children exchanged long-suffering looks and shrugged knowingly. It was Chris, astute and knowledgeable beyond his meager years, who gave voice to what they were both thinking. "They're at it again."

Author's Note

Dear Readers,

I hope you enjoyed my Australian trilogy as much as I enjoyed writing it. The Penrod men and Robin Fletcher were fascinating, often infuriating, but never boring. The women they loved were pioneers in the true sense of the word. They fought for their men with a courage and tenacity that was inspiring. No hardships were too great for them to overcome, no frontiers too far flung to conquer. Australia grew to greatness through the efforts of just such men and women.

Bold Land, Bold Love; Wild Land, Wild Love; and *Brave Land Brave Love* were all a pleasure to write. The second two books were the outcome of the tremendous outpouring of letters from readers who demanded more of the Penrods. I hope I have satisfied those readers who asked for more.

I love to hear from readers. Please write me in care of Leisure Books. Enclose a self-addressed stamped envelope for a personal answer, bookmark, and newsletter. And be sure to look for my future releases from Leisure.

All My Romantic Best,

Connie